# Tell Them I'll Be There

# Tell Them I'll Be There

*Gerard Mac*

ROBERT HALE · LONDON

ISBN 978-0-7090-9071-7

Robert Hale Limited
Clerkenwell House
Clerkenwell Green
London EC1R 0HT

www.halebooks.com

2 4 6 8 10 9 7 5 3 1

Typeset in 10.5/13.35pt Sabon
Printed in Great Britain by the MPG Books Group,
Bodmin and King's Lynn

To my parents
Danny and Ethel

# AUTHOR'S NOTE

The New York City Planners have a lot to answer for. In the early Sixties the architectural masterpiece that was Penn Station was pulled down and replaced by a soulless concourse. Why? The Romans preserved their Colosseum. They didn't destroy it.

The Visitors' Gallery at the New York Stock Exchange for many a must-see tourist attraction, was closed soon after Nine Eleven and shows no sign of reopening. Sad but understandable.

# ONE

THERE WAS A party that night at the Drummers'. There was singing and dancing and that old fool Malone danced a jig. The landlord, Matty, was drunk as usual by eight o'clock. His wife, Bridget, was run off her feet and there was a crush at the bar as the ale flowed and she had no idea who had paid for what or if they had paid at all. It was a lovely party with lots of laughter, lots of memories to share, but there were tears, too. The boys were leaving home.

Ma wasn't there. She had seen what the drink had done to her father and her brother Pat and she didn't want any part of it. As far as she was concerned the boys leaving home was not a cause for celebration anyway. But, as always on occasions such as this, her two sisters were there. Molly and Clare would shed all the tears the maudlin songs brought out. They pour the stuff down, the boys' long dead dad would say, and they top themselves up as long as someone's buying 'til it spills from their eyes disguised as tears. The real tears would be shed in private and not just by Ma. There was a girl called Kathleen.

'Cheer up,' someone told Dan. 'It will not be forever and you will come home to us a rich man, so you will.'

Malone reached up drunkenly to put an arm around Dan's shoulder. 'If anyone comes home a rich man,' he announced, ignoring the previous speaker, 'it will be this young fellow. Our very own Danny boy!'

The revellers erupted in a spontaneous rendition of the 'Derry Air' and, oblivious to the raucous chorus all around him,

Malone went on to ask, 'Why is it we must lose our best young fellows? Can you tell me that?'

'Why indeed?' Aunt Molly echoed. 'Sure 'tis a pity we cannot be rid of the likes of you.'

Dan drew his brother Tim aside. 'Are you going out to her?' he asked. 'You can't just leave without a word.'

'I can't get involved, Dan,' he said. 'You know that.'

Their brother Michael handed them fresh drinks. 'You're to be a priest, for God's sake,' Michael said, 'not a monk. You'll be dealing with the ladies of the parish and facing up to them every day.' He grinned. 'Ah, there'll be plenty of girls out to make your toes curl.'

Tim gave Michael a withering look, placed his glass firmly on the window ledge behind him and went out to speak to the girl to whom his imminent departure evidently meant so much.

'He's never a priest,' Michael said, as Tim went out the door. 'He's a man, for God's sake. Flesh and blood. He has the same needs as the rest of us.'

Dan didn't disagree but there was little to be done about it. It was Ma. She had set her heart on one of them being a priest and at one time she had high hopes it might be Dan. They had all served their time at the altar, all taken instruction. But only Tim had succumbed and from an early age. Always when someone, a relative perhaps, had asked the boys what they planned to do with their lives both Dan and Michael had answered, 'See the world.' And Ma had always added, 'But not this one. This one is for the priesthood. Sure 'tis what he was made for.' And Tim had always nodded dutifully, until he came to believe it himself, comforted by the sense of being 'special', holier than the others and one of the Lord's chosen few.

The girl called Kathleen stood up straight when Tim appeared. She had been leaning back against the oak tree, her heart heavy with the words of Mrs Dolan. 'Now you be a good girl, Kathleen, and find yourself another. Our Timothy is not for girls and settling down and you know that well enough. He's to join the Church and that's an end to it.'

But there had never been anyone else. They had been friends

since junior school, often together, seen by many as a pair. He was her friend and then he was her boyfriend and she was not going to give him up without a fight.

Tim was frowning as he left the path and crossed the grass to confront her. Kathleen clutched her thin cotton dress, held it tightly at her throat. She had washed her hair and scrubbed her face and rubbed wild thyme between her fingers to dispel the odour of onions and the kitchen where she worked. She was only just seventeen and that she was already a woman had not gone unnoticed by the men and the boys of the village. But Kathleen had eyes only for Timothy Dolan.

It was a warm summer night, the moon a pale-blue globe, the stars bright in a cloudless sky. A warm yellow glow came from the windows and the open doorway of the Drummers' Tavern and there was the muffled sound of laughter and carousing from the drunken revellers.

'What are you doing here, Kathleen?' Tim asked reprovingly. 'What is it you want?'

'You know what I want,' she whispered urgently.

'But we've been through all this,' he told her. 'I'm to leave in the morning. When you see me next I'll be wearing the collar.'

'I want us to be married, like we always planned.'

'Will you listen to me?'

She had moved back into the shadow cast by the old tree's overhanging branches and as he pleaded with her she gripped his shirt front and pulled him into the shadows.

'Kathleen!'

Her arms were around his neck, her lips fastened hard on his, the compliant contours of her body thrust against him. He turned his head away but her lips followed. Briefly he wavered and their lips met again. Both his hands were on her hips and to her delight he was responding. Slowly, gently, she tried to draw him down to lie with her in the long grass. Tim felt his resistance draining away. He sank slowly, the softness of her body luring him down. Then suddenly, with a strangulated cry, he drew back. 'No!'

It sounded strange even to him, like the voice of someone

else. But he broke away, ran to the tavern, leaving Kathleen bereft, abandoned in the grass.

A swaying group of men, most of them inebriated, blocked the entrance as Dan stepped from the shadows and gripped his arm. 'Tim! What is it?' he asked. 'What's wrong?'

Tim turned away and went on running, across the grass and down the lane into the dark. Then Kathleen came running. But she came to a halt, backed away, smoothing her dress, when she saw the men. One of them said something in a low voice and the others laughed coarsely.

'You shouldn't be out here, Kathleen,' Dan said, quietly walking her away. 'There's nothing here for you.'

She was near to tears, her voice shaking. 'I want Tim.'

Dan put his arms around her. 'I know,' he said.

Kathleen buried her head against his shoulder. 'He wants me, Dan. I know he does.'

'Cry if you want to,' he said softly. 'Let it all come out.'

'But we're right for each other. He knows it. He's always known it. We had an ... an understanding. There'll never be anyone else. There never could be.'

Dan held her close then he looked down into her eyes. 'You must go home,' he said quietly. 'Will I walk you there?'

She shook her head, seemed to regain some of her composure and tried to smile. 'I'll be all right,' she said.

'Sure?'

She nodded and reached up and kissed him on the cheek. Then she turned and walked away down the quiet lane. His brother Tim was wrong. He was sure of that. The Church was coming between two people who were clearly meant for each other. If Tim was as totally committed to the Church as he professed to be then fair enough. But Dan was not convinced. He had felt all along it was not really what Tim wanted. It was what Ma wanted. If Dad was here they might get him to put a stop to it. But if Dad was here all this priest business might never have started in the first place.

He found Tim sitting by the slow-moving river that ran alongside the churchyard. The moonlight gave the assortment of headstones and crosses a ghostly glow as Dan wondered what the dead would say if they could rise up and speak. There is no Heaven. There is no Hell. There is no God, for God's sake! All there is, all we can hope for in this world is someone to care for. Would that be it?

Some of the headstones were upright, some were sloping and some had sunk with the weight of the years. A new stone stood white and proud with fresh flowers at its feet but most of the graves looked neglected and forgotten. Tim had run here in search of solace at a shrine to the Virgin Mary. He had knelt before the pale-blue and white statue.

'Hail Mary, Mother of God,' he prayed. He felt ashamed. He had given way to a temptation of the flesh. He must be strong, maintain control. What happened was wrong. He had betrayed his calling. But he knew, too, if he was honest, he had betrayed Kathleen. He ought to have made his true intentions clear, much clearer and much sooner. The truth was he was confused, drawn in two directions, too weak to take a stand.

He had gazed in peace at the serenity of the Virgin and, as fanciful as ever, he believed he saw a reassuring smile in the fixed expression. It was there. He was certain it was there. A gentle smile. And as he watched the face seemed to change into that of his mother. He had stumbled away in confusion.

'For God's sake, Tim, what are you doing?'

Tim came to his feet, embarrassed, glad that it was only Dan and that Michael was not with him. Michael was a non-believer. He only feigned belief to avoid a confrontation with their mother. Even as a boy at school Michael had questioned and dared to ridicule the teachings of the Church. How could a man walk on water? he asked. And, with much hilarity until he was ejected from the classroom by his ear, how could a man change water into wine? Why, such a man would make a fortune at the Drummers'.

The cane, wielded ferociously by an outraged nun, and a letter of impending doom to his mother had left him in a frowned upon limbo and for the sake of a fragile peace he had accepted the imposed lessons in elementary theology from his parish priest. But his scepticism had never wavered.

Michael had kept his views to himself in recent months, since he and Dan had decided to seek a new life in America in fact. He knew he could never shake his mother's unquestioning faith even if he wanted to. She was the kind of woman who keeps a bowl of holy water in the lobby and a crucifix in every room, the kind of woman who goes on 'retreat' twice a year to beg forgiveness for her sins when her biggest 'sin' was a glass of sherry at Christmas.

Tim stood up. 'I'm going home.'

'What about Kathleen?' Dan asked quietly.

'What about her?'

'She was your girlfriend, Tim. All through school she never had anyone else. She never wanted anyone else. And neither did you.'

'We were just kids.'

'And now she wants to marry you,' Dan went on, 'and spend the rest of her life with you. Are you sure that's not what you want?'

'I'm going to be a priest.'

'And is that what you *really* want?'

Tim brushed past him, evading the question.

'It's your life, Tim. Nobody else's. Come with us to America. Things might look very different from over there.'

Tim laughed aloud, as if this was a ludicrous suggestion.

'Ma won't always be here,' Dan said quietly.

Tim turned back, angry now. 'What do you mean by that?'

'I think you know what I mean,' Dan said. 'Ma wants you to be a priest. She always has. But it's what *you* want that really matters.'

The implication angered Tim. It was his business, his own affair and he didn't want to discuss it. Not even with Dan. 'I'm going to be a priest,' he said. 'And that's that.'

'Don't you feel anything for Kathleen?' Dan asked as Tim left.

'A priest loves everybody,' he answered without looking back.

Dan followed him up the path out of the churchyard, leaving the argument for now. And as Tim trudged off, head down, in the direction of home he returned to where the drinkers were at last spilling out of the tavern and standing about in noisy groups.

Most of them were swaying with the drink, mindlessly carrying on whatever they were debating when the landlord's wife called time. Dan simply wanted to find Michael, extricate him from whatever he was up to and take him home.

'Anyone seen Michael?' he asked.

One man, with a knowing grin, signalled with a little nod. 'Sure and he went round the back, so he did.'

Dan weaved a way through the knots of mainly men gathered on the grass and was caught in a gauntlet of well-wishers. Take care now and watch out for the booze and those wicked, wicked women. If I was ten years younger I'd be coming wit' ye. If ye get to Philadelphia be sure to look up our Pat. Big man in Philadelphia. Big bag of wind, someone said and the hilarity erupted again.

Drunkenly, an old woman threw her arms around Dan's neck. 'I remember the t'ree of ye,' she wailed. 'Altar boys all. Little angels.'

With a smile Dan gently removed her arms and was at once assailed by his Aunt Molly. 'Your Aunt Clare has done it again. She knows she can't hold her drink. Will you not lend me a hand to get her home, Danny? There's a good lad.'

Towering above his aunts Dan looked around for Michael but Michael was nowhere to be seen.

'Sure and there's nothing the matter with me,' his Aunt Clare insisted. ''Tis this old fool cannot hold her drink.'

But they obviously wanted him to walk them home though home was less than fifty yards away.

'Will we see you tomorrow?' Aunt Molly asked.

'You must come in for a minute,' Aunt Clare said. 'I think we can find you a little drop of something.'

'No, no, really,' Dan said. 'I have to go. We're leaving very early in the morning. About half past five. And I have to go back and find Michael.'

'Ah,' Aunt Molly said. 'You will have to watch that one on the other side, Danny. He's a little too fond of the colleens, I'd say.'

'The wrong kind of colleens, if ye ask me,' Aunt Clare added, as Dan tried to escape. 'He was making a bit too much of that Hegarty girl early on and she of him. She is no good that one.'

Aunt Molly kissed him on the cheek and the stale whiff of what the locals called 'red biddy' filled his nostrils. 'So sad you have to go. Sure 'tis breaking your mother's heart.'

Aunt Clare did the same and clung to him as if it was she who was losing a son. 'You're a good boy, Danny. Always was. Write us now, soon as you can. Tell us all about little ol' Noo York.'

He nodded and promised he would and made his escape.

It was dark among the sheds and the outbuildings and at first he could make out only shapes and shadows. Then against a wall he saw Michael and Moira Hegarty.

'What are you doing?' he asked, though it was clear enough what they were doing. 'We have to be off early in the morning.'

Michael's speech was slurred. 'I'll be with you in a minute.'

'Michael—'

'In the name of God, can you not leave us now?'

'Well, just hurry up, will you?' Dan went back to the front of the tavern and was stopped by a little man named Teague.

'I been to America, Dan, when I was your age,' Teague told him. 'Wonderful country. Big an' empty just waiting for young fellas like you to open her up.'

'Oh yes?' Dan said politely, though he suspected Teague had scarcely been out of the village. 'So why did you come home?'

'Ah, well.' Teague pushed his cap to the back of his head and pulled at the red choker at his scrawny neck. ''Tis a long story.'

Michael emerged, swaying slightly as he tied the string that held up his rough work trousers, and some of the younger men and some of the not so young laughed and cheered.

Dan gripped his arm and hurried him away until they were well out of earshot before remonstrating with him. 'You'll go with anyone you, won't you?'

'She's all right,' Michael insisted.

'All right?' Dan echoed. 'She's been with half the men in the county. Half the men in *country*, I wouldn't wonder.'

'So what does it matter? We're leaving tomorrow.'

'It's what you might be leaving behind.'

'What?'

'What if she gets pregnant? Would you want a child of yours to be dragged up by the Hegartys?'

'If she gets pregnant? Why, it could be anybody's.'

Dan shook his head in despair. Sow your wild oats if you must, his mother's brother used to say, but don't go spilling your seed all over the place. It has a nasty way of taking root where you wouldn't want it. 'Do you not remember what Uncle Pat said?'

'Ha!' Michael laughed dismissively. 'That old reprobate.' He staggered to a halt on the moonlit road and gripped Dan by the arm. 'God help me,' he said. 'I've a brother nearly a priest and another a blessed saint, so I have. Well, come on "keeper", tomorrow we're off to see the world.'

Keeper. It was a legacy of childhood. Once, when Michael was in trouble in the village, Ma had given Dan a good clout around the ear and scolded him for not keeping an eye on Michael.

'Me?' Dan had replied facetiously. 'Am I my brother's keeper?'

And Ma had rounded on him. 'Yes! You are, Daniel, and don't you forget it.'

'Where's Tim?' Michael asked.

'He went home,' Dan said. 'He's got a bit of sense.'

'Sense, is it? If he had any sense he'd be with Kathy O'Donnell. He'll never find another girl like her.'

'He won't need to, will he? He'll be a priest.'

'Ach, he's never a priest. The Dolans are not priest material.'

They were at the front door now and again Michael pulled Dan to a halt. 'We can't let him do it, Dan,' he said and he suddenly sounded sober. 'It's not right.'

'It's what he wants.'

'It's what Ma wants and you know it.'

Dan nodded in agreement.

'Well, it's not going to happen,' Michael said. 'We'll not allow it, do you hear? He's coming to America with us. Even if we have to knock him cold and smuggle him aboard the bloody ship.'

# TWO

THEY WERE UP with the dawn. Ma shook Dan first and he saw that her eyes were already blurred by tears. It would be like that until they left, tears and more tears and tears no doubt at regular intervals long after they had gone. She was happy that Tim was going off to the seminary in England. He would not be too far away. But she worried about Dan and Michael sailing across a great ocean to begin their lives again. Dan would probably be all right. He was the one with the brains and the common sense. He would have to take good care of Michael.

She didn't want them to go but recently she had been worried that Michael was getting a bit too involved with the Maguires and the McGees and the rest of those no good Fenians. Those boys are right, Ma conceded. The English have no business to be here. But, as far as Ma was concerned, guns and bombs were not the answer. The only way to get rid of the English and their lordly ways was through the politicians, useless bunch though they were.

To her shame it was through Ma that Tim was to go to England. He could have gone to St Patrick's in Maynooth but that would have meant waiting for six months and it was too much of a risk. She wanted him away, for her woman's instinct told her he might waver over Kathy O'Donnell and that would never do. It would be a terrible waste if he put aside his vocation for what was surely no more than a passing fancy. It was not that Kathleen was a bad girl – far from it. She would make for someone a wonderful wife. It was just that she had got it into her head she wanted Tim. It was understandable, of course. Tim was a good-looking young man. But she couldn't have him. He had his vocation.

Ma had discussed the problem at length with Father Delaney who had discussed the matter in turn with the bishop and it was decided that Tim would go across to England and to Ushaw College. 'Ah, 'tis a fine an' lovely place,' the bishop said. 'Wasn't I there myself? When the boy settles down he'll be overwhelmed by the love of Our Lord and the comradeship of the many new friends he'll make. He'll soon forget such minor distractions.'

So Tim was to go to England and on the same packet steamer that would take Dan and Michael across to the port of Liverpool where they would board the big ship for America. America! The word brought a sob to Ma's throat every time she heard it. It was a long way off, thousands of miles, and it would take the big ship days maybe weeks to get there. Dan had promised he would write when they got to Liverpool, but after that it would be ages before she heard from them. And all they had was just the few pounds between them and the tickets they had worked so hard to pay for.

They were young men now, no longer her babies, no longer her boys. She couldn't stop them from going and, though they had promised they would try to get home for Tim's ordination, she knew in her heart she might never see them again. It was hard but she had to admit there was nothing for them here. Death had taken her husband, the best man a woman could wish for, now life was taking her boys.

She would see Tim, of course. Even priests have holidays. But it could be quite some time. He would have his studies and, as Father Delaney said, he was a bright boy. He might be sent to the English College in Rome. He might even get to meet His Holiness himself. She was happy to indulge such daydreams, knowing that sooner or later she would see him again. She might never ever see Danny and Michael again.

They would have to work hard to establish themselves and she was sure they would. But it would take time and with time young men meet young women. They would probably marry and have children and they would then have their own families to think about. The cost of a trip home could be out of the question for years. And Ma knew she didn't have all that many years left.

Perhaps they would meet some nice Irish girls on the big ship. Try to find a good Catholic girl if you are in need of a wife, she had ventured one evening. Both Danny and Michael had laughed and Danny had said they were not looking for wives. Maybe so, she told him, but there'll be plenty of girls looking for husbands.

But it was not Danny she worried about. Danny was a good lad with a good head on his shoulders. It was Michael. Michael was like her brother, fond of the drink and far too fond of the girls. Hadn't he been in a few scrapes already? At least, according to Molly and Clare he had – though those two 'ould fools' were not exactly reliable sources. To hear that Molly talk it was a blessing that Michael was going while the going was good. But he was not a bad lad. He was a good worker. He would work hard and long to earn a living. Might turn out it was he who made a success in America. Danny was never one for dirtying his hands.

There had been many stories of success over there, some of them true, most of them not. One of the best known concerned a certain Patrick O'Doherty who had arrived penniless in America, worked as a labourer on railways and bridges and saved every spare cent he earned. Within a few months he had sent home enough money for his wife and family to join him. Within ten years he was employing his employer and he had more than $100,000 to his name. O'Doherty was a shining example to all of what could be achieved and Ma knew his story was true because her niece had read it in a magazine. The magazine, though, had pointed out that O'Doherty was a non-drinker and a non-smoker, something that could not be said of Michael.

Dan decided there was no point in lingering, best just to say goodbye and go, and they had all agreed. They had gathered up their worldly goods but none of them had much to carry.

Dan had a small hold-all he had haggled over at a market stall. After walking away twice he had bought it for next to nothing. Tim had a trim little suitcase loaned to him by Father Delaney, 'not to be returned until the bearer is wearing the collar'. Michael, in his usual state of disarray, had a carrier bag from the corner shop.

One by one they kissed Ma and left her standing at the door of the crofter's cottage where all three of them had been born. No looking back, Michael had ordered, and again they had all agreed. But it was Michael who was first to turn and wave from the crest of the road where the house would drop away and be lost from view.

As frequently happened with Michael's arrangements – usually made in a bar at the end of a session and in an alcoholic haze – this one didn't work out. They were supposed to walk over the hill and down towards Donadea where a friend of Michael's would pick them up at the crossroads and give them a lift in his battered old truck a good part of the way. They waited by the side of the road for over half an hour without seeing a soul or a vehicle of any kind before starting to walk. Almost an hour later they came to a village where they begged a lift in an old school bus and travelled the rest of the way in comparative style.

The driver said the bus was used to pick up his boss's workmen at six every morning and take them to the quarry. He wasn't really going this way, he said, but he could take them a little of the way. They looked at each other and knew their best chance of going all the way was to keep him talking and, once they told him they were off to America, this proved easy enough.

They were off to board the packet to Liverpool, they told the driver, and from there they were off to New York. The driver said *he* was going to New York one day. He was going to 'seek his fortune' in the New World. There was nothing here. The old country was done for. But as he was already twice their age and more they merely nodded and accepted what he said, mentally consigning him to the army of dreamers they had left behind.

He took them nearly all the way and as he was reversing to drive off he broke into *Give my regards to Broadway* and with a final flourish *Tell them I'll be there.* And they laughed and waved until he was out of sight.

Standing in line, the boys had their first view of the people who would accompany them across the Irish Sea. The queue was made up mostly of men but there were several families, some with small children. Many would go to relatives in England but many would take the longer, more adventurous step and board the big ship to what those back home regarded as the land of promise.

The 'little' steamer was the biggest vessel the brothers had ever seen and they wondered, if this is small, how big is the big ship? It would take about ten or twelve hours to Liverpool, they were told, depending on the weather. Michael took a look downstairs and came back, shaking his head. It was crowded down there and airless and the throbbing of the engine would hammer your head in. Better to stay up on deck, get the wind in your face. But the decks were crowded, too, and many were sick as they huddled together. It was probably a good thing to be seasick now, was the received wisdom. Then you might not be sick crossing the Atlantic.

A young man from Waterford told them to watch out for their bags when the steamer docked in Liverpool. He had been told there were fellows just waiting to snatch your belongings. Thieves they were who hang about the docks, like gannets, and prey on the incoming passengers.

'We'll see about that,' Michael said, making a fist.

But the brothers had precious little to lose between them. Dan and Michael each had an extra pair of boots wrapped in a spare pair of trousers and a couple of work shirts. Tim had not much more. But some of the families had baggage and the boys cast a protective eye over their nearest neighbours, a young man from Courtown, his wife and his two small boys.

Michael yawned theatrically to express his boredom. 'We'll have to arrange some entertainment on the big ship,' he said.

'There might *be* some,' Tim suggested.

'For the nobs maybe,' Michael said. 'Not for the cattle in steerage.'

The passengers were so bored and weary by now that when the grey outline of the Liverpool seafront began to take shape in the mist ahead a small cheer went up. People came to their feet and prepared to disembark. Children were called to heel, bags were drawn closer to their owners. But the seasoned travellers relaxed, aware it would be another two hours before the steamer docked.

The scramble ashore was hardly necessary. It was only four in the afternoon and the big ship was not due to sail until morning. But, as the young fellow from Waterfood said, there were plenty of hazards along the Waterloo Dock. It was a perilous place for those travelling with trunks or large cases that looked as though they might contain something worth stealing.

At the quayside men with handcarts offered to carry luggage to the nearest lodging-houses. A man in a shiny suit and a bowler hat was selling his 'magic seasick remedy', a dubious-looking powder in a twist of paper. A boy of about twelve was surprising those who stopped to watch with remarkably acrobatic dancing before passing his cap round which invariably came back empty. Merchant seamen heading for a seafront bar passed through the uncertain knots of disembarking passengers and street girls in twos called coarse invitations to any man who might be a prospective client. Small children engulfed by the milling throng gazed upwards, wide-eyed and open-mouthed, at the seagulls that circled overhead.

Tim was to make his way to Lime Street Station and on to Manchester and St John's Church in Salford where accommodation would be found for him until he was due at Ushaw. He was in no hurry and he had agreed to stay with his brothers until their ship sailed before making his way inland. Michael had again and again attempted to talk him into accompanying them all the way. Now he was at a distance from home, he reasoned, and out of Ma's reach, he should give himself time to think. It was a lifetime's commitment, for God's sake, and there could be no going back. Once a priest, always a priest.

'You should come with us and then, if you decide it's what you really want, you can go into the Church in America.'

Tim had turned to Dan for support but Dan had simply told him, 'Think about it. There's no rush.'

Dan had been disturbed by the depth of feeling, the desolation, he had seen in Kathy O'Donnell's eyes and he was not convinced Tim had confronted his own true feelings. He feared that one day, when it was too late maybe, his younger brother might regret this.

Tim had simply laughed when Michael suggested he should join them on their voyage to America. He didn't have a ticket for a start. That was not a problem, they told him. They had enough money between them to buy another. But Tim knew this was money they had saved and money they had been given to help get them started. Another ticket would take all their money. And anyway, he said, he wouldn't hear of it. It would break Ma's heart.

'Let's get a drink,' Michael said in exasperation and he led the way to a dockside tavern.

The place was filled to overflowing with men standing shoulder to shoulder but Michael found the bar and soon returned with three gills of ale. As others had, they found it more comfortable to stand outside on the cobbled frontage where Michael renewed his attack. 'You're stupid and stubborn,' he told Tim. 'Come with us, make your fortune and in a year or two send for Kathy.'

'Tell him, Dan,' Tim said wearily.

'Well,' Dan said, 'there's a lot of sense in what Michael says. But I think you should go home. Be honest with Ma. Tell her it's a big step and you need time to think it over.'

'I don't want to go home and I don't need to think it over.'

Michael tried again. 'Can you put your hand on your heart and swear in the name of the Father, the Son and the Holy Ghost you never felt anything for that girl? Can you?'

Tim put his glass down on the tavern's window ledge. 'All right. I *was* fond of Kathy. There might even have been more to it at one time. But I've made a choice. I'm going into the Church and that's an end to it. Now will you leave it, Michael, or I'll go this minute.'

'Leave it, Michael,' Dan said. 'We haven't really got enough between us to buy another ticket anyway. If Tim wants to suffer eternal damnation in the Holy Roman Church that's up to him.'

All three laughed, but later, when Tim went to the overflowing cesspool at the rear of the tavern, Michael said defiantly, 'He's coming with us whether he likes it or not.'

There was a commotion at the quayside. It looked at first as if a fight had developed and Dan and Michael moved along to get a better view. But it wasn't a fight. A young woman had fainted and a small girl was clinging in terror to her limp arm. The bag containing the woman's belongings had been swiftly spirited away and lost in the crowd as a small weasel-like man prised the purse from her clenched fist and burrowed his way out from the surrounding mob.

Dan caught the man and held him in a vice-like grip as Michael retrieved the purse. The little man fought desperately to hold on to what he clearly believed was now rightfully his. But the brothers, both of them bigger and stronger, threatened to 'throw him in the drink'. When they finally released him he scurried away, spitting and snarling and calling them 'Thieving bastards!'

A dock officer cleared a way for an elderly man who claimed to be a doctor. The young woman had not come round and showed no sign of recovering as she was carried into the dock office. The small girl had been forgotten in the confusion and now, as the crowd thinned, Dan saw that she was standing alone and forlorn, her small, smudged face anxious and apprehensive.

A plump, blowsy prostitute had been watching from close by. She took the little girl by the hand and crouched low to speak to her. Then she tried to lead the girl away but the girl pulled back, unwilling to go with her.

'Do you know this girl?' Dan demanded.

'Who the 'ell are you?' the woman responded.

Tim and Michael had followed up, close behind Dan.

'Where do you think you're taking her?' Tim asked.

'She's not taking her anywhere,' Dan said firmly and the woman came out with a torrent of abuse.

'That's enough,' he said. 'Clear off or I'll have you locked up.'

'Locked up?' the woman scoffed. 'You'll have me locked up?'

Michael stepped forward. 'Yeah, you fat old hag,' he said. 'But first you can go for a swim.' He made a move towards her and the woman turned and fled.

Dan crouched before the little girl. 'It's all right,' he said.

The girl shook and sobbed but she was reassured by their Irish voices. 'I want me mammy.'

'Sure you do,' Dan said. 'I think she just fainted, that's all.'

She looked up into his dark eyes, drawn to him and his gentle way, and she nodded.

'Don't you worry,' he said with a smile. 'You can stay with us for now. Can't she, lads?'

Both Michael and Tim smiled down at her. ''Course she can.'

Tim turned to Dan and said quietly, 'Her mother should have recovered by now. I'll go and see how she is.'

He went to the office where a large, uniformed man barred his way. 'Lady who fainted,' he said, 'is the doctor with her?'

'Priest she needs,' the man said. 'Not a doctor.'

# THREE

'I CAN HELP,' Tim said. 'I'm on my way to the seminary to be trained as a priest. I can say some prayers.'

The man looked at him doubtfully then stood aside to allow him to enter the small office. In a side room the body of the little girl's mother lay on a low table. Much of the trouble had gone from her pale face now and Tim couldn't help noticing, in spite of himself, that she had once been a good-looking girl.

'*In nomine patri* ...' he began and those present, the doctor and two dock officers, stood back to allow him access.

'What was it, Doctor?' he asked.

The doctor, a rather wizened Scot, shook his head. 'Some sort of stroke, brain haemorrhage or somesuch,' he said uncertainly. 'But she wouldn'y have felt much pain. She didn'y faint. She just died. Not a bad way to go.'

'When you're old, perhaps,' Tim said. 'She was a young woman.'

'Aye,' the doctor conceded.

'What happens now?'

'Straightforward, I should think. I shall issue a death certificate and a short report for the coroner, copy to the Docks Authority, and if there are no relatives the council will take care of the rest. Shouldn'y be a problem. Plenty of witnesses to what happened.'

Tim nodded. He was about to mention the little girl, but he didn't. It all seemed sort of impersonal and routine, as if it was something that happened every day. Perhaps it was, he told

himself, with so many people making these life-changing decisions, moving whole families halfway across the world. Was it
surprising if some fell by the wayside? But he was mainly
concerned about the little girl. He wanted to know what would
happen to her before they handed her over to some anonymous
parish council.

She was sitting, wide-eyed, on the low harbour wall between
Dan and Michael. She had large dark eyes that seemed almost
too big for her small child's face, full lips, short black hair, her
reddened cheeks smudged with her dried tears. Tim saw at once
she had a look of her dead mother.

Michael was telling her some idiotic tale to make her smile.
Tim took Dan aside to tell him the sad news.

Dan sat down again beside her. 'Now,' he said, 'this is Michael
and this is Tim. These two are my brothers, for my sins. And I'm
Dan.' He smiled. 'And you haven't told us your name.'

'Caitlin,' she said in a tiny voice.

'Well then, Caitlin,' Dan said. 'Where do you come from?'

'Dublin,' she said.

'Dublin,' Dan repeated and he looked at Tim. 'Looks like you
might have to put off your trip to Manchester, Timothy, and
take this young lady home.'

The thought had already occurred to Tim.

Caitlin was looking at Dan in alarm. He put an arm around
her shoulder. There was no easy way to do this but she had to
know.

'Caitlin,' he said gently, 'your mammy has gone to Heaven.
She was taken ill and …'

The girl looked at him in disbelief. 'She's died?'

He nodded. There was nothing more to say, no way to make
it easy for her. She caught a great sob in her throat but she didn't
cry. She looked at him in a way he would never forget, her hands
clasped tight. He wanted to tell her it would be all right, to calm
her fears. But he couldn't find the words.

'Perhaps we should say a prayer,' Tim said quietly.

Michael turned away in disgust. Where are you now, God? he
asked silently. Taking that poor woman! Leaving this poor kid!

Dan had offered his hand and she was holding on to it now as if it was a lifeline. 'You'll be all right, Caitlin,' he assured her. 'We'll sort things out. We'll not leave you, I promise.'

They were silent for a while as the noise and bustle of comings and goings went on around them. Then Dan asked, 'You have family in Dublin? Brothers and sisters? Your daddy?'

She shook her head, still close to tears.

'You must have a daddy,' Michael said gently.

'No,' she said.

'No brothers or sisters?' Tim asked.

'I had a little brother but he was poorly and he died.'

'Granma?' Dan asked. 'What about your Granma?'

She shook her head.

'You don't have any family in Dublin?'

She shook her head again and her eyes filled with tears as if not to have a family was unforgivable. 'We're going to America to live with Aunty Maureen.'

'I think this young lady could do with something to eat,' Dan said. 'In fact, we all could.'

'Good idea,' Michael said and he went off to the pie stall.

Dan had the address of a lady who ran a lodging-house for Roman Catholics on their way to America. Not all landladies in Liverpool would take Catholics. Some even displayed signs that said, 'No Irish'. But this lady was recommended by Father Delaney. They would take Caitlin with them, he decided, tell the lady she was their sister. He didn't want to go into detail. The landlady might feel that Caitlin should be handed over to council workers. But that might mean she would be sent to some paupers' board school and end up in the workhouse and he was not going to let that happen.

The more he thought about it he could see no reason why Caitlin couldn't travel to the United States with them and they could somehow deliver her to her aunt. She had a ticket for the liner. It was in the purse Michael had wrested from the thief. There were two tickets, one for her mother, and the tickets bore no name. Passengers registered their names as they went aboard. Michael had already spotted the possibilities. There was no reason, he announced, why Tim couldn't use the spare ticket.

A small van had arrived at the dock office and from the look of the two men in black who got out Dan guessed they were undertakers. Caitlin's attention was focused on her pie at that moment and Tim and Michael stood before her to make sure her view was obscured. Within minutes the two men emerged with a kind of body bag stretcher that slid into the back of the van and the van honked a way through the crowd.

The lodging-house was a short tram ride away. Mrs O'Leary looked them over. She only had one room available, she said. She could make up a bed for the little girl but one of the boys would have to sleep on the floor. That was fine, Michael said. He could sleep on a clothesline if he had to.

'I'm sure that won't be necessary,' Mrs O'Leary said. 'Now you must go across to the church, see Father Kelly. He blesses all those going off to America and if you are to leave early tomorrow you must go now, right away.'

They thanked her and left their meagre luggage in the room. Dan explained to Mrs O'Leary that Caitlin had no bag because someone had stolen it at the dockside. She shook her head in despair. Ah, it was always happening. Thieves and rogues all over the place. She would see what she could do.

Tim said they would have to tell Father Kelly the truth. They couldn't lie to a priest. Why not? Michael asked. He's only a man. But Father Kelly was not what they expected. He was a solid-looking, former middle-weight boxer with a strong jaw and a broken nose. He had sparse reddish hair and pale-blue eyes and he looked as though he laughed a lot. Michael took to him at once.

'And what are you grinning at, young man? he asked.

'Well, Father?' Michael said, 'if you were not wearing the collar I'd put you down for a boxer.'

Father Kelly feinted with a right and Michael ducked. 'You'll not put me down, son,' he said. 'I was a boxer before the Good Lord called.'

Dan decided to tell Father Kelly everything, the truth from the beginning. 'We told Mrs O'Leary a lie, Father,' he said. 'We told Mrs O'Leary Caitlin was our sister because we didn't want any complications. Caitlin wants to go to America to live with her aunt and we are willing to take her there.'

'It wasn't a bad lie, Father,' Tim said. 'I mean, we had good reason.'

The priest listened but made no comment.

'We want,' Dan began, 'well, I want Tim to come with us.'

'I understood you to say he's expected at the seminary here, in England,' Father Kelly said.

'He is,' Dan said. 'But if you wrote a letter, or maybe a couple of letters I'm sure he could join a seminary over there.'

Father Kelly regarded Dan with a half smile. 'You're the "fixer" around here, I see.'

'No,' Tim said. 'Wait a minute.'

'Michael and I have nowhere to go in New York,' Dan said. 'We won't know anyone. We won't have anywhere to stay, but that's all right for a couple of young fellows. Caitlin would be so much safer under the auspices of the Church. We could all take her across. Tim could take her the rest of the way. Then, as I said, he could join a seminary over there.'

'You could take her yourselves. I could arrange for the holy sisters to meet you. I'm sure they would take good care of her.'

'No, Father,' Dan said decisively.

Father Kelly laughed. 'You don't trust the holy sisters?'

'We promised we would see she got to her aunt.'

'And how do you feel about this, Timothy?'

'I don't know, Father,' Tim said. 'I'm expected at St John's. But after what happened to this little girl today I think it's our duty to do what's best for her.'

'You're to go aboard at nine, you say?' Father Kelly asked. 'Well then I'll meet you at the dock office at eight-thirty on the dot. I'll have letters for you, Timothy. And I'll speak to Father Doyle at St John's. I'll try to speak to Father Delaney, too.' He smiled at Caitlin. 'And if we all go next door to my house I think we might find something like … chocolate cake.'

The rectory next door was built on to the church. Father Kelly ushered them into a pleasant room with two big armchairs with side tables and a large fireplace with a log fire. Caitlin had never been in such a room, but all she could remember of it later was the large crucifix on the mantelpiece.

On a low bookcase to one side of the fireplace was a framed picture of Father Kelly in a pose from his boxing days. Michael was on to it at once, wanting all the details. How many fights? How many knock-outs?

'And did you ever fight in America, Father?'

'No,' Father Kelly said, 'but I'm sure if I had wanted to I would not have had to pay my fare. The young fellow who finished my career could have knocked me there for nothing.'

Sparring in the corridor with Michael as they left, he promised he would be at the dock office at 8.30 as arranged and, true to his word, he was there when they arrived.

Caitlin was wearing a dress Mrs O'Leary had, among other small items, somehow found for her. It was a little too big but she loved it. Though probably not new it was freshly laundered and it seemed as new as any dress she had ever had.

Father Kelly spoke quietly to Tim and gave him two letters, one to a Monsignor Dunne at St Patrick's – the big cathedral on Fifth Avenue – and one to Caitlin's Aunt Maureen. The ex-boxer priest then shook hands with each one of them, Caitlin included. 'Your brother,' he told them with a smile and a nod towards Michael, 'thinks all priests are powder puffs.'

'But not you, Father,' Michael protested, jumping back as Father Kelly aimed a left jab.

Father Kelly turned to Dan last. 'Goodbye, son,' he said warmly. 'It's up to you now, Danny boy. I'm sure you'll do what's right.'

Dan nodded and thanked him for his help. They went to show their tickets and register at the desk by the gangway then, as they prepared to board, all four turned and waved. Father Kelly, in his floor-length black robe, smiled and waved back, his pugilist's face looking out of place above his clerical collar.

Caitlin was excited but scared. She was barely able to take in the events of the past forty eight hours and she was holding on to Dan's hand now as if he had taken her mother's place. She looked up at him and smiled. 'Danny boy,' she said, echoing Father Kelly.

The ship was massive, a shiny black with white-railed decks and four black, red-topped funnels. They had never seen anything like it, not even in the White Star and Cunard posters, and they couldn't wait to get aboard. But first they had to stand in a rapidly growing queue outside the purser's office to be allocated sleeping quarters.

The *Olympic* was one of the premier liners of the day. It was beautifully equipped throughout. Even in third class there was a general room where steerage passengers could relax and meet with friends, and though smoking there was not permitted, another room was set aside for smokers. There were a number of cabins for two passengers and a few family rooms sleeping four. The remaining accommodation was in dormitories. Dan asked for a family room, but when he was told they were not one family and he saw the look on Caitlin's face he said quickly that a dormitory would be fine.

'So what will I tell Ma?' Tim asked.

'Don't worry about it,' Dan told him. 'Just relax. You've got another six or seven days before you can send a letter.'

'Why is that?'

'I asked the purser how long it'll take. He said she's done it in five and a half days, but it's usually more like six, maybe seven.'

Already Michael had gone off exploring. 'They've got a little bar,' he said when he came back. 'You can buy tea and coffee. But no booze. They've got dandelion and burdock and sars'par- illa and stuff like that. But that's all.'

'I expect they have drinks in first class,' Tim said.

'Might not,' Dan said. 'There's a ban on alcohol in the US.'

Michael looked alarmed. 'A ban on alcohol? Now he tells me.'

'They can't ban alcohol,' Tim said. 'It's impossible.'

Caitlin was sitting quietly beside Dan, her head resting against his shoulder. She had not slept much the night before. Mrs O'Leary had brought in a camp-bed and some blankets and she had felt warm and comfortable there with the boys downstairs, talking in Mrs O'Leary's front room.

She didn't remember falling asleep but she awoke several times and in the grey early light she saw that Michael was lying on the floor, snoring noisily, and Dan and Tim were stretched out on the bed that was really only big enough for one of them, all three fully clothed except for their boots.

She was scared when a man stole her mother's purse, an ugly, dirty-looking little man, scared when the woman with the painted face came close with a creepy smile that looked as though it was painted on, scared even more when the woman took hold of her hand. But at that moment her rescuing hero had arrived and she had taken to him at once. Dan had put a strong arm around her shoulder and as soon as he spoke she felt safe.

Dan was lovely. He had talked to her calmly about her mother. He had treated her like a grown-up and she was grateful for that. She was one of their family now, he told her, and they would all stick together until she could join her Aunt Maureen.

Michael was lovely, too. But in a different way. He was always singing and if she was looking sad and feeling sorry for herself he would pull silly faces until he made her laugh. Tim seemed quieter, more serious. But that would be because he was going to be a priest.

The big room was filling up now and the man from Courtown the boys had met on the steamer coming over waved at Dan as if Dan was a friend he had known all his life. Dan waved back and the man brought his wife and two small boys to sit nearby.

The great ship let out a low groan and the chatter in the main cabin subsided. There was a creaking sound and a mild shudder reverberated as the seagulls squawked loudly overhead.

'We're on our way,' Dan said quietly.

# FOUR

SHE WAS LOOKING out to sea, standing by the rail on the upper deck. She was wearing a cloche hat and a slim, tight-fitting full length coat that flapped with the wind about her long legs. She didn't need the high-heeled shoes, she was quite tall anyway. But Dan got the impression this was all part of her pose as she threw back her head to take in the thin rays of intermittent sunshine, knowing she had caught the admiring attention of the lower class of mortals down in steerage.

Michael nudged Dan. 'I'm going to get myself one of those.'

'One of what?' Dan asked.

'One of those. A million-dollar baby.'

'You had better get the million dollars first,' Dan said.

Michael smiled up at her and touched his cap, then he gave her a cheeky wink. The woman ignored Michael but came to the top of the steps, removed a glove languorously and pointed a finger at Dan. Dan looked around him, surprised.

'She means you,' Michael said, nudging him again.

Dan stood up and the woman crooked her finger and signalled for him to come forward. Michael gave a low whistle and Dan looked back at him disdainfully.

'Go on, you big dope,' Michael said. 'See what she wants.'

Tim and Caitlin had been for a walk up to D deck to see what time the *Punch and Judy* show began and they reappeared now just as Dan was climbing the metal steps to first class.

'What's going on?' Tim asked.

'Looks like Danny boy's hooked a big one,' Michael said.

Caitlin caught a glimpse of the well-dressed woman who lifted the red and gold twisted rope at the top of the steps to allow Dan through and the little girl didn't like it. Dan was *her* friend.

Dan doffed his cap respectfully. 'I don't think I'm allowed up here, ma'am.'

'I invited you,' she said, and he noted her voice. It was the first American accent he had encountered in person. 'You're my guest.'

She led him along the deck to where a small metal table and a chair on either side were battened down against the cabin wall, resistant to the wind. They sat down and a waiter in tight black trousers, a white shirt and a short white jacket trimmed with the pale blue of the shipping line, passed by. He glanced briefly at Dan then came back.

'Everything all right here, ma'am?' he asked.

'Perfectly,' she said.

'Could I get you something?'

'Er ... no,' she said, then she smiled at Dan. 'Unless...?'

Dan shook his head. 'Not for me, thank you.'

The waiter nodded and moved away.

'What's your name?'

'Dan,' he said. 'Daniel Dolan.'

'Dan,' she said.

He waited, curious to know why he was here. She took out a silver cigarette case, flicked it open and offered him one. He shook his head.

'Well, I will,' she said, and he watched as she lit a cigarette and languidly blew a smoke ring. 'I thought the lower classes all smoked their heads off.'

He knew she was trying to provoke him. 'Not where I come from,' he said quietly. 'They can barely afford a drink after a hard day's work.'

'A hard day's work,' she repeated.

'Yeah,' he said. 'That's what the lower classes do. A hard day's work. Most of them anyway.'

'Got you,' she said with a laugh. 'I got him ruffled.'

Dan leaned towards her slightly. 'Why did you invite me here?' he asked. 'What do you want?'

She turned towards him, her head bowed conspiratorially. 'I'm bored. The people up here are *old*, wrapped in their blankets, sipping their port wine. I wouldn't be surprised if some of them are already dead.'

'So you thought you'd have some fun baiting the lower classes?'

'I'm sorry. I didn't mean to be insulting. I just want someone to talk to, someone who's still alive.'

'Are you here on your own?'

'Might as well be,' she said. 'My husband's a businessman. He spends all his time fiddling with papers and waiting for ship to shore telephone lines.'

'No family? No children?'

'My husband's sixty-eight. He doesn't want any kids and nor do I. Not with him anyway.'

'You don't sound very happy,' Dan said.

'Oh, I'm all right – when I'm home. It's just this boat ride gets me down. And we've another three days yet.'

'So why did you come?'

'Oh, I love coming to England. Nice hotel, nice shows. And he wants me to come. I don't think he trusts me in NYC on my own.'

NYC? thought Dan, New York City.

'Anyway,' she said, 'I'm supposed to be asking the questions.'

Dan spread his hands. 'Ask away.'

He told her he was with his two brothers, Michael and Tim. They were going to try their luck in the New World. There was nothing for them back home. Tim, he said, was going to be a priest.

'Is that so?' she said, impressed. 'And the little girl?'

'Her mother died,' Dan said, but he didn't elaborate. 'First thing we do is make sure she gets to her aunt in the US.'

'Then you're going to set about making your fortune.'

'I hope so.'

'Well,' she said airily. 'It can be done. Take my husband. A self-made millionaire.' She blew another smoke ring. 'We stayed a week at the Ritz in London. My husband was there on business and I was there for the shops. Then he had something to sort out in Liverpool so we came up by train, first class, of course, and we had three days at the Adelphi, the best hotel in town.'

Dan smiled. 'Am I supposed to be impressed? I mean, I don't know any of these places. I'm just a simple lad from the Bog.'

'Mm ... yes,' she said. 'But you don't have to stay that way. I take it you don't have a job to go to. In which case maybe I could persuade my husband to help.'

Another passing steward glanced at Dan, no doubt wondering who he was and what he was doing in first class.

'I'll introduce you to him,' she offered. 'All you have to do is say nothing, nod your head in the right places and try to look intelligent.'

'Is that what you did?'

'Don't get smart,' she said, tartly.

'Look, it's very kind of you,' Dan said, 'but I have nothing to offer in return.'

She looked him up and down, embarrassing him now. 'Oh, I don't know,' she said, then she went on quickly, 'In the morning I'd like you to take me for a look around steerage.'

'Why would you want to do that?'

'Because there seems to be more going on. More *fun*. The passengers down there look as if they actually move and talk.'

Her husband, she told Dan, was called Baker. He was Joe Baker, a financier. He was well known and well connected in the New York business community. Her name was Barbara. She was a New Yorker, she said, born and bred.

When she came down the vertical steps from the upper deck next morning Dan was there waiting. So, too, were Michael, Tim and Caitlin, all curious to meet Dan's new 'friend'. She was wearing tailored trousers and flat heels and only two rings. No eye-catching jewellery, Dan had warned. But she still looked a little too smartly dressed and well groomed for steerage.

Michael was dazzled by her elegant way of walking and her, what he called, 'class'. He danced attendance like a court jester, doing his best to make her laugh. Tim was more subdued, as usual, and she displayed a friendly deference towards him, the priest-to-be. She bought them ice creams all round but even this didn't alter the sullen look on Caitlin's face.

On D deck there was a piano that could be rolled in or out of doors as the weather dictated. Today was fine with only a gentle breeze and the steerage decks were alive with people taking the air. A little man from Liverpool was seated at the piano, playing and singing to entertain the crowd. Michael, it seemed, already knew the piano player and they had struck up a partnership where Michael joined in to harmonize some of the tunes. Michael sang and did a little tap dance and delighted the children by pretending to overbalance, just righting himself in time. The watching crowd clapped and cheered and Caitlin sucked her thumb in delight, the interloper forgotten for the moment. But the frown returned when Barbara led Dan away saying she needed to talk to him. Her husband, she said, would like to meet him and Dan was invited to join her and Mr Baker for dinner.

Dan was doubtful. He didn't want to get too involved with this Barbara but the prospect of a job was not easy to ignore. The problem was he didn't have a decent jacket or even a necktie. Barbara said this was not a problem and told him to be at the top of the steps at 7.30 the following evening.

When he arrived, one of the white-coated stewards was waiting. Dan expected to be turned back but the steward lifted the rope and beckoned him in. 'Here you go, son,' he said and he handed him a dark jacket. 'Go on, put it on.'

Dan pulled the jacket on and the steward handed him a striped tie. He looked at the steward in the half light. 'What's going on?'

'Mrs Baker's orders,' the steward said. 'Now it's my coat and I want it back. No soup stains. OK?'

'Thank you,' Dan said, knotting the tie. 'I'll take good care of it.'

'You better,' the steward said. 'Now let me look at you. Yeah. You'll do. Come on, follow me.'

It was a calm pleasant evening and as the steward led him

along the deserted upper deck Dan caught the plaintive strains of an orchestra. Then as the steward led him indoors the music became louder and close at hand. Double swing doors now and an elegant restaurant, many of the tables occupied.

Barbara, in a long silk gown, was nursing a glass of champagne. She saw Dan at once, excused herself from the people she was with and came over to greet him.

'Go get 'em, son,' the steward said, under his breath. 'Looks like you got it made.'

Dan had never seen anything like this, except in a silent movie or in a poster for one of those shows in Dublin. Men in dinner jackets and black ties, expensively clad ladies with diamonds that sparkled at their mostly wrinkled necks, and in the background on a curved stage a ten piece orchestra, in white trousers and blue striped jackets, was playing *Moonlight and Roses*.

Barbara looked him over, at his dark eyes and wayward black hair, and seemed to approve of what she saw. A waiter led them to their table and Dan saw that several of the ladies looked at him quizzically as he passed. They were all without exception, as Michael would say, 'well past it'. Nowhere was there any competition for his amused hostess.

'What's funny?' he asked as they sat down.

'You are,' Barbara said and she leaned forward and laughed. 'You have awakened the dead and the dead don't approve.'

Dan bristled. 'I don't need their approval,' he said, his chin raised as he looked around.

'Don't get upset,' she said. 'It's me they don't approve of, not you.' She leaned closer. 'Why aren't you ignorant and stupid? You're from Ireland, for God's sake.'

'I am ignorant,' he said. 'But I'm not stupid. If I was stupid I wouldn't know I was ignorant. Being stupid is tough. But being ignorant is OK. That can be put right. I'm a fast learner.'

A slightly stooping man in his late sixties had arrived to catch this last bit. 'Fast learner, eh? I'm glad to hear it, son. You'll have to be if you're gonna work for me.'

Dan jumped to his feet at once.

'Joe Baker,' the older man said. 'An' you must be?'

'Dolan, sir. Dan Dolan.'

'Well sit down, Dan. I need a drink.'

Mr Baker barely raised a finger and at once a waiter arrived. He ordered water and looked across at Barbara but she shook her head. She still had the champagne. 'What'll it be, Dan?'

'I'll have what you're having, sir.'

'An indigestion tablet?'

Dan laughed and Mr Baker ordered two beers. The menu was in French but, fortunately for Dan, an English translation in pale type was under each line. He read what was on offer and felt maybe an indigestion tablet was not a bad idea. In steerage there was a refectory with bare wooden tables where you could buy a plate of fish and chips, or cabbage and ribs, or sometimes a bowl of doubtful-looking stew that most of the passengers gave a miss.

He wanted to ask Mr Baker about America and the prospect of advancement. But he soon found it was his host who was asking the questions. He told him about the village where he came from, about the estate of the absentee English landlord he had worked for and, embellishing the facts only slightly, he explained that he had been responsible for the staff and the day-to-day running of the place. Why had he left? Limited prospects, he answered. At home, he said, America is seen as the land of opportunity.

'And so it is, son,' Mr Baker said, 'so it is. But only for those prepared to work.'

'I've always worked, sir. Even in the evenings after school. Our mother needed the money.'

'There are three of you.'

'My brothers, Tim and Michael. Tim is joining the priest-hood.'

'That so?' Mr Baker was impressed.

'We don't expect to see much of him for the next year or two. He'll go to a seminary, then when he's ordained, well, we don't know. He could be sent anywhere.'

'So you and your other brother will be looking for work?'

Dan nodded and decided to tell him about Caitlin. How they had found her alone at the dockside and were taking her to her aunt.

'Poor kid,' Mr Baker said, again impressed.

A waiter spoke quietly to Mr Baker. He nodded and stood up. 'My call came through,' he said.

'I reckon my husband was born with a telephone in his hand,' Barbara said as he went off with the waiter.

Dan was glad of the opportunity to ask questions. 'This is all very nice,' he said first of all, 'but what am I doing here?'

She shrugged. 'Joe works all the time, morning, noon and night. He knew I was bored and he didn't mind when I went down to see you and your family in steerage. I told him what a fine fella you are and he said he'd like to meet you.'

'So will he offer me a job?'

'I think he's impressed, especially with all that stuff about your brother the priest and the rescue act with the little girl.'

'Maybe he's not as cynical as you,' he said.

Her chin rose slightly. 'I wouldn't count on it.'

'Got you,' he said with a laugh. 'I got her ruffled.'

Later, when Dan left to go back to the lower deck, he had plenty to tell the others. When we dock in New York, he told them, first class passengers and non-immigration passengers will be allowed off. Then the rest of us will be transferred to a smaller boat and taken to Immigration Control. We have to go through some kind of clearance. When we get settled, he said, I'm to ring Barbara and make an appointment to see Mr Baker. Maybe he'll have jobs for us.

'So it's *Barbara*, is it?' Michael said with a grin. 'I don't think our Caitlin approves of all this. She reckons this Barbara's got her hooks into you.'

Dan smiled at Caitlin. 'Barbara is Mr Baker's wife, Caitlin.'

# FIVE

THE NEWCOMERS FLOODED the main deck in third class to gaze in awe at the hugely symbolic Statue of Liberty as the *Olympic* sailed majestically into New York harbour. The torch held high seemed like a greeting, a gesture of welcome to those filled with the wonder and excitement of their hopes for the future.

Dan's information was correct. First to disembark were the privileged few from the upper decks, the elegantly dressed met by chauffeurs or pre-booked cab drivers. Third-class passengers with unstamped tickets followed and the immigrants waited. And waited. It was almost two hours before what looked like a tugboat arrived alongside and those left aboard were corralled towards lines of rope that led to a gangplank from the liner to the tug.

An officious-looking, uniformed immigration officer checked tickets and asked the same questions as the passengers shuffled along. 'Are you carrying any liquor?'

Michael looked at him blankly.

'Are you carrying any alcohol?'

Michael exaggerated his accent. 'Oh no, sir. I'm Irish.'

The immigration man eyed him as if mentally noting his face before moving on.

'Behave, you idiot,' Dan said. 'We have to get through this.'

The entrance examination at Ellis Island was long drawn out but simple enough for Dan and the boys. They were all young and healthy as were the man from Courtown and his family and they all spoke English as their mother tongue. Tim explained

Caitlin's circumstances and produced the letter of introduction to the monsignor at St Patrick's. It helped that the officer was Irish and that Caitlin had her aunt's address to go to. When the group divided into channels, male and female, Caitlin was chaperoned by the wife of the man from Courtown.

Many people sharing a voyage and passing through Ellis Island made friends *en route*, friendships that lasted sometimes for the rest of their lives. Dan and his brothers and the young man from Courtown and his family vowed to keep in touch.

It was a long trolley ride to Brooklyn but the boys and Caitlin were enthralled, enjoying every minute as they took in their first impression of Manhattan Island. From the Dublin boat the skyline along the Liverpool waterfront had seemed somehow majestic and intimidating but here the sheer height of the skyscrapers took their breath away as they leaned forward, crouching low to see the tops of the vertical buildings.

It was fortunate. Dan realized when the trolley came to their stop, that before crossing the East River they had seen some of the better sights the city had to offer.

'Scholes Street!' the driver called. Then: 'Didn't somebody want this dump?'

'Oh yes, sir,' Dan said suddenly. And all four scrambled for the exit, thanking the driver profusely as Dan asked, 'Is this it?'

'Guess so, son,' the driver said. 'The Navy Yard down there. OK?'

'Thank you,' Dan said. 'Thank you very much.'

They watched from the grey sidewalk as the trolley car rattled on its way. Three boys in flat caps and clothing that marked them out to the casual observer as 'new arrivals', Caitlin's cotton dress barely adequate even in that oppressive and humid July.

At Immigration when asked if they had an address to go to, Dan had given the address of Caitlin's Aunt Maureen who lived in some place called Albany. Do you know how to get there? he was asked. Oh yes, sir, he said with Tim in the background shaking his head at the lie. But Dan didn't want any complications. He just wanted to get through.

On the dockside at Battery Park men of various nationalities and religions offered accommodation. A man wearing a cloth shamrock at his lapel gave them a piece of paper with the name O'Malley's Guest House, Scholes Street off Manhattan Avenue, near the Navy Yard, Brooklyn, scrawled in pencil. It sounded all right but by now Dan was not impressed. Already a blueprint of the city was taking shape in his head. He only had to experience a place once and he could find his way around. Tim was the same but Michael could get lost in their own village – or so they teased him.

Sitting quietly, watching the streets go by, Dan had noticed how the hotels and buildings looked shabbier at this ragged edge of town. He guessed that where they were heading would not be up to much and he was right. On Scholes Street they ran into trouble.

It was just going dark as they ambled along examining the brownstone houses for the name 'O'Malley'. Most of the shops now were at the Avenue end except for a grocery store and a tobacco shop. Further down was a small police station. Sailors in twos and threes on what they called shore leave were heading across the river.

As the Dolan boys and Caitlin drew near a group in their whites, exhilarated at the prospect of a night out, decided it was time for some fun at the expense of these 'micks' as they called all Irish immigrants. At once they began to hurl abuse and taunt the already disorientated four. The boys ignored them until one of them made a gesture and uttered an obscenity that was clearly heard by Caitlin.

Michael, who was closest to the sailor, reacted with a startling ferocity. He grabbed the sailor by the flapping collar of his uniform, swung him round and rammed his head against a brick wall. Two of the other sailors came to their friend's aid but, just as incensed, Dan barred their way, his fists raised, ready to take them on. Aware of the navy police patrol van where Scholes Street met the Avenue and not wanting their night out curtailed prematurely, the sailors hesitated. Then one led them away, glaring at Michael with the words, 'You wait, spud head. We'll remember you.'

Pleased to escape unscathed the boys went on down the street and Michael's shoulders took on an exaggerated swagger. It was a dubious victory but one that was to grow to inflated proportions in the telling. Caitlin was to remember the time the boys took on the navy – *six* hefty sailors! – and her story was neither modified nor denied by the others. If they were honest, all three knew there were not six, there were four, and the 'hefty' sailors were no bigger than themselves, boys in men's clothing.

O'Malley's was a large brownstone house divided into rooms to let. Dan knocked lightly on the open door, then knocked again and after a while Peg O'Malley, a small, slim, stern-looking woman came from the depths of the lobby, drying her hands on her apron. She eyed them warily and asked them who they were and what they wanted though she was, in fact, expecting them. The man with the cloth shamrock had phoned from the dock.

Peg O'Malley was slightly built and no more than five feet two. She had thick black hair, the grey roots showing through, black eyebrows, dark-blue eyes and a face that was striking rather than pretty.

She only had the one room, she told them sternly. That would be fine, Dan said. It would only be for a few nights then there would just be two of them. He looked at Tim and Tim explained that he was to take Caitlin to her aunt and then he was to join the priesthood. Peg O'Malley looked at them doubtfully and Dan asked if he might speak to her in private.

'Go into the parlour,' she told the others, 'and make sure you behave yourselves.' With a jerk of her head she indicated that Dan was to follow her.

In the kitchen he told her what happened on the dockside in Liverpool, how Caitlin now had no one but her aunt's family in some place called Albany and how they had decided to take good care of her and see that she got there.

Peg O'Malley was impressed. 'Well,' she said, 'she can't share a room with you three. I'll make her a little bed in my room.'

*

The next day the boys took Caitlin across to Fifth Avenue. It was hot and humid yet everyone seemed to be in a great hurry, dashing in and out of shops and offices. They soon found St Patrick's. It was an imposing presence in the heart of the city. Smaller than the surrounding skyscrapers it seemed somehow more grand and its wide steps and impressive portals had an elegance that was missing from the glass and concrete jungle.

'Look,' Michael said, 'I'll see you back at Mrs O'Malley's. I promised, soon as I was in town, I would go and see Nathan.'

They didn't have an appointment but a young priest took them to a small waiting room. A man in a suit came, read Tim's letter of introduction, smiled at Caitlin and asked them to wait. It was another half-hour before Monsignor Dunne arrived but when he did he seemed to know all about them.

'Your Aunt Maureen is longing to see you, my dear,' he told Caitlin. He looked at Tim. 'The lady was terribly worried when she heard what happened but we assured her that her niece was safe and in good hands.' And by way of explanation he added, 'We asked her parish priest to call and explain the situation.'

When Monsignor Dunne spoke he sounded neither Irish nor American. His voice was devoid of accent but Dan guessed right: he was English. He had the same rather cold, formal manner of the English landlord Dan had worked for back home, so unlike Father Kelly, the boxer, in Liverpool.

'And how prepared are you, young man,' the monsignor asked Tim, 'for the spiritual journey you wish to undertake?'

'To be a priest is what I want, Monsignor,' Tim said. 'It's what I've always wanted.'

Dan and Caitlin sat quietly, as Tim was cross-examined. The monsignor leaned back in his chair. 'And you think you could perform the Mass here at St Patrick's?'

Tim nodded confidently. 'I'm sure I could, Monsignor. I've played my part many times as an altar boy. I am familiar with everything that's required. Even the garments the priest must wear. The colours of the chasuble. Violet in Lent, white at Christmas and Feast Days, green at other times.'

The monsignor nodded. 'You will stay at a small church here

in New York. Good parish, West Side, mostly Irish families. Then in September, when the academic year begins, you will become a seminarian.'

'Do you know where that will be?'

'I'm afraid not,' the monsignor admitted.

Dan stood up. 'It might be better if Caitlin and I wait outside, Monsignor. You and Tim have things to discuss.'

'I need to spend some time with your brother,' the monsignor agreed. 'I'd like him to stay with me for much of the day.'

'Then Caitlin and I will explore New York,' Dan said with a smile. He shook hands with the monsignor. To Tim he said, 'We'll see you back at Mrs O'Malley's.'

Dan and Caitlin left hand in hand and spent the rest of the day exploring Manhattan. Up and down Fifth Avenue. The huge billboards in Times Square. The world clocks. Broadway. An ice cream by the fountain at the Grand Army Plaza. The itinerant musicians in Central Park. The ducks by the lakeside. Stopping to stroke the necks of the tall horses with the shiny black carriages lined up at the park gates. And a bench where they collapsed in a heap to sit back and watch as this strange new world began to unfold.

It was all arranged. They would meet Aunt Maureen and Uncle Pat under the big clock at Pennsylvania Station. Twelve noon on Friday. All arranged, and that old scary feeling was back. Caitlin had relaxed. She felt comfortable and safe with the boys and now she would be leaving them. They had kept her busy, made her laugh. She had not had much time to cry, except at night sometimes. But most nights she was too tired to cry and she just fell asleep.

The one or two times when she lay awake she felt safe and not too sad because she knew Dan was near. She loved Dan. She loved Michael and Tim, too. She would always love them now. But she loved Dan the most of all.

'Time we were going,' Dan said.

'Can we sit by the fountain again? Just for a few minutes?'

'Sure,' he said. 'Why not?' And they dodged through the swirl of Lincolns and Fords, smiling apologetically at a police officer who eyed their hazardous progress.

They sat on the low wall surround where tourists and office workers catching the afternoon sun took a break.

'This fountain,' Dan said, 'is not just for show, you know. It has a job to do. A very important job.'

'What?' she asked.

'Well, I don't know if I should tell you this, but it's a sort of State secret.'

Caitlin looked at him doubtfully.

'You see, it's not just any fountain,' he told her, 'it's a *magic* fountain. When no one's looking it shoots up in the air, catches the glints of sunlight, turns them into sparkling diamonds and stows them away in a secret vault.

'And sometimes,' he went on, 'one or two diamonds get left behind and if you look closely you can spot them in the water.'

She peered curiously into the water around the fountain. Then she looked at him again and laughed. 'You're mad,' she said. 'Absolutely mad.' And she leaned in to him, not wanting to leave, not wanting the day to end.

'What's that over there?' she asked. 'With all the flags.'

'I think it's the Plaza Hotel,' Dan said.

'It looks very grand.'

'It is,' he said. 'Too posh for the likes of us. But I'll tell you what. One day, when we're all rich and famous – well, rich anyway – and you're a grand lady with a fur coat and a little poodle on a long lead, we'll have a reunion. You, me, Tim and Michael. Afternoon tea at the Plaza Hotel.'

'Not a poodle. A spaniel with big eyes and floppy ears.'

'Sounds like you,' Dan said with a laugh.

'I haven't got floppy ears,' she said and she hit him playfully with the little handbag Mrs O'Malley had given her and chased him when he ran away.

Breathless and laughing they clambered aboard the trolley back to Brooklyn and as they settled in their seats Caitlin felt again that desperate pang of impending loss.

'When?' she asked, as the trolley gathered speed. 'When will we do it?'

'Do what?'

'Have afternoon tea at the Plaza Hotel.'

'Ah,' Dan said thoughtfully. 'Let's say when you're twenty-one.'

'But that's ages away.'

'You will be twenty-one,' he said. 'You will have gained your independence. You will be free to do whatever you want. Let's say Independence Day. Fourth of July, nineteen … thirty five.'

'But that's ten years away.'

Dan laughed. 'It'll take us ten years to earn enough money for afternoon tea at the Plaza Hotel, so it will.'

# SIX

MRS O'MALLEY HAD given Dan and Michael the name of an Irish gentleman, foreman at a company called the Acme Carriage and Transport Company. It was casual work, she said, but it would do until they found better. They did two long days, Wednesday and Thursday, stacking heavy boxes on to delivery vans and on the Thursday they worked until seven.

The Acme Carriage and Transport Company warehouses were only a few yards from the entrance to the Navy Yard and when Dan and Michael eventually signed off and left to walk back to Mrs O'Malley's they had to pass a group of sailors who were standing on a corner. One of them had spotted Michael.

It was obvious the sailors had seen their opportunity and this time there *were* six of them. Dan and Michael set off running and the sailors took up the chase. Then, as they turned into Scholes Street they found they were running towards more sailors. There seemed to be no escape. Dan grabbed Michael by his jacket and dragged him into the tiny police station along from the grocery store. The two groups of sailors met and came to a halt outside.

The place was sparsely furnished and empty but for a sergeant at his desk, reading a sports paper. He looked up at them, eyebrows raised, as they tumbled in breathless. They didn't know what to say.

'You fellas want something?' the sergeant asked after a moment.

Dan was trying to think of some innocuous enquiry he might make, but Michael blurted out, 'Do you know what time it is, Sarge?'

The sergeant looked at him for a long moment. 'Just off the boat?'

'We only arrived Monday,' Michael said with a bright smile, ready to build a conversation.

'Is that so?' The sergeant turned on his seat, looking up at the big clock on the wall behind him. 'Well now,' he said, with measured sarcasm, 'that big round thing is called a clock ...'

Dan laughed. 'All right, Sergeant,' he said. 'The truth is we had a bit of trouble with the navy. They're outside.'

The sergeant folded his newspaper and went to the door. Seven or eight of the sailors were still there. He looked at them, unsmiling, and they began to drift away. They knew that a complaint from the police was always trouble, banned shore leave maybe, whether they were in the right or not.

'What are you doing down here anyway?' the sergeant asked the boys and when they told him they had been doing casual work at the warehouse he shook his head. 'You're going to fight the navy, that's not a good idea,' he said. 'Now I don't know what you fellas been up to and I don't wanna know, but you can't come running in here unless you got a knife sticking out your back. And we don't want that, do we? If I were you I'd get a job some place else.'

He didn't want to file a report. He would be going off duty shortly. He went back to the door to make certain the way was clear. 'Go on,' he said. 'Get outa here. And stay outa trouble.'

They had told the foreman at the warehouse they would not be in on Friday. Family business. But they might work Saturday, if that was OK. They planned to say goodbye to Caitlin at Penn Station. They didn't know they were losing Tim, too. And when Tim told them Michael tried again. There's no hurry, he insisted. You have lots of time. Give New York a chance, man. You don't have to be a priest just yet. But it was no good. It was all arranged.

Caitlin was very quiet. She had not seen Aunty Maureen and her family in over a year, but she knew them well enough and she knew her mother would want her to be with them. But she didn't really want to leave the boys and she told Dan this on the brink of tears. Dan told her she was a part of his family now and she always would be. But Tim was going away and he and Michael had to find work and make a home for themselves. Aunty Maureen already had a home and she wanted her there, where she should be.

'You'll soon forget about us when you get to your new school and everything,' Michael said cheerfully. 'We've got nothing to offer, nowhere of our own and we can't stay at Mrs O'Malley's forever.' He looked at Dan. 'We need to talk about that.'

But Caitlin was still not happy on the Friday morning when they set off to the station. Both Tim and Michael tried to make her smile but without success and she held on to Dan's hand as if she would never let go.

'When we get to the station,' Dan told his brothers at the first opportunity, 'don't say much. It'll only bring on the tears.'

The bustle of Penn Station made any significant conversation difficult and instead of waiting under the clock as arranged they found themselves standing on the platform as the train from Albany steamed in. It was far from full and, as the passengers stepped down, a man and a woman in their thirties and a little girl saw Caitlin and started to wave their hands. The woman and the little girl ran forward and the man followed, all smiles.

Caitlin was swept up into her Aunt Maureen's arms and the boys stood back, forgotten for the moment in the raw emotion. Aunt Maureen's husband held out a hand. His name was Pat, he said in a quiet Trinity voice, and they'd done a fine thing.

Tim had recognized Caitlin's aunt at once. She had the darkly pretty looks of the young woman he had seen lying dead in the back room at the dock office in Liverpool. When her husband introduced the boys it was Tim, the priest-to-be, she turned to.

Caitlin and her young cousin were smiling at each other as Aunty Maureen, arms around both girls, thanked Tim and Dan and Michael profusely. The Lord would bless them. She was sure of that, she said. Her family would be forever in their debt.

There was little time between trains, not much time for them all to get to know each other, and Tim was due at St Patrick's.

For Caitlin it was all happening with bewildering speed and she couldn't hold back the tears. She hugged Tim and Michael and when she turned to Dan she looked at him in abject desolation. Then she clung to him until he was forced to draw her arms gently from about his neck. He looked deep into her eyes and whispered, 'Independence Day.'

Caitlin nodded and tried to smile and then they were gone.

In a different way saying goodbye to Tim was just as difficult. True, he would be around until September, but they knew that from now on and for the rest of their lives they were not going to see much of him. Sure, families split up all the time. Brothers, sisters, they go their own way. Of course they do. But their little trio had always been together, aware of each others strengths and weaknesses, knowing they could always rely on each other.

A brief *abrazo* on the steps of St Patrick's and Tim left, turning once and raising a hand before dissolving into the subdued light of the cathedral's dim interior. Dan and Michael, standing in the bright sunshine, raised their hands in response.

Dan wanted to sit down with the visitors and office workers on the wide steps and take in the events of the morning.

'Just you and me now,' he told Michael.

'Yeah,' Michael said, clearly raring to go. 'That's right.'

Dan sat down and pointed to the space beside him. 'Sit down,' he said, 'and tell me what's on your mind. I can see something is.'

'Well,' Michael said, 'like I told you, I went to see Nathan. I want you to come with me, now, this afternoon, and see him, see what he's doing. He's got a great job. No kidding.'

'A great job?' Dan questioned doubtfully. 'So soon?'

'He's playing the joanna and singing.'

Dan laughed. 'He can play the piano, but he can't sing. And that's not a proper job. Playing piano in some club at night.'

'No,' Michael said, his enthusiasm undimmed. 'He's playing all day at this music shop. He sells sheet music. You know, all the latest songs and everything. Come on, I'll show you.'

He set off from the steps and Dan followed.

'Where is this place'?' he asked.

'Twenty-eighth,' Michael said, as if he knew his way around. 'East or west?'

'I don't know, do I? It's down here somewhere. Just follow me. I'll know it when I see it. I was there Tuesday.'

Dan glanced up. 'Forty-ninth Street, Forty-eighth.'

The sidewalk was crowded on both sides of Fifth Avenue and Michael sang all the way. It was a long walk but part of the way they stole a ride on the step of a trolley, only dropping off when the guard appeared.

Nathan was sitting outside Levi's Music Store at a small piano that could be wheeled indoors if it rained like the one on the boat. He was banging out a tune but nobody was listening and when he saw Michael he stopped in mid-flow.

'Hey, Mikey! Dan! How're you doin'?' He already had the twang.

'What are *you* doing, Nathan?' Dan asked. 'What's the job?'

'I play the tunes and the people buy the music. I get two cents on every sheet.'

'You play on commission? No sale, no pay?'

Nathan nodded cheerfully. 'Yeah, that's right.'

'And are you selling many copies?'

'Well, no,' Nathan admitted. 'That's the problem. The manager says I gotta sing. People wanna hear the words. That's why I need Michael. He can sing. The girls'll love him.'

Michael glanced at Dan sheepishly. They had obviously come to some arrangement, something he hadn't told Dan about.

'I want to give this a go, Dan,' Michael said. 'I don't want to go on stacking boxes in that old warehouse. No future in that.'

'Mrs O'Malley has to be paid,' Dan said mildly.

'Well, that's another thing. If I'm going to be here, working with Nathan, I need to be living here.'

Dan nodded. This was something else Michael hadn't mentioned, 'And have you got somewhere to stay?'

'Well.' Michael looked at Nathan as if to say: help me out here. 'Nathan's living in this place in Greenwich Village.'

'It's not much,' Nathan said. 'But it's OK 'til we get somewhere.

This guy from the boat, he has this room an' he says we can stay for a while. As long as the landlord doesn't find out.'

Dan smiled. He didn't want to ridicule their plans but he had to say, 'And what if he does?'

'We'll take that when it comes,' Michael said. 'But we want to get in the music business, Dan. This is just a start.'

'You're going to have to sell a lot of sheets,' Dan said.

'Well, we reckon we can do this in the day,' Nathan said, 'and we can work in the bars and clubs at night.'

'Bartending?'

'No,' Michael said. 'If we work here we can get our act together. We can be first with all the latest songs.'

A short, bald man with his spectacles pushed up to his forehead came to the shop doorway. 'I don't hear no piano.'

'Yeah,' Nathan said. 'Sorry, Mr Levi. This is my friend Mike. The singer I was telling you about.'

Mr Levi looked Michael up and down. 'Can he read?'

Michael looked worried. 'He can read a bit,' Nathan said. 'But I can teach him more. Reading music ain't that tough, Mr Levi.'

'Nah,' Mr Levi said. 'I mean can he *read*? *Words*. Last guy was here couldn't read.'

Michael relaxed and Nathan laughed. 'Oh sure, Mr Levi.'

Mr Levi stared hard at Michael with his dark penetrating eyes. 'OK,' he said. 'So sing.' And with that he went back in the shop.

Dan stood aside, arms folded. It was not exactly a job but it was clearly what Michael wanted. 'OK,' he said with a grin. 'So sing.'

Totally unselfconscious, Michael struck up a pose. '*Give my regards to Broadway ...*' he sang and Nathan picked up the tune.

People passing by began smiling and glancing as they passed and a small boy stopped and gazed at Michael with his mouth open. Mr Levi came out again, still frowning. 'Hey!' he said. 'We ain't sellin' that. Sing somethin' we got in stock. Here.'

He thrust a piece of sheet music at Michael, went back inside, came out with a little pile of copies and stacked them on top of the piano. 'Sing that,' he said, and again he went inside.

Michael looked at the flimsy paper with a line drawing of a young man looking down at an old man in a rocking chair. 'Hey, Nathan!' he said with a laugh. 'Listen to this. *Daddy, you've been a mother to me.*'

Mr Levi was back in the doorway. 'Sing it,' he said.

Nathan played it through once, then he played it again and Michael hummed along until he had it and when he sang it he thought it was the corniest song he had ever heard. But a young woman stopped and picked up a copy, looked at it briefly and dropped a dime in Nathan's jam jar. 'Our first sale!' Nathan cried. 'Hey, Mikey, we're on our way!'

Dan watched, bemused. He was pleased for his brother if this was what he wanted. But whether he and Nathan could make a living at this kind of thing he had his doubts.

The dynamic duo, as Dan took to calling them, sold eight sheets in half an hour, less than a dime each. But it was a start. 'I'll bring your things over from Mrs O's tomorrow,' he told Michael when Nathan went indoors to find another song. 'Give me the address of this place you'll be at.'

'Er ... no,' Michael said. 'Better not. You might run into this guy's landlord. There isn't much anyway, couple of shirts and stuff. I can come over and pick them up first chance I get.' He looked worried. 'Listen, Dan, this doesn't seem right somehow.'

Dan smiled. 'Don't worry about it. Give it a go. Give it all you've got. And don't worry about me. I won't be far away.'

Another brotherly *abrazo* and a quick wave to Nathan who was still in the shop and Dan set off for the Avenue.

'Take care,' Michael called, his eyes moist. He was feeling guilty now as if he had broken up what was left of the family. 'And watch out for the navy.'

Dan raised a hand above his head as he turned the corner. So this is it, he told himself a little surprised. You're on your own.

# SEVEN

THE NEW YORK businessman had given Dan his card. When you get settled give me a call, son. I might be able to use you. Use me? Dan thought. As what? He had no qualifications, no experience of working in a big city. But Joe Baker had seemed serious and genuine. His last words as he and his wife, Barbara, left the ship were, 'Give me a call, why don't ya?'

Dan fished the card and an old envelope from his pocket. This was where he kept what little money he had left, eight dollars and forty cents. *Joe Baker Associates*, he read, *339 Madison Avenue*. Maybe he should telephone for an appointment. But could he afford to and what would it cost? He stopped to look at the men's suits and shirts in one of the wide windows of Manhattan's newest and biggest store, Saks Fifth Avenue. He had to find some decent clothes. Nobody was going to give him a job the way he looked. Flat cap, frayed jacket, collarless shirt. Except maybe a labouring job. There were no price tickets on the suits but they were well out of his reach anyway. Maybe he could hire a suit. But what the hell? Joe Baker knew more or less all there was to know about him. Maybe he should try him first.

He had worked out the layout of the city. It was pretty good really, made a lot of sense. Avenues going down, streets going across with the odd exception. Broadway seemed to go its own way, cutting across the rest. Maybe Madison did the same. Or why didn't it have a number? Best to ask the way. Excuse me, he said apologetically as a smart-looking young man approached. But the young man walked straight on, didn't even glance at him. Welcome to New York, Dan muttered to himself. He stared at his reflection in a shop window. He looked like a tramp. The young fellow probably thought he was going to tap him for a hand-out. I've never begged in my life, Dan told himself indignantly.

He walked on along the shabby sunless street and out to another bustling thoroughfare. Must be Fourth Avenue, he guessed. Then he saw the sign: Madison Ave. Number 339 turned out to be an office block with an open street door. Vertical blinds obscured the ground floor windows. Dan hesitated briefly but then he decided he might as well try his luck.

Through the door was a small vestibule. On the wall was a list of five or six companies followed by an invitation to 'Ring for attention'. He pressed the button next to Joe Baker Associates. Nothing. He pressed it again and eventually a girl of about his own age came primly down the narrow stairway with a fixed business smile. But when she saw Dan the smile evaporated.

'Yes?' she said archly.

Dan snatched his cap off. 'I'm here to see Mr Baker.'

'Do you have an appointment?'

'Er ... no,' he said. 'Not exactly.'

The girl frowned and shook her head as if what he asked was out of the question. 'I'm sorry ...'

'Look,' he said. 'Just tell him Dan Dolan is here, off the ship.'

Still she hesitated but then she looked relieved as Barbara Baker, laden with several expensive-looking shopping bags, came in from the street. 'Mrs Baker,' she said 'This man ...'

Barbara's face lit up when she saw Dan. 'Hey, Danny! How are you? How nice to see you.'

'I'm fine, thank you,' Dan said. 'I was in town and I thought ...'

'Here,' she said. She handed him a couple of the shopping bags and the girl took another. 'Come on upstairs. There's no lift in this goddam place. Thank you, Janet. I'll take care of Mr Dolan.'

The girl glanced sheepishly at Dan and he winked at her,

adding to her embarrassment, as she turned to lead the way up the stairs.

Janet had her desk in a small outer office. There was a much bigger office where an older man and a stenographer looked busy. Partitioned off in one corner was another office with a glazed door, the name Paul Merrick stencilled in gold letters on the glass. Facing them a closed door made up the suite.

Barbara left her shopping bags with Janet and signalled that Dan should follow. She tapped lightly on the closed door and looked in. Joe Baker was, as usual, holding a telephone. He beckoned her inside and when he saw Dan he nodded and smiled and indicated the chairs by his large desk.

'Danny boy!' he exclaimed, when he put the telephone down. 'Good to see you.' He shook Dan by the hand, kissed Barbara lightly on the cheek and asked, 'Where did you find him?'

'He was downstairs, trying to convince Janet he was on the level,' Barbara said with a laugh.

Baker opened a drawer in his desk. 'A drink?'

Dan shook his head. 'Not during the day, Mr Baker. In fact, I don't drink much at all.'

He laughed. 'I'm not asking you to get plastered, for God's sake. Just a little celebration. You'll have one, Barbara?'

'Sure,' Barbara said. 'Why not?'

He set three small glasses on his desk and poured three shots of Jack Daniel's. Dan felt he ought to explain why he had come but he didn't know how. He looked at Baker uncomfortably.

'You want a job.' Baker laughed, sensing his discomfort. 'Sure you do. Why else would you come here?'

Dan was twisting his cap as if it was wet and he was wringing it out. He felt as though he was in a court of law and he was the accused. 'I just stopped by to say hello, Mr Baker. I shouldn't have come. I mean, I expect you're pretty busy right now.'

Baker turned to Barbara. 'Will you listen to him?' he said in exasperation. 'Talking himself out of a job before it's offered.'

Barbara leaned over, took Dan's cap and threw it in the waste bin. 'You are not going to need that old thing no more.'

'So what can you do, son?' Baker asked.

'Not much,' Dan admitted. 'But I'm willing to learn.'

'Good,' Baker said. 'That's what I want. Someone who knows nothing, but ain't dumb.'

Dan had imagined Joe Baker Associates had a finger in all kinds of pies and he might be offered a small job somewhere in Baker's empire. But it wasn't like that. Joe Baker Associates seemed to do all their business from this small office.

'I want a young man I can trust totally, someone who will do all the running around and in my best interests. Not his own. This is my business, OK? Loyalty is number one.' He was watching Dan intently. 'You seen *Julius Caesar*?'

'No, sir,' Dan said. 'But I will.'

Baker nodded in approval. 'What I want is a Mark Antony, not a Brutus.'

'What would I have to do, Mr Baker? I mean, where would I work and what kind of work would it be?'

'You wouldn't do much at all at first. You would just listen and learn. Where would you be? You'd be here with me. A gofer, a Man Friday, a kind of personal assistant.'

'A gofer?' Dan queried. First time he had heard the word.

'You go for this, you go for that. When I need something, anything, from coffee or milk to the very latest Dow Jones, you go get it. You keep my diary, tell me where I'm supposed to be, who I'm supposed to ring, who I'm supposed to meet.'

Dan smiled. 'When do I start?'

Dan hadn't asked about pay or for the loan he looked as though he needed and Baker liked that. 'How about right now?' he said. 'I'll pay you twenty-five a week for three months and we'll see how it goes. After that we do things right. We set up a contract or, if you're no good, you're out.'

It was more than he could have hoped for. The talk on the boat was that a man could expect to earn around fifteen, maybe twenty working weekends. Girls could earn about ten in the sweatshops, fifteen with overtime. He stood up, hand extended. 'You won't be sorry, Mr Baker. I promise.'

Joe Baker nodded approvingly and shook his hand. To

Barbara he said, 'Take him to Polly's. Kit him out.' To Dan he said, 'See you in the morning, son. Nine o'clock.'

A colourful float was gliding slowly down Madison Avenue. Six shapely girls in striped swimsuits with beach balls and sunshades and a phoney fountain that kept sputtering out were advertising holidays in the 'Sun State of the USA'.

'Come on,' Barbara said. 'We'll not get a cab here.'

'Where is this Polly? She far away? Too far to walk?'

'This Polly is a he not a she and he's on Eighth Avenue with the rest of the rag trade. And I ain't walking nowhere. I've been on my feet all morning.'

Polly Berger was a small fat Austrian gentleman, long time friend and business associate of Joe Baker. A lovely man, Barbara said as she led the way through the humming stop-start sound of sewing machines backed up by Viennese waltzes from a phonograph. She tapped lightly on the open door to Polly's chaotic glass cage of an office. 'Ah, my best girl,' Polly cried. 'Come in, come in.'

He gave Barbara a hug and a kiss and peered at Dan through his thick-lensed glasses. 'Always,' he said, 'she brings her boyfriends to Polly for Polly to fix 'em up, make 'em look good when they take her out. But she never lets Polly take her out.'

'You never ask,' Barbara said mildly. 'And anyway, I don't think Mrs Polly would approve.'

A woman of about fifty with a tape measure round her neck made notes as Polly with another tape took Dan's measurements. 'I think we can do this from stock,' he said. 'We can fix you up now, today, and by the end of the week we'll have a real nice outfit for you.'

He looked at the lady with a tape and she nodded confidently and led Dan away. 'Should scrub up well this one,' he said, when they'd gone. 'Where did he get him?'

'Off the boat,' Barbara said.

'Will he last?'

Barbara shrugged. 'I dunno. He might do. He's no mug.'

Polly smiled. 'Poor old Joe. Will he ever find what he's looking for?'

'I don't think so. He asks too much.'

Dan came back transformed. He was wearing dark trousers, a light coloured jacket, a white shirt and an Italian silk, patterned tie. Polly laughed. 'You look like a bandleader.'

'He looks fine,' Barbara said. 'For now.'

'Couple of days or so we'll have a great suit for you,' Polly promised.

'This feels good, sir,' Dan said gratefully. 'And I think it looks good.'

'It will when we get you some decent shoes,' Barbara said. 'You can't go around dressed like that in those boots.'

'And get a nice haircut, son,' Polly said. 'Y'know, I feel sorry for you guys with all that thick black hair. I mean me, I just wash my head in the morning. Don't have to pay these Wop barbers every five minutes.' He lowered his voice conspiratorially. 'If I was you, I'd get one of those slick-back jobs. Parted in the middle. Y'know. like Valentino. You'll knock 'em dead. Girls be falling at your feet.'

It was after six when Barbara hailed a cab.

'Thanks,' he said, as she climbed in. 'See you tomorrow then.'

'You may do and you may not,' she said, looking back at him over her shoulder. 'I ain't on the payroll.'

Dan strolled down 42$^{nd}$ Street, all the way to Fifth Avenue, glancing in windows to catch his reflection. He felt great, like a new man. New shirt, new jacket, new pants, new shoes, even a new haircut. He had never had so much new stuff. In fact, he couldn't remember having anything that was actually *new*. And best of all, he had a job. He had no idea what he would have to do but he was going to do it and do it well – though something he had overheard had stayed with him. What did Polly mean: *Should scrub up well this one?* Had there been others?

The nice-looking building on his right with the two lions caught his attention. The New York Public Library. He was going to have to find out more about Julius Caesar but not now. There was time yet. He had just been walking until now, getting the feel of the city and the noise and the crowded sidewalks, and the sense that there was something in the air. In his head he could hear Michael. *Tell all the gang at 42nd Street that I will soon be there.* And now he knew he was going down to 28th Street to see if Michael and Nathan were still there. He wanted to show off the new Dan and whether he admitted it or not he had been heading there all along.

There was a small crowd outside Levi's Music Shop and Dan couldn't see what was going on. Then as he drew near he heard Michael's voice in mid-song and Nathan's hit or miss piano playing. The crowd was made up mainly of shop and office girls and they were enjoying Michael's banter. 'Hey!' he called to one. 'Did you like that, sweetheart? Bet your mother came from Ireland.'

'Sure she did,' the girl called back. 'Place called Naples.'

Undeterred Michael simply laughed, half singing, half selling. '*I'll be lovin' you,*' he sang. Then, 'Come on, girls. Lovely song. Only a dime. Learn the words. Thank you, darling. Thank you, sweetheart. Come back and sing it for me.' He was handing out sheets, taking the money, handing out sheets, taking the money. Then he saw Dan.

He stopped and stared, handed the sheets of music to Nathan and went through the little throng of onlookers. 'Look at you!' he cried. 'What did you do? Rob a bank?'

'Come on,' Dan said. 'Let me buy you some grub. Tell Nathan.'

Together Michael and Nathan wheeled the piano indoors and Mr Levi followed them outside, not happy as their audience dispersed.

'That's it, Mr Levi,' Michael said. 'See you tomorrow.'

'Sorry about that,' Dan said. 'You were doing pretty well.'

'Oh sure,' Michael said. 'All afternoon for one dollar. One dollar we made. Between two of us.'

'Fifty sheets at two cents a throw,' Nathan said. 'Fifty-two actually.'

There was a coffee shop on one corner and an Italian restaurant on the other. Dan steered them towards the restaurant. 'My treat.'

Michael and Nathan were in shirtsleeves, no jackets, and it was Dan who felt conspicuous. It was early evening and if the restaurant had a smart clientele they hadn't arrived yet. He loosened his silk tie.

'So what's going on, big brother?' Michael asked with a laugh.

Dan told them about Joe Baker's offer of a job and how Barbara helped to kit him out. But he had no idea what kind of job it was.

'Twenty-five a week?' Nathan said. 'Who cares what kind of job?'

Michael grinned. 'This Barbara will show him soon enough.'

'How about you?' Dan asked, ignoring Michael's innuendo. 'You won't be going back to selling Mr Levi's sheet music.'

'Yeah, we will,' Michael said. 'That way we can learn all the new songs as they come out. We're going to do clubs and bars and we're going to be bang up to date.'

'And have you any jobs lined up?' Dan asked.

'Not yet,' Nathan said. 'We thought we'd do the rounds tonight.'

'We're just going to go in these places and ask,' Michael said.

'Well, suppose someone offers you a date,' Dan said. 'Do you have enough songs?'

Michael and Nathan looked at each other.

'Well,' Nathan said, 'we're sort of working on that. We got about a dozen.' He pulled several sheets from the carrier bag he used as a music case.

Dan looked them over. They were all new, only just published. *Everybody loves my baby, Miss Annabel Lee, Maybe.*

'I like this one best,' Michael said and he started to sing.

Dan and Nathan looked around. An elderly couple in a corner looked across and smiled. Then the waiter came over. 'Sorry, fellas,' he said. 'Got no licence for singing.' He saw the sheet music. 'You guys in the business?'

'Well, er ...' Michael hesitated.

'They're pretty good,' Dan said. 'Looking for jobs right now. They're new to the game, just starting out.'

The waiter looked at Dan's jacket and tie. 'You their agent?'

Dan laughed. 'No, this is my brother and his pal. I'm just visiting.'

'Guy comes in here,' he said. 'Joe Bononi. He's an agent. Maybe get you started. Hangs out in the bookies on 29th every morning.'

'That's real nice of you,' Michael said. 'You're a pal.'

The waiter went off, nodding and smiling. He seemed genuinely pleased to be of help. Then he came back. 'I was thinking,' he said. 'You guys is Irish, right? Well how about the Irish Club? They got music every night. Corner of Tenth and 38th or 39th. I ain't sure.'

Michael and Nathan lost no time. They left the restaurant well fed for once and parted company with Dan at the corner of 28th Street and Fifth Avenue. It was quite a walk to Tenth and they couldn't help noticing how the streets gradually changed from upmarket chic to downmarket squalor.

A white-haired man with black bushy eyebrows stopped them at the door. 'Ain't seen you two before.' His voice was New York streetwise with an Irish overlay. 'You guys members?'

'Members of the Irish race, so we are,' Michael said.

'We're here for an audition,' Nathan lied. He looked at Michael. 'What was the name of the guy we're supposed to ask for?'

'I dunno,' Michael said. 'You did all that.'

The white-haired man wasn't helping.

'He's the club secretary, I think,' Nathan said tentatively.

'Donnelly,' the man said. 'Jim Donnelly.'

'That's him,' Nathan said. 'Can we come in?'

'Wait here.' He put his head round the door, spoke to someone inside then, as two middle-aged couples arrived, he said brusquely to Nathan and Michael, 'Stand aside. You're gettin' in the way.'

Donnelly was a big man with an overhanging stomach and an air of authority. 'What do you want?'

'We want to sing for you, Mr Donnelly,' Nathan said.

Donnelly looked them over. 'Where you from?'

'Near Dublin,' Michael said. 'Place called—'

Donnelly eyed them suspiciously, 'You're just off the boat?'

'Yes, sir,' Nathan said. 'We need to earn some money fast.'

'Is that so?' Donnelly said. 'We'll there's plenty of work in the building trade.'

Nathan and Michael stayed in the entrance, eyes downcast.

'Where's this Miller guy?' Donnelly asked the white-haired man. 'He's late. Shoulda been here half an hour ago. Let me know if he shows up.' He turned to Nathan and Michael. 'I thought I told you two ...' Then he changed his mind. 'No, wait a minute. What can you do?'

'We're a double act, Mr Donnelly,' Nathan said. 'I play piano and sing a bit. But Mikey is the real singer. He's the best.'

'You got music and everything?'

'Oh sure.' Nathan held up his carrier bag.

'They're gettin' a bit restless in there,' Donnelly told the man on the door as if still undecided and seeking support. 'You know what they're like.' Then he became a true fellow countryman, a much gentler person. 'Listen, lads.' He put his big arm around Nathan's shoulder, 'Looks as though this shitface comic could let me down. He might still show up. But until then I want you to keep 'em quiet in there. *Entertain* 'em. Can you do that?'

'Sure, Mr Donnelly,' they said together. 'Sure we can.'

'Well, get in there. Sing three songs, OK? Then take a break. And if I give you the nod sing three more.'

The club concert room looked enormous and every table was taken. Waiters in green jackets seemed to waltz and pirouette through narrow spaces in a mixture of bright and darkened lights and for a moment, through the dense fog of cigarette smoke, they couldn't see the stage. A little leprechaun of a man came over, eyes twinkling. 'This way, boys. Follow me.'

An elderly lady at the piano picked up her cigarette and left the stage with a coy smile at Michael. 'Let's hear it, big boy.'

As Nathan and Michael turned the piano and brought it forward the level of noise barely dropped. Michael stepped up to the microphone. 'Hello,' he said quietly and there was a ripple of laughter from one or two tables near the front.

The little man took the microphone. 'All right, everybody. Come on now. Will you be quiet and settle down? We have a brand new act for you tonight. Straight from top billing in the old country. Ya gonna love these two. All the way from Dublin, The Dolan Boys!'

Michael looked at Nathan.

'They wanted a name,' Nathan whispered apologetically. Nathan, whose name was O'Shaughnessy. 'It was the best I could do. And Mikey, don't sing into the microphone. Sing across it.'

Michael stepped forward. He couldn't make out any faces, just a vast shadowy tableau. 'We'd like to start with a song we know you're going to like, folks,' he heard himself say. *You brought a new kind of love to me.*

The first three songs went down reasonably well. There was a ripple of applause after each one and, though he couldn't see deep into the audience Michael sensed there were several appreciative nods. Michael had the kind of voice and range that could rise above the noise and he grew in confidence, eager for the next set of three.

Between sets the little man sat them at a small table near the stage, the table reserved for the missing comedian. 'A fast one, then a slow one, then another fast one. OK? Jim wants you on again.'

Michael and Nathan exchanged glances. It was only nine o'clock and they had just two sets of three left. But there was nothing for it. They would have to do as Donnelly said and go on again.

'Try to spin it out,' Nathan whispered.

A man near the front was waving his arms and shouting abuse at the people at his table as Michael took the microphone. 'Come on, pal,' Michael called. 'Settle down. We're here to have a good time.'

'Who asked you?' the man cried.

Michael appealed to those in the man's party. 'What's going on there? Time he was back in his cage?'

There was laughter and an appreciative cheer and the shadowy figure sat down. The next three songs went even better than the first and all the way Michael and Nathan were inter-acting and learning fast how to charm the audience, Nathan holding their attention with jokes and anecdotes between songs. 'We're coming over on the boat, so we are,' he said, 'and this guy says to me ...'

Even so when their repertoire finally ran out it was still only 10.30 and Mr Donnelly's shiny red face was beaming, the missing comic forgotten. He held his glass high in salute and made it clear that he and the audience wanted more.

'What are we going to do?' Nathan asked. 'Play the first set again?'

'We can't do that,' Michael said.

The leprechaun reappeared. 'Come on now, fellas. Jim wants you up there. You're doing great.'

Michael took the microphone and the noise level dropped in expectation. But he had no songs left and he'd run out of jokes. His best option was to say goodnight and retire gracefully but he knew that Donnelly would not be happy with that and they hadn't been paid yet. Then inspiration struck. High above the entrance at the back of the hall a large green shamrock carved in bas-relief adorned the once white, tobacco-stained wall. This was an Irish Club. Of course it was. He looked back at Nathan and mouthed the words, 'Follow me.'

'Can we have the lights turned up?' he asked over the micro-phone. 'I want to see who's not singing.'

There was a slight pause then lights came on down both sides of the hall. He could see their faces now. Then, softly at first, he began to sing: *There's a tear in your eye, and I'm wondering why ...* ' And when he came to the chorus he led the whole hall into a heartfelt rendition of *When Irish Eyes are smiling*.

Prohibition or no Prohibition, it was as if half the audience was inebriated. Michael had his lead and he knew exactly what to do. As the cheers and the applause died down he asked, 'Is there anyone here from the west of the old country?'

Several hands went up at a long table and around the hall a number of hands waved. 'Well now,' he said, 'this'll bring the tears to your eyes, so it will.' And he launched into Galway Bay.

They listened enraptured and joined in with spirit when invited. *The Mountains of Mourne* and *The Rose of Tralee* followed and when he sang *Phil the Fluter's Ball* the place erupted. Nathan started it. The pace was too fast for him to follow on the piano but not to be outdone he stood up and danced a jig and this was the signal for three or four ladies who, it was said, ought to have known better, to join in.

When Jim Donnelly at last called a halt the boys were 'stars', an instant hit, at least in the Irish Club. 'A grand old hooley,' Donnelly declared, 'but what it was in aid of I have no idea.'

'Sure and it was to celebrate our arrival in the New World, sir,' Michael told him, waiting for him to offer payment.

Nathan was not so shy. 'It's fifty, sir,' he said confidently.

'Fifty what?' Donnelly asked.

'Fifty dollars.'

Donnelly laughed. 'Fifteen more like. That's what we pay, take it or leave it.'

'Fifteen?' Nathan looked affronted.

'Listen,' Donnelly said reasonably, 'if you're going to do this that's what to expect. You did well, but you're a couple of kids. You're just learners and fifteen's what I'd have paid the comic.'

'But there's two of us,' Nathan protested.

'All right,' he said at last. 'Twenty. And I'll book you Fridays.'

'You will?' Michael was delighted. '*Every* Friday? Well, that's great! We can get all the new songs as they come out and all the old favourites and we can always finish with a bit of the Irish.'

He nodded. 'That's up to you but if you're no good you're out. Now come on, get yourselves home. I have to lock up.'

'One thing I don't get,' Nathan said. 'How come they all seemed sort of merry as the night wore on.'

Donnelly laughed and tapped his nose.

'I thought this was a dry town, Mr Donnelly. No booze.'

'And so it is,' he said as he paid them off and ushered them on their way. 'See you Friday. Seven thirty and don't you forget it.'

They discovered later that nearly all the men had a hip flask and the ladies brought their supplies well concealed in the fashionable underarm bags most of them carried. It also helped that the three police officers who patrolled the nearby streets were Irish and all three were members of the club.

# EIGHT

IT WAS A small parish, home to second and third generation Irish immigrant families. In the beginning, almost without exception, they had come through Ellis Island with little to offer except, in most cases, a will to succeed.

Inevitably the impact on the younger generation of the glare and glamour of the New World was causing problems. Working girls were willing to contribute some of their hard-earned sweat-shop wages to the family budget but not all of it. And they now wanted freedom, the freedom to spend money on clothes and make-up, the freedom to go out with boys and not always *Irish* boys. The newly street-wise young men were ready and waiting.

Often an older brother would be called upon to accompany a younger sister to the ice-cream parlor where she might meet her friends, usually her workmates. But by 9.30 she must be home, back in the safe custody of her family. On no account must she allow herself to be drawn into the wicked world of the ten-cent dance hall, even though on three evenings each week 'ladies' were admitted free.

Many a brother would make a deal with his sister and arrange to meet her at a given hour, see her safely home then resume his own interrupted night out. It was not uncommon to see a brother storm into the local dance hall and drag his indignant charge from the arms of some would-be Casanova. Often, not surprisingly, this would result in raised fists and a scuffle and all three being thrown out by uncompromising bouncers. But the times were changing and there was little the black-shawled matriarchs could do about it. Many a bewildered father, torn between laying down the law as his wife demanded and not wanting to alienate his daughter, wayward or not, would seek refuge in the bar at the corner.

The parish priest, Father Costello, didn't discuss any of this with Tim. In a couple of months or so, the time-served priest decided, Timothy Dolan would become a seminarian. He could spend his time here on the front line. We can see what kind of a boy he is, see what he's made of, see if he learns anything before he leaves.

Pat Costello was born in Beacon, New York. His parents had come from County Mayo and they had never really settled. But Pat had known from an early age that he wanted to be a priest and he had set his heart on working with the poor Irish families on the Lower West Side. It had not been easy but now after forty years he was known well beyond the parish as a man who could be trusted, a man who really did care about his parishioners. As a young man serving with an older parish priest he had been known to all as Father Pat not Father Costello and he still was.

Tim, wary of him at first and his sometimes sharp tongue, soon came to like and respect him. When he saw first hand how people in the parish responded to Father Pat he decided this was the kind of place where he wanted to work and he wanted to get involved. He didn't have long to wait. Almost every day Father Pat was out visiting people in their homes or at the shops or in the RC school, even calling in at the local bars. Now he took his new acolyte with him.

This is Tim, he would say without further explanation and men and women alike would nod respectfully, taking in Tim's black jacket, his black trousers and black collarless shirt, but there were no questions, no explanations needed. Not until a small boy sitting on the stoop of the run-down brownstone where he lived with his family and eight other families addressed Tim as 'Father'.

'I'm not a priest,' Tim said apologetically.

'He's just Tim,' Father Pat said. 'Can't call him Father yet. He has to learn the job first.'

'That why he ain't wearing the collar?'

Father Pat smiled. 'That's it, Francis. Is Ma home?'

Francis nodded. 'Bad mood though.'

Tim followed the stooping priest up the steep steps. The door to the tenement block was open. It was always open, night or day. There was dust and dirt in dark corners. Dimly lit stairs, a single gaslight the only guide. The scent of stray cats twitched Tim's nose. To his right he caught a glimpse through an open door of a bleak interior, bare floors, an old lady, head covered by a black shawl, eyes closed in a battered armchair.

Father Pat knocked on a door that, after a while, was opened by a tired-looking woman, drably dressed in a full-length black shift, a small square of shawl about her shoulders. She looked at the priest, her face without expression, then she turned and went back inside, leaving the door open for him to follow.

'What's the problem, Mary?' the priest asked quietly.

'Everything. This place. This stinking …' She threw her arms up in the air as if she was carrying the weight of the world and she just wanted to be rid of it.

Tim looked around, a little surprised by the freshly painted walls and the sparsely furnished but neat and clean living room, such a contrast to the rest of the place. As Father Pat explained later most of the tenement blocks had a housekeeper who was responsible for keeping the hallway and the common areas in reasonable condition. This was usually one of the women who lived there. She would do the job in exchange for paying less rent and it was up to her to ensure the place was well kept and, in most cases, to collect the rent and pay the landlord.

The housekeeper had the power to recommend eviction and if a resident behaved badly, or caused problems for the rest of the tenants, or failed to pay the rent in good time she could, and sometimes did, have them thrown out. If it was just about the rent the housekeeper might persuade the landlord it was a temporary problem and the tenant might be given a little more time to pay. But it was not uncommon to see some unfortunate woman, her children and her few belongings at her feet, out in the street. Sometimes, too, tenants in arrears would move out of their own accord, usually at night, to another district. This was known as 'jumping the rent' or 'doing a moonlight'.

It so happened that the housekeeper of Mrs O'Reilly's block had fallen out with the landlord. At the end of the month she had absconded with most of the rent she'd collected. Nobody's sympathy was with the landlord. Without exception landlords were reviled as 'leeches' and 'bloodsuckers'. But so far the landlord had failed to replace her and the common areas – stairs, landings, the water closet – had rapidly deteriorated.

Though she hated the thought of having to keep the public areas, especially the water closet, clean, Mary O'Reilly had considered applying for the housekeeper's job herself if only for the reduction in rent this would bring. She had lost her husband to the tuberculosis that terrorized the Lower West Side and her eldest son, Tony, now seventeen, was proving unwilling to help out with the family budget.

As a homeworker sewing and finishing garments for the clothing factory on Mott Street, Mary could earn at most just a few dollars a week and she had herself and Francis to feed and clothe. She didn't know where Tony was all day, or what he was getting into, and she was worried he might be mixing with the wrong people. Father Pat said he would see what he could do.

As they left the tenement block Francis was mobilizing what he called his 'truck', a cardboard box on wheels. He did a regular tour, scouring the ground around the railyards for pieces of coal and sometimes filling his truck from an unattended open wagon. It wasn't exactly stealing, Father Pat told Tim. It was more an economic necessity. Most of the kids did it.

'Hey, Francis,' Father Pat called. 'Where does your Tony hang out these days?'

Francis seemed reluctant to talk. 'I dunno, Father.'

'Sure you do,' the priest insisted. 'Come on, who's he with?'

'He's usually with Marty Rip and Declan down the pool hall.'

Father Pat nodded and left the boy with his usual parting shot, 'Take care of your ma, son. She's the only ma you got.'

The landlord wanted Mary O'Reilly out, Father Pat told Tim. When her husband died he had guessed correctly she would have trouble paying the rent. Since then he had twice put her rent up. The first time he called he advised her to take in a lodger. But she didn't want to bring a stranger into her home though she knew many of her neighbours did. Lodgers take over the place, she had been told. They expect the best room and an evening meal and for just a few dollars a month.

Mary's son, Tony, had come home one night with two large cans of paint. Fallen off the back of a lorry, he said with a grin. Mary had painted the two biggest rooms herself in bright fresh colours and she thought the landlord would be pleased. Still without a housekeeper and still collecting the rent himself he was impressed with the newly painted walls. But instead of congratulating her he said the apartment was now worth more than the others. He would have to put her rent up again.

Father Pat told Tim he had called on the landlord on behalf of several tenants who had appealed to him but he had met with complete indifference and a refusal to even discuss the matter.

'The man's a complete asshole,' the priest said, startling Tim.

Dan arrived early that first morning, long before Joe Baker. He went through to the general office and into Mr Baker's private office. He looked at what was on Baker's desk but there was no note or instruction for him. He went to the window. It was not yet nine o'clock and the pavements of Madison Avenue were flooded with office workers and others, most of them hurrying to their work. They were like columns of ants, passing in opposite directions, halting at the roadside, crossing in unison.

The door opened behind him and a tall, slim man in a business suit looked in. He had dark hair and a neat black moustache like the smooth-looking leading men in the new movies. He was not exactly handsome but he wasn't ugly either.

'We better get you a seat outside,' he said with a faintly unfriendly air. And then, pointedly, he added, 'This is Mr Baker's office.'

Dan remained seated. 'Thank you,' he said, 'but if you don't mind I'll wait here until Mr Baker arrives.' He smiled pleasantly. 'Mr...?'

'Merrick. Paul Merrick.'

Since becoming a traveller, Dan had taken to observing people and guessing their nationality. Ellis Island had been a revelation. Italians, Russians, Middle Europeans – an education in itself. Paul Merrick, he thought. He was used to the imperious ways of the English landowning bosses back home, but this fellow with the English-sounding name was not like them. There was something about him that was definitely not English, Dan decided. But he was to learn that many people coming to a new life in America, for a variety of reasons, changed their names.

'And what do you call yourself?' Merrick asked.

Dan smiled and stood up. 'What I've always called myself,' he said and he extended a hand. 'Dolan. Dan to my friends.'

A frown crossed Merrick's brow fleetingly. He had expected a not so bright 'Mick'. He ignored the outstretched hand but bowed his head slightly. 'Mr Dolan.'

The door closed behind him and Dan sat down again. Perhaps Merrick didn't want him here. Well, if so, that was too bad. As far as Dan knew, Joe Baker was the boss.

The door opened again and the stenographer backed into the room, struggling to hold up one end of a narrow desk. On the other end was the older man he had seen earlier.

Dan went at once to help. 'Dan,' he said, holding up the desk with one hand and offering the other. 'Dan Dolan.'

The girl shook his hand quickly and, slightly flushed, said, 'Lois. I'm Lois.'

'Nice to meet you, Lois,' Dan said, as they set the desk down. 'I look forward to working with you.'

'Harry,' the older man said. 'I'm in charge of the general office.'

'No, you ain't,' the stenographer said. 'He's just a clerk, Mr Dolan. He's not in charge of anything.'

Dan shook the man's hand. 'I'm pleased to meet you, Harry.'

Harry was a short stout man with a bald head. He was wearing a red bow tie, a check shirt and glasses that glinted and flashed in the sunlight from the tall office windows. 'Mr Baker said you were to have a desk in his office.'

'Did he say where?'

'Well, I think he meant over here in the corner.'

'Fine,' Dan said, pushing the desk as far into the corner as it would go. 'Do you think I could get a chair of some kind?'

'Oh sure,' Harry said, flustered now as if the oversight was entirely his. 'Right away.'

'I love your voice,' Lois said coyly. 'It's nice.'

'It's just Irish,' Dan said with a smile.

'Yeah,' she said, 'but not like *some* Irish.'

Lois retreated and Harry returned with an office chair. Dan asked him to wait as the door closed on Lois. 'As you can see,' he said, 'I'm, new to all this. What's going on here, Harry?'

Harry looked at him blankly. 'Far as I know, you'll be working with Mr Baker.'

'Doing what? I don't even know what Mr Baker does.'

Harry didn't look surprised. 'No,' he said, 'they never do. Mr Baker likes to start them from scratch.'

'Start who from scratch? Who are *they*?'

Harry looked worried. 'Listen, Mr Dolan,' he said, 'I think you should wait until Mr Baker comes in. He'll explain everything.'

'You don't want to help me out here, Harry?'

'It's not that. I just don't want to get into trouble. I mean, it's nothing to do with me.'

Dan nodded. 'OK. I understand. But tell me this. What kind of business are we in? And is it legal?'

Harry looked offended. 'Oh yes, of course. It's absolutely legal.'

'So what do we do?'

'Mr Baker is a stock operator.'

'And what the hell is a stock operator?'

'Mr Baker will explain. He'll be pleased if you know nothing. The less you know the better. He'll want to teach you the business from the start. He always wants someone with no preconceived ideas.'

'I don't have any ideas, preconceived or otherwise,' Dan said. 'So what about Mr Merrick? Is he Mr Baker's partner?'

'Oh no,' Harry said quickly. 'I'm sure he'd like to be. No wait, I shouldn't have said that. He's a sort of speculator, too.'

The telephone on Baker's desk came to Harry's rescue. He picked it up and as he did so the door opened and Joe Baker came in. 'Yes, sir,' Harry said into the phone, 'Mr Baker is here now.' He handed the receiver to Baker. 'Mr Meehan.'

Joe Baker nodded at Dan and Harry went out. 'Michael, hi!' he said. 'What? Down three points? No. Far too soon. Wait a while. It'll turn around. Sure I'm sure. Leave it for now.'

He put the phone down. 'Dan!' he said with a big smile, his hand extended. 'Welcome to my world.'

# NINE

JOE BAKER'S WORLD revolved around Wall Street and Broad Street in Manhattan Island's Financial District. This was where the money markets operated: the New York Stock Exchange, the New York Curb Market. There were brokerage houses on every street and at 23 Wall Street the offices of the powerful banking company J.P. Morgan.

After sipping coffee and making several brief telephone calls Joe turned his attention to Dan Dolan. 'You're coming out with me this morning, son. I want you to stick by me, see everything, hear everything, say nothing. OK? Any questions, you save 'em and you only ask what you want to know when we're alone.'

Joe Baker, small and slightly built, walked with brisk, short steps and Dan had to hurry to keep up as they set off down Madison to 42nd Street then by cab to the Financial District. In his head Dan could hear Michael again and the sheer exuberance of his *Give my regards to Broadway*. Joe Baker glanced up at him, sensing his enthusiasm. 'Great city, eh, son? This is where it all happens.' Then, as the cab turned into Wall Street, he added, 'And this is the money-go-round.

'In the old days,' Joe went on to explain, 'trading stock was done out in the streets. These guys, the traders, would stand under the lamp-posts and along the curbs on Broad Street and Wall Street. Nowadays trading is done on the floor of the Exchange. It begins and ends when the bell rings. Trading can only be done between those bells. OK?'

Dan was fascinated. So this was where the money was! All day millions of dollars were traded at posts on the Exchange floor. But only, he soon discovered, Stock Exchange members could do business here. The members were traders. They bought and sold stocks for themselves. Or they were brokers who bought and sold stocks for their customers.

Joe Baker bought and sold stocks for himself and once they were inside the Exchange it seemed to Dan that his boss knew everyone and everyone knew him. The first of Joe's friends they encountered was a man Joe had spoken to that morning on the office telephone. Dan read the name of the member at Post 12: Michael J. Meehan.

It turned out that Michael J. Meehan was a Stock Exchange celebrity, well known throughout the New York financial world as a smart operator. He was around forty years old, the son of Irish parents who came to the United States at the beginning of the century. He'd had little formal education but he was a natural born salesman and he had got where he was with his ability to charm and impress.

Meehan had started out as a cigar salesman before becoming the manager of an agency selling tickets for Broadway shows. At the ticket agency he concentrated on his better off clients and always ensured they had excellent seats. In return he would sometimes receive stock-market tips. He was doing all right at the time but the more he learned about the stock market the more he became convinced he could do better than spend his days selling theatre tickets. Taking the plunge he went into business on his own and, after a difficult start, he steadily built a thriving business. After only two years he could afford to buy himself a seat on the prestigious New York Stock Exchange for $90,000.

Joe Baker and Meehan shook hands warmly but Meehan merely glanced at Dan. Another of Joe's protégés, he guessed. Always on the look-out for the one true kid he could trust and teach the business and no doubt, eventually, leave his fortune. And that was some fortune. Joe Baker was one of the richest men in the city. But, apart from Barbara, he had no one, no family of his own, and as Michael Meehan's wife said, 'Poor ol' Joe, always looking for the son he never had.'

Standing up at the lunch counter on the corner of Broad Street and Pine, Joe Baker and Dan had coffee and sandwiches in a ten-minute break, then they were back at the Exchange. By 4.30 they were walking back up Madison, Joe as brisk as ever, Dan's head awash with new faces, new scenes, the Exchange floor, trading posts, numbers chalked up on blackboards, numbers, numbers and more numbers. But he was excited, too, excited at the prospect of learning the job, of making an impression and maybe, too, of making a fortune, *his* fortune.

Dan had never valued money for its own sake. He came from a background of a sometimes dire poverty. His family were poor but they didn't worry about it. So were most of their relatives and friends. Now, with a privileged glimpse of what seemed untold wealth with millions of dollars changing hands by the minute, ambition stirred in his previously unambitious soul.

Back at the office he faced Joe Baker across the big desk. Joe waited until Lois had delivered their late afternoon coffee and they were alone. 'So,' he said. 'First day. How did it go?'

'Absolutely fascinating,' Dan said truthfully.

'You learn anything?'

Dan nodded. 'I think so.'

Baker raised his eyebrows expectantly.

'I think we should be holding Radio shares,' Dan said seriously.

Baker laughed. 'Why? Because Mike Meehan is a super salesman? That guy could sell fur coats in the desert.'

'No, sir. It's not that.'

'You trust him because he's Irish.'

'No,' Dan said with a laugh 'I think we should buy into Radio shares, lots of them, because every household in the country wants a radio. More than that. Every household in the country *needs* a radio. The demand is there and it can only increase.'

Baker nodded. 'Correct. But you can relax, son. We already hold Radio shares. Lots of 'em.'

The Irish Club was full as usual that Friday evening, the third Friday of Michael and Nathan's regular bookings. The Dolan's, as they were now known, had just come off stage after their first set of three numbers, just sat down at the small table reserved for them, when a man they had never seen before approached.

'Hi!' he said. 'Can I sit down?'

Michael shrugged. 'Sure,' he said.

The man was short, thick-set with a squashed face and several chins. He didn't look or sound Irish. Italian, Michael guessed.

'Well listen, fellas,' he said, immediately leaning forward as he sat down, 'I've got a proposition for you. We've been hearing good things about you two. How you pull in the customers, give the people what they want.'

'We do our best,' Michael said.

'Well, I mean look at this place,' he said. 'They were lined up outside but they had to close the door. The joint was full.'

'How come they let *you* in?' Nathan asked bluntly.

'I'm a booker,' the man said. He took out a printed card and handed it to Michael. 'They got to let me in.'

According to the card he was a licensed booking agent and he was authorized to book concert and variety artists and artistes in the state of New York.

'You don't have an agent,' he said, 'so I came to you direct.'

'You seem to know a lot about us,' Nathan said.

'I do,' he said, 'and take it from me you need an agent. Guy who'll take good care of you. I don't do that. I work for the clubs and theatres.'

'You know a good agent?' Michael asked.

'Joe Bononi. Tell him I sent you.'

'Yeah,' Nathan said. 'We heard of him.'

'Well anyway, like I said, you got this place buzzing.'

'Oh, I don't think that's because of us,' Michael said with a laugh. 'This place is buzzing every Friday night.'

'That's not true,' Nathan said, throwing Michael a withering look. 'They couldn't drag people in here before we came.'

'Well anyway,' the man said, 'there's this place on Canal Street. Arnie's. They have shows like this every night of the week. I'd like to book you in there. Just a couple of dates at first. See how it goes.'

'Oh great!' Michael said. 'What do you say, Nathan?'

'Yeah, fine,' Nathan said, less enthusiastically. 'If we're free, that is. When did you have in mind?'

'Next Saturday and Sunday. Not tomorrow. Tomorrow week.'

'Is it Irish?' Michael asked. 'I mean, what are the people like?'

'It's not like this,' the man said. 'It's not an *Irish* club. They get all sorts of people in there. Tell you the truth, it's a bit rough. Tough guys with their molls. But you'd be fine.'

'What would they want exactly? We do a lot of Irish here.'

That's OK,' Nathan came in. 'We get all the new songs just as soon as they come out.'

'Well, fine,' the man said. 'One or two Irish is OK. Italian, too, if you can. Y'know, what's-her-name from sunny Italy. That kind o' thing.' He leaned forward. 'They're funny these guys. They may be tough, but they sure like soppy songs. Y'know, about your mother or your daddy left home when you were a kid, that kind of crap.' He laughed and his squashed face looked even more squashed. 'It cracks 'em up, the crazy bastards.'

Michael grinned. 'Daddy, you've been a mother to me.'

'Yeah,' the man agreed. 'That sort of stuff.'

'We'll be fine,' Nathan said. 'So how much? We get fifty here.'

The man regarded him coolly. 'You get twenty here.'

'This is Irish,' Nathan continued unabashed. 'It's kinda family. Outside of here we want the going rate. Fifty for the two of us.'

'Twenty five,' the man said.

'Nothing doing,' Nathan said.

'Fifty five for two nights.'

'Sixty,' Nathan said.

The man leaned forward, hand extended. 'Done,' he confirmed. And then: 'You should be an agent. You'd do all right.'

The pool hall was on Thirty-first Street and, according to Father Pat, it was a den of iniquity. He walked in, passed the glass-fronted cashier's desk, ignoring the large notice ordering members to sign in. Tim Dolan followed.

Father Pat looked along the two rows of tables. Cue in hand, a man at the first table, his tie loosened at his open-necked shirt, his hat on the back of his head, eyed Father Pat with an air of amusement and undisguised contempt.

'Something bothering you, rat-face?' Father Pat asked.

Here we go, thought Tim. But the man walked away and round the table, intent on taking his next shot.

Tony O'Reilly was leaning back against the wall four tables down.

According to another notice displayed on both sides of the long room gambling was strictly prohibited yet there was a little pile of money on a window ledge.

'Good morning, boys,' Father Pat said expansively to Tony and the two friends he was with. 'Shouldn't you all be at work?'

'Shouldn't you, Father?' the one called Declan asked with a cheeky grin and they all laughed, including Father Pat.

Declan was a short, wiry young man with a shock of thick black unruly hair and a pock-marked face. Holding his cue upright like a paddle in a punt, he rocked to and fro, enjoying his joke. Marty Rip, ignoring the priest's arrival, carried on assessing the shot he was about to make. He was three or four years older than Tony and Declan, Tim noted, and better dressed in a smart jacket and a polka-dot bow tie.

'What in God's name are you doing here, Tony?' Father Pat asked, forthright as ever. 'There's no future in this.'

Tony shrugged, embarrassed by the priest's presence. He was a good-looking boy, blue-eyed with light-brown hair and, despite the tough stance he affected there was something angelic about him.

'We've been to see your ma,' Father Pat told him. 'She's having a rough time. That leech of a landlord is sucking her dry. Keeps on putting up the rent. She needs you, Tony. Do you want to see her out on the street? She needs you working, son, not wasting your time in this shit-hole.'

Tim didn't flinch. He was getting used to Father Pat's colourful use of language.

'I'll see to it,' Tony said.

'You'll get a job, help her out?'

'I said I'll see to it, Father, and I will.'

'Do me a favour, Tony?' Father Pat asked. 'Five minutes?'

'What do you want, Father?' Tony asked, impatient now.

'I just want to talk to you. But not here. Five minutes?'

Tony looked at Declan and Marty Rip, shrugged helplessly and followed Father Pat and Tim out to the street.

'Thanks,' the priest said when they were outside. 'I just want to say this, Tony. I care about you. Your ma cares about you. She hasn't had things easy this last couple of years. You know that and she doesn't need any more trouble. The thought of you hanging around with those two in there worries her and so it should. Declan is just a silly lad. But this Martin Ripley is trouble and it's pretty obvious where he's heading.'

'Yeah?' Tony said tolerantly. 'And where would that be?'

'It's either six feet under or Sing Sing. That's not for you. You're a smart boy. You have a future. They haven't. I can help. I can get you a job.'

Tony laughed. 'Doing what? Laying sleepers on the railroad?' He turned away then he looked back. 'I'm OK, Father. I told you. I'll see Ma and I'll sort things out. Now, please, leave me alone.' And before Father Pat could say another word he walked back into the pool hall.

'Come on,' Father Pat told Tim, 'we're gonna pay a visit.'

The block where Declan O'Connor's family lived was in a short alley close to the freight yard. On the way Father Pat told Tim that at one time Declan's father regularly beat up his wife. He was warned, first by Father Pat then, when the police department failed to act, by three or four brawny parishioners. He had been subdued for a while but the word was that he was at it again. Mrs O'Connor had turned up at Mass first with an ugly bruise on her forehead, which she tried to hide by combing her hair forward, then with a badly blackened eye.

'Why do people do these things?' Tim asked.

'Well,' Father Pat said, 'in O'Connor's case I reckon it's because he suspects Declan is not really his. The lad doesn't look like anyone in their family and, despite Mrs O'Connor protesting her innocence, every now and then this great eejit flies into a rage and beats her up.'

Mrs O'Connor was in alone when Father Pat knocked on her open door. She looked up and smiled and Tim saw that her once pretty face was clearly disfigured. Her nose had been broken at some time and right now there was a bruise over her left eye.

'Angie!' Father Pat exclaimed. 'How are you?'

'Fine, Father,' she said. 'Just fine.' She held up a roll of cloth. 'Lots of work in.'

'Good, good, pleased to hear it,' the priest said. 'This is my new assistant – Tim.'

'Father Tim?' she asked.

'Not yet,' he said. 'Just Tim for now. Thought we'd say hello. Now where's O'Connor? I want a word with him.'

Mrs O'Connor's eyes registered alarm. 'Oh no, Father. Please. There's no need. He's fine right now.'

'Where is he, Angela? He has to be told.'

'I don't know,' she said. 'He was outside, on the stoop.'

And before she could protest further the priest said, 'See you at Mass on Sunday and don't you worry about a thing.'

Tim nodded and smiled at Mrs O'Connor and followed his mentor out and down the bare stairway. 'Doesn't seem like a woman taken in adultery,' he ventured.

'Sure and you'd have an affair if you was married to a great bonehead like O'Connor,' Father Pat said.

'She seems like a nice lady,' Tim said.

'And so she is. But according to the gossips – and we've plenty of them, Timothy, so we have – our friend Angela got into a little trouble one time over some Christmas hamper she was buying. O'Connor was working at the yards then and giving her a little help to pay for it. This slimy kike was collecting instalments by the week but Angie O'Connor had not been able to keep up with the payments. Declan has two older sisters and they were little girls in those days. They were expecting this big hamper for Christmas so, the story is, Angie paid the man in kind. And that's why Declan's birthday is early in September.'

'Sounds like malicious gossip to me,' Tim said.

Father Pat looked at him sharply. 'All right. So it could be just gossip and I shouldn't be repeating it. But if you want to get to know the people you need to know all this background stuff. And anyway, the fact is, this used to be one of the little kike's best rounds and we ain't seen him since Declan arrived.'

Assholes? Kikes? thought Tim as they emerged from the alley. They don't sound like words your parish priest should be using. But then, Father Pat was no ordinary parish priest.

O'Connor was coming back from wherever he'd been. He was large and untidy, bleary-eyed and unshaven, with a crumpled workshirt open to the waist displaying his hairy chest. He was not especially tall, but he had big hands and long muscly arms with bulging shoulders.

Father Pat stopped him in his tracks. 'O'Connor!' he bellowed and the big man froze. 'I want a word with you.'

O'Connor looked from Father Pat to Tim and back.

With a few brisk steps Father Pat confronted him threateningly. 'Do you want to die? Is that it?'

O'Connor looked down at the little priest. It seemed to Tim that the man could swat Father Pat with one sweep of his hand. Yet O'Connor cowered back as if genuinely scared.

'One more go at Angie and you're dead. The boys will be round and they'll be scraping you off the sidewalk. An' that's a promise. They'll batter you so's you never wake up. Have you got that?'

O'Connor looked at him stupidly.

Father Pat stepped up even closer. 'I said, "Have you got that?"'

O'Connor backed off. 'Yeah, yeah.'

'Final warning,' the priest said. 'All right?' And again, 'All right?'

'Yeah, yeah,' O'Connor said.

'Get out of my sight,' Father Pat said with a jerk of his head. 'And get a job, you idle bastard.'

O'Connor slunk away as Father Pat and Tim watched him

go. 'Useless sod,' the priest said, and he looked at Tim as if he'd forgotten he was there.

Tim was smiling. This was a new one. The hoodlum priest with the colourful language.

'It's all people like him understand,' Father Pat said.

# TEN

**D**AN WAS EARLY again that second morning at the office but Lois and Harry were already busy at their desks. He raised a hand in greeting and went through into Joe Baker's office where he sat at the desk he had been allocated. Nothing in the drawers, nothing on the desk, not even a pen. Today, he thought, maybe Baker would give him something to do.

The door opened and Paul Merrick came in. Without a glance at Dan he went to Joe Baker's big desk and dropped some papers in the in-tray Then he turned to leave but Dan stood up.

'Mr Merrick,' he said.

Merrick paused at the door and looked back, his hand on the door handle, his face without expression.

'I ...' Dan began. 'I just want to say, I get the feeling there's – I don't know – a sort of atmosphere here. You don't seem too happy to have me around.'

Merrick didn't deny it.

'If that is so,' Dan said, 'I'd like to know why and what, if anything, I can do about it.'

'You are working with Mr Baker,' Merrick said at last. 'Let us keep it that way.'

'Well,' Dan said, 'the thing is, I don't know why the hell I'm here or what I'm supposed to do. I expect both you and Mr Baker have forgotten more than I'll ever know about the stock market so I thought maybe you would put me right if I go wrong. I'd like us to get along, Mr Merrick. I mean, I don't know anybody, I don't have any friends. The last thing I need is enemies.'

Merrick shrugged.

Dan smiled and held out a hand. 'Dan Dolan.'

Merrick seemed to need a second or so to think about it then he relented and shook Dan's hand. It was a brief business-like handshake, lacking in warmth. But at the door he looked back. 'You had better call me Paul.'

Dan nodded and smiled. Progress, he thought.

Joe Baker came in. 'Morning, Daniel. Ready for the lion's den?'

'Sure am, Mr Baker,' Dan responded and soon he was striding as before to keep up with Baker's short brisk steps.

'You know something, Dan,' Joe Baker said, not even short of breath. 'There's something going on and I'm not sure what.'

There was a change in the air, he tried to explain. Echoes of the war were fading fast and the whole country was gripped by a new feeling of prosperity. Everyone seemed to be a bit better off than they were last year and things were getting better. On the Avenue, *Fifth* Avenue, on Madison and certainly along Broadway, people seemed to have a spring in their step.

Dan knew what he meant. There was music everywhere, a crazy rhythm. Crotchets and minims seemed to dance out of doorways and fill the air with the infectious bounce of the Charleston, the Shimmy and the Black Bottom. Song sheets rolled off the presses and spread their words as every day a new breed of popular songwriter, underwriting the buoyant mood of the people, came up with something new.

New goods filled the shops. Washing machines and refrigerators, gadgets galore, with bigger and better advertisements to announce their arrival. Radios were in great demand with broadcast news and entertainment from far and wide. And all this added up to a new awareness. A pretty face could sell a thousand products and now, at long last, the older generation was forced to acknowledge there was such a thing as sex.

Girls cast off their drab heavy dresses and took to wearing the new slimline skirts cut just below the knee. They bobbed their hair and wore make-up and turned a deaf ear to their critics. They had won the vote. They could do as they liked and they did, captivated and seduced by the blandishments of a newly empowered advertising industry. From every vantage point big bold advertisements beamed invitations: 'See what wonders await you at our brand new store.' And reprovals: 'Still using that old wash tub? Throw it out! Throw everything out! Start again.'

Shoppers were shamed into realizing they needed toothpaste, perfume and skincare products, longer eyelashes, redder lips and rouged cheeks and, most of all, smart new clothes. And with a down payment of just a few dollars or sometimes no down payment at all the average American could buy a new car or a new home on the instalment plan. And there was something even newer to engage and dazzle the populace. For the first time in history the old and the young, the worker and the housewife were actually *buying* stock. Stocks were rising in value by the day or by the hour and people who had never dreamed of owning a stake in a prospering company were rushing to buy. Cab drivers, bellboys, waiters, stenographers, shopgirls – all of them eager for a piece of the spiralling bonanza. The paper gold rush was on.

'It's boom time,' Joe Baker told Dan. 'There's big money to be made and there's big money to be lost. And that's OK. The trouble is, there's *small* money to be lost. Too many newcomers, ordinary people who can't afford to lose are risking their life savings, their homes, everything. And that's a problem. It's storing up trouble.'

'But the radio, newspapers – we're being told things are good,' Dan said, 'and they're going to get better.'

'Maybe,' Baker said. 'But too many people are buying blind. They don't know what they're buying. We don't do that, Dan. Take Radio. This is something everyone wants. Better still, something everyone *needs*. It's a good, solid investment. Even so, we've got to keep an eye on that investment. If we get a sniff something better is coming along we've got to be the first to know about it.'

'Something better than radio?' Dan queried.

'You never know,' Baker said. 'Some nutty professor might be inventing something new in his back room right now.'

'So what do we do?'

'We keep our eyes open and our ears to the ground. Never discount a rumour until we've checked it out.'

'And what do I do?'

'Ah,' Baker said. 'The way we work is this. Something big like General Motors or Radio comes along and we buy into that in a big way. Knowing what to buy and when is important, yes. But we always keep a close check. Knowing when to sell is essential.

'Now, we go for the big stuff like radios and cars, sure we do. But our business was built on spotting future winners and it still is. That's what we do. We look out for the genuine company with a solid long-term product. Then we go see them, see how they operate. We find out if they are open to investment and, if so, how open. I prefer to deal with small closed outfits who need just one backer. If we like what we see we buy in and grow with 'em. If things change and they run into trouble, sometimes we'll stay with 'em, sometimes we'll call in our investment.

'Once you get the hang of this place,' he said, waving an arm over the Stock Exchange floor, 'I'll send you out on a few jobs. I don't know where yet. We operate all over the country.' He laughed. 'One way to see America, son. I send you to meet the board or the boss of some growing outfit, tell you what to look for. You look at the product, you look at the premises and you look at the work-force. Then you come home, make a report and we discuss what you got.'

'Sounds good,' Dan said.

'Lots of travelling, couple of nights in some hotel, maybe more, and you've got to make your mind up fast about people you never met before. Think you can handle that?'

'Yes, sir.'

'Good. We'll talk about this some more. Right now I want to check out US Steel. So let's see what's new at Post 2.'

Arnie's was a theatre club on Canal Street. It was also one of the many illicit drinking joints that had sprung up and proliferated with the advent of Prohibition. The long low wooden building had been a neighbourhood bar. Now it was, officially, a stone dry variety club, a place of entertainment, though everyone, including the police knew it was a place to buy and consume bootleg liquor.

Patrons were carefully vetted and, if admitted, they were handed a slip of paper with the title of a popular song. Drinks, mostly gin, would be served in teacups and if the three-piece band at any time during the evening struck up this song it was the signal to drain your cup, drink up fast. Arnie's was about to be raided. This week's song was *Yes, we have no bananas*.

The poster outside promised an 'All Star Cast' but Michael and Nathan, listed as the Dolan Brothers, found the only other 'star' that night was a ripe old stripper billed as 'Legs Akimbo'. Michael was the first to meet the lady. The house manager had pointed him towards a dressing-room down a dingy corridor but when he opened the door he was met by a stream of abuse and a high-heeled shoe that narrowly missed his head.

The stripper refused to let them in and they had to settle for a tiny table and two chairs by the stage.

'She's got a point,' Nathan said. 'We can't share a dressing room with a lady.'

'She's a stripper, for God's sake,' Michael said. 'What would we see that she won't be showing on stage?'

The audience at Arnie's was nothing like the audience at the Irish Club. The house manager was not the only gorilla looka-like. Half the men at the tables looked as though they had done a mass breakout from the zoo and raided a tuxedo store. And they had girlfriends to match.

Michael was worried. 'How do we know what they want?'

Nathan shrugged. 'We give them what we've got and we get out of here and as soon as possible if you ask me. Tomorrow night we take the money and run.'

The only way on to the stage was up three steps close by the table where Michael and Nathan were seated. The three-piece band – piano, bass and drums – had been playing a selection of Eddie Cantor songs. Now, as the lights went down, there was a drum roll to bring the audience to heel. Some of them actually looked up and listened.

Michael found the stripper, enveloped in pink fans, standing immediately in front of him as she waited to go on. She had her back to where he was sitting and she was wearing exceptionally high heels. This brought her naked and ample backside almost level with his chin. She looked over her shoulder and winked at him as if their previous encounter had never happened. Then, deftly handling the fans, she mounted the steps.

Nathan looked hard and long at Michael. 'Forget it. OK? We do the gigs and that's it.'

Michael feigned innocence. 'I never said a word.'

Their act went down without incident, a ripple of applause here and there but nobody was really listening and there was proof of this when, after midnight, they were out of songs and they repeated some they sang earlier. The following night, Sunday, was more eventful.

The stripper had been replaced by a moustachioed magician who twice inadvertently set himself on fire, but nobody seemed to notice. Then in the small hours Michael was surprised to find when he began to sing an Irving Berlin song – *When I lost You* – there was a quietening down, an unexpected hush. He glanced back at Nathan but Nathan merely shrugged, as puzzled as he was. The audience was suddenly respectful and the reason for this seemed to come from a table where several well-dressed men who looked like mobsters presided.

Michael and Nathan were almost through when the boys of the three-piece ran up the steps to the stage and made for their instruments, the piano player bundling Nathan unceremoniously off the stool. In seconds they were into the chorus of *Yes, we have no bananas*. Nathan joined Michael at the microphone and together they took up the words. The pianist looked round and nodded in approval, but again no one was listening. They were too busy consuming their gin. Arnie's was being raided.

The main doors burst open and eight uniformed police officers led by a stern-looking inspector entered wielding batons.

Everyone was now relaxed, smiling at the officers, as Michael and Nathan backed by the trio launched into a further chorus of *Bananas*. The raid took less than ten minutes, the house manager chatting to the inspector as the officers walked around, sniffing here and there at the drained teacups.

As inventive as ever, Michael couldn't resist breaking into the policemen's song Nathan had taught him on the boat coming over. Nathan joined in as the drummer picked up the beat. Then the bass player came in, then the pianist.

It was when they sang the chorus, 'We run them in ...' the audience laughed and applauded and very soon joined in.

The police inspector gave a sardonic smile, signalled to his men that the raid was over and they trooped out. Again the audience broke into a cheer.

'You did all right,' the pianist told Nathan and Michael. 'You even made old Vinnie smile.'

They looked at him enquiringly. 'Vinnie?'

'The guy with all the bodyguards. That's Vin O'Hara. His ma died last week. That's why we all had to be quiet when you sang *When I lost you*.'

'Who is he?' Michael asked.

'Who is he?' the drummer said incredulously. 'You mean you don't know?'

'He's the big gang boss around here,' the bass player said. 'Got a stake in all the dives. All the top showplaces, too. Music halls, vaudeville, even a stake in Broadway shows. A guy could go a long way with Vinnie pushin' him.'

'Or die,' the pianist said soberly.

Later, when they had been paid their sixty dollars, Michael and Nathan set off walking. It was a warm, balmy night, with a bright moon washing the empty streets and the steps of the tenement buildings. The place where they were still laying their heads was only a few blocks away but, as they turned into Bedford Street, they realized they were being followed. A couple of rough-looking characters had emerged from an alleyway to fall in behind them.

Michael was ready for a fight, but Nathan nodded to indicate they should make a run for it. The two men behind were very close now and one said clearly, 'This says you won't.'

They looked back, down the barrel of a handgun. The one without a gun stepped forward and gestured with his fingers. 'Come on,' he said. 'The money.'

'What money?' Nathan asked.

The man looked back at his partner and jerked his head. The one with the gun took over and they heard a click. 'Where do you want it?' he asked. 'Arm? Leg?'

'Give him the money, Nathan,' Michael said.

Reluctantly Nathan put his hand in his pocket, wishing he had a gun, and drew out the three twenty-dollar bills they had just been paid. 'This ain't right,' he said. 'We had to work for this.'

'Look at us,' the first man said. 'We're crying.'

The man with the gun snatched the notes. 'Now on your way.'

Nathan hesitated, furious at the loss of their hard-earned cash.

'OK, so where do you want it?' the man asked again. 'Arm? Leg? How about in the balls?'

'Come on,' Michael said. 'We can't win.'

Father Pat was expecting a representative of the bishop on one of his quarterly, sometimes half-yearly, visits. He didn't want Tim around because Tim might be one of the items up for discussion. He was as forthright as ever. 'I want you to get lost this afternoon, son,' he said. 'The bishop's man is coming and he might want to know how you're doing.'

'Right,' Tim said. He was already planning to call on Dan or Michael, or maybe both.

'So I want you to go around the parish in the usual way. Look in on the school, look at the diary, see who's sick. And don't come back until after five.'

Tim nodded and that was why he was walking rather aimlessly towards Tenth Avenue. By the railway sidings he saw Francis, Tony O'Reilly's kid brother. Francis was trundling his trolley on one of his foraging expeditions.

'Hey, Francis!' Tim called. 'How are you doing?'

Francis waited as Tim came over. A group of children, all girls, had formed a circle in the road and one girl in the middle was skipping as two girls swung a rope. Tim hurried round them to catch up with the boy.

'How's your ma?' he asked.

'She's OK,' Francis said. 'Fine now.'

'Now?' Tim queried. 'Something happen?'

'Oh sure,' the boy said. 'Somebody leaned on the landlord.'

'How do you mean?'

'Some guys told the landlord to lay off her, quit asking for more rent.'

'Yeah?' Tim was genuinely interested. 'Who was it?'

'I don't know,' he said. 'Some pals of Tony, I think.' He looked worried now, as if he had said too much. 'Hey, I don't know who it was. Just some guys.'

Tim nodded. 'Don't worry. I won't tell anyone.'

'See you, Father,' the boy said. 'I mean, well, y'know …'

'Yeah,' Tim said and, as the boy turned to go on his way, he added, 'Call me "Father" if it's easier.'

The boy came back. 'Hey, Father. I want to ask you something.'

Tim nodded. 'Go ahead.'

'Will you do me a favour?'

'If I can,' he said. 'Sure.'

'Will you tell Father Pat folks round here don't call me Francis?'

Tim smiled. 'What do they call you?'

'Frankie,' he said. 'I don't mind Frank. But I don't want Francis. It's kind of sissy.'

'OK, I'll tell him.' This was obviously a matter of some concern to the boy. 'I'll tell him tonight.' Tim raised a hand. 'See you, Frankie.'

The boy's round face broke out in a big smile as he turned to tow his coal wagon. 'Gee thanks, Father. I won't forget this.'

Along the street one or two of the older residents nodded at Tim or murmured hello. Already he was recognized as Father

Pat's protégé, the new sidekick for the uncompromising priest. Tim decided to call on Mrs O'Reilly. The place still looked neglected – no sign of a new housekeeper's handiwork – but when he knocked on Mrs O'Reilly's door she greeted him with a smile and invited him in.

'Father Pat's busy today, Mrs O'Reilly. Visit from the bishop's man.'

'So you have to patrol the parish.'

'Something like that,' Tim said.

She seemed much more relaxed than the last time and she seemed to want to talk. She asked him about the old country, his family and how was his mother. When he mentioned he had two brothers she wanted to know what they were doing. Dan was working on Wall Street and Michael was trying to make his way as a singer. A singer? She made a face. 'The music business is mixed up with criminal gangs,' she said. 'And they are nearly all Irish, so they are. Fellows like that Vincent O'Hara.'

'He's a good lad, our Michael,' Tim said loyally. 'But I'll warn him.'

'You tell him from me. The music business is full of crooks. But then so is Wall Street.' She laughed. 'Whole country's crooked.'

'Why do you say that?'

'Because if alcohol is prohibited, how come we got so many drunks?'

Tim nodded in agreement. 'I guess you're right, Mrs O'Reilly. So how about that landlord of yours? Still giving you trouble?'

'Nah,' she said. 'He's OK now.'

Tim had done his rounds, chatted briefly to a few parishioners and looked in at the pool hall. He was hoping to run into Tony O'Reilly, but Tony was not in or around any of his usual haunts. He started to walk back to the church and then he saw him. Tony was sitting on a bench outside a soda fountain. He looked like a carefree young man-about-town in baggy flannels, a white shirt, lovat pullover and two-tone shoes, a navy-blue blazer with silver buttons over his arm.

'Hello there,' Tim said. 'Mind if I sit down?'

'Free country,' Tony responded, but not in an unfriendly way.

'You're looking pretty snappy, if you don't mind me saying so.'

Two girls passing by glanced at them shyly and one ventured, 'Hi, Tony.'

'Hello. gorgeous,' he said, revelling in his youthful good looks. He glanced at Tim. 'See what you're missing, holy man?'

'I saw your mother today. You took care of that landlord.'

'She tell you that?'

'No, but somebody took care of him and if you didn't do it someone did it for you.' Tim waited but Tony made no comment. 'Dangerous game. The way I hear it, nobody does anything for nothing. Sooner or later you're going to have to return the favour.'

It was then that Tony erupted. 'None of your business, right? You keep your nose out, OK? Or it might just get flattened.'

'I'm not a priest yet, Tony. Never dodged a fight in my life.'

'Look, I don't want to fall out with you. Just stay away from me. Go preach to those sad bastards who keep you in business.'

'And what sad bastards are those?'

'Mugs around here got a houseful of kids 'cos that's what the Church wants. Poor suckers who work day and night to pay through the nose for Easter clothes so's their kids can traipse round the streets after parasites like you with your stupid banners and statues. Church don't pay the rent when some poor guy gets sick and he can't work. Who takes care of 'em then? Not you.'

'Sorry you feel like that.'

'What do you expect? You drag little kids to church. You make 'em confess their sins. What sins? Poor little sods are seven years old. What sins have *they* committed? You brainwash 'em at seven years of age so as they're scared of you. And they're scared for the rest of their lives. Well, not me, holy man. I ain't stupid.'

'OK,' Tim said mildly. 'It's just that I care about you. The Church cares about you.'

'Don't give me that. Father Pat's the church around here. He didn't go round and beat up the landlord when Ma told him what was going on. He was useless. All he could say was, "Your Tony's mixing with the wrong crowd". Well, it was the wrong crowd that sorted things out and that's why Ma's got a smile back on her face.'

'He just doesn't want to read about you in the *Daily News* with a bullet in the back of your head.'

The children playing in the road were running to the sidewalks, clearing the way as a smart new Model A Roadster with the top down appeared, its three horns playing a jaunty greeting. Martin Ripley was driving with Declan at his side. The children laughed and raced in its wake, enchanted by Marty Rip's new toy.

Martin Ripley and Declan, like Tony O'Reilly, were dressed in the kind of fashionable clothes most young men who lived on the Lower West Side couldn't afford.

Tony stood up, slinging his jacket over his shoulder. 'Be seeing you,' he said with a smile. Then, as he climbed into the jump seat he looked back and called, 'Why not come with us, holy man? Take the rest of the day off. Coney Island. See the girls.'

Declan curved the shape of a girl with his hands. 'Lots of girls.'

Marty Rip said something Tim couldn't catch, Tony and Declan laughed, then the roadster roared into action and sped away to the cheers of the children.

An elderly man in a drab jacket and a collarless shirt stopped by the bench to watch them go. 'Up to no good those three,' he said, shaking his head. 'Car like that cost about four hundred. Where do kids like them get that kinda money?'

# ELEVEN

D AN DIDN'T HAVE long to wait for his first assignment. A company in a small town near Baltimore had come to Joe Baker's attention. They were making collapsible cardboard boxes for industry, Joe told him. Easy to produce, easy to assemble, easy to transport. The potential was enormous, but Baker had heard the company was in need of an urgent injection of cash. Dan's brief was to 'go down there, see the operation first hand and report back'.

Joe Baker gave Dan his initial instructions on the morning stride down Madison. The man he was to see was called Fox. Joe Baker had never met the man but he had 'checked him out', as he put it. Fox was around forty, he'd had a varied career, mainly in sales, but no great managerial experience. By the end of the afternoon Dan had all the details Joe could give him and he was ready to set off early the next morning.

That evening Dan was the last to leave or so he thought. Harry and Lois had gone and Barbara Baker had arrived to whisk Joe away to the Plaza for dinner. He had been neglecting her, she complained. 'See you when you get back, son,' Baker called as they left. 'Should only take a couple of days.'

Dan checked he had everything. Rail tickets, reservation at some hotel called The Commercial, his file on Fox Boxes. Then, ready to leave, he was surprised to see Paul Merrick was still at his desk in the glassed-in office. He knocked lightly and put his head round the door. 'Know where we can get a drink?'

Merrick looked up. He had been poring over what looked like a movie magazine. His eyes and his expression seemed for a moment as though he was far away. Then he came back. 'I do,' he said.

Just off Madison, Merrick led Dan down some steps to a little café called Joey's. 'Not one of Baker's?' Dan asked.

'Could be,' Merrick said, and ushered him into a back room.

Dan wanted to know why there was this frosty feeling between Merrick and Joe Baker, had it always been that way or was it an association that had soured? He looked around. The bar was only about half full. Elegantly furnished with oak panelling and ceiling fans and subdued lighting, there was a men only feel about the place. Men in business suits with an hour to kill before their train was due, or maybe not eager to get home yet anyway. Who knows what a person's motives are for hanging around a bar after work? Dan paid for the drinks and handed Merrick his glass, but there wasn't really room to stand at the bar.

'Over here,' Merrick said, and he led the way to a corner table. 'So. What do you think?' he asked when they were seated.

'About what?'

'About the job, about America, about everything,' Merrick said, clearly trying to be friendly now.

Dan was trying to place his voice. He had an English name but it was not an English accent. Middle European. Hungarian, maybe. Or something like that, he guessed.

'About everything?' he said. 'Well, certainly, everything is one heck of a puzzle to me at the moment. About America? Well, I just can't imagine what it must be like. Looking at a map it's just so ... so *big*. New York is about all I can take in right now.'

'And the job?'

'Scares me,' Dan admitted. 'Every time he takes me down to Wall Street I try to remember what I learned yesterday and I find I didn't learn anything. I don't *know* anything. I need to make a start.'

'I would say you made a good start,' Merrick said quietly. 'You say you know nothing. Not everyone can do this. When you say to yourself you know nothing, you are OK.'

They talked about the job Dan had been given and Merrick

told him what to look for. 'They want your money,' he said. 'You must remember that. They tell you what they believe you want to hear. But they don't always tell you the truth. You can listen, but you don't have to believe everything they tell you. You find out the truth, the way things really are, in your own way.'

'And how do I do that?'

'Talk to the workers, listen to what they say. Ask the people no one ever asks.'

Merrick seemed genuinely willing to help and answer his questions and Dan was grateful. They were only there for a half-hour but he felt it was the most profitable half-hour he had spent since joining Joe Baker Associates. Then, after a couple of drinks, as they were leaving, he ventured, 'Can I ask you something? Straight answer?'

'Certainly,' Merrick said.

'Why does Joe Baker care about me?'

Merrick drained his glass. 'He doesn't care about you. He wants to *change* you, to make you like himself. Then, when he's done that, he will care about you. He's tried it before and it hasn't worked out. The men he chose were either too clever or too stupid. If you like the work and you like the money you have to accept this.' He smiled. 'The scientists call it "cloning".' He laughed. 'If you don't mind being cloned you'll be OK.' He leaned forward now and said quietly, 'Mr Baker thinks he has found a simple country boy from Ireland. I think perhaps in you he is mistaken.'

On the trolley back to Mrs O'Malley's Dan was pondering all this when a young fellow in a cloth cap and overalls caked in dried mud from the knees down came aboard, sat beside him and pulled out a copy of the *Daily News*. The headline screamed STOCK PRICES THROUGH THE ROOF! WALL STREET BONANZA!

The young man, who was no more than twenty, his face as yet unworn and unlined by age and his daily manual toil, grinned at Dan. 'Stock market gone crazy. Stocks going through the roof.' He showed Dan the headline. 'Everybody's buying. Can't lose. Time to get in on the act, I guess.'

'OK if you have the money,' Dan responded.

The young man regarded him frankly. 'You should be OK,' he said, noting Dan's suit, his collar and tie. 'Work in the City?'

Dan didn't know it but this meant Wall Street. 'Yeah,' he said.

'You do!' the young man's eyes lit up. 'Then what's to buy? What's the hot ticket right now? I got a few bucks put aside.'

Dan was suddenly alarmed, anxious not to mislead him. 'Oh, I don't know. I'm sort of new to all this.'

'Come on,' the young man urged. 'You must know something. Give us a break. What's everybody buying?'

'Well,' Dan said reluctantly, 'Radio, I guess. Radio stock is on the up and going higher.'

'Yeah? Radio, huh? Sounds good.' The young man stood up. 'This is my stop. Well listen, thanks for that. I'm getting married soon. Few dollars more will be great. See you around. I'll look out for you.'

Dan nodded and smiled uneasily as the young man swung from the trolley, raising a hand in gratitude. He felt even more uneasy when he heard a much older man in the seat behind murmur to the lady beside him, presumably his wife, 'Radio. He said Radio.'

Inadvertently he had become one of Mike Meehan's salesmen, pitching for Radio. The fact was, stocks and bonds were the newest craze and everyone was on their trail as they gave off the scent of easy money. But Dan Dolan was not qualified to offer investment advice. He was not even sure it was *good* advice. Feeling chastened, he resolved to keep his lips sealed and his amateur predictions to himself in future.

But the young man's eager quest for tips and scraps of 'inside' information was simply a manifestation of the popular hysteria. A wave of euphoria, it seemed, was carrying people, ordinary people, into the strange new world of stocks and bonds. They couldn't lose, they told each other. It was the surest thing since night followed day. People wanted in and the salutary warning signpost with the message that investments could go down as well as up had been trampled underfoot.

*

Ted Lewis was asking if everyone was happy. Eddie Cantor was making whoopee. Al Jolson was crying for his mammy. A young lady called Helen Kane was stealing the show with her boop-boop-a-do version of *I wanna be loved by you*. And Michael and Nathan were back plugging songs for Mr Levi. All they had was the Friday night job at the Irish Club. They needed to make some money fast.

Three o'clock in the afternoon and Twenty-eighth Street was quieter than usual. Things would improve later, probably around six when the office workers and the girls from the clothing factories were making their way home. Most of the time it was the girls who bought the sheet music. The boys might sing snatches of the latest song but they wouldn't buy a copy. Not unless they were aspiring crooners. The girls were more sentimental and the songs were mainly sentimental that year. Songs like *Someone to watch over me, Among my souvenirs, Melancholy Baby, Tea for Two* – songs Michael loved to sing. He had this gnawing ambition now. He wanted his name up there in lights with the top entertainers. He was going to take Manhattan, the Bronx and Staten Island, too. He was going to take the whole country – by storm.

Nathan was playing his way briskly through *Tea for Two* for the third or fourth time when Mr Levi appeared in his shop doorway. 'You,' he said, pointing a finger. 'Why aren't you singing?'

'There's no one to sing to,' Michael complained helplessly.

'Sing!' Mr Levi ordered, and he turned to go back inside. But then a black sedan pulled in close by and two men got out. One was just another gorilla with bulging shoulders and dead eyes under a Derby hat. The other was short with a big overcoat and a thin face rendered almost comic under a hat that looked two sizes too big.

'All right, boys,' the short man said. 'You're coming with us.'

'To where?' Michael asked.

'Get in the car,' was all he would say.

Mr Levi, jacketless and in shirtsleeves, held his hands out humbly and with excessive deference. 'Mr Pickles.'

The short man said, 'It's all right, Sol. They won't be long. And I'll see they get back here.' He looked at Michael and Nathan who were still standing by the piano. 'Get in the car,' he repeated testily. 'A piano player with no fingers is no good to anyone and a canary with it's throat cut can't sing.'

Michael and Nathan looked at each other and decided to get in the car. 'What do you want us for?' Michael asked.

The gorilla was in the driving seat. Pickles swung in beside him and looked back at his captives. 'Boss got a job for you.'

'The boss?' Michael said. 'And who might that be?'

'The only boss there is around here. Vin O'Hara. Mr O'Hara was at Arnie's Sunday night. Must have seen something in you bums.'

'Well, listen,' Nathan said. 'We need to know what kind of job you got in mind. We ain't working in a dump like that no more.'

Pickles laughed shortly. 'You don't work where the boss sends you, you don't work at all. Simple as that.'

'You mean he owns that dump?' Nathan asked.

'Arnie's? Nah, he was just visiting. He didn't like what he saw, but if he takes it over everything will change. Anyway, you did all right so what's your problem? You got paid, didn't you?'

'Oh sure,' Nathan said. 'We got paid. We got rolled, too.'

Pickles looked back with a grin. 'You did?'

'The Greek pays us off, we walk home and two guys follow us with a gun. Goodbye dough and two nights' work.'

'Hey, Bluey,' Pickles said to the gorilla. 'Do you hear this?'

Bluey's shoulders were shaking as he drove along. They seemed to think Nathan's story was hilarious.

'Glad you think it's funny,' Michael said.

'Why, it's the oldest trick in the hook, you dumb bastards,' Pickles said, still laughing. 'The Greek pays you off, two of his boys come after you, he gets his money back.'

'Well, we might be paying him a call,' Nathan threatened.

'No need,' Pickles said. 'Bluey.'

Bluey nodded and drove to the Village. He pulled up outside

Arnie's. The place was closed and shuttered in the quiet, sleepy afternoon. No one about. Pickles hammered on the door.

After a while there was the sound of bolts being slid back and the voice of the Greek club owner. 'OK, OK! Wait-a, can't you?' He peered round the door and immediately his attitude changed. He drew the door open wide. 'Mr Pickles! Nize to see you. Come in.'

'It's not a social call,' Pickles said. He looked back and signalled that Nathan and Michael should join him.

The Greek saw them and seemed to withdraw within himself as if to hide from their hostile stares. He led them down a dingy corridor to a room with no windows, a pile of showbiz magazines on top of a filing cabinet and a desk overflowing with assorted papers.

'These boys,' Pickles said, wasting no time. 'You owe them.' He looked back at Nathan. 'How much was it?'

'Sixty,' Nathan said.

'I pay them already,' the Greek protested.

'And you took it back. Now come on. We don't want to do you over but we will.' Pickles smiled. 'Then we'll close down the club.'

The Greek was shaking. He opened a deep drawer in the desk, took out a metal box and unlocked it with an unsteady hand.

'Eighty bucks,' Pickles said.

The Greek looked up meekly. 'He said sixty.'

'And I said eighty.'

Nathan's eyes lit up as the Greek counted out four twenty-dollar bills and handed them over. Pickles gave the Greek one back. 'Make this two tens.'

The Greek changed the twenty for two tens.

'Thank you,' Pickles said and he led the way out to where Bluey was waiting and keeping watch. All four climbed back in the car.

Pickles handed Nathan three twenties, gave Bluey a ten and put the other ten in his top pocket. He smiled sweetly at Nathan. 'Our expenses,' he explained. The whole operation had taken less than ten minutes. 'Now you're going to meet the boss.'

Vin O'Hara's town house was a well-kept brownstone at the better end of Bedford Street. Bluey parked outside and stayed in the car. Pickles led Michael and Nathan up the steps, through the open door and down the hallway. There was a bar in the living room and three of O'Hara's men were sitting around, drinks in hand. They sat up straight when Pickles appeared.

'Wait here,' he told Michael and Nathan. He went back down the hallway, knocking lightly on a door on the right before going inside. Almost at once he reappeared and gestured for Michael to join him.

O'Hara was sitting behind a large desk in the gloom of the late afternoon. The only light came from a shaded desk lamp that threw a bright little circle on the papers before him. From what Michael could make out the office was furnished with dark heavy furniture, dark-brown sofas, floor-to-ceiling, heavy-looking brocade curtains and an ornate drinks cabinet.

He couldn't see O'Hara clearly but he had the impression of a man who was overweight, heavy-looking, but bear-shaped with narrow, rounded shoulders. He also appeared heavy-jowled with small eyes and fleshy, cherub's lips. Quite ugly, in fact. But Michael was only interested in what work he might have to offer.

'This is the kid, boss,' Jimmy Pickles said, with a nod at Michael.

'Leave us,' O'Hara said and Michael thought he caught even in those two simple words the hint of an Irish brogue.

Pickles withdrew at once and Michael was left standing awkwardly in the middle of the darkened room.

'Close the door, son,' O'Hara said, 'and come and sit down.'

Michael closed the door and sat on an upright chair, facing him.

'You sing good,' O'Hara said.

Michael nodded. 'Thank you, sir.'

'So where are you from?'

'Little place just south of Dublin,' Michael said.

'Ah now, myself I'm from County Armagh, so I am. Heartland of the resistance.' He laughed and started to sing in a hoarse, wheezing voice. '*O Paddy dear, now did ye hear the news that's goin' roun'*…'

Michael laughed and joined in and for a moment they were linked like a couple of rebel soldiers ready to fight for the cause. Abruptly O'Hara asked, 'And how's your mother?'

Michael was surprised. 'She's fine, as far as I know. I mean, she was upset when we left but she didn't try to stop us.'

He nodded. 'You and your brother?'

'No, sir.' Michael thought he had better explain. 'Nathan, the boy who plays piano, he's not my brother. He's a friend, came over with us on the boat. We call ourselves the Dolan Brothers. It was Nathan's idea. His name is O'Shaughnessy. He reckons that's a bit too long to go up in lights.'

'Sure an' I know *he's* not your brother. Your brother's a priest.'

'Going to be,' Michael said, again surprised. 'Tim's waiting to go to the seminary. Working with a priest called Father Pat just now.'

O'Hara nodded. 'I know Father Pat.'

'There's three of us. Me, Tim and Dan.'

'Oh? And what does Dan do?'

'He's working in Wall Street. He's going to be a stockbroker.'

'Is he, be God? Bigger crooks than us that lot.' O'Hara leaned forward into the light from the desk lamp and for the first time Michael saw his face clearly, the pink bloated cheeks, the small eyes with the disconcerting cast. 'Who's he with?'

'Man called Joe Baker. I thinks it's Joe Baker Associates.'

'Is that right?' O'Hara seemed impressed. 'Well listen, Michael, I heard you the other night at that shithouse in the village. I'd say you can do better than that. We can find you some work.'

'Yeah?' Michael's expression said it all. 'That's just what we need right now, Mr O'Hara. We'll work hard, sir. We got lots of stuff.'

'Well, don't tell me. Tell Jimmy. He'll put you right.'

'Mr Pickles?'

'Yeah, yeah. Jimmy.' O'Hara seemed to withdraw into his high-backed leather chair as if submerging in the mist of some private world. Softly he said, 'You write to your ma?'

Michael nodded dutifully.

'I lost my ma just a week ago. Lovely lady, so she was. The only person in this lousy world ...' His voice trailed.

Michael remained silent, not knowing what to say.

'One day she's fine,' O'Hara said quietly. 'Next day she's gone.'

A silence descended on the darkened room and for the first time Michael noticed the flowers in the window bay. It was like sitting in a chapel of rest. Maybe they haven't had the funeral yet, he thought. He sat still, scared to look round in case the old lady was laid out in her box. He could just make out O'Hara's eyes now as they glistened in the dark. He seemed to be crying.

'Sing it,' O'Hara said.

'Sir?' Michael was startled.

'That song. Y'know, I lost the sunshine....'

Michael stood up. He peered at O'Hara uncertainly.

O'Hara seemed to give a brisk nod. 'Sing it.'

Standing in front of his shadowy audience of one, Michael began to sing.

He sang with feeling, thinking this might be O'Hara's idea of an audition. O'Hara's head went back and his eyes closed and when Michael came to the end he opened his eyes. 'Again,' he said. 'Sing it again.'

Michael sang it again and this time, at the end, there was silence. 'Mr O'Hara,' he ventured, after a moment, 'are you all right?'

O'Hara was perfectly still, his eyes closed.

'Mr O'Hara?' Michael said softly and he moved a little nearer.

Then suddenly O'Hara sat up straight and startled him. 'Get out!' he bellowed, erupting violently. 'Go on, damn you! Get out!'

Jimmy Pickles hurried in and bundled Michael out and into the hallway. 'It's OK,' Pickles said. 'Go get a drink.'

Pickles pushed Michael down the corridor and went back into the darkened room. Puzzled and bemused, Michael found Nathan was standing with a drink in his hand with O'Hara's men chuckling at his jokes about his fellow countrymen.

'Hey, Michael!' Nathan said. 'It's OK to tell jokes about the Irish as long as you're Irish. That right, fellas?' The heavies rocked to and fro, laughing as if this, too, was a joke. Quietly, to Michael, he murmured, 'What's going on?'

Michael shrugged. 'You tell me.'

The parish church was old. It had been there since the 1840s. It was constructed of wood originally and though much of it had been rebuilt, the west wing, the side most exposed to the Hudson, was desperately in need of repair. The contractor for building maintenance throughout the diocese had made a report a year ago and the news was not good. Not only did the roof and the west wall need replacing, there were the early signs of termites in the timber. The estimated cost of repair ran to several thousand dollars of which the diocese could only fund around fifty per cent.

'We're going to have to find the rest, Timothy,' Father Pat said.

'From where? Not from the parish surely. Our people haven't got any money.' They were silent for a moment then Tim said jokingly, 'Maybe we should get Tony O'Reilly's pals to help out.'

'Those boys have got more chance than we have,' Father Pat said.

He sat down on a low bench, his flowing cassock sweeping the gravel path as he drew Tim down beside him. 'Tell me some good news. How did you get on today?'

Tim told him about Mrs O'Reilly and her landlord, about an old man whose wife they buried a month ago and who was still so distraught he was contemplating suicide. 'I had to sit with him for over an hour,' he said.

'All in a day's work,' Father Pat said. 'What else?'

Tim told him about Tony O'Reilly and Martin Ripley and Declan. They were dressed in the kind of clothes nobody else around there could possibly afford. And Marty Rip was driving a brand new car.

'Envious?' Father Pat teased him. 'Like to join 'em?'

'I would not,' Tim said with conviction. 'But I'd like to know where the money comes from.'

'Well,' Father Pat said in a drawn out sigh, 'it's always been the same around here. Ever since I've been here anyway. There's always been a gang with a big boss. And it's always our own people. The Irish gangs have ruled the Lower West Side for the past sixty years. Police, politicians, even the coastguard – all sewn up. You get to know all the big shots in this job. One guy I knew well was Big Bill Dwyer. He had a fleet of trucks hidden away right across the West Side. He was running booze from all over the place. Europe, Canada and, like I said, border patrols, coastguards, all on the payroll. He was just an ordinary working fellow 'til the Volstead Act. You know, that crazy law created more criminals than the IRS. Anyway, they caught up with him in the end. Got two years. Out after twelve months for good behaviour.'

'I hear he went legit,' Tim said.

'Yeah,' Father Pat said drily. 'He fixes fights and hockey games for a living. Trouble is, what we got now is ten times worse. A crazy killer, calls himself The Englishman. Reckons he's from Yorkshire, England. He's killed more men than died in the last war. Got sent down when he was still a kid. Twenty years in Sing Sing. Served about half and now he's out, back to his old tricks. But he has better cover this time. He bought this night spot called the Club de Luxe, bought it from the boxer Jack Johnson. I hear he smartened it up. Made it a *whites only* club and he brings in all the top black entertainers. Ellington is the resident band.'

'It's a *whites only* club with black entertainers? *Why?*'

'I told you, he's mad. They're all mad. Anyway, he's got night-clubs all over the place but he's still a killer underneath.'

'And he's the big boss now?'

'Until someone fills him full of lead, as they say.' Father Pat was quiet for a moment then he said, 'Termites. People like him are like termites gnawing away at the very fabric of the Church. We have to eliminate them. But don't ask me how.'

'You think Tony O'Reilly and those boys are involved with this Englishman?'

'Not directly. He splits his territory into sections. Divide and rule, I suppose. The madman running our patch is an oddball, a lapsed Catholic. Lapsed brain, too, if you ask me. Fellow called Vincent O'Hara. Lives on Bedford Street. You're sure to come across him sooner or later.'

Tim nodded. 'Oh, Father, before I forget. I promised young Francis – you know, Tony O'Reilly's kid brother? – I promised I'd mention to you he wants us to call him Frank or Frankie in future. He thinks Francis is too sissy.'

'Does he now? Wait 'til I tell St Francis.'

'It seems to mean a lot to him, Father.'

'Tell him if he turns up for altar duty on Sunday I'll call him anything he likes.' Father Pat looked at Tim sideways. 'And, by the way, a message from the bishop and I'm not sure if it's good news or bad.'

Tim waited.

'They're not quite ready for you yet at the seminary. Or maybe you're not quite ready for them. They want you to wait a while. Maybe next year. The bishop wants you to stay here for now, keep an eye on me, make sure I don't get myself a gun and blow everybody's brains out – including my own. God knows, I feel like doing just that sometimes.'

Tim had mixed feelings. He was not really disappointed. He wanted to join the seminary, prepare for his ordination, of course he did. But he felt he had become involved here. The people of the parish were important to him. The unorthodox Father Pat was important to him. And there seemed to be so much to do, though he was not sure what or where to start.

# TWELVE

PENN STATION. IT was Dan's second venture into this
magical place but his first chance to appreciate the high
vaulted ceiling, the enormous classical columns. It was a
colossus, more like an old world cathedral than a railway
station and he was entranced. The first time he came here
Caitlin was his main concern then he was rushing off to say
goodbye to Tim at St Patrick's. Now he had time to stand and
stare. Twenty minutes, anyway, before his train was due out.
And there was something romantic, he felt, about a railway
station, especially one as big and as grand as this.

He had read about the great steam engines traversing conti-
nents, the magnificent railways constructed by the British Raj
and until now most of his knowledge had come from books,
books from the travelling library that arrived in the village in an
old bus once a month. He would tell the library lady what kind
of book he wanted and on her next visit she would nearly
always have something for him. In the village he had become
known as the boy with a book mainly because once when a
cousin he had never met arrived and went looking for him Uncle
Pat told him to, 'Look for the boy with a book.'

It was not that he was a brilliant scholar or anything like
that. In school he was usually engrossed in something other
than what was under discussion, a dreamer with a thirst for
knowledge. He was good at reading and writing but he was no
good at all at what the teacher called 'Ritmatic. And this
worried him a little in view of his job on Wall Street.

Now, at Penn Station, though he had been here only once

before, he felt that he knew the place and it seemed somehow very special as people swirled around him. Anxious eyes peering at timetables. A slim black porter in a pillbox hat. Trolleys loaded with luggage. A beggar with a tin cup. Smoky, noisy, alive with arrivals and departures. Dan loved it and he had plenty of time, then he had no time at all.

He found an empty compartment, a seat by the window. He had only just made it and the train was already moving when a young woman and a small boy arrived. The woman, pretty in a demure way, smiled at him with a shy twitch of her lips and told the small boy to sit down and be quiet.

Dan watched the tracks as the train moved forward smoothly and slowly. Images gently glided by. Iron posts, high-wire cables, abandoned wagons, a railroad worker walking down the middle of a line. Then the train gathered speed, sped along unimpeded then slowed and came to a halt as a freight train clanked over the points then eased slowly past his window.

As the last of the linked freight wagons went gliding by the train set off again, slowly at first then picking up speed as if it was chasing lost time. Dan closed his eyes and for no obvious reason he thought of Paul Merrick. He liked Merrick. It was not just that he had found no reason to dislike him. Merrick seemed a genuinely nice fellow and this made Merrick's clear alienation from Joe Baker all the more puzzling.

When he was in the mood Merrick could be good company and Dan looked forward to their occasional drinks after work, though he sometimes had to endure Merrick's forthright advice. 'You look intelligent,' he told Dan, 'and this is an advantage. If you are not sure what is going on, you must say nothing. Just look intelligent. And – how do they say it? – always keep the cards close to the chest.'

It was all a bit patronizing, the time served soldier talking to the rookie. But Dan knew it was well meant.

He must have fallen asleep because when he opened his eyes the young woman and the boy had gone and he was alone. He looked anxiously at his watch but there was still an hour to go.

Again his thoughts turned to Merrick. What was it with him and Joe Baker? Something must have happened between them. They were partners once or, at least, close associates. Now all that was over. Something Paul had done? Double-crossed on a deal? He didn't think so. He trusted Merrick. He had no reason not to. Yet Merrick's own, rather stark maxim was, 'Do not trust any man in business.'

There was a restaurant car but Dan wasn't hungry. He stayed in his seat. Not bored. Not restless. An empty carriage on a rhythmically moving train is a great place to think, he decided, a great place to take stock. He thought of Tim in his colourful vestments and with a white collar, baptizing babies, solemnizing marriages. Tim holding a golden chalice high before a large congregation then handing out the Blessed Sacrament. And Michael with that endearing Irish grin, full of the Blarney, charming his audience with ballads and Nathan making them laugh with his Irish jokes. Tim and Michael had gone in very different directions. Although, the thought occurred to him, maybe not. They were each in their own kind of show business, Tim with his vow of poverty and service, Michael with his quest for fame and fortune.

And what of himself? Dan knew now that what he wanted was money. Not as an end in itself but as the means to an end. Hard cash in the bank, solid investments. He knew what it was like to be poor, to live from week to week on a paltry hand-out called wages, to be a wage slave. He wanted to be rich enough to be independent, indebted to no man. He had seen the men at the Stock Exchange in their smart suits sporting the silver spoons they had been handed at birth. This was supposed to be the land of the free, equal opportunities for all, yet there was a class system here just as there was at home.

It was built on old money and no matter how wealthy a man might become certain doors would always be closed to him. The only entry to the periphery was through the marriage stakes. It was like a horse race in which only a very few unknown runners are allowed to enter. But none of this concerned Dan. Financial independence, the freedom to choose – these were his aims now.

He stood up, a little stiff from sitting so long, as the train hissed and puffed into his station. His hotel was close by. It was a quiet commercial hotel and it was called exactly that, The Commercial Hotel. His room was small, over-furnished with two time-worn armchairs, an old bedstead and a large wardrobe. Incongruously, a dead spider was trapped and preserved behind the glass of one of the nondescript pictures that adorned the walls. But otherwise the room was clean and probably comfortable and he would only be there for one night. The bathroom was down the hall. Dan freshened up and went to work at once, his appointment for three o'clock.

'A cab?' the tall, thin, rather imperious lady at the reception desk asked severely. 'Where to?'

'The boxmakers,' he said. 'The company that makes boxes.'

She peered at him over her spectacles. 'Which one?'

'You mean there's more than one?'

'Sure. There's the Davis plant and there's the new one out on the 'pike. Fox Boxes, something like that.'

'Yes,' Dan said. 'That's the one. I didn't know this other place – Davis? – made boxes.'

'They didn't until this Fox started up. But they do now.'

'Competition, huh?'

The lady frowned. 'Old man Davis owns just about everything in this town, including this place.' She waved a hand to indicate the hotel. 'Start a new business and sooner or later he'll run you out.'

'Doesn't sound like a very nice fellow,' Dan said mildly.

'He ain't. Reckons this town is his territory. Davis family owned everything here from way back. Don't take kindly to upstarts.'

'But Fox specialize in boxes. They're nationwide. Every state in the union. Surely they get all the business.'

'Nah. Davis'll lose money just to bankrupt 'em.' She peered at Dan through her ornate spectacles. She had lost her polished veneer now and, clearly bearing some private grudge, she added, 'Kinda shit he is.'

Dan swallowed, surprised. 'I see. It still doesn't seem right though. I thought Fox were providing employment for local people.'

'They were,' she said. 'But that don't bother Mr High and Mighty Davis. Fox laid off half its workers Friday.'

'Will Davis take them on?'

'Nah. He reckons they been disloyal. They're black-listed.' Again she peered at him. 'You thinking of taking a job with this Fox? If so, I'd think again. Sure as hell they ain't going to last.' She looked at him quizzically. 'Still want that cab?'

Dan had a half-hour wait for the cab and when it came he noted the circular logo stencilled on the doors. *Davis Cabs*. He chose to sit up front with the driver. 'Davis Cabs?' he queried. 'Sounds like this Davis owns just about everything around here.'

'Just about,' the cab driver confirmed. 'You official?'

'How do you mean?'

'You come to wind up this place?'

'Wind it up? Why, no. Fox is a good business.'

'Oh yeah? It's dead on its feet, washed up. Everyone knows that. Old man Davis killed it off.'

'I heard about this Davis,' Dan said. 'He's your boss, right?'

'He owns the cab company. He's everybody's boss in this town.'

'Isn't it time somebody fought back? I mean, Fox is just trying to run a legitimate business, make a profit, provide employment.'

The driver glanced sideways at him. 'That's true. But around these parts it ain't allowed.'

The Fox plant was housed in a long, low building that had once been part of an army compound. On the facing wall a large sign announced FOX BOXES and there was an arrow pointing to the reception office. There was plenty of space around the building but a roadster and a couple of trucks were the only vehicles on view and the place didn't exactly appear to be a hive of activity. It was too quiet and there didn't seem to be anyone about. Maybe they've already closed down, Dan thought for a second. Then, as the cab drew in, a man of about forty came from the office.

'Want me to wait?' the driver asked, as Dan was paying him off.

But the man from the office put out a hand and with a big smile said, 'Mr Dolan, I presume.' To the cab driver he said tersely, 'I'll see this gentleman gets back to town.'

The cab moved off and the man introduced himself. His name was Hugo Fox, owner and managing director of the Fox Company. Mr Dolan had arrived at a difficult time but, of course, he was very welcome. The order book was full, Fox said, as he ushered Dan into his office, and the product was in great demand.

'Maybe we should take a quick look around,' Dan suggested. 'Then we can come back and talk. I'd like to know what we're talking about, Mr Fox.'

'Oh sure,' Fox said at once. 'Sure you would.'

He led Dan down a narrow passage into a long corridor with a brick wall on the right and windows into several bays along the left. The workshop seemed to be divided into these bays and Dan could see into each one from the corridor. In the first bay large sheets of cardboard were stacked high. In the second there were three long tables covered in equal lengths of board and a cutting machine that was not in operation. In the third, feeding the sheets of board to a new-looking machine that folded and turned out the finished product was a man in blue overalls. A conveyor delivered the flat packs to the fourth bay where two men were stamping them and packing them into large cartons.

No girl on reception, no secretary, just three men. No trucks waiting to be loaded, no drivers ready to race to the railyard or hit the highway. Nothing much. Fox led Dan back along the corridor to the first bay and through to a similar set up beyond. There was the same machinery, the tables ready and waiting but there were no workers. Nothing at all going on here.

In silence and in single file Dan and Fox trooped back to the office. Fox began talking, explaining, even before they sat down. 'I know it seems pretty quiet right now. But we just need to get this order out of the way.'

'Only three men?' Dan said.

'Well, that's all it takes for this particular order. But when we're going full blast I bring everybody in. Both sides full. Eight bays buzzing away. Great sound!'

Dan nodded, unconvinced. 'What about the work-force?'

'Well, they're mostly casual. But I can call them up at any time. There's a lot of unemployment.'

'When you have no work you lay them off?'

'It's not that. We got the work. Look at the order book.'

Dan listened politely. He liked Hugo Fox. He was so desperately earnest, so obviously eager to assure him he had a good product, a good set-up, the will to succeed. But the place had an aura of defeat. The quiet corridor, the silent telephone. It seemed more like a failed business closing down than a thriving business bursting to expand.

Dan smiled pleasantly. 'Mr Fox,' he said, 'can we be absolutely frank here? I can see you have the orders. But you have not been paid yet for the work you have done. And you have not paid your suppliers. You are short of cash. That's why you have come to us.'

Fox nodded, looking down at his desk.

'It's not just that you need money for expansion, you actually need money to carry on. Is that not the position we are in here?'

Fox looked up at him. This young fellow with the pleasant, slightly Irish brogue, was quite a lot younger than himself, but he seemed someone he could talk to, man to man, and he was obviously no fool. Maybe it would be better to level with him. 'You're right,' he said. 'I need the money to carry on. I've got the work and there's plenty more. I can get the workers, they're ready and waiting, but I need a backer. It would be a great shame to let this opportunity go, Mr Dolan. This business has great potential.'

'But this fellow Davis is making things tough,' Dan said.

Fox was taken aback slightly. 'You've done your homework.'

'It's my job,' Dan said mildly.

He nodded. 'OK. Davis is a tyrant with a big ego. But we can fight him. I know we can. I sank all my savings into this game,

Mr Dolan. I'm not going to let him win. The Davis family run more or less everything around here, but that's not going to stop me. They make it tough and they fight dirty. Well, so will I.'

'In what ways do they make it tough?' Dan asked.

'Right of way, access points. They make it difficult for my trucks to get out on the main routes. They blocked the entrance to the freight yard. One of their vehicles breaks down at the gate so we miss trains, that sort of thing. My post goes missing; my telephone line goes dead. I can't prove any of this is deliberate or that they are responsible. But we all know they are. With your backing we can kill them off once and for all. Together we can make it work. We can beat him. I know we can. All I'm asking is two fifty grand.'

'And that would be just the beginning.'

'But then you would see what a great business you were in and you would want to put in more.'

You had to admire his enthusiasm, Dan conceded, and he didn't doubt that Fox had the determination to make it work. 'You need a partner, Mr Fox, a full time working partner. Not a company like ours. We would just provide the money for expansion. We don't get involved. You need a partner with money of his own to invest and a one hundred per cent commitment.'

Fox looked crestfallen and Dan felt genuinely sorry for him.

'You could take Davis on as a partner,' he suggested tentatively.

Fox shook his head. 'He'd take that and he'd put the money in. But I wouldn't be a partner. I'd he working for him.'

Dan was silent for a moment. He wanted to help. Fox was a genuine pioneer, ready to work and put his life into making his dream come true. He'd already put his own money in. But the odds were stacked against him.

'Look,' Fox said, 'you've seen all this in the worst possible light. The place is quiet for the moment. You need to see it when it's really buzzing. Why not take some time to think things over, Mr Dolan? How about I take you back into town then I pick you up later, about seven? Dinner on me and we can talk some more.'

Dan smiled appreciatively. 'Thank you, but I'd like to take a look around town tonight, get a feel of the place, maybe talk to some local people.'

'That it then?'

'No, no,' Dan said sincerely. 'I agree. Lots of potential here.' He stood up to leave. 'I'm sure of that and if you do beat this Davis there'll be a lot of people on your side. I'll go back, write my report for the boss and I promise it'll be fair. I'll give him the full picture.'

'I've heard a lot about Joe Baker. What's he like?'

'Tough, shrewd, but he likes a fight.'

Fox brightened a little as Dan held out a hand.

'Whatever happens, Mr Dolan,' Fox said, 'it's been a pleasure meeting you.'

'Things are looking up,' Michael said, and they were. They had six weeks booked on the Vaudeville circuit with the promise of more and better bookings. Vin O'Hara had said Jimmy Pickles would look after them and he had. Early on he had introduced them to the agent, Joe Bononi, who represented most of the entertainers on the West Side and certainly all of the Irish acts.

'Hey, Nathan,' Michael said. 'Why do you suppose this Bononi is the top agent around here? He isn't even Irish.'

'He's probably Paddy Baloney from Blarney. Everybody changes his name in America.'

'Like you?' Michael said with a grin. 'Nathan *O'Shaughnessy*.'

They were in high spirits. There were so many burlesque shows and vaudeville theatres – not to mention the dinner clubs – and Joe Bononi was the key to them all. With the right contacts the only way, it seemed, was up. Yet it was on their very first date, at a dinner club on 34th Street, the fateful seeds of what lay ahead were sown.

# THIRTEEN

THE DINNER CLUB was several steps up in style and elegance from Arnie's in the village. Michael did a mixture of slow and upbeat songs, some of them new and just off the press. He was dedicated to the job and totally focused, always trying to gauge the mood of the audience, forever worrying about his performance, dancing on his toes, eager to get on again. Was his breathing right? Did that nuance actually work? Had he had to strain to make any of the high notes? Was he completely comfortable with the music? No matter how well his performance went, no matter how much the audience applauded, Michael was never satisfied.

Every table in the place was taken now and everyone was talking, laughing, not really paying much attention to the acts on stage. But there was a noticeable drop in the level of noise each time Michael stepped up to sing. He seemed to command most attention, he had noted, and engage his audience best when the lights were lowered and he sang a slow song like *Always* or *What'll I do?*

The raucous Charleston dancing, Black Bottom stomping, secret drinking masses apparently had a suppressed yearning for romance and an unabashed weakness for sentimental lyrics. But the surprise hit of that first evening was not the Dolan Brothers. A house chorus of eight gorgeous girls provided what Nathan called 'the hip-hooray and ballyhoo' and it was when all eight were on stage and seven of them, arms outstretched, made a ballet-like withdrawal and left one girl alone, centre stage. The girl paused for a moment and most of the audience stopped talking and waited expectantly.

She was slim like the rest of the girls. She'd had her black hair bobbed like the rest of the girls. She wore a coloured band around her head, a waistless dress fringed with tassles to just below her knee and flat shoes like the rest of the girls. But she was not like the rest of the girls. At least, Michael Dolan didn't think so.

Mascara seemed to enlarge her dark eyes and she wore a bright red lipstick. She sang in a childish, petulant voice that was somehow both amusing and provocative and the whole audience paused to listen as she stepped to and fro in the simple little dance that accompanied her words.

'*He's got eyes of blue,*' she sang and each time, on the verge of what promised to be a suggestive line, she would go into a '*boop boop-a-do*' routine to replace the words. But in her voice and in the dance there could be no mistaking the meaning and every coy, bashful '*boop boop-a-do*' had the audience calling for more and roaring approval. It was the first time, Joe Bononi said later, anyone got a standing ovation in that place.

As she danced off, after several bows and little girl curtsies, the other girls took over with a faster version of the same song.

Michael Dolan was waiting to go on when the dark-haired girl passed by and bumped into him slightly in the narrow space provided. He saw then she was even prettier close up.

'Hey!' he said spontaneously. 'You were great!'

She looked back at him and smiled. 'Well, thank you, sir.'

'You could go a long way with that act.'

She shook her head. 'I don't think so. It isn't mine.'

'How do you mean?'

'Where have you been?' she asked in disbelief. 'A girl called Helen Kane dreamed that one up. She's knocking 'em out on Broadway.'

Michael grinned. 'I bet she's not as good as you.'

The girl smiled and turned away.

'Wait,' he said. 'What's your name?'

'Why?' she asked, eyebrows raised. 'Who wants to know?'

'Me,' he said. 'Michael Dolan.'

'OK, Michael Dolan. It's Annie. My name's Annie. Now I've

got to go. I've got to get changed. We're on again after you.'

Later that evening they literally bumped into each other a second time. 'Hey!' Michael said, with a smile. 'We can't go on bumping into each other like this.'

Annie stopped. 'You were good,' she said. 'I mean it. I think you have a great voice.'

'Right.' Michael looked down at her. 'And do I hear a *but*?'

'But you're not the finished product. You still have a lot to learn.'

'Oh, I know. I'm sure I can learn a lot from you older performers.'

'What do you mean *older* performers?' she demanded. But she was not really offended. She was obviously no older than him, probably even younger.

'Would you care to join us for supper, ma'am?' he asked hopefully.

She hesitated. 'I can't. We're goin' to a party. The boss says so.'

'And who's the boss?' Michael asked.

'The only boss there is, of course. Mr O'Hara.'

Michael nodded, not knowing what to say.

'I would like to talk to you though.'

'You would?' he said, brightening.

'Yeah,' she said seriously. 'About your voice. Like I said, I think you have a great voice. But you need to sort one or two things out. I mean, take just now. In the slow numbers it was fine. Then when the tempo picks up you're not quite on the beat. Or maybe it's not your fault.'

'How do you mean?'

'Well,' she said tentatively, 'I think the problem could be with your piano player. I think, maybe, he ain't good enough at this level and he sure ain't good enough for where you can go with a voice like that.'

One of the girls passed by. 'Come on, Annie,' she said. She fluttered her eyelashes at Michael. 'Great voice,' she said and she was gone, taking Annie with her.

Michael was left to ponder what Annie said. He knew what

she meant about the faster numbers. There were times when they were not quite synchronized. Not too noticeable in a crowded room, but Michael had one eye on the up and coming record market. They couldn't get away with anything like that in a recording studio.

'Everything OK?' Nathan asked, 'She turn you down or something?'

'No, no, nothing like that,' Michael said. 'Let's eat.'

Father Pat handed Tim the evening 'paper: GANGLAND KILLING. WEST SIDE KID ARRESTED. Tim scanned the story swiftly. A man called Devlin had been shot dead in a warehouse just off Tenth Avenue. The police wanted to interview two men who had been seen, by several witnesses, to run from the building soon after the shot was heard. A third man, named as eighteen-year-old Anthony O'Reilly, had been arrested and was being held in custody.

'We'd better get down there right away,' Father Pat said.

A small crowd, mainly women, had gathered on the steps and on the pavement in front of the house where the O'Reillys lived.

Father Pat, with Tim in tow, skirted the crowd. 'What's going on, Ed?' he asked a fortyish, untidy-looking man in a shabby suit, a collar and tie and a lapel badge that read PRESS.

'They reckon it's kids from round here,' Ed said. 'Tony O'Reilly, Martin Ripley and that kid Declan. But we don't know for sure. I want to get a few words from O'Reilly's ma.'

'Wait here,' Father Pat told Tim, and people moved aside to let him through. Two women who had taken it on themselves to bar the entrance to the house acknowledged him at once.

'Doc's with her, Father,' one called, as he went in and up the stairs.

Tim turned to the reporter. 'You sure it's Tony?'

'Absolutely, and from what I hear it was him pulled the trigger.'

'How is she?' Tim asked when Father Pat returned.

'Shocked,' he said. 'She doesn't know the full extent of it yet but, according to Officer Healey, Tony's in deep, deep trouble.'

'Where is Healey?' the reporter asked.

'He'll be out in a minute,' Father Pat told him. To Tim he said, 'Officer Healey is our neighbourhood cop.' To the reporter he said, 'Who's handling it, Ed?'

'Dennis,' the reporter said.

Dennis Casey was a young man who had hauled himself out of the gutter and landed on the right side of the law. Qualified as a lawyer, he was always ready to help and advise the less fortunate, especially people from his old neighbourhood. A good Catholic boy, Father Pat called him. They went straight to his office.

Casey had light-brown hair and brown eyes yet there was something distinctly Irish about him. Father Pat introduced Tim and Tim and Casey shook hands.

'So what's the story?' Father Pat asked.

'Looks bad for Tony O'Reilly, Father,' Casey said. 'Seems the three of them – Tony, Martin Ripley and Declan O'Connor – went to this warehouse to deliver a message to this Devlin fellow.'

'A message from who?' Father Pat asked.

'Vincent O'Hara, according to Tony.'

'You seen Tony?'

'Yes, of course. Police are not too helpful right now. Mayor Walker is demanding a crackdown on organized criminals and the police commissioner is on his toes. Cops have clammed up and they're not saying much.'

'The police commissioner is part of the problem,' Father Pat said.

Casey laughed. 'You can't say things like that, Father.'

'He's in O'Hara's pocket,' the priest said scornfully. 'So what did Tony have to say for himself?'

'He said they went off to meet this Devlin on the top floor. They were told that when they met, Devlin would say, "Where's the money?" Marty Rip, as they call him, was to say, "Mr O'Hara says there is no money. Not now, not ever." Eamonn Devlin only got out of Sing Sing three days ago. He must have contacted O'Hara and set up this meeting right away. Far as I remember he went up the river for twenty. He did four but last Christmas new evidence came up. It proved he couldn't have done the job he was in for because he was robbing a bank in Queens at the time.

'Anyway, the four years he'd been inside covered what he would have got for the robbery so they let him out. My guess is Vin O'Hara owed him money, but O'Hara thought he was in the clear because Devlin was away for twenty.'

'So he sent these boys to start the war?'

'Yes,' Casey said. 'But, according to Tony, when Devlin says, "Where's the money?" Ripley doesn't say there isn't any. Instead he pulls out a .38 and shoots Devlin right between the eyes. But Devlin was not quite as stupid as O'Hara thought. He actually told the police he was going to this meeting to collect money he was owed and he thought he might need protection. So, when the shot was fired, Tony and Declan O'Connor were not expecting it and they were scared out of their wits. Seems to me Ripley had his orders but they were not in on it. Declan was keeping watch. The shot was fired, Declan shouted "Cops!" and Martin Ripley threw the gun to Tony. Tony caught the gun just as the cops burst in. Ripley and Declan made it down the back stairs and Tony was stuck there with his hands in the air and they were telling him to drop the gun or they'd blow him apart. Looks as though he was caught in the act, but he swears he didn't shoot anyone. Still with me?'

'Just about,' Father Pat said.

Tim thought about Tony and Declan. They probably didn't figure in O'Hara's plans. They were surplus to requirements. Not Martin Ripley though. He was criminal material. 'We must find Declan,' he said, speaking up for the first time. 'He's not a bad lad. I'm sure we could get the truth out of him. We need to find where he's hiding.'

'We sure need something,' Casey said. 'Keep in touch, Father. Good to meet you, Tim.'

'I'll go up and see her again,' Father Pat told Tim, as they walked back, 'tell her Dennis is on the case.'

Tim nodded and Father Pat went up the steps to Mrs

O'Reilly's place. Already, though he had no evidence and no good reason to believe Tony O'Reilly's story, Tim did believe him. Some people are just evil and some are not, he decided. Maybe that was not a very Christian conclusion, he acknowledged, but that was how he saw it just then. He was prepared to believe Martin Ripley was evil, one of the bad apples, like O'Hara, that contaminate the rest. But Tony O'Reilly wasn't. Neither was Declan O'Connor. They'd been caught up in the phoney glamour of O'Hara's world and now it looked as though Tony might have to pay the price. It doesn't bear thinking about, he told himself, but they have something called 'the electric chair' here for murderers. It was a monstrous, barbaric practice. But that was what they did. They strapped people in a chair that was all wired up and electrocuted them.

At the corner of Tenth and 52nd Street Tim saw Tony's little brother. Frankie was at the centre of a group of small boys. In their eyes he was the brother of a gangland hitman with the dubious respect that commanded. Tim quickened his pace but Frankie had seen him coming. He detached himself from the group and backed off, but Tim was not going to let him get away. 'Hey, Frank! Frankie!'

The boy stopped reluctantly and waited for him to catch up as the others drifted away. 'Bit off your home patch, eh Frank?'

'I can't go near our place, Father.'

'People want to talk to you?'

'Yeah, that newspaper guy. Creeps like that.'

Tim noticed that Frankie had adopted the hunched shoulders pose of the tough guy and he was talking out of the side of his mouth like some mobster in one of the new gangster movies.

'Father Pat's with your ma. Come on. I'll walk back with you.'

The boy lost his swagger. 'What happens now, Father?'

'Well, I don't believe Tony did this. He told Mr Casey he's innocent. He didn't do it, he says, and I believe him. But we're going to have to prove it.'

'He *is* innocent!' Frankie said. 'I know he is. It was Marty Rip shot that man. Declan told me.'

'You've seen Declan?'

'Yeah,' the boy said. 'He's hiding. I promised not to tell anyone, but I can tell you, can't I, Father? I mean, you won't tell anyone, will you? It's sort of like Confession. You're not allowed to say anything, are you?'

'Only if it's in Tony's best interests,' Tim said.

They walked on in silence until Tim said gently, 'So what did Declan say exactly?'

'He said they were sent to meet this guy at the warehouse and give him a message. But when they get there Marty Rip pulls out this gun and shoots the guy. Then he throws the gun to Tony and just then the cops arrive.'

'And Declan said this?'

'Yeah. He said it wasn't Tony shot the guy. He was there and he saw it all. It was Marty Rip, definite.'

'So where did you see Declan, Frankie? He's our answer.'

'It was down at the yards. He was hiding in a wagon. He said he'd got to get away. People are after him.'

'So can you take me to him?'

'He ain't there, Father. He gave me a nickel and he asked me to get him some water and something to eat. Then when I went back he wasn't there. He told me he was going to hop one of the big freights. They come through real slow down there. He said he wanted to get to Philadelphia, anywhere, away from here.'

'Do you think someone might have seen you coming or going?'

'Nah, I don't think so. It's pretty quiet, especially afternoons.' The boy gave Tim a sidelong glance. 'That's when I go there. If those guards is around they're probably sleeping.'

'I think we should write this down, Frankie,' Tim said. 'You'll need to make a statement for Mr Casey.'

'Aw, I don't know, Father,' the boy said.

'You want to help Tony, don't you? We've got to find Declan, make him tell what he knows. Marty Rip isn't going to help us.'

It was in the *Daily News* two days later. The badly mangled body of a Declan O'Connor, one of the two men police wanted to interview about the shooting at the warehouse on Tenth

Avenue, was found on a rail line near the 30th Street freight terminal. At first, a police spokesman told the *News*, it was thought the man had simply been hit by a train. Officers now believe he was strangled and his body was thrown on the track.

In the beginning Dan was unsure of himself. He knew almost nothing about the stock market. Now he was more confident. There didn't seem much to it. It was simply a kind of 'respectable' gambling. When he asked Joe Baker questions Joe would merely shrug and say, 'You'll soon figure it out.' Paul Merrick was more helpful. Early on he had patiently explained fundamentals such as the difference between a bull market and a bear market.

'Basically,' he said, 'bulls are optimists and bears are pessimists. Bulls believe prices will go up, bears believe prices will go down. When the vast majority of investors are on a buying spree it's a bull market and right now we are on the biggest buying spree in history.'

Perhaps it was the Irish connection and the fact that Dan Dolan was quiet, diffident and respectful, not in the least a noisy boastful Irishman that endeared him to Michael Meehan, but the older man approved of Joe Baker's new apprentice and said so. Dan quietly went out of his way to get to know Meehan's young assistant and he learned in a roundabout way that Joe Baker had three seats on the Exchange. Apparently to own one of these was the ultimate goal and Paul Merrick had been expected to take one but he hadn't. It may simply have been the cost, Dan guessed. A seat had to be bought and the price was currently around $100,000. Dan's confidante said it wasn't that. Merrick had been like a partner to Mr Baker, but something had happened and he'd been frozen out.

Mike Meehan was a specialist in Radio Corporation of America stock. If an investor wanted to buy Radio stock – the big seller at that time with one in three households in the country owning a radio – he would do it through a broker who would contact a member of the Exchange who would go to Meehan at Post 12.

Watching for significant changes in the day's trading could be a tedious job. Business could only be done between the opening gong and the closing gong, a large brass bell that everyone obeyed, and already Dan found he was relieved when the bell rang at the day's end. The business of the Exchange seemed little different to the gambling on the horses that went on at home and he had never found that exciting or even interesting. He would probably have a small bet on the Gold Cup at Cheltenham the same as most people in the village. But it was a once a year thing. Here the men in their business suits, some with black jackets and striped trousers, and always with a carnation or at least a fresh flower in their buttonholes, would stand around, apparently doing nothing but swap jokes. Even Joe Baker bought a flower each morning from the old lady with the flower stall on the corner of 42nd Street. Still, he told himself, it was better than labouring in the streets, digging up the road as so many of his countrymen did.

He had been back almost a week now but Joe Baker had not mentioned his trip. Then at the lunch counter he suddenly said, without expression, 'Read your report.'

Dan waited. He had spent two evenings going over all aspects of Fox Boxes. He'd been given a printed list to cover – strengths, weaknesses, prospects for the future – and the most difficult section to fill in he found was the last: Recommendation.

What could he say? He liked Fox. He could see what the man was up against and he felt very strongly about the kind of stifling stranglehold people like this Davis had on local enterprise. But could he really recommend investment? Probably not. Yet he felt that Fox was a genuine pioneer, willing to work hard himself, a man who would be a good employer, an honest man. He decided to write: Would like to discuss.

'So you want to discuss the future of Fox Boxes?'

'Well,' Dan said soberly, 'I don't think they have a future, I spent the afternoon with Mr Fox and that night I talked to some of his workers in a couple of bars. I got a feel of things from other people, too, and I have to say, without a really big investment, he's on a loser. What he's asking for would just be the start. Trouble is, Fox is a good man. I'd like us to help him but I guess we can't. This Davis is too powerful.'

'Good,' Baker said. 'You got that right. Fox has been fighting a losing battle for the last two years He's got no chance.'

'You knew that?'

'Oh sure. I got the full picture when he first contacted me.'

'In that case, why send me down there?'

'I wanted to know if you would get the full picture.'

Dan remained silent.

'It's not a waste of time, son. You did a pretty good job. But one thing you didn't do.'

'What's that?'

'You didn't check out this Davis, see how solid he is. He could be in the same boat as Fox.'

Dan shook his head. 'No, no. I checked on the properties he owns, the companies he runs, his family background. He's from what we used to call in Ireland *old* money. He's rich all right.'

Baker nodded approvingly. 'Correct, but you should have put all that in your report.'

'Too bad we can't take him on,' Dan said.

'First rule,' Baker said. 'Listen to your head not your heart. I'll write to Fox, give him a gentle no. From what you say he sounds the kind of man who'll soon be back on his feet. He'll be OK.'

'I hope so,' Dan said.

'Something else I want to sort out,' Baker said. 'You can't go on calling me Mr Baker, Dan. Too formal.'

'I don't mind.'

'Well, I do. You got a choice. You can either call me Joe, like everyone else, except Barbara that is. Or you can call me Pops. Barbara calls me Pops.'

Paul Merrick had warned Dan about this. He will give you a choice, Paul said in his precise English, and he would like you to choose Pops. He is always saying we are a family at Joe Baker Associates and I suppose with Pops he is the head of the family. 'I got it wrong,' Paul added. 'I chose Joe.'

Dan pretended to give it some thought. 'Well,' he said at last. 'Joe seems a bit disrespectful somehow. I mean, you're my boss.

I owe you a lot. I think I'd like to call you Pops, if you don't mind.'

Joe Baker's wizened face, wreathed in a wrinkled smile, told him he had chosen right. 'Then Pops it is.'

'And to mark the occasion,' Dan suggested, 'perhaps you will allow me to pay for our lunch.'

'That's another thing,' Baker said. 'How are you for money, Dan? Do I pay you enough?'

'I'm OK. I reckon I'm doing all right for someone just off the boat.'

'Don't put yourself down. You learn fast and you've learned a lot these past few months. I'm sure you know what to buy and when, but you haven't bought any stock.'

'I bought lots of stock. You give me orders every day.'

'I mean, you haven't bought any for yourself.'

'Oh, I wouldn't do that. You might not approve.' He laughed. 'In any case, if I was risking my own money I'd consult you first. And also, right now I'm saving what I can to find a place in town. I'm still living in Brooklyn. It'd be a lot easier if I was over here. I'd like to be nearer the office.'

Back at the Exchange Joe Baker joined a group of his cronies and Dan went back to his post but not before he had paused to confront himself in the great mirror in the reception hall. 'Uncle Sam is turning you into one hell of a creep, Dan Dolan,' he told his amused eyes. Then he laughed. *Pops* Baker! What would Dad make of that?

That evening when he got back to the office he wanted to see Paul Merrick, arrange to go for a quick drink. He wanted to tell him he was right. He had been given a choice. There was no sign of Merrick, but Baker's wife Barbara was sitting on Baker's desk.

Dan was in an ebullient mood. 'Do you realize, madam, you are sitting on the very site where momentous decisions are made, the very spot where letters of national importance are written. This is no seat for a lady, no matter how elegant and curvaceous.'

Barbara gave him a long, sensual look. 'Elegant and curvaceous, I like that. Is that how you see me, Daniel?'

Dan was sorry already. 'I think you are a very elegant lady, yes.'

'And curvaceous?'

He laughed. 'All right, yes. Now Pops is with Mr Meehan. Maybe he wasn't expecting you.'

'Pops, huh?' She raised her eyebrows. 'You joined the family. Well, I'd say that calls for a celebration. You must take Mama for a little drink.'

'I can't, Barbara,' Dan said, suddenly serious. 'Got to get going.'

'Pops would expect you to take care of me,' she said petulantly. 'One little drink. Come on. What do you say?'

'Drinking alcohol is prohibited, Mrs Baker.'

'Well, we'll have coffee like everyone else. And a dry martini.'

There was no escape as she led the way downstairs.

Out on Madison she drew a second glance more than once and Dan noticed, not for the first time, she really was a good-looking woman. The illicit bar where he normally went with Merrick was the only one he knew that was near enough and classy enough.

On the way in they met Paul Merrick on his way out. 'Hello,' he said pleasantly. 'I was just about to leave.'

'Good,' Barbara said coolly.

Merrick bowed stiffly.

'Nice fellow,' Dan said, when he had gone.

'Mm,' Barbara murmured.

On the nod of the manager they went through to the inner room. It was filled with the usual after office crowd and again Barbara drew appreciative glances as they found a corner table.

'What is it with Paul?' Dan asked, determined to find out.

'How do you mean?' she asked.

'Well, I can't help noticing there's something not exactly friendly between him and Pops. And now you treat him the same way. They must have been on good terms once. So what happened?'

'Leave it, Dan,' she said and she wouldn't be drawn.

# FOURTEEN

THE AGENT, Joe Bononi, pulled up in his 1927 Roadster. Michael was singing *Someone to watch over me* and Nathan was at Mr Levi's moveable piano. 'Hey!' he cried. 'What are you doing?'

Michael walked over to the car. 'Mr Bononi!'

'You don't sing for free on the street.'

'We're helping Mr Levi out,' Michael said. 'Gives us a chance to go through his new stock. He's got some great new sheets.'

'No more singing for free. You understand?' Bononi jerked his head in Nathan's direction. 'OK for him, but not for you.'

Michael frowned. 'Why is that?'

'We don't need him no more. He ain't good enough.'

'Hey, now!' Michael said. 'Nathan's my partner. We're a double.'

'Not any more,' Bononi said. 'We talk about this another time. Not now. Mr O'Hara wants you to sing Friday at his house.'

'We're working Friday. The Showcase. You booked us in there.'

'I'm talking about later. After the show. We'll send a car to pick you up. Mr O'Hara is having a party. He wants you there.'

'OK, fine. What about Nathan?'

'He can come, too.'

'No, no. I mean, he's always been with me. He knows the act.'

'Not now, eh? We do this later.'

'What can I tell him? He's nowhere to go.'

'Tell him nothing yet. We do this later. OK?'

Michael frowned as Bononi drove off. He was right, of course. Michael had realized this now. Nathan was all right for the bars and sing-alongs, but he was not really good enough for the big time. Annie had noticed it in the fast numbers. But Michael had noticed it now in the slower numbers, too. Listening to Jolson at a matinee performance on Broadway he felt the pianist was fantastic. And he'd gone along with Annie to hear Helen Kane. In her slow numbers like That's my weakness now and I wanna be loved the back up and the beat from her piano player were perfect. And there was the guy who played piano with Louis Armstrong. Earl Hines! Nathan was not in that league, nowhere near. But he was not going to say so. Nathan was his pal.

After their appearance at the Showcase on the Friday night a car was waiting, as promised, to take them to O'Hara's house. Michael had arranged to meet Annie but had to call it off. His boss wanted him at a party, he explained. Annie smiled and said OK without telling him that all the girls from her show, including her, had to be there, too.

The party at O'Hara's was held in a surprisingly large converted basement. Thirty or more people were already there when Michael and Nathan arrived. They were sitting at tables or standing around in little groups and everyone seemed to have a drink. A bartender in a short white jacket was behind a curved bar in one corner and a waiter was going around with a heavily laden tray. A young black man was playing piano unobtrusively with a quietly bouncing beat.

A floppy-haired young man with a handheld microphone seemed to be the Master of Ceremonies. 'We got a song now from a lovely little lady,' he announced. '*I'm nobody's sweetheart*, she says, and we all know that ain't true. She's everybody's sweetheart. Annie?'

Michael looked up quickly. He hadn't realized she was there. He shook his head at her reprovingly and she winked back at him before going into an upbeat version of her song. Annie could sing, no doubt about that, but the piano player was amazing, pushing the beat along, making the whole room swing. Several of the watchers went into a spontaneous Charleston, arms raised in response to the music, until Annie and the piano player bounced to a breathtaking end and the audience erupted in cheers and applause.

Annie replaced the microphone and kissed the piano player lightly on the cheek, bringing a frown of disapproval here and there. Even here there were some who thought the black man should not be encouraged. But the thought didn't even occur to Annie. For Annie, a piano player was a piano player and this boy was brilliant.

She came over to Michael and he lifted a drink for her from a passing tray. 'So you have to sing for your supper,' he said with a grin.

'Yeah,' she said. 'Same as you.'

'Some pianist,' Nathan said admiringly.

Annie glanced at Michael and Michael could only nod his head in agreement. Michael had been studying those present. A number of girls looked too young to be there, flushed with excitement and banned gin. Older men, late thirties or early forties, some in their fifties even. And many with the look of hardened criminals, no nonsense 'enforcers' with notoriously short fuses. These were Vincent O'Hara's friends or, at least, his associates and Michael knew, if he wanted to succeed in show business, he was going to have to get along with these people. They had the entrée to the big time, the classy theatre clubs that were springing up all over town, the new venues, the new openings for ambitious young entertainers. They had the power to push a talented newcomer all the way to the top.

'You thinking what I'm thinking?' Nathan asked.

Michael grinned and nodded. 'They all look as though they've been inside, or that's where they're going.'

At Mr Levi's music store they had found a number of new songs, among them one or two Al Jolson had introduced on Broadway. One in particular had intrigued them. It was about a 'three-time loser', as criminals who were going to jail for a third and lengthy time, twenty years or more or maybe life, were called. In the Al Jolson song the doomed man is trying to say goodbye to his little boy, trying to explain gently that Daddy was going away for a long time and he wanted the boy to grow up into someone far better than he had ever been. It was a real tearjerker, sentimental and sad at the same time, and Michael, as mischievous as ever, wanted to lay it on thick with this mob.

The party had settled back into its talk and sporadic laughter after the high spirits of Annie's song and after a while the self-styled MC came over to Michael. 'Hey, Mikey!' he exclaimed with an expansive grin and an arm around Michael's shoulder though he and Michael had never met. 'Jimmy says you're going to sing for us.'

'Sure,' Michael said and Annie squeezed his arm.

Nathan handed him the sheet music and Michael raised his eyebrows. 'He can play it,' Nathan said. 'Looks like he's the house piano player.'

Michael went over to the piano. 'It's a bit slow,' he said apologetically.

'Dat's OK,' the piano player said, glancing at the sheet. He looked up at Michael with a slow, knowing smile. 'You sure you wanna do this?'

'Why not?' Michael said, with a grin.

He laughed and tinkled a few notes of introduction. 'Lets's go, man.'

'Hi, everybody,' Michael said into the microphone. 'I'm Michael Dolan. You can catch my act any night next week at the Showcase.'

'Cut the crap!' someone called good-humouredly.

'No advertising, Michael!' Jimmy Pickles shouted from the back. 'You don't have to tell everyone you're at the Showcase all next week with two shows Wednesday and Saturday.'

Everybody laughed and someone called, 'We'll be here 'til next week if he doesn't get going.'

Michael held up his hands. 'I was looking through some of the new tunes coming up right now,' he said as the piano played softly behind him, 'and I came across this little beauty. It's about a guy who's going up the river for a very long stretch and he's trying to say goodbye to his little boy.'

He looked back at the piano player, then he went into the song. The audience listened with rapt attention as the gentle words unfolded. Then, when he came to the line, '*And if someday you should be, On some new daddy's knee,*' there was an audible sob from a table nearby.

Michael had the audience of hard men spellbound and when he came to the end there was a moment's silence. Then Vin O'Hara, standing by the bar, broke the spell. 'Good lad, Mikey!' he called and the audience erupted in applause.

A large, bleary-eyed fellow with a bulging waistline left his table and came over. He grabbed Michael by the arm. 'You made me cry, you Mick prick!'

'Hey!' Michael was incensed. 'Nobody calls me that.'

The diminutive Nathan stepped between them, then Jimmy Pickles, who was not much bigger than Nathan, took over. 'Go and sit down, Joe,' he told the big man. 'You've had enough booze for one night.' To Michael he said, 'It's his idea of a compliment. He's as Irish as you are.' Then he whispered in Michael's ear as if this knowledge was worth imparting, 'He runs the Cabaret Club on 43rd.' To the piano player he said, 'Come on, Lou. Play!' To Michael, 'Sing something else.'

Michael spoke quietly to the piano player then, as the party settled down, they went into a swinging version of *Somebody stole my gal*. An understanding, a true rapport, had developed between them and Michael was enjoying singing with him. Lou was in a class of his own.

Luis, Luis without the O, as Joe Bononi explained, had come to New York from Chicago. Already he had played with some of the biggest names in Chicago jazz. He was sure to make it big here. 'But you can forget about teaming up with him,' Bononi said. 'Luis has his own plans.'

The thought had crossed Michael's mind. He had enjoyed Luis' back-up. It was so different to singing with Nathan and he knew now people were right. Nathan did OK, but he was just knocking out the beat. Luis provided a whole new dimension, a framework for a variety of subtle yet unobtrusive little phrases and grace notes. The difference was, he supposed, that Luis was a natural, a born musician, and Nathan was just a barroom piano player.

Later, when it was time to go, O'Hara came over. With his big fleshy smile he took Michael by the lapels of his coat and drew him close. 'We're going places, Mikey boy. You and me, we're going right to the top.'

'I hope so, Mr O'Hara,' Michael said.

O'Hara patted Michael's face, grabbed his lapels again and kissed him on both cheeks. 'The sky's the limit, son.'

Michael nodded and smiled gratefully, backing away. The man was crazy. He was convinced of that but if he could open doors then so be it. Might as well stay with him.

He turned away as O'Hara went back to his main guests and his men closed in automatically around their boss. But there was no escape yet. 'Hey, Mike!' O'Hara called and he came over a second time. 'I meant to ask you, how's that brother of yours doing? The big shot on Wall Street. I'd like to meet him.'

'Sure, Mr O'Hara,' Michael said. 'But I wouldn't say he was a big shot. He just works there.'

'If he works for Joe Baker he must know something.'

Michael was puzzled. Why would O'Hara want to meet Dan? He looked for and found Annie. Had she seen Nathan?

'Nathan went home,' she told him. 'He said you would want to walk me home.'

'Was he all right?'

'I don't know. He seemed sort of quiet. I think maybe the piano player got to him. He knows he was outclassed.'

'Luis would outclass most piano players,' Michael said.

'So are you going to walk me home, Mr Crooner? Because if you are you better understand it's three o'clock in the morning and I am going straight to bed – on my own.'

Annie was staying with the rest of the showgirls at a rooming-house called the Lennox. They strolled up Seventh Avenue, hand in hand, under a starlit sky. Even at that time, the middle of the night, there were people about. Girls with cloche hats, clutching fur collars. Young men in racoon coats and fedoras. Everybody talking loudly, calling from group to group with no respect for the stillness of the night.

Nineteen twenty-seven was drawing to a close and they were riding on a giant roller coaster, holding on as the stock market climbed higher and higher and screaming in a wild delight as they cashed in their gains and splashed them around, dollar bills floating down like dissolving snowflakes. They felt rich, they *were* rich, richer than most of them had ever been.

'We can make it here, Annie.' Michael was flushed with his part in the evening's entertainment. 'You and me, we're going places.'

'You are, you mean,' Annie said. 'With Vinnie O'Hara behind you, you can reach for one of those stars. Make it your own.'

'Yeah,' he said. 'And wherever I go I want to take you with me.'

Annie smiled up at him. She knew he meant what he said. At that moment, anyway. But she knew, too, he would do better on his own. At least, until he made his mark. It was a tough business and those who made it to the top rarely carried passengers.

He was dancing along on the balls of his feet, like a boxer in training. 'I want to dance, Annie. Maybe you could teach me.'

'You want to do high kicks in a chorus line?'

'You know what I mean. Basic steps. Tap dancing. Charleston. Just imagine – if I was in a movie I might have to dance.'

The loss of Declan O'Connor was a major blow to Tony O'Reilly and his case. Only Tony's little brother, Frankie, could add anything and there was no proof Frankie had seen or spoken to Declan.

Dennis Casey was not optimistic. The police had interviewed Vin O'Hara and he had denied ever having met Eamonn Devlin, the man shot dead. Tony, when interviewed, admitted he had never met O'Hara. He knew the man by sight but that was all. His connection, he said, was with Martin Ripley and Ripley's boss, a man called Jimmy Pickles.

Pickles was well-known to the police. He was also well primed on police procedures. Yes, he admitted, he knew this

Martin Ripley but he had only seen him once or twice, usually when Ripley was hanging around the pool hall, hoping to take some poor sucker for a ride. From what he had heard, Ripley was pretty good with the cue. This kid Tony O'Reilly, he said, he didn't know, he had never met him. If he was one of Ripley's pals he might have seen him, too, at the pool hall. But he didn't know O'Reilly and he'd never had any dealings with either of them, Ripley or O'Reilly. As far as he was concerned they were kids. Lots of kids hung around the pool hall.

Without Ripley, Tony O'Reilly had no real defence. 'What does it mean?' Tim asked, dreading the answer.

'First degree murder,' Casey said. 'It's the chair.'

Tim was appalled. He turned to Father Pat. 'We've got to do something, Father. He's just a kid.'

'Tony O'Reilly is eighteen years old,' Casey said. 'And killing people is not a good idea, especially now. Mayor's determined to clean up the city and he's getting really tough.'

'We have to go and see him, appeal to him,' Tim said earnestly. 'We can't let this happen.'

'Jimmy Walker is on a roll just now,' Father Pat said. 'Everybody likes what he's doing – everybody except the criminals.'

'Tony's not a criminal,' Tim said.

'According to the police he is,' Casey said. 'They've charged him.'

'So what can we do, Dennis?' Father Pat asked.

'Find Martin Ripley, I guess.'

But the only person who knew where Martin Ripley was hiding was Jimmy Pickles and Pickles was in trouble with his boss. Vin O'Hara's puffy, self-indulgent face was flushed with rage. 'You were supposed to handle things,' he roared and he threw a glass vase at Pickles' head. The vase hit the door behind him and shattered, shards of glass flying off. He had seen O'Hara like this many times but the anger had never been directed at him. Now that it was he did the only thing he knew might calm his crazy boss. He stood quite still, his head down, saying nothing and taking it all.

'I've never been arrested in my life until now,' O'Hara raged. He had not, in fact, been arrested. He had been asked to call in at the precinct to answer a few questions. His name had been mentioned, he was told, so it had to be followed up. It was just routine.

'And *who*,' he demanded of Pickles, 'mentioned my name?'

'I suppose it was the kid they're holding,' Pickles said meekly.

'You suppose? You don't *know*?'

'Yeah, boss. Sure I do. Look, let me take care of this. There won't be any more trouble. I promise.'

'Kid is saying I ordered him to shoot that sonofabitch Devlin.'

'Nobody believes that. He ain't one of us anyway. I don't know where he got your name. But for some reason he fingered you and the cops have to follow it up.'

'I don't want my good name coming up again, OK?'

'Sure. Sure, boss. Let me deal with it. Please.'

O'Hara was mopping beads of sweat from his brow with his big pink handkerchief. He poured a glass of water from a jug in his office ice box and popped a couple of pills in his mouth. He had been advised to watch his blood pressure, but now and then he went out of control. He confronted Pickles once again, glowering down at him. 'Last chance, Jimmy. I'm warning you. Last chance.'

'Sure, boss. When have I ever let you down?'

O'Hara's pained expression was evaporating slowly as his fury cooled down. 'All right,' he said and he put both arms around a relieved Pickles and gave him a bear hug. 'All right.'

Pickles was furious now, furious with himself. He had chosen this new kid – Marty Rip they called him – for the job. He wanted to see what the kid was made of, blood him so to speak. But the crazy kid had taken his two sidekicks along. He wasn't supposed to do that. He was supposed to do the job alone. He was supposed to meet Devlin, kill him and get lost. Fast. Five-minute job, that was all it was. Nobody else around. Maybe he should have made that clear at the outset, Pickles conceded. Maybe it was partly his fault. Kid was showing off no doubt to his pals. It was just inexperience. More than one killer is always trouble, he told himself. The best jobs are done alone.

According to Tony O'Reilly, this Martin Ripley had joined the O'Hara gang and he and Declan O'Connor were hoping to join, too. Martin Ripley's orders, Tony told the police, came through a man called Pickles and this had resulted in Jimmy Pickles being called in for interview. Well, it should be fairly easy now, Pickles decided. They had taken care of the one called O'Connor. All they had to do was take care of Ripley.

Martin Ripley was scared, running scared. He was in trouble for taking O'Reilly and Declan along. That was just bravado, stupid. He realized that now. Declan had seen it all. He had tried to keep Declan with him but the crazy kid had run off. He was in trouble over that, too. Losing the kid. But what scared him most was the way they dealt with Declan. It was in all the newspapers. They strangled him and threw him on the rail track.

Jimmy Pickles had been furious with him. He had given him a wad of notes and told him to go to this place, the Poplar Hotel in Trenton. Ripley had never been to Trenton but he went by train and he soon found the hotel. It was a cheap-looking joint with a lot of people – business types and travelling salesmen – coming and going. He was to stay there until he was contacted. Stay in the hotel, lie low for a while. Meals in his room. Keep to himself. No visitors. And no hookers! Just as soon as things quietened down he would be told what to do next. He would not be safe, Pickles warned him, until they fried O'Reilly.

Ripley was standing by the window in the hotel room, watching people go by. The hotel was in the centre of town and the early evening was the worst. Young people going out, meeting friends, out for a good time. And here he was, cooped up in this dump. He was going slowly crazy. Why couldn't he call a hooker? What harm would it do? But he knew he had better not. The look of barely controlled fury in Jimmy Pickles' eyes told him that. All right, he acknowledged, so it was a mistake, a big mistake to take them along. Although, if he hadn't, the cops might have got him instead. It could have been him, not O'Reilly, facing the chair.

Bluey knew the Poplar Hotel. The boss had used it before for some guy who was lying low. He pulled into the gas station on the toll road, squinted at the number and the name on the piece of paper Jimmy Pickles had given him and rang the hotel.

'Sammy.' he told the desk clerk. 'Tell him it's Sammy.'

Martin Ripley had been told to expect a call from someone called Sammy. He took the call with a sense of relief. Maybe the waiting was over at last and he could get out of here.

'There's this park with these big gates,' a gruff voice told him. 'Just by the hotel. Wait there. Ten-thirty. I'll pick you up, OK? Make sure there's nothing left in the room with your name on it case someone goes snooping around. And pay your bill. You're moving out.'

'Sure will,' Ripley said, eager to get going. He had booked in under a false name and there was nothing there to identify him. He had not received any post and there was only the one phone call. But it was not the kind of hotel where they asked too many questions anyway.

He took a last look round, checked out and found the entrance to the park with the tall wrought-iron gates in less than a minute. Almost at once a black sedan drew alongside, the passenger door opened and the man called Bluey said, 'Get in.'

'So what's new? What's been happening?' he asked, as soon as he was seated and the car moved off. He recognized the big dark hulk of the driver as the man who usually accompanied Jimmy Pickles. He had never actually spoken to him before. He had always been a kind of sinister, threatening presence, hovering behind his boss. But Ripley wanted to talk to someone now, anyone, even the less than friendly Bluey. The only person he had spoken to these last few days was the guy who brought him room service. But Bluey was not exactly responsive and Ripley soon realized he was talking to himself. They had been driving for over half an hour, leaving the city behind, when he asked at last, 'Where are we going?'

'A place where you'll have no worries,' Bluey told him in his slow, ponderous monotone.

Ripley looked out uneasily at the road ahead. It was quiet now, moonlit from time to time as the dark clouds moved on. There were no other cars, no trucks, and the only sound was the steady purr of the motor.

Bluey drew the car to a halt. 'What's that noise?'

Ripley frowned. 'I can't hear nothing.'

'Better take a look,' Bluey mumbled and he got out of the car, went to the front and raised the hood. His hands hidden now he pulled on a pair of skin-tight surgical gloves. 'Hey, kid,' he called. 'Come here. Take a look at this.'

Ripley came forward and looked in. 'What? I can't see nothing.'

From behind him Bluey placed his big hands around Ripley's neck and held him in a vice-like grip. Ripley's eyes bulged as the pressure increased. Bluey had done this several times and he enjoyed it. He enjoyed feeling the life slowly drain from his victim's body, leaving it limp, lifeless. He drew Ripley back, dropped the hood into place, lifted his body as if it was a life-size doll and put it in the trunk.

Less than a mile down the road he turned off to where a van was partially hidden from view. A torch flashed twice and two men came forward. They lifted Ripley's body from the trunk and threw it in the van. One of the men smirked at Bluey. 'This guy's still warm.'

Bluey just grinned and drove off, his part of the job done.

It was a convenient arrangement. Vin O'Hara had connections in Trenton where they had a highly efficient method of disposing of potentially incriminating corpses. The Dog Patrol Unit was on the streets daily, collecting stray dogs, mostly mongrels, of which there were many. If no one claimed the dog or no suitable home could be found the dog was put down and cremated along with an assortment of rodents at the City Council incinerator.

A member of the council staff with links to a local crime lord would, from time to time, in order to reduce the 'back-log', the superintendent was told, work a late shift all alone and collect a generous pay-off from his gangland friend for doing a little more than disposing of dogs.

That night, Martin Ripley would burn and be gone forever along with a number of other unwanted animals.

# FIFTEEN

'HAVE YOU HEARD of a man called Vincent O'Hara?' Dan asked.

Harry glanced at him sharply, sharply enough for Dan to look surprised. 'I've heard of him,' Harry said quietly. 'Most people have. He's not a friend of yours?'

'I've never met him,' Dan said.

Lois looked up from her desk. 'He's a crook, Mr Dolan. A big-time mobster. A racketeer. Not a nice fella.'

'All right, Lois,' Harry said.

'Well, actually,' Dan said, 'I thought he was a kind of showman.'

'He is,' Harry said. 'He owns nightclubs and speakeasies and dance halls and things. He's even got his fingers in Broadway.'

'And he's a crook,' Lois insisted.

Dan laughed. 'My brother's working for him. He's a singer.'

'Not *Michael* Dolan.' Lois was excited. 'Michael Dolan is your brother? Wow! I hear he's a great singer. And if he's as good as people are saying he is, he can't miss with Vincent O'Hara.'

'You've heard of him?' Dan was intrigued.

'You should take a walk to the corner of West 44th and Ninth Avenue, Mr Dolan. There's a big poster there saying: Michael Dolan, everybody's favourite singer.'

'I've seen one or two posters,' Harry said to confirm this. 'And it's true, if anyone can help him get to the top O'Hara can.'

'He's all over the place,' Lois went on. 'Saturday night he was with the band at the Alhambra. And later on he was at the Black

150

Cat on Tenth. My boyfriend says he'll take me there but I'll bet it's too expensive.'

Dan was surprised. This was rapid progress. Better check on his little brother, he thought with a smile, and he decided to call a family conference. Check on Tim, too. It would soon be Christmas anyway and it was time they arranged something about that.

It was less than a week since he casually mentioned to Joe Baker that he was looking for a place to live nearer the office so he was surprised when a prospectus and some keys appeared on his desk.

'Check it out,' Baker said. 'See what you think. The firm will pay the deposit and you should manage the rent OK. Especially if you get a raise.'

It was a two-bed apartment in an end block on West 59th Street. It was on the fringe of what was known as Hell's Kitchen, but it was quieter and more elegant than lower down. Dan liked it at once. It was far better than he had expected, but his problem now was his landlady. Peg O'Malley had grown fond of her young lodger. She treated him well and he knew she would want him to stay. In the short time he had lived there he had become fond of her, too, and he wished things could have been different for her. Running a lodging-house with no family of her own and, as far as he knew, no close friends was not exactly a wonderful life. She was forty-two and still a good-looking woman. It was none of his business, of course, but he wished she would dress herself up a bit sometimes and go out more, maybe go some place where she would meet a good man who would take care of her. Dan laughed at himself. It was nothing at all to do with him. Peg was her own woman and she would do what she wanted. For all he knew she might be perfectly happy. But he didn't think so. Anyway, he acknowledged, what worried him most was having to tell her he was moving out.

'Ah, Danny boy,' she said when he told her. 'I don't want you to leave but I always knew you would. And soon. You look too much of a city gent to be living around here, in Mrs O'Malley's flophouse, so you do. The big wide world is calling and you have to go.'

'This is not a flophouse,' he told her sternly, 'and you know it.'

'It's not the Waldorf, either,' she said. 'No, you have success written all over you. You're going places, Dan. And so is that Michael. He's everybody's favourite singer. It says so on a poster down on Atlantic Avenue.'

'I must go and hear him,' Dan said with a laugh. 'He was never *my* favourite singer. I was always telling him to shut up.'

'Well, listen,' she said. 'If you're moving out we'll have to have a little farewell party, so we will. And it can be this Saturday. Few drinks here at home. What do you say?'

'Mrs O'Malley,' Dan said, 'have you not heard of Prohibition, the Eighteenth Amendment, the Volstead Act?'

'I have, too,' she said, 'and I've seen the drunks on a Saturday night. So you'll not be talking to me about Prohibition.'

'I promised Tim I'd call and see him on Saturday night.'

She looked at him as if this was a feeble excuse. 'That the priest?' she said. 'We'll, I'm sure he won't be staying out all night painting the town. We'll have a little drink when you come in.'

That Saturday evening Dan met Tim in town and took him for a meal. The swank restaurant Dan had in mind stopped them at the door. Tim was dressed all in black as he usually was these days, but no clerical collar. The man on the door said he couldn't let Tim in without a tie so they were out on the sidewalk. As resourceful as ever Dan stopped a young man who was passing and offered him a dollar for his necktie. The young man summed up the situation at once and said, 'Five. It's yours for five.'

Tim pulled Dan away. 'Leave it, Dan. We can go to that Italian place on 28th, see our waiter friend.'

Dan had noticed Tim was unusually quiet, withdrawn even. 'So,' he said, 'I'll be calling you "Father" soon.'

'I don't know, Dan,' Tim said. 'Maybe. But there's a long way to go yet and, sometimes, I'm not sure.' He faced his brother earnestly. 'Things happen that can sort of stop me in my tracks.'

'What sort of things?'

Tim told him about Tony O'Reilly, about little Frankie, Declan O'Connor and the missing Ripley. 'Everything is stacked against Tony O'Reilly,' he said, 'and if we don't find this Martin Ripley he could be sent to the electric chair.'

'It won't come to that,' Dan said confidently.

'That's what I thought,' Tim told him, 'but Tony's lawyer says it's looking more and more likely.'

'What about Father Pat? He must know this kid O'Reilly and his family if they're from his parish. What does he say?'

'Not much up to now. But I'm pretty sure this boy is innocent. I just feel the Church should be doing more. I think we should at least go and see the mayor, or even the governor.'

'Not both,' Dan advised. 'One of them yes, but they probably wouldn't work together. If there's any political mileage in this and you can get *one* of them to take it up – fine. I'd try Jimmy Walker first, then if there's nothing doing try the governor.'

He drew Tim to a halt on the darkening street. Going down Ninth Avenue they had come to a corner where a newly pasted poster with a list of coming attractions at a night club called The Black Cat had caught his attention. Top of the bill was the name Michael Dolan and the boast: Everybody's favourite singer. They gazed with a mixture of amusement and pride. Then they both laughed aloud, genuinely thrilled at Michael's rapid progress.

At the Italian restaurant there was no problem about ties and the same waiter served them. 'I think I should thank you on behalf of my brother,' Dan told him.

'Oh, yeah?' the waiter said politely.

'Yeah,' Dan said. 'I was in here with my brother, not this one, my other brother. He's a singer and he was looking for work. Do you remember? You told him to try the Irish Club.'

The waiter's face was wreathed in smiles. 'Oh sure. I remember. But there were three of you.'

'That's right,' Dan said. 'My brother Michael and his pal Nathan, the piano player. Anyway, they did all right. They got a job at the Irish Club and they've gone on from there.'

'Good. That's great. So he's doing all right?'

'He's doing fine,' Dan said. He wanted to ask if the waiter had heard of him, but he didn't want to embarrass the man.

Tim didn't hesitate. 'His name's Michael Dolan,' he said. 'Posters going up all over the place.' He laughed. 'Famous overnight.'

'The Irish boy? You're not ... he's not this Dolan? Michael Dolan? The girls are going crazy over him.'

'That's what we're worried about,' Dan said.

'He should go a long way,' the waiter said. 'Good-looking boy.'

'Don't tell him,' Tim said with a laugh.

'He's really going places,' the waiter said enthusiastically. 'I ain't heard him yet. But my sister and her husband went to this place in the Village and they said he was great.'

Later, when they were walking back to the church house where Tim was living, Dan mentioned Vincent O'Hara. According to Tim, Tony O'Reilly and his pals were doing a job for O'Hara when Ripley pulled out this gun and shot someone. The police questioned O'Hara but he said he knew nothing about it and he had never heard of Tony O'Reilly. That was the story.

'And now,' Dan said with a frown, 'it looks as if our Michael is working for O'Hara.'

'Trouble is,' Tim said, 'they tell me O'Hara is pure evil, a ruthless killer. Cross him and he wouldn't think twice. Crazy, by all accounts.'

It was eleven o'clock when Dan climbed in a cab. He wanted to get back to Brooklyn before midnight when the cab fares doubled. And anyway, if Peg O'Malley was having a party in his honour he ought to be there. They would have to meet up with Michael soon, Tim said as they parted. Time they found out what he was up to and what he knew of Vincent O'Hara.

The party had already started. Friends and neighbours, most of them quite a lot older than Dan, filled the place with Irish accents. One woman was singing loudly *Come back, Paddy Reilly, to Ballyjamesduff* and never getting any further. Yet another asked Dan at every opportunity if he had ever been to Skibbereen. An old lady, whose hat had been knocked sideways, was making a face every time she took a sip of the unlabelled gin. But it didn't stop her drinking the stuff. And nearly everyone was inebriated, Dan noted with a smile. It was almost two o'clock in the morning when the last guest left and he started to help Peg O'Malley clear up.

'Ah, you can leave all that,' she said, as Dan went round picking up empty glasses, and she sank to the sofa. 'Come here and sit beside me.'

Her blue eyes were sparkling and she looked as though she had enjoyed herself but compared to her guests she was relatively sober. 'You're not a drinker, Daniel,' she said.

'Only in moderation,' he told her.

'Most of the young fellas coming over get drunk out of their skull Saturdays. Work all week and drink all Saturday.'

'I know,' Dan said, 'but not me. And not Tim. We've seen what the drink can do to people. Our Uncle Patrick drank himself to death. And his father was just the same.'

'And what about Michael?'

'We have to watch him sometimes.'

She snuggled up close. 'Put your arm around me,' she said.

He put his arm around her shoulders and she turned towards him and kissed him on the lips. He smiled down at her as she curled up beside him. 'Have you had a lot to drink?'

'No,' she said, 'and I do know what I'm doing.'

'Oh yeah?' he said. 'And what *are* you doing?'

'I'm losing you. My best boy. So I'm seducing you. I want you to take me to bed – tonight. Just this once.'

Michael was a natural showman and with every engagement he was getting better. The Wednesday evening following the Friday night party at O'Hara's he was singing with the dance band at the Alhambra. The crowd loved him. When he sang a jazzy number he whipped them into a frenzy. When he sang a slow number the spooning couples slowed down and hovered around the stage.

'You got to enjoy it,' Joe Bononi told him. 'When you enjoy it the audience enjoys it.' And Michael was loving every minute.

Nathan was waiting as he came off the stage. 'Guy here wants to talk to you,' he said. 'Name of Al Marco. He's in the passage.'

'Who is he?' Michael asked.

'Reckons he's an agent. He says he's with the Jean Goldkette Organization in Detroit. They send bands out on tour. He says right now they're looking for a couple of singers. Boy and girl. I thought you and Annie might be interested.'

'In touring? The main action is here, Nathan. You know that.'

'Yeah,' Nathan agreed. 'But I'd listen to what he has to say. Can't do any harm.'

A small, bird-like man, he wore a heavy black moustache that was too big for his pale, creased face. He was dressed in a black overcoat and a black trilby hat. Looks more like an undertaker than a talent spotter, was Michael's first impression, as he went down the passage that led to the tiny dressing room he shared with the twelve-piece orchestra.

'Hey, Michael Dolan!' the man called by way of greeting and he came forward, hand outstretched, his face shrouded in clouds of smoke from a cigarette that seemed to be welded to his lower lip. 'Al Marco from Detroit. I represent Jean Goldkette and I have to tell you we're putting together a really great band. The very best musicians. Jazz, swing. And we need a couple of ballad singers – boy and a girl. It's a touring band with great prospects.'

Michael smiled and nodded politely but showed little interest.

'Band is almost in place. Guy called Glen Gray running things.'

'I don't know anyone in Detroit, Mr Marco,' Michael told him. 'And I'm OK here for now. Plenty of work.'

'Yeah, well, this is different,' Marco said. 'They start with a tour of the Midwest. But before that they got a recording date. Their stuff is going to be out in all the music shops. Swingin' on one side for the fellas, ballads on the other for the girls. I reckon the girls'll go crazy for the records if you're doing the vocals.'

Michael was more than interested in the record deal.

'Then when they come back, what do you think?' Marco was thrilled with his news. 'They got *six* radio spots.'

The idea of touring didn't appeal to Michael but the recording contract and the radio shows were exactly what he wanted. Radio stations all over the country were playing dance music and regular record programmes were starting up every week. He shook hands with the smoke-enveloped Marco and said he would think it over.

Al Marco gave him a card with a Detroit telephone number. 'Don't leave it too long, son,' he said. 'Chance of a lifetime.'

When he told Joe Bononi of Marco's approach, Bononi was not pleased. 'Sonofabitch,' he said. 'Not supposed to do that. Supposed to come to me. Did you tell him you got an agent?'

'No, I didn't,' Michael admitted. 'I'm sorry. I didn't think.'

'Well think next time,' Bononi ordered, as if chastising a child. 'You're going to get all kinds of creeps coming round.'

Michael didn't say so but he didn't think Marco was a creep. The man was just doing his job and Michael didn't like Bononi's reaction. It was as if they owned him. He decided to hold on to the business card with the Detroit telephone number.

Friday night, Bononi told him, Mr O'Hara was coming to the Showcase. Michael would be at the Alhambra with the band until midnight. Then he had two spots at the Showcase, first around one, the second an hour later. Mr O'Hara was bringing a party of his friends. He would be accompanied, too, by some girl who was said to be eager to meet 'the new singing sensation'.

When Michael arrived at the Showcase that Friday evening, Jimmy Pickles was waiting for him. 'Boss is here,' he said, 'and he wants you to put on a good show.'

'I always put on a good show,' Michael said with a laugh.

'Yeah well, he's got some big shots with him tonight and he wants them to have a good time. The Englishman and his boys. You heard of these guys?'

'I think so,' Michael said. 'Crooks aren't they? Mobsters.'

Pickles looked around in alarm. 'Don't say that, you idiot.'

'Well, I heard this English guy was in Sing Sing or some-where.'

Pickles put his face close to Michael's. 'You're a singer, not a funny man. OK?'

'OK, OK,' Michael said, backing off. 'So who's this girl?'

'She's Mr O'Hara's niece. He's very fond of her so you better treat her real nice.'

'How?'

'Well, she's only a kid. Can't you sing to her or something?'

'Sing to her? How old is she exactly and what's her name?'

'She's about seventeen and her name's Rose.'

The way it turned out O'Hara was more concerned about his main guest than he was about his bright-eyed niece. The man he clearly deferred to was the man they called The Englishman.

The Englishman was slim and wiry. He had black hair, flat-tened down and parted in the middle. He had blue, unblinking eyes, a beak-like nose and a pale face that rarely smiled or expressed any emotion. He had come to New York from England with his family, aged ten, to grow up in the cauldron of Hell's Kitchen.

In 1915 he was sentenced from ten to twenty years in Sing Sing. Out after serving less than eight he now had a piece of many, if not most, of the clubs and speakeasies on Manhattan Island. Michael didn't look at him directly, but he gained the distinct impression he was not a man to cross, an instinct confirmed when he heard The Englishman was also known as 'The Killer'.

Michael's first three numbers had gone down reasonably well, but his audience, hunched over the tables in the darkened room, seemed more intent on their own affairs than listening to him. This was fine. He was tired and he would be glad when the night's show was over. But as he came out for the next set to a mild ripple of applause, Vin O'Hara beckoned him to come over. The piano player carried on tinkling his introduction as Michael walked over to O'Hara's table.

Always aware of how to please without appearing over syco-phantic, Michael said respectfully, 'You want me, boss?'

O'Hara liked this and he stood up and slapped Michael on the back. 'Mikey!' he said. 'I want you to say hello to my special guest and very good friend, the chief himself.'

'Pleased to meet you, sir,' Michael said, feeling like a hypocrite.

The Englishman was toying with a coffee spoon. He nodded once, his pale face unsmiling.

'How about something for the boss, eh Mikey?' O'Hara said, giving Michael a problem. 'Got a song for the head man?'

Michael got the message. O'Hara was desperately anxious to please this fellow. He nodded, backing away. 'I'll do what I can.'

He walked back slowly to the small stage, trapped between these massive egos. Jimmy Pickles had warned him this might happen. If you have to sing for The Englishman, Pickles told him, make sure it's nothing too soppy and lay off the Blarney. He's *English*, OK? He's from Yorkshire and he's proud of it. And don't try any of that three-time loser crap, he warned. Mention of the stammer might not go down too good with a guy who did eight in Sing Sing.

Michael was left with few options but by the time he reached the piano he had an idea. There was a streetwise song about fellows who were always on the town and never seemed short of cash. He saluted the thugs at The Englishman's table to indicate this was for them and went into a song called Ace in the hole. Well before he reached the end he knew, from their grinning faces, it was a good choice. Even The Englishman almost cracked a smile. Michael milked the song mercilessly. He sang the last few lines twice and most of the audience, sensing there was a certain tension in the air, were quick to join in the appreciative outburst of applause.

O'Hara's niece was watching Michael's every move with rapt attention and, though Michael didn't realize it at the time, he had made one new fan who was about to cause him serious problems.

# SIXTEEN

FOR SOME REASON – his own safety, perhaps – Tony O'Reilly was being held at the old Raymond Street Jail in Brooklyn. It was a dark, forbidding place with high walls and high corner turrets like some medieval house of correction. His cell was a small square with four bunks and like all the others it was fully occupied, many of the prisoners, like himself, awaiting trial.

The Tony O'Reilly who appeared now, handcuffed, in the bare, drab visitors' room shocked Father Pat and Tim Dolan. He looked pale, thinner and his shoulders sagged despondently. He looked scared, too, his dark-ringed, sunken eyes fearful as if he was wary of being attacked.

Father Pat glanced at Tim, his eyes registering his deep concern. He had kicked up a fuss when refused permission to see Tony and he had refused to leave. True, they had arrived unannounced and without an appointment but he had railed at the prison officer who refused them entry, demanded to see the warden or better still, he said, a telephone so he could ring his friend the mayor. He caused such a disturbance that a senior guard or someone in authority had finally relented. Even when admitted, with Tim in tow he had raged all along a corridor, 'You cannot refuse a man permission to see his priest! Visiting hours or not!'

When the wan, diminished figure of Tony O'Reilly was brought in Father Pat calmed down. 'Can you not leave us alone?' he asked.

But the prison officer delegated to keep a watchful eye and

stand guard at the door shook his head. 'It's not me, Father,' he said, full of apology. 'It's orders. I *have* to stay.'

'Well sit down, man,' Father Pat said, 'make yourself less conspicuous.'

They faced Tony across a rough wooden table, Tony with his head down, not wanting to look at them, not wanting them, especially Tim, to see him like this.

'How are you doing, son?' Father Pat asked.

Tony raised his head slightly but he didn't answer. He looked instead as though he was about to cry. Nobody spoke and the only sound in that bare, unpainted room was the relentless tick of the wall clock as the second's finger followed its prescribed route. To Father Pat he was the little O'Reilly boy who served at his altar before the bright lights of the city and the illusory promise of the criminal life led him up the wrong path.

Tim's heart went out to him. He really was like a frightened little kid and, watching him now, Tim was even more convinced of his innocence.

'What's happening, Father?' Tony asked at last, his voice shaking. 'When will I get out of here?'

'We're doing our best,' Father Pat said. 'You just have to hang on, keep your trust in God and pray we can get you through this.'

Tony looked at Tim Dolan, all self-respect gone. 'I can't stand it,' he sobbed. 'They're crazy, mad, the whole lot of them. I can't sleep. I *daren't* sleep. They … they won't let me alone.'

Tim nodded, not knowing what to say. There was nothing left of the cocky, confident young man about town who, just a couple of weeks ago in his snazzy new outfit, was inviting him to join him and his pals on a jaunt to Coney Island. Now one of those pals was dead, another was missing, hunted by the police, and he was incarcerated in this God-forsaken hell hole.

'Have you seen your mother?' Father Pat asked.

Tony shook his head violently. 'No! I don't want her to come. I don't want her to see me like this. Promise me you'll not let her come, Father.' He looked again at Tim. 'You'll tell her I'm OK? I don't want her coming here.'

Tim nodded. 'Sure, Tony. We'll tell her.'

'Is Frankie OK?' he asked pathetically.

'He's worried about you, of course he is,' the priest said. 'He wants to come but they won't let him. Partly because he's just a kid but also because he's a witness. You seen Dennis Casey yet?'

'He's been here every other day,' Tony said. 'It was looking OK, he said, until they found Declan. Well, that's down to O'Hara and that Jimmy Pickles. They're killers, Father. They killed Declan and they'll kill Ripley if they get their hands on him. I should never have got involved.' He glanced at Tim, aware of the irony. 'I know. It's all my own fault, no less than I deserve.'

'You don't deserve this,' Father Pat told him, 'and you must not give up. Do you hear me? You mustn't even think about it.'

'They won't kill Ripley,' Tim said with a confidence he didn't feel. 'All Ripley has to do is lie low, hide away somewhere. Well, it's up to us to find him.'

'You don't know what they're like,' Tony said bitterly. 'If they think Ripley might squeal they'll make sure he doesn't.'

'Let's not talk about this now,' Father Pat said, aware the officer sitting quietly by the door was trying to let him know it was time to go. 'Let's talk about you for a minute. Can we bring you something? Books, a magazine? We can ask Dennis to bring something in.'

Tony's eyes were filling up again as he realized their time was up. 'It's no good, Father. If I had anything they'd take it off me.'

'Who'd take it off you? The guards?'

'The guys in my cell. They're criminals, Father. Hard men. I'm not like them. I shouldn't be in here. I have to scream out at night for the guard. I have to fight them off but there's three of them. They're like animals ...' His voice trailed. 'I wish they'd get on with it, find me guilty. Anything's better than this. I'd rather be dead.'

'I'll see the warden,' Father Pat promised, his indignation rising.

Tim was affected deeply by the desperation in Tony O'Reilly's eyes, his voice, his whole body. He didn't want to leave him here yet there was nothing he or Father Pat could do.

Dennis Casey was doing what he could but he didn't seem to be getting anywhere. Dennis had talked to Sam Leibowitz, a Manhattan defence attorney who was making a name for himself as a man who enjoyed taking on difficult cases. Leibowitz had conducted the defence of several high-profile clients with considerable success. But after studying all aspects of Tony's case Leibowitz, Dennis Casey had told Father Pat, was not optimistic. He simply repeated what they already knew. Even if Martin Ripley was found there was no proof he had even been present at the scene. All they had was the testimony of a ten-year-old boy, the testimony of the accused's little brother, a boy who may or may not be telling the truth, and even if Frankie *was* telling the truth, the only person who could corroborate his testimony was Declan O'Connor and Declan was dead.

'We'll do everything we can to get you moved,' Tim promised. 'We need to see the warden.' He turned to Father Pat. 'This is crazy. Tony's not a criminal. He's not been convicted of anything and we *know* he's not guilty.'

'All right, all right,' Father Pat said to calm him. 'We'll do what we can, of course we will. But for now ...' He turned to Tony. 'For now, son, all you can do is pray. Nobody believes you did this. You have the whole parish behind you and, among other things, we're getting up a petition to the mayor. I'll take it to Jimmy Walker myself.' He reached across the table and put a hand on Tony's bowed head. 'Bless you, my son. Have faith.'

The guard stood up. 'No touching, Father. It's not allowed.'

'Is that right?' Father Pat said scathingly.

The guard banged on the door and almost immediately two more guards appeared. 'Time's up. Father,' one said. 'Come on now.'

One on either side, they took hold of Tony O'Reilly and drew him to his feet.

'Let the boy alone,' Father Pat said indignantly. 'Sure and he's not going to run away.'

'Time's up,' the guard repeated and Tony was led from the table, his eyes imploring them to do something soon.

'We'll do everything we can, Tony,' Tim told him.

'We'll be back, son,' Father Pat promised.

Back at his church Father Pat went straight to the altar and knelt to pray and Tim joined him, questioning in spite of himself the value of this ritual. He couldn't help thinking it wasn't prayer Tony O'Reilly needed just then, it was positive action and the sooner the better. 'Where's the justice, Father?' he asked later. 'If there was any justice,' he said and what he really meant was the justice of the Almighty, 'this rat Ripley would be found and dragged screaming into court.'

'This rat Ripley,' Father Pat repeated, slowly and deliberately. 'I'm afraid you don't know Martin Ripley, son. *I* do. And have I not failed him? It's my job to keep these boys out of trouble.'

'But how could he do something like that and let Tony take the rap? Is he going to lie low until it's too late? See Tony go to the chair then get on with the rest of his life? What kind of man is he?'

'I'll tell you what kind of man he is. Martin Ripley is a young man who had a rotten start in life. His father was no good, a petty thief who disappeared when he got Martin's mother in trouble. The poor girl was only seventeen and she walked the streets to feed herself and her baby. The vermin who lived off her filled her up with cheap booze until she didn't know what the hell she was doing and she became an alcoholic. She couldn't live without the stuff and in the end it killed her. But before that they took her little boy away and that only made things worse. They took Martin to the orphanage at Mount Loretto over on Staten Island and they managed to keep him there until he was old enough to run away. He went missing for a long time but then he showed up around here again and by then he'd learned how to take care of himself. That's what he's good at. Taking care of himself. And that is what he's doing right now. He ain't going to come forward and tell the cops, "Hey! You got the wrong man." Oh no, not Martin. Martin Ripley knows only one number and that's number one. He has had to live that way.'

Tim was caught up in a mix of emotions. Everything was so

much more complex than it appeared. 'So what's going to happen, Father?'

'Well, at the moment,' the priest said, 'the inevitable is going to happen. Tony O'Reilly is going to the chair.'

The rise and rise of Michael Dolan seemed unstoppable, a showbiz phenomenon. The notable and the notorious were flocking nightly to the cabaret at the Showcase and it soon became necessary to turn those without the cachet of a big name or influence with the management away at the door. The Showcase had long been a cut above most of the night spots in midtown Manhattan but now it was the place to be and be seen, and this was undoubtedly due to the appeal of the new singing sensation, Michael Dolan.

On one memorable night 'Mr Showbiz' himself, George M. Cohan, curious to know what was going on here, came in with a party of friends. Michael always seemed to be ready on these occasions and he delighted his much celebrated guest by opening his act with one of Cohan's best loved songs. *For it was Mary*, he sang. Now, as Michael broke into *Give my regards to Broadway*, Cohan actually stood up and danced a few steps in the way he had made famous. And when he joined Michael on stage they had the whole audience singing with them. George M. Cohan had been in the business for almost fifty years, most of that time at the top and though his star was fading in 1927 he was still revered by many as a true Irish New Yorker.

Another night the mayor himself, Mr Jimmy Walker, arrived with his girlfriend Betty Compton. Jimmy Walker was noted for his many affairs with dancers and show girls and now he had left his wife for this lady, yet such was his popularity in New York city that he was still well received wherever he went. A smart dresser and a flamboyant character he had in his younger days wanted to be a songwriter and the legacy of this period was just one song of note. Again Michael was prepared and with a majestic wave towards the honoured guest he went into the song, a song that was very popular in its day, *Will you love me in December as you love me now in May?* The good-time mayor stood up and took a bow.

Vincent O'Hara owned a half share in the Showcase and the place was well protected from the incursions of other gangs by his boss, The Englishman, who owned the other half.

O'Hara was well aware that much of the club's recent success was due to Michael Dolan and his power to draw in and charm his audiences. He was also aware that Michael Dolan might be getting a little too big. He had to be tied down or shackled in some way. In Vin O'Hara's world contracts could be bought by force or intimidation or simply torn up and he felt he needed to tighten his grip on the boy. He began this process the night Dan was invited to be his 'special' guest. Michael warned Dan to be on his guard. Whatever O'Hara wanted would be for his own benefit, nobody else's. But Dan had already guessed this.

It was a quiet night tonight, O'Hara told Dan when they were introduced, no big name celebrities, but it was also a 'special' night. Not only was he getting the chance to meet Michael's 'big shot broker' brother, it was his niece's eighteenth birthday. Dan bowed to the girl, who was pink cheeked with excitement, and wished her 'Happy Birthday'.

She was a smallish girl with a kind of fresh-faced innocence, not yet tarnished by life in the city, her newly bobbed hair at odds with her country girl demeanour. Dan guessed she was not long 'off the boat'. Nothing wrong with that, of course. She was young, she had her whole life ahead of her and he hoped her overbearing Uncle Vinnie would allow her to live it.

Her name, as Jimmy Pickles had said, was Rose. She had brought along a girlfriend to keep her company, a girl as enthralled as she was, and they were mesmerized by the line of scantily clad dancers who opened the show. These dancing girls, were not much older in years than Rose and her friend but they were veterans in the ways of the world. They had already performed two shows that evening and now, feeling dead on their feet, their job was to inject a little chorus-line glamour into what was really an intimate cabaret.

O'Hara had rather rudely turned away from his other guests

and was intent on quizzing Dan. Despite Dan's assertion that he was not a 'big time broker' and was simply learning the job, O'Hara ignored his protestations. 'I would like you to come into our little family, Dan,' O'Hara told him, as if he knew him well and had always known him. 'Michael is doing great and there are more rewards ahead, many more. He's going a long way. So I would like you and me to get to know each other. You know, *real* well.'

Occasionally Dan had heard people say they had taken an instant dislike to someone, but this had never happened to him until now. He found Vincent O'Hara and everything about him repellent. The moment he shook his damp, fleshy hand, watched the small mouth with the cherub lips and saw the ingratiating look in those insincere eyes he knew he could never warm to the man. O'Hara didn't look like a man you could trust, he told himself, and all Lois's libellous claims that he was an evil crook were easy to believe. Dan had not yet met any of New York's feared and fabled Irish mobsters but he didn't doubt that this O'Hara was one of them.

The man kept on about stocks and bonds and which stocks were sure to rise and which were sure to fall, but Dan had little to add and would only shrug or nod here and there. He didn't want to appear discourteous. This man had a stake in Michael's future. But it wasn't easy, he found, to humour him. O'Hara went on talking even when a rather suave comedian came on and had the audience rocking with laughter. He only stopped talking when Michael appeared.

Michael had his instructions that night. He must sing something for the birthday girl, something special. 'Ladies and gentlemen,' he began, 'do you remember when you were just a kid? You were seventeen and you couldn't wait to be eighteen. Forget twenty-one. When you were eighteen you were grown up. You could smoke cigarettes and stay up late and do all those things grown ups say you shouldn't do. Well, tonight we're lucky enough to witness that beautiful transformation. Put a spotlight on that lovely girl over there. Stand up, Rose. That's it. Tonight this young lady is here with us to celebrate her eighteenth birthday! Eighteen! So lets have a big round of applause for one of our very own, our true Irish rose. Miss Rose O'Hara!'

Dutifully everyone joined in the applause and at that moment a chef walked in carrying a two-tier birthday cake with sparklers flashing in the darkened room as, overwhelmed, the girl sank back in her seat. Then, led by Michael, the whole room erupted into *Happy Birthday*. And, as the tribute ended, Michael immediately went into a Jolson-like rendition of *Rosie, you are my posie....*

Dan couldn't help smiling. Michael! Where did he get it from? He'd always been a show off. Well now he was a show*man* and he was pretty good at it, too. O'Hara was sitting back in his chair, his pink puffy cheeks shining, his flabby lips closed now in delight. He turned to Dan. 'That brother ... that brother of yours. He's ...' Words seemed to fail him.

Across the table Dan noticed the girl. For all the thrill of being the centre of attention in this usually sophisticated night spot she was watching Michael. She was fascinated, couldn't take her eyes off him, and Dan wondered if Michael, as usual, was getting into a situation he couldn't control.

Despite all the fuss and the noise and the exuberant excitement of that evening, Vincent O'Hara was calm and cool-headed enough when Dan was leaving to grip his arm and tell him confidentially, 'Like I was saying, Dan, you and me, we can do business. I got the dough to invest. You got the big tip-offs.'

'What tip-offs are those, Mr O'Hara?' Dan asked innocently.

'Don't tell me you don't know where Joe Baker and the smart money go. You see it every day. And don't tell me you're just a learner around the office. From what I hear you're Joe Baker's number two. So what I'm saying is, when the big deals come along, all you do is call this number.' He handed Dan a business card. 'We back the same winners as your boss and his associates. We make our money and so do you. A big rake off on every deal. Ten per cent just for you.'

'You forget, Mr O'Hara,' Dan said, 'we make losses, too.'

'Small deals, maybe. I'm talking about the big deals. Your boss always gets those right and those are the ones where you call me. Just a little phone call.'

'I don't think so,' Dan said.

O'Hara's fixed smile never faltered as he followed Dan out to his cab. 'You will,' he said, 'I promise you.'

As the cab drew away O'Hara's words hung in the air. There was an implied threat in there somewhere and Dan was not sure what it was. What could the man do? Well, he could damage Michael, call a halt to his remarkable progress. That was the worst he could do, he supposed. But he didn't know O'Hara.

# SEVENTEEN

MRS O'REILLY AND Frankie were in court when Tony was brought over from Brooklyn to stand trial. They had not seen him for more than a month and Mrs O'Reilly caught her breath. She was shocked to see how pale he was, alarmed at the dark rings under his eyes. He had lost weight, too.

When he appeared between two burly prison officers Tony looked around for a friendly face. Father Pat nodded, smiling in encouragement, but Mrs O'Reilly simply broke down. Yet it was Frankie's look of anguish that affected Tony most of all and his tears welled.

The hearing was held at the Supreme Court on Chambers Street in Lower Manhattan. At four o'clock in the afternoon Tony O'Reilly took the stand. The charge was Murder in the First Degree and each time he had been asked how he would plead he had replied, loud and clear, 'I am not guilty. I didn't do this.' Now he was asked again and with quiet exasperation he said, 'Not guilty.'

Dennis Casey found the case against Tony so overwhelming he decided the only sensible course was for him to plead guilty. He could then ask for leniency in view of his youth and because he had been led astray and used by older criminals. But this didn't work because the district attorney said fine, in that case, I'm sure the judge will opt for leniency if O'Reilly can prove he was connected to some criminal organization.

Tony couldn't prove any connection. He had never met Vincent O'Hara and he had never claimed he had. In the line-up when he was first taken into custody two police officers had no hesitation in picking him out as the person holding the gun that shot and killed Eamonn Devlin. But all Casey's manoeuvring came to nothing anyway because when it was put to him Tony refused to consider changing his plea. He was not guilty, he insisted, and he absolutely refused to say he was.

The list of cases awaiting trial on charges relating to prohibition violations and gang crime was unacceptably long. Both the police and the judiciary wanted things to move fast. In Tony O'Reilly's case there was little excuse for delay. In just over a week, with a unanimous verdict, he was found guilty of First Degree Murder.

Tony was dragged, protesting his innocence, from the dock. His mother collapsed. Frankie screamed at the judge, the tears rolling down his young cheeks and Tim Dolan took him from the courtroom. Father Pat stayed to comfort Mrs O'Reilly with gently reassuring words but, though Dennis Casey said he would lodge an appeal, Father Pat knew there was little hope.

In a letter featured on the front page of the *Morning News* under a two-line banner headline PRIEST BEGS WITNESS PLEASE COME FORWARD Father Pat pleaded with Martin Ripley. Yet, though it meant a boy barely nineteen years old would go to the chair, there was no public outcry at the verdict. And when members of the public were interviewed on radio there was little support for, as one New Yorker put it, *'these young hoodlums terrorizing our streets'*.

Tim said he was going to try to see Tony and he went back into the courtroom. But when he found a court official he was told that Tony O'Reilly had left. Already he was on a boat on the Hudson going 'up the river' to Ossining and the dreaded Sing Sing prison.

The barely credible now seemed unstoppable. Never for a moment had Tim believed the judge would send a boy like Tony O'Reilly to the electric chair. The whole procedure was obscene, he raged in his head, as he rode the trolley back to the church. They couldn't let it happen, he told Father Pat later that night. But Father Pat simply said, 'We can make all the noise we like, but it's too late. Dennis has no grounds for appeal. The best thing Tony could have done was plead guilty and he may well have got away with ten to twenty years.'

'We've got to *do* something,' Tim raged.

'Nobody's interested,' the priest told him, 'except maybe the anti-chair gang and they're crazy anyway. I'm working on the Mayor. We might get the sentence commuted to life because of Tony's youth. And that's the best we can hope for.'

Within days members of the Anti-Chair League were marching up and down the avenues with protest banners and posters, 'The electric chair is evil!', 'A crime against Humanity!' they proclaimed as a variety of slogans appeared on walls. A large van with 'Burn the chair!' stencilled on its sides crawled the streets with a loudspeaker calling for civil disobedience and a national outcry against this method of execution. But most members of the public were indifferent to such demonstrations and the van with a loudspeaker soon found it was in competition with an even larger vehicle with *four* loudspeakers playing the latest records available in the music shops. Street and gang crime had to be stopped was the general feeling and nobody was more in favour of the police and a stringent regime of law enforcement than Mayor Walker.

Tony O'Reilly was again opposed to his mother visiting him in jail. He didn't want her to see him handcuffed and in chains and he would not be persuaded otherwise. Mrs O'Reilly took to her bed. Frankie was being cared for by her sister who had moved into the tenement block where they lived. Frankie desperately wanted to see Tony, too. But the prison authorities said he was too young and a visit was out of the question.

Dennis Casey was the first to visit Tony and he spent most of his allotted half-hour urging him to change his plea. Without that, he told him emphatically, there was no chance of an appeal. But Tony seemed traumatized. He simply shook his head and stared at the floor. Father Pat also tried without success.

Tim wanted to see Tony, talk to him. Rightly or wrongly, he felt there was a kind of bond between them, a grudging respect perhaps, and he might somehow get through to him. Dennis

Casey made the necessary application on Tim's behalf but it was turned down. He was not a relative. He was not a minister of the Church. He wasn't anything. But he so desperately wanted to see Tony he suggested to Father Pat maybe he should borrow a collar and apply as a priest. He was only half serious yet for a moment Father Pat seemed to consider the idea. But then he pointed out if Tim was found to be an impostor not only would he enjoy a little spell in jail himself he would probably be barred from ever entering the seminary, *any* seminary.

Father Pat made regular trips to the prison via the railroad station at Ossining and though he wanted Tim to remain on duty in the parish, Tim insisted on travelling with him. When Father Pat went through the tall gates at Sing Sing Prison, Tim would join the ever present vigil of the supporters of the condemned men along with members of the Anti-Chair League. They were angry and they were noisy but they were on the outside looking at a dense bureaucratic wall and there was little they could do.

It was only two weeks after his first visit to the Showcase that Dan Dolan was cornered into going again. Joe Baker had gone into the NY University Medical Center where he spent a night each year for a health check. Baker's wife, Barbara, was left 'all alone', as she put it. It was time, she insisted, Dan took her to hear his brother sing. He couldn't take her out for the evening, he told her, without checking first that Pops wouldn't mind. But she brushed his objection aside. Of course Pops wouldn't mind. She had already mentioned it to him and he had simply said, 'Fine'. But Dan was not convinced and he was not enamoured of the idea anyway. He didn't want to meet O'Hara again unless he had to. He was wary of Barbara, too. The last thing he intended was to get involved with her. It was not that he didn't think she was a very attractive woman. He just didn't trust her. He felt there was something devious about her. He had the feeling, too, that she had been in some way involved with Paul Merrick and that this was why Merrick was *persona non grata* with the boss. It could be, he guessed, that she was setting a trap for him, some kind of test of his loyalty and maybe Pops was in on it. If so, he told himself with a wry smile, he would just have to resist whatever temptation she might put in his way.

The Showcase was full again that night but O'Hara had reserved a table by the dance floor for Dan and Barbara. He greeted them effusively, sat with them briefly and before he left to rejoin the party at his own table told Dan he and Barbara had met before. He had seen her with Joe, he said, on numerous occasions. But when he left Barbara was adamant. She didn't know the man.

Tonight Barbara looked elegant and almost beautiful and it was difficult not to appreciate her air of cool sophistication. She was only *almost* beautiful, Dan decided, because there was a certain toughness about her, a hard edge that dented her charm.

She bristled noticeably when an unusually pretty girl came over to introduce herself. Perhaps it was because the girl was younger than her but she was less than welcoming and she only relaxed when the girl told Dan she was Annie, Michael's friend.

Dan had heard about Michael's Annie and he was more than a little impressed. She really was a lovely girl and Dan could well understand now why Michael had described her in such glowing terms. He was on his feet at once. 'Good to meet you, Annie,' he said. 'Michael's told me all about you. Won't you join us?'

'I can't,' she said. 'I'm on soon and I have to get changed. It's just that Michael wanted me to come over and say hello.'

'Well, I'm glad you did,' Dan said, sitting down.

As Annie left Jimmy Pickles hovered. He came forward now, speaking quietly to Dan. 'I hope that girl wasn't bothering you, Mr Dolan. She ain't supposed to talk to the customers.'

'Not at all,' Dan said. 'She's a very nice girl.'

'Boss says the girls should know their place.'

'Like I said,' Dan told him, 'she was no bother at all.'

'Can I sit down for a minute?' Pickles asked. Dan nodded and he sat down. 'Mr O'Hara wants you to know he's delighted you decided to join us. We can do great business together.'

Dan looked at Barbara but she just smiled weakly. Why

would he say a thing like that in front of Barbara? Was she in on something? 'I don't know what you mean, Mr ... er ... Pickles. I'm here tonight to support my brother and to escort Mrs Baker.'

'Sure you are,' Pickles agreed with a knowing grin. 'Good to have you on board.'

'What's going on, Barbara?' Dan asked, when they were alone.

'I suppose they're looking for some financial advice,' she said.

'What kind of financial advice?'

'When to buy and when to sell. That's what you and Pops do. You buy and sell at the right time. I expect O'Hara and his gang want to be in on all that. The way they see it, I suppose, is if they're helping your brother to further his career you can help them further their business interests.'

'You *do* know these people, don't you?'

'Oh, all right, yes,' she admitted. 'If you must know, I've known Vin O'Hara for years. Since I was a kid anyway.'

'So why did you say you didn't?'

'Because he's a crook.'

'Everybody knows O'Hara is a crook,' Dan said.

'Listen,' she said, 'I didn't come here to talk about Vin O'Hara. The man's a – what do they call them in the movies? – a *gangster*. So what? He's helping Michael. You're in a position to help him. So you help each other. That's the way these people work.'

'I work for Joe Baker, nobody else. I can't stay here, Barbara.'

'Aw come on,' she said with a smile. 'Sit down and don't be silly. You can't ruin my evening. I'm not leaving until I've heard your brother sing. And anyway, you can't leave me here on my own. Pops wouldn't like it.'

Dan felt trapped. He didn't want to be there and even when Annie's chorus-line came on to galvanize the audience with an infectious dance routine he barely noticed.

'They're pretty good,' Barbara said, trying to interest him in what was going on. 'Especially the one called Annie.'

'She's lovely,' Dan said quietly. 'Michael's very lucky.'

'I expect he's got lots of girlfriends. Like that kid over there.'

Michael was standing at O'Hara's table and O'Hara's niece was gazing up at him in pure adulation. But even from where he was sitting Dan got the impression Michael was not happy. He was arguing with Jimmy Pickles and shaking his head vigorously until O'Hara stood up and stepped between them, said something to Michael and waved Pickles away.

Barbara wanted to dance and they danced for a while until the music stopped and people drifted back to their tables. The lights were lowered and there was a drum roll. Then people were on their feet, applauding as Michael appeared. In a large spotlight he came on singing, *If I could be with you one hour tonight* ...

'You know,' Barbara said, across the small table, 'that young man has got the world at his feet right now. But if he doesn't toe the line he's going nowhere.'

'Very special guest here tonight, ladies and gentlemen,' Michael announced from the small stage. 'My brother Dan.'

A second spot swung round and picked out Dan and Barbara. Embarrassed, Dan felt obliged to stand up and bow to acknowledge the unwarranted applause.

'And just for Dan,' Michael said, 'a special song.'

All eyes were on Michael as he hesitated. He seemed uncertain, unsure of what he was doing, reluctant to begin. 'I'm sorry, folks,' he said. 'It's not easy for me to do this.'

There was a further pause, an expectant hush now, the audience wholly attentive. Michael nodded at his pianist and Dan sat upright as he recognized the first few bars of the piano introduction. Surely not, he told himself. He can't do this. But he did. Michael broke into the *Derry Air* and Dan shaded his eyes.

Barbara laughed. 'What's wrong, Danny Boy? Embarrassed?'

'He's not supposed to sing this. He knows that.'

'It's just a song,' Barbara said.

'You don't understand,' Dan said, but he didn't want to explain.

Michael sang the song beautifully, both verses, and the audience loved it. But as soon as he sang the last note, not wanting to wait for the applause that was about to break, he led the piano player into a fast swinging number.

'That was lovely,' Barbara said, a question in her eyes. 'But he couldn't wait to move on. Now why was that?'

A waiter silently handed Dan a piece of paper. It was a note from Michael. '*Couldn't get out of it*,' he read. '*O'Hara insisted. Sorry.*' Dan folded the note and put it away.

'Not going to tell me what it says?' Barbara asked, amused.

'It's a note from Michael. He says he couldn't get out of it. He had to sing it. O'Hara insisted.'

'Well, he's the boss. But you shouldn't be so sensitive, *Danny boy*.' She laughed. 'What does it matter? It's a lovely song.'

'It wasn't about me,' he said. 'But I don't want to talk about it.'

Jimmy Pickles was coming over. 'Hey, Danny!' he said. 'Michael did you proud there.'

'Well, he didn't want to. Somebody put the pressure on him.'

'Ah, sure. He didn't want to embarrass you. But you know how it is, if the boss tells you to do something you got to do it.'

'Is that right?' Dan said, his tone less than friendly. 'So what do you want, Mr Pickles?'

'I reckon it's time you called me Jimmy,' he said, undeterred. 'Everybody else does.'

'Well, I'm not everybody else.'

Pickles shrugged. 'OK. But listen. The boss wants to see you tomorrow. Lunch on him. Car will pick you up at one.'

Dan shook his head. 'I don't think so.'

'OK,' Pickles said. 'Nice to see you, Barbara.'

'I think we should go,' Dan said, as Pickles moved away.

'We can't let them drive us off,' Barbara said. 'I like it here and you are supposed to be taking me on a night out. All we've had up to now is long faces and arguments.'

Dan felt trapped. It was true. Tonight had been all about him and his brother and the problem of O'Hara. He gave Barbara a conciliatory smile. Encouraged, she pulled her chair round closer to his and leaned forward as if she was about to say something. But as he turned towards her, she planted a kiss fully on his lips and at that moment a camera flashed.

'Hey!' Dan reacted angrily. 'What's going on?'

A photographer gripping a huge flash-bulb camera was dodging between tables and making for the exit. Dan stood up to follow him but the head waiter, a large bulky man was in his way, full of apologies.

'I am so sorry, Mr Dolan,' he said, impeding him purposely. 'We never allow cameras in the club. I promise you there will be a full investigation into how that man got in here.'

'Oh sure.' Dan said scathingly. 'I don't suppose anyone spotted his camera.' He sat down, knowing the man had got away with a compromising picture of himself and Mrs Joe Baker. He stood up again. 'We're leaving,' he told Barbara. 'At least, I am. You stay if you want to.'

Pickles was there again. 'So sorry about that, Mr Dolan. The boss is furious. He wants to know how that creep got in here.'

'I bet he does,' Dan said.

'Well, look. Mr O'Hara has influence, *lots* of influence. That guy was from one of the dailies. The boss can stop that picture being spread across the gossip pages.'

'Is that right?' Dan was furious with himself, angry that he had allowed himself to be set up.

'Sure it is. We'll get on to it right away. Don't worry about it. And, like I said, the car will pick you up at one. OK?'

'No,' Dan said. 'It's not OK.'

'Well, we'll see it doesn't get in the morning papers but we can't promise it won't be in one of the evenings. Unless you change your mind, of course.' He smiled smugly, sure of himself. 'Car will come for you at one anyway. And if you are not there at one o'clock we will still have time to make the late editions.'

Dan called for the check but Pickles waved the waiter away. 'That's OK, Mr Dolan. Tonight was on the house.'

Barbara led the way and as she called for a cab Dan gripped her by the arm. 'Why did you do that?' he demanded.

'I didn't know they had a photographer, did I? You were very close and I wanted to kiss you. That's all there was to it.'

She tried to hold on to him but he pulled away and they

stood apart, waiting for the cab. They didn't speak again until the cab stopped outside Joe Baker's Park Avenue apartment.

'Are you coming up?' she asked.

'No,' he said emphatically.

'OK,' she said mildly. 'Just tell me one thing. Why did you get so uptight when your brother sang *Danny Boy?*'

'It's a family thing. We don't sing that in our family.'

'Why not?'

'Because when we do someone we care about dies.'

# EIGHTEEN

NATHAN WAS DOING all right. He had found his forte, he said, and it was not a pianoforte. It was his natural flair for publicity. He had asked for a job at one of the new record companies and he had been taken on part-time. But Nathan had little idea of time. He was soon seen to be working full-time, putting all his efforts into promoting the company and its records, and as soon as a rival company tried to poach him he was taken on as a properly paid, full-time member of staff. But he didn't stop there. Soon he had music shops like Mr Levi's branching out and selling the latest records and popular music blared all day from shops along 27th and 28th, Vans with loudspeakers toured both the East and the West Side, stopping like ice cream vendors, to sell their latest products, the newest sheet music with hit records from Jolson, Cantor and Michael Dolan. And Nathan was the driving force, coming up with new ideas week after week and promoting his pal Michael at every opportunity.

He had his own office now and he was surprised one afternoon when the receptionist buzzed him to say a young lady who said her name was Annie was asking to see him. 'Show her in,' he said at once and he was on his feet to greet her.

Annie looked a little pale and she was clearly agitated.

'Annie!' he said. 'What is it? What's happened.'

'Nothing,' she said. 'Yet. But I want you to help me, Nathan.'

'Sure. Anything. You know that.'

'I'm leaving town. Now. Tonight. I want you to tell Michael for me. I didn't want to leave a note and just go.'

Nathan nodded, frowning. 'So go on. Tell me. What brought this on? Things not working out for you two?'

'Oh no,' she said. 'It's not that. It's … Well, I've been warned. I've got to leave Michael alone, get out of his life.'

'Says who?'

'O'Hara. He sent Jimmy Pickles to see me after the show last night. He said Michael doesn't need a girlfriend. Michael's going places and he's not carrying any baggage. If I know what's good for me I'll go, disappear, get lost. Michael doesn't need me.'

'Of course he needs you.' Nathan was furious. 'They can't do this. Mike won't have it. You know what he's like. He'll just walk out. He'll tell 'em where to put their job.'

'But I don't want him to. He'll never get another chance like this. I don't want him to throw it all away because of me.'

'I'm telling you, when Mike hears about this …'

'Pickles says I have to leave before he knows.'

'And if you don't?'

'They'll deal with me.'

'Pickles threatened you?'

'You know what they're like. They're criminals, killers. O'Hara is mad and so is Pickles, couple of psychopaths. I have to go. I'm scared, Nathan. I just want you to wish Michael all the luck in the world from me. Tell him I'll always love him and maybe one day …'

'Don't talk like that,' Nathan told her. 'You live here. Your work is here. You don't have to go just because some mobster says so.'

'Nathan,' Annie said quietly, 'I do and you know it. I've had my warning and I've got to leave. Now. Tonight. Just tell Michael I hope he goes all the way to the top or wherever he wants to be.'

She came round the desk and embraced him, even managed a smile. 'It's been great knowing you, Nathan. You've been a good friend to both of us. You're a lovely man and I'll miss you.'

'Where will you go?'

'I'll go home until I can find a job. Touring, maybe.' She tried to smile again. 'Take care and take good care of Michael for me.'

'I think you should see him before you go. I'll give him a call.'

'No, please,' she said. 'I have to go. There's a train from Penn Station in about thirty minutes. I have to be on it.'

'Train to where?'

She shook her head. ''Bye, Nathan. I hope everything goes well. For you and for Michael. But I have to go.'

'Annie, wait!' he pleaded, but she turned on her heel and left.

Nathan grabbed the telephone on his desk. 'Michael!' he said urgently. 'Meet me at Penn Station, main steps. Now! You have to. We've no time to waste. It's about Annie. I'll explain later.'

It was raining hard, slanting sidelong in windswept sheets, as the cab dropped Michael at the station steps. Nathan was waving frantically from the cover of the wide entrance.

The concourse was flooded with shoppers and commuters.

'She said she was going home?' Michael demanded.

Nathan nodded. 'So where is that? Do you know?'

'Place called Paduca,' Michael said. 'Chicago line.'

People swirled around them as they stared up at the giant departures board. Six o'clock from Platform 17. The New York-Chicago Pullman. It was already a minute past six.

A porter was at the gate to Platform 17 as they raced through, brushing him aside. 'Too late, fellas,' he cried. 'She's on her way.'

The train was gathering speed, all doors locked, and there was no way Michael could climb aboard. Desperate now, he raced alongside. All along the train passengers were leaning out, hands raised at those they were leaving behind. He scanned the carriages and then he saw her and she saw him. She was at a window too far down for him to reach. She raised a hand and he stopped running, his eyes asking a question as the train took a bend in the track and curved away and Annie was lost from view.

'Come on, Mike,' Nathan said, catching up. 'She's gone. It's probably for the best.'

'What do you mean *for the best*?' Michael said angrily.

'Come on. Take it easy. Let's go home, talk about it.'

Nathan followed him down the wide steps as Michael called up one of the waiting cabs. 'Bedford Street,' he said.

Nathan was worried. 'You can't go there. Not yet. You've got to calm down, think this through.'

'Nothing to think about. I need to see O'Hara, let him know he doesn't own me.'

'Well, that's the trouble,' Nathan said. 'He thinks he does. And if you want to go on singing you have to accept that. He brought you a long way, Mike, and he can just as easy drop you.'

'So let him drop me.'

'Is that what you really want? Annie wouldn't want you to give up everything. You got too much to lose.'

'I've lost the only thing that matters and I'm going to get her back.'

The cab pulled in on Bedford Street, a few steps from O'Hara's door. One of O'Hara's men was on duty. He recognized Michael and immediately swung open the door for him. Jimmy Pickles was in the hallway with three more of what Nathan called 'O'Hara's gorillas'.

'Where is he?' Michael demanded. 'Where's O'Hara?'

Pickles raised his eyebrows in surprise. 'Mr O'Hara is not expecting you, Dolan, What can I do for you?'

'I want to see the organ grinder,' Michael said.

Two of the gorillas moved over to block the door to O'Hara's office.

'Something ruffle the canary's feathers?' Pickles asked with a grin and the gorillas laughed.

Michael moved towards him but then the door opened and O'Hara's bulky frame filled the gap. 'What's going on here?' he asked.

He saw Michael at once, 'Ah, Michael!' He smiled expansively. 'Come in. Come in.' Pickles put two fingers to Nathan's chest but O'Hara said, 'It's OK. He can come too.'

Nathan and Pickles followed Michael into the room O'Hara used as an office, the room with the half closed slatted blinds, the room that always seemed to be in semi-darkness as if to hide from the outside world the true nature of the business.

O'Hara sat behind his large desk, his hands together, fingers interlocked. 'You look as though something's bothering you, Michael,' he said mildly. 'So what's the problem?'

'You are,' Michael said bluntly and the other two flinched.

O'Hara laughed 'Lot of people think that, so what's your beef?'

'You know well enough,' Michael said, the anger still churning inside him. 'You told my girl to leave town or else '

O'Hara looked at Jimmy Pickles. 'Did we say "or else", Jimmy?' he asked innocently.

Pickles raised his shoulders, spread his hands, but didn't speak.

'We told her to leave town,' O'Hara acknowledged, his voice hardening, 'and I hope for your sake she's gone.'

'But why?'

'Because you don't need a girlfriend. Not that one anyway. We can fix you up seven nights a week, as many broads as you want. But you don't need a *girl*friend, someone who might get serious.'

'We're already *serious*. We're going to get married.'

O'Hara laughed again. 'Listen, son,' he said. 'I've sunk a lot of dough into smoothing your way. Why do you think you get these singing dates? Why do you think your pan's in the papers nearly every day? Why do you think you got a record deal? You owe me big time and I say when you can get married.'

'Makes sense, Michael,' Pickles said. 'Good-looking young guy singing his way to the top. Single, no strings. Much bigger deal than some married guy with a wife and kids.'

Nathan nodded. He could see the sense in that, but Michael turned on Pickles. 'Who asked you?' To O'Hara he said, 'Listen, I don't care about you and your big plans. Annie is my girl and that's all there is to it.'

O'Hara stood up, a large, shadowy presence behind his desk. 'We can do this two ways,' he said. 'I can work out what I spent on you to date and you can buy yourself out. Or you show up at the club tonight, you put on the performance of your life and we forget we ever had this conversation. OK?'

Michael shook his head and made for the door.

'And Dolan,' O'Hara said calmly. 'If you don't show up tonight you'd better find a good hiding place because we'll find you, no matter how long it takes, and you'll be sorry.'

Michael left and he was striding up the street, Nathan running after him.

'Slow down,' Nathan begged and he tried to draw him into a sidewalk café. 'Let's sit down, talk about this.'

But Michael was not listening. He simply flagged down a passing cab. Back at the apartment he swung a suitcase up onto the bed and began opening drawers and packing his clothes.

'You can't do this,' Nathan warned him. 'It's too dangerous. You got to stay for now. You can't afford to buy yourself out and you can't just go. They'll come after you and it won't just be you. You'll be risking Annie's life, too. You know what they're like.'

'This has been coming for a while,' Michael told him quietly. 'I knew I'd have to make my mind up soon. Be O'Hara's slave or be my own man. Well, I've had enough. I'm not going to be a slave for anybody. Especially a slimy crook like O'Hara. I'm leaving and that's it.'

'You'll be throwing away a lot,' Nathan told him. 'Everything you've worked for since we arrived. From where you stand now you can see the top. People know your name. You're Michael Dolan. Walk away and you'll be just one of thousands again, a nobody, just another warbler in some bar or some cheap dance hall. You know how tough it is out there.'

'You don't know the whole story, Nathan,' Michael said calmly, 'That crazy psycho had other plans.'

'What other plans?'

'He only wanted me to get involved with his little niece, the one who sits out front with the dreamy look in her eyes. Seems she wants a guy who can sing her to sleep at night.' He laughed bitterly. 'It's not the kid's fault. It's him. He lets her think she can have anything she wants.'

'He can't make you do that,' Nathan said.

'He thinks he can make me do anything. He cracks the whip and I jump. Well, this time he's mistaken.'

He put both his arms around Nathan. 'You can manage this place, can't you? You've got a good job.'

'Oh, sure,' Nathan said, resigned now. 'Don't you worry about me. I'm going to miss you, sure I am. All that gargling first thing in the morning. All that running up and down scales. But I'll manage.' More soberly, he said, 'Be careful, Mike. And better not try to get in touch. Not for a while anyway.'

Michael nodded. 'When you get the chance, do me a favour? Tell our Dan what this is all about. Tell him I didn't have time to see him before I left. But when the dust settles, could be a year or so, I will be in touch.' He smiled. 'And don't look so worried. I'll be back. I'm your original bad penny.'


Dan was eager to see Joe Baker before the late 'papers came out. As there was no sign of Paul Merrick that morning, he left Harry in charge of the office. Pops was not at the NYU Center. He had been sent for a couple of nights' stay to a hospital out on Long Island. But the trains were frequent enough and before noon Dan was walking up a long driveway. At first he thought he had come to the wrong place. The sign over the entrance said 'St Mary's Hospital, Institute of Oncology'. It was a cancer hospital. He looked back at the long driveway and decided to ask at the desk if this could possibly be the place. The receptionist said yes, there was a Mr Joe Baker here. She would check, she said, if Mr Baker wished to see him.

A nurse approached Joe Baker who was sitting out on a back porch that overlooked a long pleasant stretch of green. 'You have a visitor, Mr Baker,' she said. 'Young gentleman. A Mr Dolan.'

Baker nodded in surprise, pulling his pale-blue hospital dressing-gown into place. 'Bring him through.'

Dan followed the nurse through the elegant hallway and an even more elegant lounge to where Baker was waiting.

'Who's minding the store?' was his first question.

'I'm sorry, Pops,' Dan said. 'Harry's in the office, and Lois.'

'So what's this about?'

'I'm sorry to turn up unexpected like this, but I have to see you and, maybe, offer my resignation.'

'What are you talking about?'

'Well, I think I may have let you down last night. You trusted me with things but I got it wrong.'

The only person nearby was an old man in a dressing-gown similar to Joe's and he was fast asleep.

'Pull up a chair,' Baker said. 'Tell me all about it.'

Dan told him that Barbara wanted him to take her to this club, the Showcase, to hear his brother sing. He told her, he said, he would have to check with Pops first, see if it was OK. But she insisted that wasn't necessary. Pops wouldn't mind.

Baker nodded. 'Why would I, if it keeps the girl happy?'

'Yes,' Dan said, 'but it wasn't that simple.'

He told Baker he had been approached earlier by the crook who owned the Showcase, a man called Vincent O'Hara. This O'Hara said he 'wanted to get to know him better' and for that reason he didn't want to go there again. But Barbara wanted to go. She made out it was all about his brother. She had only heard Michael on the radio and she wanted to hear him in person.

'I couldn't turn her down,' Dan said. 'Anyway, we went and O'Hara set us up. He put us at a little table on our own and when we were pretty close he had a press photographer ready to take a shot.'

'You were pretty close?' Baker said.

'We were pretty close,' Dan admitted. 'Then, when I turned towards Barbara she kissed me on the mouth and the creep with the camera got his shot. I swear I didn't know she was going to do that. She had absolutely no reason to but she did and I don't suppose anyone would believe I wasn't expecting it. So I guess the honourable thing to do is apologize and offer my resignation. So I'm sorry and that's it.'

'You're sorry because you kissed a girl?'

'I didn't kiss her. She kissed me.'

Joe Baker laughed. 'This is kid's stuff. You sound like a coupla schoolkids being naughty.'

'It wasn't like that,' Dan insisted. 'It was a set-up and I fell for it.'

'You were set up by O'Hara?'

'Well, I don't like to say this, Pops, but I got the feeling Barbara was in on it, too.'

Baker nodded but made no comment.

'Now the press have got the picture and if I don't have lunch with O'Hara today it will be in tonight's 'papers.'

'And you missed your lunch.'

'Yes,' Dan said. 'I wanted you to know the full story before it came out.'

'O'Hara wanted to get to know you better. Why was that?'

'So I could shadow your dealings on Wall Street for him, tip him off when you're buying big. He's convinced you have the magic, the Midas touch.'

Baker nodded again.

'You don't seem surprised by any of this,' Dan said.

'It's all happened before, son, with O'Hara. And it's time I did something about it.'

Dan stood up. 'Well, I'm sorry for my part in what's happened but I feel better now that I've told you. Thanks for everything.'

'Sit down, for God's sake,' Baker said. 'You're sorry, but this is not entirely for my benefit, is it? O'Hara has another hold over you. If you don't go along with him he could pull the plug on your brother's remarkable rise to fame. But if you're not with me you can't help him.'

Dan smiled. 'True,' he admitted.

'Well,' Baker said, after a moment, 'you're not resigning. I need you in the business and I need you to help me fix O'Hara once and for all.' He leaned forward confidentially. 'What you should know is this is not all about O'Hara. Vincent O'Hara is a stooge. The real boss is a man they call The Englishman. Controls most of what goes on illegally in NY. The police know it and quite a lot of top people, including cops, are on his payroll. The thing is, he has a finger in most pies – clubs, cabs, booze – but he's never satisfied. He wants a piece of Wall Street, too. Now I've no beef with him but I have with O'Hara. Maybe I can figure something out here. Let me think about it.'

'What about Barbara?'

'I'll deal with her. And don't worry about the newspapers. For the kind of people who read that stuff today's news is tomorrow's ass paper.' He stood up. 'And get back to work, you big dope. I'll be in the office Wednesday.'

He walked Dan through to the reception and out front in his dressing-gown. Dan glanced at the dressing-gown. 'Was everything OK?' he asked. 'With the doc?'

Baker hesitated. 'Not entirely. But don't ask me now. I'll tell you later. Few things I need to think about just now.'

When Dan arrived back at Penn Station the late editions of the evening papers were out. He bought one of each and it was right there on the gossip page across three columns in the first of the papers he opened. The headline, WHEN THE CAT'S AWAY, was above a picture of himself, Barbara Baker and a pretty convincing kiss. *As high finance king, Joe Baker,* he read, *takes a break and a medical check, his young wife, Babs, and up-and-coming Wall Street whizz-kid, Danny Dolan, brother of the new singing sensation, Michael Dolan, get it together at the Showcase.*

# NINETEEN

IN LATE 1928 the new prosperity was still gathering momentum. This was the land of opportunity, the promised land where poor men could join in the financial fun and games and become dollar millionaires overnight. These were games that anyone could play. Anyone with a few dollars to spare could buy stock and a stake in some prosperous company and almost all of the larger companies *were* prosperous in 1928.

Most Americans that year were intoxicated, not with bootleg liquor but with the lure and promise of the stock market. Every day there were tales of spectacular overnight gains fuelled by the euphoria of those lucky enough to have bought a little stock and watched it soar in value. Stock prices had become hot news, as keenly read as the baseball results. Each weekday newspapers listed Wall Street prices and the radio stations gave a running commentary on the day's highs and lows. And in late 1928 there were very few lows.

The relentless rise of the market was avidly discussed in the clubs and coffee shops and in the workplace with a riot of jazz and crazy dance music orchestrating the excitement. The masses had become infatuated with the stock market. It was the newest craze, as mad and as popular as the latest dance. It was as if Wall Street had become an all-embracing casino where everyone was welcome and nobody could lose. Place your bets and carry on dancing was the order of the day. And beneath all this was an underlying anxiety. Shop girls and cab drivers and the man drilling the road all wanted to be in on the act and those who couldn't afford to gamble away their meagre earnings felt they were being left behind, losing out on the chance to hang on to the coat-tails of the soaring stock prices and get rich in the process along with everyone else.

In the midst of all this Dan Dolan was embarrassed and had the grace to blush at what was featured in the press as a cold betrayal of his ailing boss. He folded the newspaper and turned to the page he ought to have been reading, the daily trading figures. Despite the explosive gains across the market, Dan felt a nagging unease. He had felt this throughout the year and now, as the year was drawing to a close, he felt it even more. It was like watching a giant bubble grow bigger and bigger with the suspense of feeling it was about to burst. He was out of step, he told himself. Everyone else is on a trip to the moon and undreamt of wealth. So what was wrong? Well, if you wanted a house, a car, clothes, there was no problem. Whatever you wanted you could have. All you had to do was find a small deposit, or maybe no deposit at all, and the credit company would stump up the rest. The Easy Payment Plan was all the rage. But the promises to pay of many of the Easy Payment customers had little substance. They were built on insecure jobs, jobs that could disappear overnight, fall to the domino effect of some failed enterprise. Then who would pick up the bill?

To an innocent Irish peasant not *that* long off the boat, it all seemed like 'funny money' and he couldn't bring himself to believe it would always be this way. He had tried to raise the subject with Paul Merrick, but even someone as level headed as Merrick was not prepared to take him seriously. 'If that's what you think, line your pockets while you can,' was all he would say.

Now, when he got back to the office that evening, he had to put such negative thoughts aside. Nathan was waiting for him. Michael had left town. He was going to pick up Annie and they were going to disappear for a year or two. Dan listened in stunned silence.

'It had to come,' he said at last. 'Michael won't be pushed around by anyone, especially someone like O'Hara.'

'But he's giving up so much,' Nathan argued. 'It could take him years to get back to where he was.'

'Maybe he doesn't want to be where he was,' Dan said.

'O'Hara will make sure he doesn't work anywhere,' Nathan said.

'Can he do that?'

'Sure he can. That Bononi, the thief who calls himself an agent, he can warn people in the business not to touch him. He'll be lucky if he gets a job in a barber shop quartet.'

'It's a big country. O'Hara can't stop him from working everywhere.'

'He can,' Nathan said sadly, 'and he's started already. Michael had a business card a guy from the Goldkette Organization gave him. Jean Goldkette is this French Canadian who puts out touring bands across the country. Good outfits. Based in Detroit. Anyway, this guy came down one night to hear Michael sing and offered him a job. Michael gave him a call before he left but there was nothing doing. Seems the guy had a visit from some of O'Hara's gorillas.'

'He'll be OK with Annie,' Dan said confidently. 'I'm glad he's left O'Hara. Annie's a good girl and they'll make a decent home somewhere, somewhere safe. And they'll get work. I'm sure they will. Michael's a good singer and Annie can dance.' He thought for a moment. 'He should be OK for cash, shouldn't he?'

'Should be,' Nathan agreed. 'But he ain't. Bononi handled all his earnings, paid him a weekly salary. A pretty good one, Michael said, but I told him he was crazy. It was his money not Bononi's and not O'Hara's. But you know Michael. He's no businessman and so long as things are running smoothly and he can sing he's happy. He said Bononi was investing it for him. Buying stock.'

'In whose name, I wonder?' Dan said. Then: 'Maybe I should send him some dough.'

'We don't have an address,' Nathan said. 'Michael doesn't want anyone, including us, to know where he is. He thinks O'Hara might try giving us the works if he thinks we know where he is.'

Dan had a number to call. He picked up the phone, indicating Nathan should stay. Jimmy Pickles answered. 'Dan Dolan here,' Dan said, 'and I don't want you, Pickles. I want your lord and master.' There was a pause then Dan said, 'Just put him on, will you?' Nathan sat upright, facing the desk.

'O'Hara? Dan Dolan. Lousy picture in the paper. You need a better photographer ... Oh sure, I know he was working under difficult conditions. Dangerous, too. If I'd got hold of him I'd have strangled him ... It was the Press? Sure it was the Press and I reckon in a really classy club the management would have come over and apologized for the intrusion ... No, no. No hard feelings and there'll be no inside information for you either. Just stay out of my life in future. Oh and by the way, I hear you ran my brother out of town. Was that a good idea? Your biggest earner?'

Dan listened patiently. 'Yeah, well, you listen to me now. I've no idea where Michael is, or where he's going and neither has Nathan so there's no point sending your monkeys round.' Dan listened again. 'No, I'm not sore. I'm glad he's gone. I'm glad he got you off his back ... I know, I know you did a lot for him but with the talent he's got he'd have made it on his own anyway.' Listens again. 'Yeah, OK. Have it your way. I just want you to know if he comes to any harm, or you bother me or Nathan, I have a dossier on you and your activities. It's in a very safe place and if there's any trouble it'll turn up on the DA's desk and on the front page of the *Daily News*. And that's a promise.'

Nathan could hear O'Hara's raised voice, then Dan said quietly, 'Who? Oh, it's in safe hands. A guy called Walker. Happens to be the mayor. You'd like him. But he won't like you if he reads what you've been up to. You know Jimmy. The clean-up man ... No, *you* listen. Through you I've lost a brother. Michael left a note to say I won't be seeing him for a year or two.' Pause. 'I don't know. Maybe he means until you're dead. And with the kind of games you play maybe that won't be too long.' Pause again. 'All right, Mr O'Hara. As long as we understand each other.'

Nathan shook his head as Dan put the phone down. 'You're just stirring things up.'

'I haven't finished with O'Hara,' Dan said. 'Not by a long way.'

'We had a recording deal set up for Michael,' Nathan said sadly.

Dan decided he'd had enough for one day. He looked at his desk. Whatever there was could wait until tomorrow. Talking to O'Hara, even by phone, had made him feel nauseous. He needed fresh air.

It was a crisp, clear night and in the dark oblong of sky above the towering office blocks of Madison Avenue the stars glistened hard and bright. Dan walked part of the way with Nathan, taking in the sights and sounds. There were plenty of places they could go, all of them illegal and overlooked by the Police Department, but neither needed a drink. When it came to alcohol, illegal or not, Nathan was like Dan. He could take it or leave it.

Most of the shops and offices were closed now and the city was dressed for the evening. Taxicabs disgorged black ties and fox furs. Restaurants and dinner clubs, some noisy and brightly lit, some discreetly subdued, were filling up and, as Dan and Nathan walked through a dark side street to Fifth Avenue, it seemed there was music from every door. A lightly bouncing piano, a swinging band, a soaring trumpet, an urgent tenor sax and, incongruously, from somewhere high up, the plaintive strain of a solitary violin.

Looking down as far as the Flatiron Building, Fifth Avenue was a long narrow canyon festooned with lights that shimmered in the mild evening breeze as if gently dancing to the music of the night.

'Aren't you going the wrong way?' Nathan asked.

'I just wanted to walk, take another look at this crazy city.'

'It's our home town now,' Nathan said.

Dan nodded in agreement. 'Watch your back,' he said, as they parted and he walked through the knots of revellers on 42nd Street, the college boys with their dangling scarves, the party girls with their bobbed hair, their tight-fitting, knee-fringed dresses and their child-like, high-pitched laughter. He was twenty-three years of age yet already he felt too old to dive into the sparkling fountain of youth these kids revelled in.

Amidst all this hedonism and *joie de vivre*, squatting by a hard wall and wrapped in a black shawl, an old lady held out a begging bowl. Dan dropped a dollar bill in the empty bowl and the lady's lips moved silently as she bowed her head in gratitude.

'You're crazy.' He could hear Michael's voice, knowing what he would say. 'The old girl's probably got a mansion in Palm Beach.'

A shadowy figure, face mostly hidden, asked in a hoarse cigarette smoker's voice, 'Hey, mister. Wanna do business?'

Dan smiled and shook his head as he went on his way.

The evening had barely started by Manhattan standards but already it was over for someone who was being stretchered to an emergency ambulance, its lights flashing front and rear. At a theatre club on the corner of West 45th an early drunk repeatedly made his way in via the revolving door and was repeatedly bounced back to the sidewalk. On West 45th an orderly queue had formed outside the Five O'Clock club. On West 56th the Napoleon was being raided and protesting men and women were being hustled into waiting police vans. Dan laughed. It was like a hooley at the Drummers on a Saturday night. He had started walking to clear his head, help him think through what was to be done about O'Hara. But he had been sidetracked by the night and the city.

It was quieter and darker when he turned into West 59th Street, but Dan saw at once that someone was sitting on the stoop outside the apartment block. He looked around for other figures that might be lurking in the dark. O'Hara's men, perhaps. But, as he drew near, the man in black came to his feet and Dan relaxed.

'Hey! What's the idea, sitting out here in the dark?'

'I'm waiting for you,' Tim said.

Dan led the way and let himself in and without another word Tim followed him inside and up the two flights of stairs.

'How long have you been out there?' Dan asked, putting a match to the gas fire and without waiting for an answer he went into the kitchen and filled the kettle. 'Have you spoken to Nathan?'

Tim shook his head. 'No. Should I have?'

'I thought maybe he told you about Michael.'

'What about Michael?'

'He's gone, Tim, and we've no idea where,' Dan said. 'O'Hara ran him out of town and he's going to have to lie low for a while.' He told Tim what Nathan had told him.

'They'll find him, Dan,' Tim said, 'and when they do they'll kill him. Killing people is nothing to them. This boy we need, Martin Ripley, he left town and he's not been seen nor heard of since.'

'Doesn't mean he's dead. They'll probably hide him 'til it's all over.'

'Something has to be done about O'Hara.'

'I'm working on it,' Dan told him. 'So how is your boy?'

'I don't know. They won't let me see him. Father Pat can go but anyone else has to be family. And he's on Death Row, Dan.'

'Is there no hope?'

'Not much. And there's no publicity. I got a petition going and the whole parish signed it but that's not enough. To most outsiders Tony O'Reilly is just another young hoodlum. The papers promised to do what they can but just now they're full of this Ruth Snyder story.'

Ruth Snyder and her partner in crime, a corset salesman called Judd Gray, were big news, not just in New York but throughout the country. She was a bored and not very bright housewife on Long Island when she started an affair with Gray, the even less bright salesman, and eventually persuaded him to help kill her husband. She had taken out a valuable insurance policy on her husband and once the deed was done, she believed, they would be able to live happily ever after on the proceeds. But the plot they devised was a disaster. Ruth Snyder said the house had been burgled, she had been tied up and her husband murdered in his bed. The police didn't believe a word of it and, blaming each other, Snyder and Gray confessed, were arrested and put on trial.

The trial, well attended by crime writers and movie people, attracted enormous publicity. Ruth Snyder was now a media phenomenon. The tall blonde was a source of endless speculation. Was she really to blame? Surely she won't go to the chair! Across the country her story had gripped the attention of the ghoulish. She had also become an accidental icon for oppressed women.

The ill-thought-out murder plot had so obviously little chance of success Damon Runyon labelled it 'The Dumbell Murder'. Asked why, he said, 'Because the whole thing is just so dumb.'

Snyder and Gray were sentenced to death and, as the date of their execution drew near, and opinions divided on whether or not a woman should go to the chair, the radio and the press went into a frenzy. If Ruth Snyder was executed she would be the first woman, apart from a few black women who didn't seem to count, to die in the chair since 1899.

There was little interest and no space in the press for the plight of an unfortunate kid like Tony O'Reilly.

Dan looked at his brother curiously. 'You didn't know about Michael, so why *did* you come here tonight?'

'I had to see you,' Tim said. 'It's Ma. Father Pat got a phone call from the bishop's office. She was taken ill last Wednesday. She's in the Cottage Hospital. Sounds pretty serious.'

'Did they say what it is, what's wrong?'

'Father Pat tried to make a transatlantic call but he couldn't get through. Seems there's a letter from Aunt Molly on the way with more details. But that'll take ages.'

Dan didn't know what to say.

'If she's really bad,' Tim said, 'maybe one of us should go home.'

'Take a couple of weeks at least,' Dan told him, 'and it would have to be you or me. Way things are we can't even let Michael know.'

Tim smiled wryly. 'Have to be you, I guess. I couldn't afford it.' He was waiting for a lead from Dan who was usually quick to make decisions but for once Dan seemed unsure. 'You can't go, is that it?'

'Well,' Dan said, 'Mr Baker is in hospital. In for a couple of days. I had to see him about something today so I went over there. He said he was just in for an annual check-up but it turned out it was a cancer hospital. He wouldn't tell me why he was there. He said he'll tell me tomorrow when he gets home.'

'He may need you here in the business.'

Dan shrugged. 'If Ma's ill one of us should be there.'

'Well, you know how it is. I would go, but it's the money.'

Everything seemed to be happening at once. Dan needed to know exactly what, if anything, was wrong with Joe Baker. He wanted to be in town if Michael tried to contact him and he wanted to be in on any arrangements Joe might make to deal with O'Hara.

'How are things in the parish?' he asked. 'Does Father Pat need you?' There was a look on Tim's face he hadn't seen before. 'Tim?'

'The Church,' Tim said disparagingly. 'Useless. Waste of time, Dan. Tony O'Reilly is locked up in a cell on Death Row and what is the Church doing? What is the Holy Catholic Church doing for its ex-altar boy framed for a murder he didn't commit? Absolutely nothing. And take me. What am I doing? I'm not a priest. They can't make up their minds if they need me or not. Well, I'm beginning to wonder if I need them.'

'Hey, come on!' Dan said. 'Ma wouldn't want to hear you talk like that. And you can't blame the Church over Tony. What can they do? No witnesses for the defence and a couple of cops who say they actually saw your man holding the gun.' They were quiet for a moment then Dan said, 'Maybe you need to get away for a while, go home, see Ma. Things might look different from a distance. What do you say? I find the money, you go see Ma.'

Vin O'Hara was in one of his frequent rages, the kind that came when things were not going exactly the way he wanted. Find Dolan by tonight or else, he bellowed at Jimmy Pickles. But Pickles didn't know where to start. Then it occurred to him that if Michael Dolan had gone, the girl, Annie, was probably with him and if so it might be worth grilling her girlfriends, especially the blonde dame who always had a lot to say. He went at once to the Vaudeville Theatre. The girls, he knew, were part way through a four-week booking.

Flanked as usual by two gorillas, he burst into an office on the mezzanine floor where the far from young theatre manager was startled out of a midday clinch with his very young and innocent-looking secretary.

'Dancer called Annie,' Pickles demanded, straight to the point. 'Michael Dolan's girlfriend, no less. Where's she from?'

Flustered and anxious to adjust his clothing, the man blinked at Pickles, clearly aware of who he was and what he represented. 'They all stay at the Lennox. It's a rooming-house on Third.'

'Her home address, dumb-head.'

His hands shaking, the manager took a ledger from a shelf and said doubtfully, 'I don't think we have—'

'Well, look,' Pickles ordered, 'and make it snappy.' He looked at the girl. 'You know this Annie?'

Terrified, the girl shook her head.

'We don't have any other address,' the theatre manager said, equally scared. 'They come and go all the time.'

'Yeah, yeah,' Pickles said, and he turned to his two men. 'Do we know this Lennox joint?'

The one called Bluey nodded, the other was leering at the girl. With a flick of his head Pickles indicated they were leaving. From the doorway he looked back at the girl. 'Keep your pants on, kid,' he said. 'With this old ram around you'll be taking home more than your pay check.'

Bluey drove over to the rooming-house on Third Avenue. It was where theatre people and others in the business stayed anything from a week to a year depending on how long a project lasted.

A well-upholstered German lady intercepted them in the hallway. 'You bring the rent?'

'What rent would that be?' Pickles asked.

'Das little dame, Annie. She one of yours, ain't she? Vell she skip out vid'out paying up for the last three veek.'

'She ain't one of ours, no,' Pickles told her, 'but we want her and when we find her she'll pay up in more ways than one.'

The woman looked worried. 'She do something wrong?'

'Where do we find her pal? Susie or Sue, something like that. Blonde dame, thin.'

Sue, the girl in question, was part way down the stairs. 'Don't you mean *slim*, Mr Pickles?' she asked coyly.

'We're looking for your sidekick,' Pickles told her.

'Annie?' she said, biting her lower lip. 'She went home.'

Pickles advanced up the stairs and his men followed. 'If you don't mind,' he said, 'we'd like for us to have a little talk.'

The German landlady turned to Bluey and opened her mouth, but he gave her a look that said clearly: Keep out of this.

They came up the stairs slowly and with measured steps and Sue was forced to back into the room she had shared with Annie and another girl. The other girl was still in bed but she sat up now and pulled the bedclothes up to her neck.

Pickles focused on Sue 'What do they call you? Susie?' She nodded. 'Well, Susie,' he said quietly. 'You're Annie's pal and Annie's gone home.' She nodded again. 'And you're going to tell us where home is. We need an address, Susie.'

Sue shook her head. 'I don't know, Mr Pickles. Honest. She left in a hurry and she just said she would be in touch.'

Pickles looked back at Bluey and indicated he should step forward. Bluey stepped forward, put an arm around Sue's neck and held a narrow bladed switch knife to her face. The girl in the bed stifled a scream.

'Please, Mr Pickles,' Sue whimpered. 'I don't know where she's from. Honest. If I did I'd tell you.'

Bluey held the knife against her cheek so she could feel the smooth cold blade that was ready to mark her for life.

'Please,' she begged 'Not my face. I'd never work again ...'

'Where did you say she came from?' he demanded.

'It's somewhere near Chicago,' the girl in the bed said.

Pickles put his face close to Sue's. 'If we hear she's been in touch and you haven't told us we'll be back. Understand?'

Sue nodded, her eyes wide and fearful, and she collapsed into a chair as they left.

At the foot of the stairs the German landlady was waiting. 'Vat about the rent? The boss vill stop it from my vages.'

Pickles smiled sweetly. 'If he gives you a hard time, Mama, just call us. We'll take care of him.'

*Never was a country so happy and so prosperous as America is today.* So claimed the newspaper and magazine advertisements. Successful businessmen were celebrities and there was no escaping the mass euphoria. Talking pictures had Movietone News, almost every household had a radio and newspaper boys yelled the latest developments daily through several editions.

Never before had the working man, the housewife, the man in the street taken such an interest in the day-to-day business of the Stock Exchange. And perhaps with good reason. Ten thousand dollars of stock held in General Motors in 1920 was now worth one and a half million.

Radio stock, along with General Motors, was one of the market leaders and Michael Meehan, the man mainly responsible for its rise in value now organized an 'insider' group who collectively bought Radio to boost it still further. Investors, large and small, took note and so did the media. The impression was created that Radio stock was on the way up and the scramble was on to buy in. With a little help from Mr Meehan's friends, Radio stock had swiftly become the 'in' thing. The smart investor bought Radio and, with so many outsiders eager to buy, Radio stock climbed more than twenty dollars in two days to a new high of $125.50 per share. The rise and rise of Radio soon became front-page news and within a few days Post 12 became the busiest spot on the floor of the Exchange.

Investors, large and small, were now fighting to invest in Radio. In just eight days the stock gained fifty dollars. Across the country, coast to coast, speculators were whipped into a frenzy of buying. Anyone and everyone, whether they could afford to gamble or not, wanted to be in on the bonanza and the myths grew daily. An elevator boy made half a million dollars; the girl in the office quadrupled her money in three days. The stories poured in and nobody wanted to check if they were true. At $195, Radio was now even higher than General Motors. In less than a month the price had doubled. And more than ever, organized crime barons, like Vincent O'Hara's Englishman, were eager to muscle in and manipulate the market. But the market had its own manipulators.

Dan Dolan was spending most of his days on the floor of the Exchange, alerting his boss to trends in the market, and despite his brief spell in hospital Joe Baker was as active as ever.

'You realize we missed lunch?' he asked one day.

'No time for lunch,' Dan said with a grin, as he followed him out to Broad Street. And this was true. There was so much going on people were reluctant to leave the floor.

'Let's get a coffee and you can tell me what's bugging you.'

Dan raised his eyebrows in surprise, but he didn't speak as they walked up to Pine and the coffee shop.

Baker was looking at him knowingly. 'Come on,' he said. 'I know you. What's your mind?'

'Couple of things,' Dan told him. 'First of all and most important, you said you would tell me why you were in a cancer hospital.'

Baker glanced at him sidelong. 'I was there,' he said, 'because it's a hospital for people with cancer.'

Dan gripped Baker's arm. 'What is it, Pops?'

'We all have to go some time,' Baker said without expression.

'What is it?' Dan asked in alarm. 'Tell me. What's going on? Come on. I need to know. We have to get you the best doctors, the experts.'

Baker smiled, his elfin, wise-old-man smile. 'They're all the same, Dan. They know nothing. All they're expert at is writing out death certificates.' His expression softened. 'Don't look like that. It won't happen for a while yet. So what was the other thing?'

Dan shook his head. 'It's not important now.'

'What was the other thing?' Baker insisted.

'I need a note from my employer to the bank,' Dan told him.

'To say what?'

'To say that I'm good for a loan. I need to borrow a couple of hundred dollars. There'll be no problem. They seem to be happy to lend money just now. All I need is a note from you.'

'You going to tell me what the money's for?'

'My brother Tim. He got a message through the Church to say Ma's been taken ill. Seems she's pretty bad and we reckon one of us should go home and see her before it's too late.'

'You want to take some time off?'

'No. Tim would go but he has no money and I don't have enough to give him.' He smiled. 'The banks won't lend to a trainee priest.'

Baker laughed. 'But they'll lend to the crooks on Wall Street.'

'That's about it,' Dan agreed. 'And, as I told you, Michael has gone missing, thanks to O'Hara.'

'Don't worry about it,' Baker told him. 'You don't need a bank loan. We'll work something out.'

# TWENTY

TIM HAD NOT expected to see the old country again so soon. But nothing, it seemed, had changed much. It was raining as they left and it was raining now, the clouds low and grey.

A loudspeaker on the quayside at Liverpool had summoned him to the office of the dock manager. He had been here before and he remembered that hectic day, the day Caitlin's mother died, her lifeless body in that narrow back room, the small black van that took her away, the lost little girl with Dan and Michael. The place was associated with death and loss then and it was now. The manager was waiting for him with a note, a message received by telephone.

Ma was dead. She had died before he left New York and all the time he was sitting patiently in the main cabin, gazing out at the dull, timeless Atlantic, she was lying dead. He was too late. He was even too late for the funeral. The funeral was yesterday and already she was underground, that lovely face he had known all his life was gone and gone forever.

The boat to Dublin had moved slowly, the bus had moved slowly, and the hours had only memories to pass the time. Then at last the bus dropped him at the crossroads and he began the half-mile walk, steadily, resolutely, his head and his shoulders wet with rain, to the house where he and his brothers had been born.

The cottage was as he knew it, as he had always known it, yet it was different. He had never realized how small it was until now. His mind's eye, filled with images of Manhattan skyscrapers, tall tenement buildings and majestic bridges, saw it now for what it was. A tiny house, scarcely big enough for two. A place where once his mother had presided over a noisy household.

She had them all in those days and somehow she kept them all under control A large amiable husband, three growing boys and much of the time their clumsy, beer-swilling Uncle Patrick. Sure and they must have all got in each other's way, he told himself with a smile, then a sadness in the knowledge that those days were gone, gone forever and now Ma had gone with them.

The front door, he noticed, was slightly open and, as he went down the uneven path, he could see through the window a fire was burning brightly. He had forgotten to bring the only key they had and he expected he would have to go down the road to Aunt Molly or Clare. But they were here already, waiting for him.

'Will you look at him!' Aunt Clare said reproachfully as if it was his fault he was wet. 'He's wet through, so he is. Come on now, take off that coat. And that shirt. And take a towel to your head.'

She was talking to him as if he had come in wet from school, as Ma did in the old days. But he held up his hands. 'I need to go down there and see her.'

'No, no, son, not now,' Aunt Molly said. 'We have a hot drink for you. With a little something in it. And you must get yourself dry.'

The rain spattered the window. 'You'll get yourself soaked to the skin,' Aunt Clare said, as he backed away.

'I'm already soaked to the skin,' he said with a smile. 'It'll only take a few minutes and I'll come straight back. I promise.'

They shrugged helplessly, accepting he was a man now with a will of his own. 'We'll have something hot for you. So don't you be long.'

He dodged out the door and back into the rain and set off down the lane, skirting the Drummers'. The tavern was closed until 5.30 and he was glad. He didn't want to be dragged in there by well-meaning sympathizers. It was a place he hoped to avoid this trip. He couldn't face the commiserations and then the inevitable questions about New York City and all the blarney they would expect in return. Maybe tomorrow, he told himself.

He saw the newly formed grave at once. It was covered by flowers, the flowers pounded by the relentless rain. They were mostly wild flowers gathered for free from the hillsides and the edge of the woods. The newly turned soil was looser and blacker than the surrounding soil, crossed now by little rivulets of rain-water. The gravestone was a dull, worn grey. He would leave some money for the stone to be cleaned and for his mother's name to be added to those of his father, a baby girl his parents had lost and Uncle Pat.

He stood in silence for several minutes, thinking of this lovely selfless lady who now lay in peace, ready to meet her God. And if there is a God, he thought, he'll welcome her with open arms. That troublesome phrase brought his train of thought to a halt. *If there is a God* … It had rarely occurred to him that there might not be and he had always dismissed the possibility. Slowly, confused, he turned away and he saw the statue of the Virgin in her light blue robe. He had run to her that last night, the night before they left, when he was running from Kathy O'Donnell. He had escaped then yet he knew that now he was home and before he left again, though he didn't know why or what he wanted to say to her, he would have to, he *wanted* to see Kathy O'Donnell one more time.

Father Delaney was in the vestry. He knew Tim was home and he was ready with his condolences as he greeted him and led him through to the house that adjoined the church. It was a large house by local standards, on three floors with a comfort-able sitting room, a large kitchen and a housekeeper, Bridie Friel, who as far as Tim could remember had always been there. She appeared to have no family of her own and seeing her now with her scrubbed moon face and her mouse-like, quietly scur-rying manner he wondered why she wasn't a nun.

His mother, Father Delaney told him, had not suffered much,

except perhaps for a day or two towards the end. A day or two? A minute is an eternity for someone in pain, Tim thought but he didn't say so. It was a carcinoma, the priest said and Tim merely nodded. Typically, without any frills, Aunt Molly had said it was breast cancer, so it was, a malignant tumour. It must have given her terrible pain, she said, and she never told anyone she had it until it was too late. Aunt Clare simply shook her head and with a doomsday frown said, 'Ah 'tis always too late with the cancer.'

Father Delaney was droning on about the better place Tim's mother had gone to where there was sure to be a seat for her at the table of the Lord and other such platitudes. He was talking to Tim as if Tim was a small boy in one of his Saturday morning religious instruction lessons. But Tim was feeling sleepy, kept awake only by the angry buzz of a large bee as it rammed a window in a vain attempt to escape. If it only knew, he thought, it's far better inside than out. It was throwing it down outside and it was warm and dry in Father Delaney's sitting room.

It occurred to Tim that Father Delaney had known him all his life. He had been the parish priest here for more than thirty years and he had always seemed a towering presence in his flowing robes and the more colourful garments he wore at Mass or Benediction. Father Delaney had known Tim and his brothers since they were born, were baptized, made their first Confession and received their first Holy Communion, and he had known, too, that from an early age Tim Dolan was being groomed by his mother for the priesthood.

It was a process he had been subjected to himself and he was not sure he entirely approved. But this was Ireland and the mothers were Roman Catholic.

As the boys grew up Dan and Michael had become less close to the Church. But not Tim. He had served at the altar from eight to eighteen and it was only his recent departure that took him away. Fate had taken Tim across the Atlantic and now as Bridie brought in the tea and the little cakes she had made herself Father Delaney offered Tim 'a drop of the hard stuff' to stiffen his tea. Like everyone else he wanted to hear all about New York.

Father Delaney seemed to acknowledge now that Tim was already a man with a greater experience of the wider world than himself and he began to talk to him as an adult. Tim, sensing the subtle change, felt he could now tell Father Delaney about Father Pat, the Lower West Side and Father Pat's sometimes startling use of language. But first he told him about Michael's remarkable rise to fame.

'Ah and he could always sing that one,' the priest said and he recalled the time they tried to get Michael, as a small boy, to sing solo in church one Easter Sunday. He was to sing *Ave Maria* but he refused point blank. He threatened if he was forced into it he would sing *Paddy McGinty's Goat* instead. 'And the way that boy was,' Father Delaney said with a laugh, 'we couldn't risk it.'

He listened carefully, nodding from time to time, as Tim told him of some of the problems that faced a parish priest in what New Yorkers called Hell's Kitchen. 'You know how sometimes people say, "It would make a priest swear"? Well, Father Pat does. He swears all the time. He calls Jewish people Kikes and Italians Wops. He has a terrible tongue on him.'

Father Delaney laughed. 'Ah, these are just words. 'Tis of no consequence. 'Tis how he deals with his people that matters. I'm sure he does what he can to guide them.'

Tim nodded. 'They love him, Father,' he said. 'They really do. But things go wrong.'

He told Father Delaney about Tony O'Reilly and his response surprised him. Yet, he decided later, it was predictable.

'It doesn't matter much how we die,' Father Delaney told him. 'If they sit the boy in the electric chair and he's innocent the Lord will know he's innocent and he'll still be welcome upstairs.'

'But the people he leaves behind ... his mother, his little brother.'

'Ah, the whole of life is a problem, Timothy,' he said. 'It was never meant to be a bed of roses. Life on this earth has always been a mess and sure it always will be.'

There was to be a private family Mass for his mother before he returned to the US and he arranged for this now. Then, as if he was propelled by some inner force he set off down the lane to the house where several generations of O'Donnells had lived. Along the lane was the elementary school where Tim and his brothers and Kathy O'Donnell and most of the children of the village first grappled with the complexities of what Mrs Yeats, the seemingly ageless schoolmistress, called readin' an' writin'.

From somewhere at the back of the school came the sound of the school choir singing tunefully and for now the playground was deserted. Tim paused to gaze fondly at the playground. This was where Michael and a boy called Padraic Cleary came to blows at every opportunity from the age of seven to thirteen. Then when Padraic's family emigrated to Australia the two of them had clung to each other in a tearful farewell.

As with all the boys, as the brothers reached the age of fourteen, they went out to work. Michael in the fields. Tim himself at the General Post Office delivering mail, Dan in the estate office of the English Lord who, despite Independence and Partition, still owned and in all but law ruled the county.

Just a short distance from the school there was a narrow turning off to the right. It was almost hidden from the lane by the bushes that reached out as if wanting to embrace across the opening. Here there were fewer footprints in the mud and a stranger to the village might think the path led nowhere.

The O'Donnell house, a house Tim knew well, was one of three in a two-storey terrace of crofters' cottages. He stood quite still for a moment, again struck by how small the houses were. It was like coming to Toytown but it was not a pretty sight. There were too many overgrown bushes that should have been trimmed or cut back, there was a broken drain, rusty and leaking, and the thatch looked tired and black in patches.

The O'Donnells' was the first of the three, the front door closed, the windows grimy with neglect. Perhaps the family had moved but where would they go? They had always lived here. He knocked at the dingy front door. Kathy might not be here, of course. She had worked at the kitchens in the market hall but he felt sure she would have left that job by now. It was a job she had never enjoyed and she was always looking in the newspaper for something better.

Tim just wanted to know where she was working and he would go and see her. A little apprehensive now, he knocked again at the door. If Kathy was in what would he say to her? Why had he come? He couldn't answer that. He just knew he couldn't leave and go back to the States without seeing her.

He waited but no one came, He went down the side of the house and round to the back door. It was open. He knocked lightly then pushed the door inwards. Kathy's older sister, Bridget, was at the kitchen sink. She looked up at him sharply, her hands in water. 'Jesus, Mary and Joseph, and what do *you* want?'

'Hello, Bridget,' he said and he started to cross the threshold but she rounded on him, a large bread knife in her hand.

'Don't you dare step foot in this house,' she warned him. 'You are not wanted here.'

'I just want to see Kathy.'

She looked at him curiously. 'Is that right?' she said, her head on one side.

'You will have heard we lost Ma. I came over soon as I could but I was too late.'

What he was saying didn't help. It sounded as if he had only called because he happened to be passing and he just thought he would look in on Kathy, see if she had got over the shock of losing him. At least, that was the way Bridget chose to see it.

Bridget was only two years older than Kathy but she had always seemed so much more. She had aged, too, and she looked far older than her years. She was notorious in the village for blaming all the troubles of the world on men and the fact that she had never married, never had a male friend, was not surprising. Her two brothers had gone off to Australia when Bridget and Kathy were still at school and when their mother fell ill with what the doctor called pleurisy their feckless father had gone off to God knows where with his fancy woman never to be seen nor heard from again. Times had been very hard and Bridget had left school a year early, the deed done before the school board found out, to work in a laundry.

Now, faced with Timothy Dolan, Bridget erupted. First she threw a dishcloth at him, then a ladle and, as he ducked and, swayed his way in, he caught and held her arms to her sides.

'Get out!' she screamed.

The commotion had alerted Mrs Lynch, the lady next door, and she came running now. 'What, in God's name?'

'It's all right, Mrs Lynch,' Tim said, gingerly letting Bridget go. 'I'll go. I shouldn't have come.'

Bridget screamed again and ran at him but Maggie Lynch was a heavyweight and she caught Bridget, came between them.

'You better go, lad,' she said. 'What you did to young Kathy was wrong and you'll find no forgiveness for that around here.'

'I just want to see her,' he said quietly.

'Well, she's at the church,' Bridget told him. 'If you want to go down on your knees and say you're sorry then that's where she is.'

'You robbed that girl of her future, Timothy Dolan,' Mrs Lynch accused him. 'You were going to marry Kathy and you were going to spend the rest of your lives together.'

'You don't understand,' Tim said feebly.

'Oh, I understand all right,' Mrs Lynch assured him. 'You held on to that girl and then you left her.'

'I know,' Tim said. 'But look, I just want to see her.'

'I've told you,' Bridget yelled at him. 'She's down at the church.'

'I've just come from the church.'

'Well, that's where she is. Now go, will ye? And don't come back.'

Still Tim hesitated.

'Is your Jim home, Maggie?' Bridget asked Mrs Lynch. 'Will you get him to throw this one out?'

'No need,' Tim said. 'I'm going.'

They were right. He should have finished with Kathy long before it became so serious. There were other fellows after her and he should have made his intentions clear much sooner than he did. But hey! he told himself. She's still only a young woman.

He walked back to where the path met the lane. This was where he would wait for Kathy when they were both in standard seven, aged fourteen. Most days she would be walking a little eight-year-old called Marie to school. Marie had red hair and a smiley face full of freckles. She would walk between them, holding them by the hand, and every few yards they would swing her up in the air and she would squeal with delight.

Now, as he approached the school, the children were spilling out into the lane. He saw Marie at once, same red hair, same smiley face, and she saw him at the moment he saw her. *She* was fourteen now but, apart from growing taller, she didn't seem to have changed much. He raised a hand and smiled, but she simply stared back at him, her face without expression, before turning away and running to catch up with her friends. Tim felt like a leper, an outcast in his own village.

He hurried back to the church and the deserted churchyard. Sometimes in the church a girl from the village would arrange the flowers from a funeral with just the family flowers left at the grave. But there was no sign of Kathy and the church was empty. He went to the sacristry but the door was locked and he found himself back at the main door. Then he saw Bridie Friel. She was coming up the path with her shopping basket.

'Bridie!' he called. 'Have you seen Kathy? Kathy O'Donnell?'

She looked at him blankly, her mouth open.

'I was told she was here, at the church.'

The poor lad, she thought.

'She's here all right,' she said in her gentle way and with a nod she indicated that he should follow.

Tim followed her down a neatly edged path, away from the church to where she came to a halt and looked down at an oblong mound of earth with a simple wooden cross. It was starting to go dark now in the grey dismal late afternoon but he could make out the carved wording on the small cross: Kathleen Mary O'Donnell (1908-1926). He fell to his knees.

'I'm sorry,' Bridie said softly. 'I didn't realize you didn't know.'

Tim stared up at her in disbelief. 'What was it? What happened?'

She shook her head. 'I don't know. I believe she started to stay at home, wouldn't leave the house, wouldn't go to her work. They say she sort of wasted away.'

'When was this? How long...?'

'It was soon after you and the boys left.'

'It was my fault, Bridie? Is that what you're saying?'

'That's what everyone says.' He was suffering and she wanted to help him, reassure him, say what he wanted to hear, but she couldn't. 'You were together for a long time. Everyone expected you to marry and become a part of the village but you chose the Church.'

'So did I do wrong?'

'What you did wrong was you didn't end it soon enough. Kathleen never believed you would leave her until you did.'

'She didn't have to die.'

'No,' Bridie agreed. 'But you still don't understand, do you? She didn't want to *live* and she just allowed herself to waste away.'

'But what did she die of? I mean ...'

'I don't know what Dr Murphy called it but the folk in the village, they say ... well, you know what they are like.'

'What? What do they say?'

She looked at him with genuine compassion and with her head on one side she said gently, 'They say she died of a broken heart.'

# TWENTY-ONE

BACK IN Joe Baker's Madison Avenue office Lois had a message for Dan. A Mr O'Shaughnessey had called to say he needed to speak to Mr Dolan urgently, would he please call. Dan called the music agency where Nathan was employed but the girl on the switchboard said he had not been in. They hadn't heard from him and nobody there had any idea where he might be. Dan decided, as soon as the bell went for the end of the day's trading, he would call at the apartment Nathan had shared with Michael.

He knocked several times, tried the door handle and was about to leave when the housekeeper intercepted him on the stairs. She was a little Irish lady, a Mrs Daly, and she knew Dan was Michael's brother.

'You're a friend of Mr O'Shaughnessey.'

Dan smiled. 'I'm Michael Dolan's brother.'

'Oh, Mr Dolan,' she said, her hands shaking. 'I didn't know what to do. Your brother's gone and Mr O'Shaughnessey ...' Her voice trailed.

'What?' Dan asked quietly to calm her down. 'What's happened, Mrs Daly? Is Nathan all right?'

'No,' she said. 'He is not. They took him to the County Hospital. Three men came very early this morning, about six o'clock, and they ... they beat him up real bad. He was in a terrible state I thought they'd killed him.'

'Three men.'

'A small man and two big ugly brutes. Cowards they are. And you know Mr O'Shaughnessey. He's not a big man.' Mrs Daly

had clearly been shaken and she was still sca͏ʳ
yesterday. They said they were looking for Mr ͏ˎ
but he wasn't in, so they said they would come b͏ˎ
did.'

'The County Hospital?' He dodged by her in the hallw͏ˎ
was in a hurry now. 'Don't worry, Mrs Daly,' he said. 'I'll let ͏ˎ
know what's going on. And thank you for calling the ambulance.'

'I called the police, Mr Dolan. The police called the ambulance.'

He nodded and left her wringing her hands in the apron at
her waist. It turned out that Nathan was not at the County
Hospital. He had been transferred to an emergency unit at a
hospital in Jersey where a specialist could examine his badly
damaged eye.

It was 6.30, the traffic was heavy and it took Dan over an
hour to get there. The man at the desk was reluctant to let him
through but he walked through anyway, determined to find
Nathan if he had to look in every room in the place. The man
at the desk called Security but Dan was in luck. Both the
Security men who appeared were Irish and when he told them
his friend, Nathan O'Shaughnessey, had been beaten up and left
for dead by a couple of hoodlums they couldn't have been more
helpful. Within minutes they had found where Nathan was and
one of them led him there.

Dan was shocked at what he saw. Nathan lay perfectly still,
his head and his face heavily bandaged, a neck brace for
support. The young doctor on duty told Dan that Nathan was
lucky to be alive. 'Whoever did this,' he said, 'was out to kill
your friend and they darn' near did.'

Nathan's left eye was patched up but he succeeded in opening
his other eye. He tried to grin at Dan but the effort looked
painful.

Dan looked down at him and smiled. 'So how's the other
fellow?'

Nathan opened his mouth but the young doctor looked
concerned. 'Don't try to talk,' he said. 'It's too soon.'

Dan said, 'I just want to ask you a couple of questions, Nathan. If it's yes give me a wink. If it's no, give me two. OK?'

Nathan winked his good eye.

Dan smiled. 'You're a tough guy, O'Shaughnessey.'

Nathan winked in agreement and Dan grinned down at him.

'This was two of O'Hara's men?' he said, grimly serious now. Nathan winked once. 'They wanted to know where Michael was?' He winked again. 'You told them you didn't know and they didn't believe you?' He winked again. 'So they tried to beat it out of you?' Winked again.

The young doctor decided this was enough. 'I guess—'

'It's OK, Doc,' Dan said. 'I've got all I need to know.' To Nathan he said, 'I'll be back and don't you worry about a thing. You're in good hands here.'

There was a telephone booth in the hospital foyer. Dan was furious. Nathan's wounds were much worse then he had expected and it was obvious it would be a long time, if ever, before he fully recovered. Dan wanted to do something about it, fast. He rang Joe Baker's apartment.

'Pops!' he said, and he realized he was trembling with rage. 'I'm just calling to tell you I may not see you for some time so I want to say thanks, thank you for everything.'

'Sounds serious,' Baker said.

'It is,' Dan said.

'So where are you? What's going on? When you didn't come back to the office we thought maybe something had happened.'

'It has. And I'm sorry. But I can explain. I'm at a hospital in Jersey.'

'Hospital! Why? What is it?' Baker asked in alarm. 'You OK?'

'Yeah,' Dan said. 'I'll tell you about it when I see you. But that might not be for some time. I'm going along to O'Hara's place right now and I'm going to kill him.'

'Whoa! What's this? You are not going to kill anyone.'

'I'm going to do it now, so I am. He's going to get what he deserves.'

'You do nothing 'til you've seen me. All right? Whatever he's done he's not worth doing time for. Now you do as I say and come over here.'

'Is Barbara there?'

'Yeah, she is.'

'Well, I can't talk to you there.'

There was a pause then Baker said, 'Right. I think I know what you're saying. Well, why not go home, get some sleep and we'll talk about it in the morning.'

'Can't do that, Pops. I need to do something now, tonight.'

'Just calm down, son. Come over here and I'll be waiting for you downstairs. OK?'

'O'Hara sent a couple of thugs to beat up a boy called Nathan, friend of ours, wouldn't harm a fly. And they left him for dead. Well, he's not going to get away with it. Not this time. I'm going to kill him.'

'No, you're not,' Baker said. '*I* am.'

The crowd had been growing since early morning. Word had gone out that three condemned men were to die in one day and the Anti-Chair League and other protestors were there in force. News reporters were broadcasting from outside the prison gates and listeners across the country could hear the chants and the hymn singing of the demonstrators that drowned the loud-hailers of the large contingent of police officers detailed to keep them under control. Three executions in one day seemed an unsavoury act of defiance on behalf of the authorities and this had provoked a feeling of outrage amongst even the most passive of objectors.

Beyond the gates Father Pat felt there was an air of unease, a kind of guilty briskness about the proceedings as if everyone on duty wanted to get the day's gruesome work over and done with as quickly and efficiently as possible. Even the minute finger on the large round clock in the main hall seemed to be in a hurry, the little time left eroding rapidly.

The brick walls of Tony O'Reilly's cell were pale grey with here and there a lighter patch where some message left by a previous occupant had been painted out. There was a small wash basin, a single upright chair for visitors and a low iron bed, the last place where Tony would lay his head. Tony's cell was in a row of eight. Two were empty, six were occupied by men awaiting execution.

The wide passageway outside the cells led to a brown door that led to another door, a green door that opened on to the slightly raised area where the dreaded chair with its retaining straps awaited. Facing the platform were the seats from where members of the Press and around twenty 'witnesses' would watch. In just ten minutes' time Tony O'Reilly would make his entrance and a few minutes later he would make his exit.

In his cell he sat on the bed, his head down, his hands covering his face, as Father Pat, seated in the chair, spoke to him quietly.

Tony's head had been shaved as if to render him anonymous. He looked up, terrified. 'I don't want to die, Father.'

Father Pat didn't know what to say. Tony was just a boy, barely out of school. But the priest knew he had to keep talking, help the minutes tick away. 'These people are wrong, son,' he said. 'They don't know what they're doing. But I guess it's too late now to stop them. They think what they are doing is right. But God knows what is right. You must be brave, hold your head up high. You're Tony O'Reilly. And you're innocent. Let them see that. Look them in the eye and be proud. I want to be able to tell your Ma and Frankie that you were brave and strong because you were innocent and you knew that your God was with you.'

The governor was at the cell door. He nodded at Father Pat to indicate the time had come. Father Pat drew back his chair as a guard came in and took hold of Tony's arm. Tony stood up. Neither the governor nor any of the guards knew what to expect. They never did. Sometimes the condemned man would cower back and have to be dragged from the cell. Others would come quietly, often as if in a kind of stupor.

Tony's eyes mirrored his terror as he looked at Father Pat. 'Will you walk with me, Father?'

Father Pat nodded. The governor had already agreed to his request that he should take the place of the prison chaplain.

'As far as the Gates of Heaven,' he told Tony and together they began that last walk, passed the cells of others awaiting the same fate, to the brown door then on towards the green door.

'Go on, kid,' one of the condemned men cried. 'Show 'em you can take it.'

Tony's young, lithe, athletic body seemed to have collapsed from within. He looked thinner, smaller, shrunken in on himself as if his spirit had already left his body and what remained of him had come to accept his role in this obscene and indefensible charade.

Beyond the green door the audience fell silent as the six guards, lined up in twos, trooped to a halt. As if perplexed by the part they were playing, they seemed to hang their heads in shame.

Tony O'Reilly turned his tear-stained face to Father Pat and tried to smile. 'Tell Ma an' Frankie ...'

Father Pat nodded and gripped his hand for the last time.

'I'll put in a good word for you, Father, when I get up there.'

He squeezed the priest's hand and with that he turned away and was led to the waiting chair where he was swiftly strapped in, a black mask went over his face and a wired-up helmet was placed on his head.

Father Pat looked at the governor. It was all happening so fast. But the governor simply nodded at the executioner and without a moment's grace or time even for a collective prayer the switch was thrown. There had been reports that on occasion the electrics had failed at the last moment and the doomed prisoner had been reprieved, his sentence commuted. But there were no such hitches today and the strong, young but diminished body of Tony O'Reilly slumped forward.

The greying priest had closed his eyes and if, as the myth-makers maintained, the lights dimmed as the surge of electricity took all the power, he had not noticed. For the moment he was traumatized, his heart and his mind scarred for the rest of his days.

The procedure had taken seconds, a young man was dead and even as they were being ushered out the apparently insensitive newsmen were scribbling their lines, their lives intact, their earthly pressures paramount. From behind the phalanx of guards and the straight-backed governor, the diminutive figure of Father Pat stepped forward.

'That's it, fellas,' he cried. 'You can do your job now, write your grubby little stories. Or you can try telling the truth. The State has murdered an innocent boy today, a mere child. And you lot sat there and watched it happen. Have you no shame?'

The governor and a large guard stepped before him. 'Please, Father,' the governor said quietly, 'we must have some respect.'

Father Pat gave a hollow laugh. 'Respect? Respect for what? We're murderers,' he cried at the dwindling audience, 'all of us, because we were here and we let it happen.'

The governor looked shocked, open-mouthed, at the priest's outburst, but some of the scribes were already adding a new dimension to their reports. And then, in the shamefaced silence that followed, Father Pat shook himself free of the guard's gently restraining arm and turned on his heel to the green door.

'Shame on you!' he cried as he left. 'May God forgive you.'

On the train home Father Pat could not contain his tears and to the consternation of those nearby he sobbed bitterly. Back at his church and well into the night, he composed a letter to the *Times*.

*I am sixty-eight years old. My parents came here to a free and democratic country where they could live and work at peace with their fellow human beings. I was born here. I loved this country. I have loved this country all my life, until today.*

*Today I was ashamed of what I saw. Today I saw a young man, a mere boy, strapped to a chair, a ghastly contraption was clamped on his head and thousands of volts of electricity shook his petrified body. To think that one man, any man, could do this to another is unbelievable, the work of the Devil himself. But it happened. I was there. I saw it with my own eyes. And I was ashamed. And now I find that today, here, in the State of New York, two more men were murdered on our behalf in this barbaric way. Three in one day! How can this be? Millions of decent people go about their business, allowing this to happen. What is it? Ignorance of the facts? Indifference? I am guilty and so are you. Every one of us is guilty. This sinful spectacle, carried out in the name of justice with the ravenous wolves of the newspaper business snapping up every morsel, must be stopped. We cannot allow such a practice to continue in our country in the twentieth century.*

*Oh, and by the way, there can be little doubt that the boy I saw die today was innocent. God knows he was innocent and God knows, too, that we are guilty – all of us.*

*

Dan Dolan was doubtful. He had wanted to beat O'Hara to a pulp, kill him even, and when he thought of Nathan, helpless in that hospital bed, he still did. But Baker had calmed him down.

'What you plan to do,' he said, 'is not very clever. It's not worthy of you. You can do better than that.'

Dan shook his head, murder in his heart.

'Look at me,' Baker ordered. 'You're not some crazy Irishman. You got to think this through. You go round there and if you get anywhere near O'Hara you kill him. How? With your bare hands? Have you got a gun, a knife, what? You got no chance. And even if you did somehow get to kill him, what would happen? There'd be a contract on your head. The lowlife of this town would be scrapping to get to you first. You wouldn't last the weekend.'

'So I do nothing'?' Dan demanded. 'Sit back and let him get away with it. That what you're saying?'

'I'm saying you use your head. You don't win with a gun, you win with your brains. And anyway, he's not just yours. I want him, too.'

So Dan had listened and now here he was, walking up to O'Hara's brownstone on Bedford Street on a Sunday afternoon as if he was paying a social call.

The door was opened, as expected, by one of O'Hara's henchmen. The man was dressed in a sober Sunday suit. He looked as though he'd just been to church and now he was expecting family visitors for lunch. Dan brushed passed him into the hallway with its garish pink wallpaper and yellowish oilclothed floor.

Jimmy Pickles was at the foot of the stairs, a glass in his hand. To his right in what would have been the living room in a normal set-up was a bar where three of O'Hara's men were sitting around, apparently half-asleep. Pickles looked up in surprise and said loudly to alert the three in the bar. 'Mr Dolan! To what do we owe this pleasure?'

'I'm here to see Mr O'Hara,' Dan said mildly.

'Yeah?' With a flick of his head at the doorman, Pickles came forward. The doorman frisked Dan for concealed weapons and was satisfied. 'Wait here,' Pickles told Dan as he knocked lightly at the door to the parlour, O'Hara's office, and went inside. Then, though not without a brief delay, he came back to usher Dan in.

O'Hara was seated, as usual, behind his desk in the semi-dark room and Dan wondered what sort of life this was. Sitting in a gloomy office with all visitors vetted and frisked and with one eye on security day and night didn't seem much fun. For all his power and alleged wealth, O'Hara was as trapped as anyone else.

Pickles hovered at the door as O'Hara stood up. O'Hara pointed to a chair and Pickles sat down. Hand extended O'Hara offered Dan a seat by the desk. Then he returned to his own chair, leaning into the light from the desk lamp. 'So what can I do for you, Mr Dolan?'

Dan found his next words difficult to say but he had promised Joe Baker he would go along with his plan. 'I want to put things right between us, Mr O'Hara. I mean, you've won and well, OK, I have to accept that.'

O'Hara made an arch with his fingers. 'Go on.'

'Well, you showed what you could do to my brother. He stepped out of line and you ran him out of town. Now Michael was wrong to disappear like that. He owed you a lot. Not just in the way you smoothed his path as a singer, but financially, too. You must have paved his way with dollars. He couldn't have made it so fast without your help. You were good to him and the way he repaid you was wrong. But I'm asking you to stop hounding him, Mr O'Hara. His career as a performer is over. Surely that's enough. You don't have to find him and … and do whatever you plan to do with him.'

O'Hara remained silent, not giving anything away.

'And then there's Nathan,' Dan went on. 'Your boys beat him up pretty bad. He's in hospital right now and he'll be there for a long time. I went to see him and he swears he has no idea where my brother is. He says he would tell me if he did. So I'm hoping your boys will leave him alone.'

O'Hara's watery eyes never left Dan's. He was silent now for several seconds. Then he said, 'I understand your concern for your brother and your friend, Mr Dolan, but I should tell you that neither I nor my boys admit to any responsibility for what-ever happened to – what was his name? – Nathan. Nor do we admit to putting out what some people in the criminal commu-nity would call "a contract" on your brother's life. But if we did, if we were to admit responsibility for these despicable acts and promised to refrain from such activity in the future, what would be in it for us?'

Dan looked over his shoulder at Pickles, then he leaned forward and lowered his voice. 'You know when I came to the club and you wanted me to help you place your bets on the stock market? Well, if I had your assurance you would call off the hunt for Michael I'd be willing to work for you in that sphere one hundred per cent.'

O'Hara sat back out of the light. 'Interesting. Very inter-esting,' he said quietly. 'An interesting proposition, Mr Dolan.' He was quiet for a moment as if turning the idea over in his mind. Then he said, 'And how would we communicate? Through Barbara Baker?'

It was the clearest admission yet that Baker's wife was involved.

'Oh no,' Dan said emphatically. 'Not Mrs Baker. I don't know why but Joe – I mean, Mr Baker – doesn't like me to have much contact with Mrs Baker.' He smiled wryly. 'Maybe those rather compromising pictures in the newspapers have something to do with it. Better if we do this direct. Or, if you prefer, I could deal with Mr Pickles.'

O'Hara nodded and stood up, holding out a hand. 'Fine, Mr Dolan,' he said with a smile. 'It's a deal.'

Dan stood up, too, and shook the damp, clammy hand, determined not to cringe. 'I don't think we should do the small day-to-day stuff, Mr O'Hara, or people might see me as some kind of financial adviser and that could cause problems on the floor of the Exchange and with Mr Baker. I would prefer to contact you only when the big boys get together to rig the market. It goes on from time to time and the really big money is made. This is what I'm offering. Inside information on the big stuff.'

'Fine.' O'Hara was beaming now. 'That's what we're after. Stay in touch with Jimmy. And if you need to see me at any time you only have to ask.'

'And Michael?' Dan asked.

O'Hara smiled. 'Michael who?'

# TWENTY-TWO

TIM LOOKED OVER his shoulder as he left the village, knowing he was probably seeing it for the last time. There was nothing there for him now, nothing but memories and what remained of a girl, a girl whose lovely wistful face and trusting eyes were gone now. She was gone forever but not from him. Her searching look and the questions he had refused to face for far too long were still there and would always be there, ready to confront him in quiet moments. Kathleen, her hair blowing in the wind or framing her face in the driving rain, her thin cotton dress clinging to the contours of her body, would haunt him, stand before him from beyond the grave and ask him why. Why had he let her love him when he didn't love her? He didn't know why. Maybe it was because he *did* love her. Certainly he had come back aching to see her. He had come back for his mother's sake. But that was only part of it. He knew, if he was honest, he had wanted more than anything to see Kathleen. But he knew, too, that even when he arrived and was ready to face her he had no plan, nothing to offer. He was still confused, his true motive unrealized, and even if Kathleen had been alive he had no idea what he would have said to her.

Would he have held out his arms, renounced the Church, turned his back on the path smoothed out for him? Did his calling count for nothing? Was his vocation gone? Was it ever there? Or was it something others had ordained for him? He didn't know. All he knew was that this all-seeing God Almighty he worshipped had let him down, deserted him and left his head and his heart in turmoil.

He had watched his native shoreline slowly recede, grow fainter, then indistinct and finally disappear in a damp mist that left his hair wet. Only the grey, swelling Atlantic remained. Next stop New York. He didn't know what he would do now in his adopted city. He didn't know what he would tell Father Pat. He was no longer sure of anything and his days at sea did little to help.

Going ashore as a bona fide passenger and not as an immigrant whose next stop was Ellis Island, Tim looked across at the hopefuls detained by a boatswain's rope. Just a few years ago he and his brothers had been like them and it was the same mix now. There were a few older people who had left everything behind to be with their families, but it was mainly young married couples and single men in search of a better future and a prosperity that eluded them at home. And there were children, children of all ages, wide-eyed and bewildered, unaware that *they* were the future and that most of the promises this new country made were made to them.

He walked off into a chilly but bright sunlight and at once the newspaper billboards caught his eye. Four posters in a row said the same thing: DEATH PICTURE INSIDE! READ ALL ABOUT IT! The partial headline he could see under the newsboy's arm read: SING SING. He bought a copy and opened it out as the disembarking passengers swirled about him. RUTH DIES IN SING SING.

The *Daily News* carried a picture of Ruth Snyder, the Brooklyn woman convicted with her boyfriend of murdering her husband. Somehow, by some means that could only have been devious, the man from the *News* had snapped a picture of Ruth Snyder in the electric chair. It was a scoop, a sensation, sordid and sickening. It was all of those things and it was gruesome, too, yet people were clamouring for copies. Tim was jostled, brushed aside, cursed, but he read on, eager now to rejoin the crusade circumstances had forced him to leave.

A *Daily News* reporter had smuggled a camera strapped to his leg into the death chamber and at the moment of Ruth Snyder's death had taken a surreptitious shot as she slumped forward in the chair. Printing a picture like this was disgusting, an insult to every decent human being, Tim told himself. But maybe some good would come of it. Maybe it would put an end to the mindless barbarity or, at least, force the authorities to reconsider.

On every page, it seemed, the paper was filled with righteous indignation at the inhuman killing of a woman in this manner at the same time celebrating its 'world scoop'. A front-page comment condemned the use of the chair as 'savage and archaic, an affront to civilization.' Not content with despatching a woman in this way, Tim read, our *"guardians of Justice" sent three men to their deaths in one day.'*

According to the newspaper the so-called Death Row at Sing Sing had come to resemble a factory floor with an assembly line where prisoners were disposed of in threes. Lower down he read that a Father Patrick Costello had accused the State of whole-sale murder when three men including one of his parishioners, a nineteen-year old boy, were executed within hours of each other. Furthermore, the priest had claimed, the boy, Anthony O'Reilly, was innocent.

Tim closed his eyes. He couldn't believe it. No date had been set for Tony when he left. It usually took a couple of months before any date was confirmed. But, as the paper hinted, Sing Sing had become a fast track conveyor belt. Three in one day and one an innocent boy. He knew he would be haunted now by the spectre of Tony O'Reilly, the boy he had truly believed would be spared, the boy whose sentence, he felt certain, would be commuted.

He was at the bus stop, waiting to go back to his temporary home at the parish church. His first instinct was to see Father Pat, hear what he had to say. But when the trolley came he changed his mind. Without knowing why he stayed on as far as Times Square.

He didn't want to see Father Pat just yet. He was not ready for him. He didn't want to think about Tony O'Reilly. He didn't want to think about Kathy. He didn't want to think about anything.

It was early evening but darkness was falling fast. Already the bright lights of the city were spread out before him. Nearby the green and blue neon of Hannigan's Irish Bar looked warm and inviting. He pushed open the door and was surprised to find the place empty. It was set out like a coffee shop with little bowls of sugar and place mats on the tables. Tim had planned to have a few drinks to help him forget and this was not what he expected. Then he remembered this was the United States and Prohibition.

A short fat man, black hair slicked down in thinning strips, a black walrus moustache and an apron from the waist down was behind the bar.

'Well, hallo there?' he exclaimed genially as if surprised to see a customer and, with a nod at Tim's suitcase, 'Leaving town?'

'Just come back, so I have,' Tim said, matching the man's accent. 'I've been home for a few days.'

'Across the water?' he asked, placing a cup of coffee on the bar.

'Across the water,' Tim confirmed. 'We heard our Ma was ill, my brothers and me, so we decided one of us should go home.'

The barman was impressed, impressed probably that Tim could afford the fare. 'That's good,' he said. 'And how was the lady?'

'She died before I got home.'

'Ah now, that is a shame. And where is home? Dublin?'

'Not far from Dublin.'

'Now we're from Down and some us from Armagh,' he began and Tim felt obliged to listen and nod and look interested as the man went through his family history of the last fifty years. 'Did you not want your coffee?' he asked at last.

'I was looking for a bar, to tell you the truth,' Tim said. 'But I forgot. They don't allow it over here.'

The barman looked at him closely for a moment then held out a hand. 'Gerry McKenna.'

Tim shook his hand. 'Timothy Dolan.'

'Well now, Timothy,' he said. 'You look to me like you're on the level.' He was taking off his apron. 'Come along wit' me.'

Tim lifted his suitcase. 'Could I leave this here?'

'Sure you can.' McKenna put the suitcase behind his counter.

They left Hannigan's Bar, turned off the square and went down a side street. Tim followed the rolling gait of his new found friend. It was much darker here but they had only gone a few yards when McKenna led him down some steep steps between two apartment buildings. He opened an outer door and led Tim down a flagged passage to where he knocked on another door. A grating appeared in the door at eye level and they were scrutinized from within.

'Open up, for God's sake,' McKenna said impatiently and the door opened. 'You'll get yourself a drink in here, Timothy, so you will. Enjoy the crack.'

Tim turned to thank him but McKenna had already gone. He followed the door opener to the end of another passage, wondering where he was being taken, but this time, as the next door opened, the level of noise hit him in the face. The place was tightly packed with people holding drinks chest high.

'You'll get a drink at the bar if you can find it,' the door opener told him and returned to his job.

Tim edged his way gingerly through what was no doubt Hannigan's former clientele. Irish voices everywhere. A burly waiter ordered two swaying drunks to shut up and sit down or he would throw them out so they could fight in peace. Tim smiled. He liked the place already.

Clumsily he bumped into a raised arm, almost causing the owner to spill his precious drink. 'I'm sorry,' he said at once. 'I'm trying to find the bar.'

'Follow me, laddie,' the man said, emptying his glass. 'I'll show ye the best spot to get served and ye can buy me a drink.'

'So I can,' Tim said with a laugh, following him through the crush.

He was a large man and he looked as though he was fond of his drink. He was from a village down in the south east not far from Skibbereen, he told Tim, and as they waited at the bar he started to sing. '*Ah, well I do remember the year of forty eight, we joined the boys of Erin's Isle to fight against the Fate. I was hunted in the mountains, a traitor to the Queen and that is why, my mother dear, I left ol' Skibbereen.*'

'Shut up, Murphy,' the bartender said, 'you'll turn the stout sour.'

'Yes,' Murphy said. 'That's what we'll have. Two pints of the Murphy's, barman. Got to be Murphy's. Me gran'daddy started the brewery in 1848, so he did. Murphy's, the finest stout in the whole of Oireland.'

'Well, if that's the truth,' the bartender said as he drew the pints, 'your gran'daddy must have cut you off without a penny. You never have one when you come in here.' He put the pints on a ledge behind him. 'And who'll be paying?'

'Me, I guess.' Tim put his hand across the bar. 'Timothy Dolan.'

'Was him blew up the Post Office in O'Connell Street,' Murphy said.

'And it was me won the Grand National, so it was,' the bartender said, shaking Tim's hand.

As they watched the stout settle in the time honoured fashion Tim had to smile. Draught stout! Prohibition? Then the moment the drinks were put before them Murphy took a long swig. 'Now that's what I call stout,' he said, a line of froth on his upper lip.

Murphy was full of the blarney but for now Tim was happy in his company. He wanted to drown himself in the black stout and he was deaf to the tuneless singing and the relentless repartee of those around him. Two more pints and they were joined by a large blonde lady in a cheap-looking fur coat.

'Matthew Murphy,' she said, slurring her words as if like most of those present she was already well into the drink. 'You got this fine-looking young fella here and you have not the good manners to introduce me. What kind of friend are you?'

Murphy's eyes seemed out of focus. 'A good friend,' he said and he nodded vaguely in Tim's direction. 'A good friend to him.'

Ignoring the intended rebuff, the blonde lady thrust her large bosom between them and introduced herself. 'Sophie,' she said and she offered Tim her chubby fingers.

Light-headed and flamboyant now, Tim kissed the back of her hand. 'Timothy Dolan, at your service, ma'am.'

'Ooh!' she said suggestively. 'I hope so. And I'll have a jar of the bathtub.'

Tim was quietly amused that he had been picked up so swiftly by a couple of drunks. It was what he needed, an hour or two of brainless banter. He had little idea of time and as the evening wore on others joined their party. Some stayed and some came and went and the only indication that the session was drawing to a close was the increasing number of slurred songs.

All three were wilting now. Tim's eyes were closing, the gin was dribbling down Sophie's chin and even Murphy looked as though he'd had enough.

'And what will you do now you're back, Timothy lad?' Murphy asked, putting an arm around Tim's shoulder.

Tim swayed. 'I'm to join the priesthood.'

'You're to be a priest?' Murphy was astonished. 'Lord God Almighty, Sophie!' he exclaimed. 'We're drinking with a man from the Holy Roman Church. Wasn't I an altar boy myself?'

'Get away with you,' Sophie said scornfully. 'You wouldn't know one end of the church from the other.'

'I was I tell you. Born and bred a Cat'lic, so I was. And you know what they say. Once a Cat'lic, always a Cat'lic.'

'So you're having a last fling, Father?' Sophie asked. 'Is that it? Well now, good for you. There'll be no more of this when you get yourself co-ordinated.'

'*Ordained*,' Murphy corrected her disdainfully.

'That's what I said,' Sophie challenged him.

'Ah, there'll be plenty of this,' Murphy went on. 'Every priest I ever knew was a drinker.' He laughed. 'And that does for you, old girl. You cannot go to bed with a priest.'

'He's not a priest yet,' Sophie said drunkenly. 'I'll take you home, Timo ... Timothy lad, and I'll show you what you'll be missing.'

'If I thought it would save me from that,' Murphy said, 'sure and I would take the collar meself.'

The bartender took Sophie in hand and led her towards a door behind the bar. He smiled at Tim. 'We cannot let her leave here in this state,' he said. 'She would get us closed down, so she would.'

The crowd had thinned now and a small table and a couple of seats were free. Tim and Murphy moved in. 'What does he mean *closed down*? I thought they were not supposed to open up.'

'Ah,' Murphy said, 'the polis know all about this place and so long as it's quiet and there's no trouble, they look the other way.'

Murphy sat back in his seat, legs splayed, his eyes beginning to close, and without realizing it Tim began to talk. He told Murphy about Kathy O'Donnell, how he had found she was dead and that he was responsible. 'I killed her, Murph,' he said. 'It was me.'

Unaware that his companion was barely capable of listening, he confessed to Murphy that he felt unfit to be a priest. He told him about Tony O'Reilly and how he had been unable to help the poor lad, how he failed to keep him out of trouble. He told him, too, how Tony had died in the electric chair and, his mood darkening, how it was all Vincent O'Hara's fault.

He went up to the bar and told the bartender, 'I need to get to this club. It's called the Showcase.'

'Is that a good idea?' the bartender asked mildly. 'They'll be just about opening up and the way you look right now I reckon they wouldn't let you in.'

'Sure they would,' Tim told him. 'I got a date with O'Hara.'

The bartender was impressed. 'You know Vincent O'Hara?'

'I know O'Hara all right,' Tim said, swaying boastfully, though he had never met the man.

'Well, look …' The bartender was worried. He didn't want any trouble with O'Hara's boys and that little rat Pickles. If this kid was supposed to be meeting O'Hara he didn't want O'Hara to think he had been allowed to get into this state here. He put an arm across the bar top. 'Timothy,' he said. 'Come in the back. Let's get some coffee down you, straighten you out.'

'I don't need straightening out.'

'Maybe you do,' he said gently. 'We'll get you a good strong coffee then we'll get you a cab to take you over there.'

# TWENTY-THREE

DAN WAS SEEING Annie's friend, Sue, now. Each week on her free night they would go to one of the top restaurants then on somewhere for a few drinks. Sue was good company and he was fond of her, nothing more. Then one night she made it obvious she wanted to stay the night. It would be a pleasant change, she said, to stay in Dan's elegant apartment, a pleasant change from the room she shared at the German lady's rooming-house.

Dan had misgivings. He had not wanted things to get serious, but he said, 'OK, you go to bed. I'll have the sofa.'

'I don't want the bed,' she said.

'Well, you have the sofa,' he said.

'I don't want the sofa either.' She laughed. 'I can see I'll have to spell it out. What I mean is: I don't want to go to bed on my own.'

'Sue,' he said quietly, 'I thought we were just good friends.'

She laughed again. 'Oh my! You are a country boy, aren't you? We *are* just good friends. But we can be *very* good friends.'

'With no strings?' Dan said. 'There's always strings.'

'No strings,' she said. 'I promise.'

Dan thought of Peg O'Malley. That was fine. No strings and no come backs. But it was Christmas and they had both had a few drinks. Now, with Sue, they were both relatively sober.

'You sure about this?' he asked.

'Absolutely,' she said, and she drew him into the bedroom.

It was good and he was very fond of her and she was fond of him and so far there were no complications. Nobody was getting hurt and few people were any the wiser.

Then one night this happy arrangement was interrupted. They had just come in from dinner and a dance at the Rainbow Room and both were in a pleasantly mellow mood. But then there was a telephone call and it was Jimmy Pickles.

'Hey, Dolan. Jimmy Pickles. I'm at the Showcase. You better get down here – now.'

'Why? What's going on?'

'We got your brother. He's kicking up a stink and I want him out of here – fast.'

'You've got Michael?'

'Nah. It's your other brother. The priest guy. He wants to see the boss but I can't let him do that the state he's in. Looks as though he's been out on the town. He's loaded and he's using some pretty choice language for a holy man.'

'You've got Tim? I didn't know he was back.'

'Well, wherever he's been, he is and you better get down here and take him away or I can't be responsible.'

'Yeah, yeah. I'll be there.' Dan put the phone down and turned to Sue. 'They've got my brother Tim at the Showcase. I don't know what he's doing there but Pickles wants me to pick him up. Seems he's had too much to drink and he's creating a disturbance.'

'You want me to come with you?'

'No, no,' he said decisively. 'I don't want you getting involved with O'Hara or Pickles and I don't want them to know about us.' He kissed her lightly on the cheek. 'You go to bed.'

At the Showcase there was a police wagon outside and a disturbance in the foyer. Pickles, his henchmen alerted, was urging two police officers to restrain Tim. When he saw Dan he hurried over. 'I don't get it,' he said. 'He's quiet one minute, crazy the next.'

'O'Hara!' Tim cried. 'Come out here, murderer!' He was telling the police officers as he struggled, 'It's him you want, not me. He's a murderer. He should be behind bars. No, that's too good for him. He should be in the chair. He's not like Tony O'Reilly. Oh no. He's a *real* murderer.'

The police officers were doing their best to handcuff Tim.

Dan stepped between them and gripped his brother by both shoulders. 'Tim!' he said harshly and he slapped him hard across the face. 'Stop it! Pull yourself together.'

Tim stopped struggling and shook himself free.

'This is my brother, Officers,' Dan explained. 'I'm sorry about this. I'll take care of him now.'

'Oh no,' one of the officers said. 'He's comin' with us. A night in the cooler is what he needs.'

'No, please,' Dan said. 'I'm sure that won't be necessary.'

Vincent O'Hara had appeared now and he, too, intervened. 'Let Mr Dolan take him, gentlemen. I shall not be pressing any charges.'

Dan acknowledged him with a nod. 'Thank you,' he said.

But then Tim looked up, saw O'Hara and erupted again. 'So there you are. White tuxedo, Havana cigar, fancy night club. I'm going to expose you, O'Hara. I'm going to tell the world what you really are.'

'Get him out of here,' O'Hara said, through his teeth.

Dan turned Tim away, pushing him towards the door and out of the foyer on to the sidewalk. Pickles and the two police officers followed.

'Tell Mr O'Hara I'll call him tomorrow,' Dan said apologetically.

Tim seemed to have sobered a little. He glared at Pickles and with a slightly deranged look in his eye he said quietly, 'You tell your boss he is not going to get away with this. He sent that boy Tony O'Reilly to the electric chair and I'll have him if it's the last thing I do.'

Dan hailed a cab but as the driver slowed down he didn't like what he saw and he accelerated and sped away. Dan turned to one of the police officers. 'Any chance of a lift?'

The officer made a face but opened the rear door of the wagon and as they climbed in it occurred to Dan that, though Tim was clearly inebriated, not even the police had asked where he got the booze.

Dan had gone to his office by the time Sue dragged herself from the bed. She was not due at rehearsal until 11.30 but she was not looking forward to it. They had a new choreographer, a young guy eager to make his mark and, as the stage manager said, he was 'a regular pain in the ass'.

She staggered to the bathroom and was surprised to see a man she had never met sprawled out on the sofa in the living room. He appeared to be sleeping, his face creased as if he expected to meet one hell of a hangover the moment he opened his eyes. She went back into the bedroom and pulled on Dan's bathrobe.

When she eventually emerged from the bathroom Tim was sitting up, his head in his hands as he stared at the floor.

Sue laughed. 'As bad as that?'

He looked round. 'Hey! I'm sorry,' he said. 'I didn't know.'

'That's OK,' she said. 'I expect Dan didn't want to wake you. You look as though you've been hit by the hangover to end all hangovers.'

He tried to stand up but she indicated there was no need.

'I've got coffee,' she said, amused by the look on his face.

'I'm Tim,' he said. 'Dan's brother.'

'I guessed that,' she told him, still amused. 'I'm Sue. I worked with Annie, Michael's girl. That's how I met Dan.'

'So now you're Dan's girl?'

'I wish,' she said.

Tim was surprised. 'A fair assumption?'

She laughed. 'I guess so. We're just good friends, as they say. And before you say it, yes, we're *very* good friends.'

'Hey, look!' Tim said. 'None of my business.'

She handed him a cup of coffee. 'So what's with the hangover? I understood you were the one going into the Church.'

'Yeah,' he said, with a grimace. 'So did I.'

This was not just a flippant response. Recent events had seriously questioned his commitment. Did he have a vocation? Did he really want to live the celibate life of a priest? He was not sure. The only thing he knew for certain was that if Kathy O'Donnell was here he would sweep her into his arms.

'Second thoughts?' Sue asked.

'I don't know. I don't know what the hell I think. But hey! Let's talk about you.'

'Nothing to say. I'm crazy about your brother, but if I tell him I lose him and I'd rather have him on his terms than not at all.'

'That's sad,' Tim said, thinking again of Kathy and the pain and sadness of a lost romance. 'Does he know how you feel?'

'I guess not. There's something …' She hesitated. 'Sometimes, when I'm with him, it's as if he's not really there as if he's with someone else. Is there someone? Someone back home maybe?'

'I don't think so. Always plenty of girls, but no one special.'

'Well, there's something holding him back.'

'Probably ambition,' Tim said. 'He's wrapped up in this job of his right now. Maybe when he's made his millions …'

'If that's all it is, fine,' she said. 'But if he's carrying a torch for someone else I'd like to know.'

'Ah!' Father Pat said. 'You're back, so you are. I'll be with you in just a minute and you can tell me all your news.' He was standing on the path outside his church as he looked up to where two workmen were examining a corner of the roof.

'What's going on?' Tim asked, well aware that before he left the restoration fund had nowhere near reached its target.

'Great news, Timothy! We're to get a new roof after all. Just this morning a benefactor came forward promising to put up all the dough we need. Hoping to book his place in Heaven I guess.'

'That's great,' Tim said. 'Who is he?'

'A local businessman,' Father Pat said evasively, 'Good Catholic boy he was once, or so he tells me. Fallen away a bit since, fallen quite a long way, in fact.'

Tim gripped his arm. 'Who is he, Father?'

'Welt,' Father Pat said, pulling away, 'I don't suppose you'll approve, but if we don't accept this very generous offer and fix this roof now we'll have much bigger problems later on. How the man came by his money is between him and his God. The Church will be here when he's gone.'

'You're talking about O'Hara,' Tim said in disbelief.

'If he wants to ease his conscience that's—'

'The man's a murderer. He sent Tony O'Reilly to the electric chair. His money comes from organized crime, booze, extortion, protection rackets, prostitution. He stole that money.'

'And we're stealing it back,' the priest said. He put a fatherly arm around Tim's shoulder. 'Listen, son. Men who live like O'Hara don't live long. Sooner or later they get what's coming to them. Give it time. He'll be dead and we'll have a new roof.'

'And what does he expect in return?'

'Well, I know you've been back a bit longer than you're letting on and you've been giving him a hard time. Preaching about the evil gangster in our midst. He wants me to call you off.'

'No chance,' Tim said, inwardly fuming.

'That's what I told him,' Father Pat said and he laughed. 'But not until I'd taken his cheque.'

'It'll probably bounce.'

'He can't pull out now,' the priest said. 'I told the newspapers.'

Spring came early that year, the sun slanting down between the tall buildings, the park an inviting green oasis at the top of the Avenue, out of the swirl of hurrying feet and away from the clamour of honking automobiles. It was one Saturday morning when, as he often did, Dan took a stroll as far as the boating lake and back to find a bench where he could sit for a while.

The previous Saturday morning he had run into Paul Merrick. Merrick had been sitting on a bench, enjoying the new green leaves on the overhanging trees and the rippling sunlight on the water, and he was there again today.

'We can't go on meeting like this,' Dan said with a grin.

Without a word Merrick moved along the bench for Dan to sit down.

'You OK?' Dan asked after a moment.

'Yes and no,' Merrick said. 'I can see where I want to go but I am not sure how to get there.'

'Want to tell me about it?'

He shrugged. 'Where to begin?'

'You can start by telling me what it is with you and Joe Baker.'

Merrick looked at him sidelong then appeared to make up his mind. 'If you wish.'

Dan leaned forward.

'My partner and I set up this company,' he said. 'Bailey and Merrick. I was the junior partner. It was Bailey's money. We put up the capital for small businesses to expand. Same as Baker, only he was much bigger. We did well and Baker wanted to buy us out. He made us a pretty good offer. Bailey wanted to retire so he took the money and the deal was Baker must keep me on for three years or pay me fifty thousand dollars.

'This was fine by me. I wanted to go and the fifty thousand dollars was just what I needed. Baker said he was happy with this and I could leave at the end of the month. Then I made my mistake. Big big mistake. I got involved with *Mrs* Baker, the dangerous Barbara.'

It was beginning to make sense. 'And Joe found out?'

Merrick nodded. 'Barbara went to Miami for a few days, the Fontainebleau Hotel, and I met her there. She told Baker she was visiting an aunt or something and I was to check on a company in St Louis. I spent one day in St Louis then I flew to Miami. But Baker called the Fontainebleau to speak to Barbara and I picked up the phone.'

Dan shook his head. 'Not a good idea.'

'We were expecting a call from room service.' He laughed. 'I expected to be fired. But I didn't mind. I was happy to take the fifty thousand dollars and go. But no, Baker wouldn't have that. He's kept me on for three years and he knows this isn't what I want.'

'What *do* you want, Paul?'

'I want to go to the coast, out West, go into the movie business. This is the future, Dan. I want to make movies.'

He became animated at the mention of the movie business.

'Two friends of mine, fellow countrymen, boys I came with to America, are there now and they're doing OK. They put up fifty thousand each and the offer was for me to join them. But I can't.

I don't have the money. The three years will soon be up and I won't even have a job.'

'You know plenty of people at the Exchange.'

He shook his head. 'Baker has finished me there.'

'He wouldn't do that.'

'He would and he has. There is a side to Joe Baker you don't know, Dan. I put a little money together and he let me believe he and his friends were buying big. This is what they do. They pick out a stock. They all buy at the same time and they all sell at the same time. Make big money.'

'Is that legal?'

'They make the law at the Exchange. The little man can't win. I bought a share I thought would bring me close to my fifty thousand. Then when they all sold and he knew the price was going down he didn't tell me. I lost the little money I had and now I have nothing. I have to start again.'

'So he was paying you back.'

'He was.'

They were silent for a moment as a group of boys rode by on bicycles. Young mothers paraded new babies in their sparkling high-handled perambulators. A couple of ice-cream vendors gesticulated angrily and argued in Italian over who the corner pitch belonged to. And Dan didn't know what to say.

'So what about Barbara?' he asked at last. 'Why didn't he kick her out there and then?'

'Good question,' Merrick said. 'He knows now what she is because I told him.'

'Why?' Dan asked innocently. 'What is she?'

'She's a high-class whore. Or she was until she met Baker. All those girls are linked to criminals. Barbara was one of Vincent O'Hara's girls. I wouldn't be surprised if she still is.'

'Joe must know that.'

'I am sure he does,' Merrick agreed. 'But he works in some strange ways. He'll get rid of her when he's ready.'

Dan's loyalties were divided. 'He's not a bad guy, Paul.'

'He's OK,' he conceded, 'and if I hadn't betrayed him ...' He shrugged resignedly. 'I thought I could do anything I wanted, but I was wrong. And Joe Baker doesn't forget. I was a fool and when Barbara said come with me I followed.'

'Why does he need her? She's not like a real wife.'

'She's not a wife. They're not married. Joe is a big man at the Exchange. He attends dinners, functions. He needs something on his arm.' Merrick stood up. 'And I need a drink.'

They strolled out of the Park and dodged their way across to the back alley bar where they knew they would be welcome and the bartender would be pleased to serve them. Merrick wanted to talk about his plans for the future. He'd had enough of his problems with Joe Baker.

He was Hungarian, he told Dan. Jewish. His name was not Paul Merrick. It was Ferenc Matthau. Like so many immigrants he had changed his name. He wanted to get into the film business. He was convinced he could make it big in the movies. Not acting, he said with a laugh. He wanted to produce. Two of his fellow Hungarians were already big producers in Hollywood. William Fox was running his own Fox Film Company and there was Adolph Zukor, another big name. But it was no good starting at the bottom. It could take years.

'Why don't you go to Joe?' Dan suggested. 'Tell him you made a terrible mistake and you've regretted it ever since. You let him down and you're sorry. Not just because you were found out but because you know now it was a lousy thing to do. You were young and stupid. OK? Tell him you want to go out West. You want to make movies. Convince him it's the next big money spinner. He's a businessman. He likes to be in on things, especially new things. He might even back you.'

Merrick shook his head. 'To Joe Baker I'm nothing.'

Dan was grateful to Paul Merrick. The picture was much clearer now and he was convinced more than ever that Barbara Baker was still working for O'Hara. He wished Merrick well and he wished, too, he could help him get into the movie business. He was right. Movies were big news. Already there were over 350 movie houses or nickleodeons in New York City. According to Paul, thousands went to the movies on week nights, many a bored housewife went in the afternoons and probably half a million people went on a Sunday, and now there were the new talking pictures. It was only a nickel to get in, ten cents for two.

He remembered soon after they arrived, when they were living at Peg O'Malley's, the newspapers were full of pictures of the funeral of the silent movie star, Rudolph Valentino. The 'papers reckoned that over a hundred thousand people lined the streets of Manhattan to catch a glimpse of the cortége as it made its way to St Malachy's, the Catholic church on West 49ᵗʰ. Then there was the first big 'talkie', *The Jazz Singer* in 1927 with Al Jolson, and the next big thing was a musical, *The Broadway Melody*. If Michael is in California, Dan thought fondly, maybe we'll see him singing on the screen one day.

He was still thinking of Paul Merrick and how he could help him when he turned off the Avenue and saw that his brother, Tim, was there, waiting for him. 'Getting to be a habit,' he said with a laugh. 'Turning up unexpected.'

'I want to talk to you,' Tim said, clearly agitated.

Dan sat beside him on the stoop and listened as he raged against Father Pat. 'That crazy Costello,' he complained. 'You know what he's done. He's only made a deal with that evil bastard O'Hara.'

'Tell me about it,' Dan said, 'and watch your language. I thought you were back to being a priest.' Dan was aware that Tim had been causing trouble with his denunciations of O'Hara around the parish and close to O'Hara's house on Bedford Street. It was a dangerous game he was playing. He listened to what Tim had to say then told him, 'Father Pat is right. Take the money. Fix the roof. And you stop rocking the boat.'

'What!' Tim exploded. 'You, too?'

'Listen to me,' Dan said. 'I don't want to tell you this, but if it'll stop you from getting yourself bumped off I will.'

'Tell me what?'

'You keep getting on O'Hara's back and you'll probably have a little accident. Go and work in the Church where you're needed. Trust me, O'Hara will be dealt with once and for all. My boss, Joe Baker, can pull a lot more strings than either of us and, I promise you, he's working on a plan to put O'Hara out of business.'

'What can *he* do against a mobster like O'Hara?'

'Don't ask questions. Believe me, Vincent O'Hara will be well and truly fixed.' Dan put his hand up as Tim opened his mouth. 'I said no questions.'

Tim was reluctant to drop the subject but he recognized the look on his brother's face. 'OK, but it had better be soon.'

'Just do as I say,' Dan insisted. Then he smiled. 'Have you eaten today? No, of course not. Well, let's go see your pals at Hannigans.'

Tim laughed. 'They won't be open at this time.'

'It's a coffee shop. We can get a sandwich or something.'

They set off walking and Tim was quiet for a while, then he said, 'I saw your girl.'

'Sue? Yeah, she told me. But she's not exactly my girl.'

'She's lovely, Dan. You should hold on to her. You know, sometimes we don't realize what we have until we lose it.'

# TWENTY–FOUR

I N 1928 AND 1929 the good times were still rolling. New Yorkers were enjoying the biggest, the longest binge in history. Yet at the NYSE few counselled caution as small investors, many of them first time buyers in the market, still rushed to risk their precious savings. Everyone was getting rich. Why shouldn't they?

But behind the scenes, unknown to the vast majority of investors, an exclusive group of 'insiders' was controlling and manipulating share prices and one stock in particular, Radio again, pioneered by the indefatigable Michael Meehan, was the focus of their attention. In the early months of 1928 Radio had climbed to an unprecedented $420 a share. Radio executives, noting that the price was too high for the small investor, decided the shares would be divided on a five for one basis, each shareholder receiving five new shares for every one old share held.

It was when the new shares began trading that Michael Meehan took a hand. Contacting fifty or so prominent traders he invited them to join with him in a syndicate to trade a million Radio shares. It was an offer most of them found impossible to refuse. Within a few days Radio was heavily traded between members of the syndicate, the stock began to climb again and the newspapers took the bait. Radio shares were portrayed as 'the next big thing', 'a real buy', 'a must have stock'. The surge in buying, it was said, had come because the company was about to launch a huge programme of expansion. Orders came in from all over the country.

Few questioned what was happening. Apart from the odd wry comment from a perceptive columnist that this was simply about 'whipping up the market', the newspapers excited people with lines like 'a chance to make easy money' and 'too good to miss'. Within a week the price of a new Radio share jumped to $109.

Joe Baker, long time friend and confidante of Michael Meehan, was well aware of what was going on. He saw, in his membership of the syndicate, the opportunity he had been waiting for. Just before the new Radio shares started to take off he instructed Dan Dolan to contact Vincent O'Hara and tell him what was about to happen. He should buy big in Radio stock, sit back and watch his money grow. O'Hara invested a quarter of a million dollars.

The wily old veteran then explained his plan. The big boss, as Dan knew, the controller of all the criminal gangs in the city at that time, was known as The Englishman and Manhattan Island was divided into well-defined areas for the purpose of organized crime. O'Hara's patch, mainly on the Lower West Side included Broad Street and Wall Street and the NYSE. The Englishman had long set his sights on what he believed should produce rich pickings in that corner of his domain and it was O'Hara's job to find a way in.

O'Hara had hoped Barbara Baker, a girl he knew as Barbara Barosnikov from a Bulgarian immigrant family, a girl who was a high-class hooker when he recruited her into his favoured circle, could find that way in. He had engineered her first meeting with Joe Baker, but since moving in with Baker, a man at the centre of the Wall Street action, she had achieved little. The fact that O'Hara now had Dan Dolan under his control was none of her doing either and in O'Hara's eyes she was enjoying just a little too much the high life and easy time she was having with Baker.

Joe Baker fully understood O'Hara's position. The Englishman, he guessed, had become more than a little disenchanted with O'Hara's failure to deliver. What O'Hara wanted, *needed*, was to find a cast-iron certainty for his boss.

Now Dan was beginning to understand. O'Hara is given the big tip, he invests heavily and the syndicate pull the plug. It was more than that, Baker told him. Just watch what happens. As expected, O'Hara invested his own money and with an air of triumph he couldn't wait to pass on his inside information to his boss. The Englishman invested more than $2 million.

Dan was wide-eyed. 'So if they fall, O'Hara falls with them.'

'With any luck,' Baker said with a grin, 'yeah.'

They didn't have long to wait. On Monday, March 18, almost all the Radio shares held by members of the syndicate were sold and the price fell dramatically. Thousands of small investors were left holding stock they had bought when the price was at its peak.

At Post 12 that day Dan caught up with Baker on an Exchange floor littered with paper and crowded with frantic shirt-sleeved clerks as the ticker tapes went wild. 'Looks like it worked,' he shouted above the din. 'I reckon I better get lost for a while.'

'No,' Baker called back. 'You're OK. I got Mike Meehan to pull O'Hara's shares at the top so he's done pretty well.'

'You did what? I don't get it. What's going on?'

Baker ushered him out of the hall and into the relative quiet of a corridor. 'I want you to call O'Hara. OK? Tell him Radio shares have taken a big dive. But he needn't worry. You pulled his out at the top and he's made a nice little pile.'

Dan still didn't understand.

'You didn't know anything about The Englishman's invest-ment,' Baker said, 'so you couldn't save it. He loses the lot. Cool couple of million. So when you've called O'Hara you call this number and ask to speak to the man himself.'

He handed Dan a piece of paper with a telephone number.

'Do I call him that? The Englishman?'

'Yeah, you do,' Baker asserted. 'A lot of people assume he's Irish like most of the clowns he employs – no disrespect, Daniel – but he doesn't like that. For some reason he's very proud of being English. OK? So you call him up, tell him he's been double-crossed. Vin O'Hara pulled his own money out at the top and he expected him, The Englishman, to lose all his dough. The word is O'Hara is planning to take over Manhattan.'

'Will I get through to him?'

'Use your natural charm, Danny Boy. But don't forget to call O'Hara first. Oh, and you don't call The Englishman from the office and you don't tell him who you are. OK? You can call him from a drugstore. Get off now, do what you have to do.'

'What about you?' Dan asked him. Pops didn't look well. He seemed to be more short of breath than usual and, though he never looked the picture of health, his thin, lined face now had a greyish tinge. He seemed very tired, weary almost. Tired of life maybe, Dan thought. He had never seen the old man like this before. 'I'll make the calls and I'll come back for you.'

'No need,' Baker said airily. 'I'll call a cab.'

Whether Pops liked it or not, Dan decided, he would consult the doctor at the first opportunity. Just as soon as he had made these two calls, in fact.

He took a cab part of the way then he walked up to Madison. At Pershing Square there was a corner café. He would make his calls from there, he decided, get them over with, but there was only one booth and it was occupied. Dan ordered coffee at the counter. He thought of O'Hara and his sidekick Jimmy Pickles. What would happen to them? The Englishman was crazy, well known for his unforgiving nature. It could mean the end for O'Hara. But Dan had no qualms about that. O'Hara was a parasite. He used people and he didn't care who he hurt. If his time was up, then so be it.

Across the way several tall posters of boxers in a fighting pose advertised forthcoming fights. There had not been a really great fighter since Jack Dempsey, Dan thought. But then, it was said, the crime lords controlled much of boxing these days. Many fights, even some of the biggest fights, were fixed.

The girl from behind the counter was out front clearing tables. 'Hey, mister!' she called. 'Telephone's free.'

Dan nodded and went into the booth, closing the door behind him. When he got through it was Jimmy Pickles who answered.

'Dolan,' he said. 'I need to speak to your boss.'

'About what?' Pickles demanded.

'Boss, please,' Dan said.

Pickles swore but handed the receiver to O'Hara.

'What do you want?' O'Hara asked.

'That's no way to greet a colleague,' Dan told him with a laugh. 'I don't know if you heard the news but Radio shares took a big dive this morning and they're still diving.' He waited for this to sink in, then he said, 'But no need to worry. I saw it coming and I pulled you out at the top. Plenty of people have lost money and they're still losing, but not you. You've done pretty well, I'd say. Made quite a killing.'

'People have lost money?' O'Hara asked weakly.

'Oh, sure,' Dan said. 'Big time. But not you.'

The line went dead and, with a smile, Dan immediately called the number Pops had given him.

'Yeah?' a rough voice answered.

'I need to speak to The Englishman.'

'Oh yeah? About what?'

'If you're not The Englishman you put him on fast or you'll be sorry. I've got some very hot news for him.'

'Who is this?'

'I said put him on. Now! Or I hang up and he won't thank you when he finds out what's happened and he didn't know about it.'

Dan could sense the tension, then a calm even voice came on and asked quietly, 'Who is this?'

'Doesn't matter who I am,' Dan said, matching the reasonable tone. 'If you *are* The Englishman I have some information.'

'Go on.'

'Your investment in Radio shares, the shares Vincent O'Hara recommended, they took a big dive today. O'Hara told you Radio shares were the next big thing. And they were. Until today. Push up the price and get out at the top. Let the suckers take the rap. That was the deal and you thought you were in on it. Well, looks like he double-crossed you, Mr English. He pulled his dough out last night when the price was almost double what he paid. But then they went into a pretty steep dive and they're still diving. He didn't warn you, did he? Oh no. He wants you cleaned out. Rumour has it O'Hara plans to take over the whole of Manhattan, leave you out on a limb. Be seeing you, Mr English. Begging for dimes, no doubt. It's goodbye the Big Time, hello Skid Row!'

'Who is this?' the voice that was rarely raised almost screamed down the phone but Dan Dolan had hung up.

When Nathan O'Shaughnessy was at last discharged from the hospital he was ready for work and raring to go. Sadly his job had already gone. He was bitter at first. Promoting music was the only business he wanted to be in. But then he decided maybe O'Hara's gorillas had done him a favour. He had a steel pin in his jaw, he conceded, but his head was still screwed on OK. He decided this was a chance to make a fresh start.

Like radios, sound boxes, phonographs and gramophones were selling in thousands nationwide and 75r.p.m records were selling with them. Already Columbia, Decca and HMV were household names and the little dog listening to His Master's Voice was a national treasure, recognized by everyone. The knack is, Nathan told himself, to provide the masses with what they want and he was sure he could do this. He would go into business on his own. He would launch a new record label and he would begin by changing his name. Overnight he became Nathan Shaw. All he needed now was the necessary capital.

Anxious to help, Dan arranged an interview for him with Joe Baker then one rainy afternoon in late March Nathan made his pitch. He would target the mass market, popular acts singing popular songs. Jolson, Cantor, Rudy Vallee, some young guys called The Rhythm Boys, Paul Whiteman, the Casa Loma Orchestra, the list was endless.

'And how will you get these people?' Baker asked, quietly amused. 'Surely they'll all be under contract.'

'I'm working on it,' Nathan told him. 'But that's the big stuff. To start with I got a good line in bread and butter records. These will provide a steady flow of funds to build on. Specialized music for immigrant groups.'

One of his first records, he explained, would be a mixture of traditional Italian music, Neapolitan love songs, operatic tenors, heart-breaking stuff aimed at the homesick. And Yiddish songs for the many Jewish communities across the country. 'I can corner the market in this stuff,' he said. 'Give the business a solid base.'

For half an hour Nathan enthused over his plans and Joe Baker listened, his lined face giving nothing away. Then Baker glanced at his watch and held up a hand. 'Thank you, son,' was all he said and he indicated the interview was over.

Nathan was desperately anxious to know what Baker thought but there was no way of knowing. He left the building wondering if he had overplayed the sales patter. He couldn't wait to meet up with Dan later. Dan had said his boss was a man who would make up his mind fast, not keep him waiting. If it was no, Dan said, that would be the end of it. There were no second chances with Joe Baker. If it was yes, he would say so and the money would be up front right away.

When Dan arrived that evening Nathan studied his expression but Dan kept a straight face. 'So it's no dice,' Nathan decided despondently. 'Down the pan! So what do I do now?'

'You start making plans, Mr Nathan Shaw. That's what you do' Dan told him quietly. 'You're up and running.'

Nathan let out a yell of delight, his fist in the air.

'Baker,' Dan told him, 'was impressed with your energy and enthusiasm, but not with all those big names you reeled off. That was a mistake. You don't have any of them and you have no chance of getting them. But he did like the idea of the specialized stuff. Italian music, Jewish music. Reckons you're on to something there. He believes you can build that solid base you mentioned, then maybe go for the big names. Good foundations, he says. What every business has to have if it's going to succeed.

'He's offering twenty-five grand start up,' Dan said seriously, 'and maybe more as you go along. For that he wants a twenty per cent share.'

Nathan was delighted but then he thought again about the offer. 'Twenty per cent? That's a big share, Dan. Only leaves me with eighty per cent and I do all the work.'

'Well, right now you've got a hundred per cent of nothing.'

'So what does it mean exactly?' Nathan was calculating the cost. 'If I make fifty grand, he gets ten.'

'But that's after you've paid yourself a salary and covered your costs. What have you got to lose?'

'You're right,' Nathan said, 'but what's he like to work for?'

'He's OK,' Dan assured him. 'He'll expect a financial report at the end of the year and maybe he'll have something to say. But you will own eighty per cent of the company remember.'

'Yeah,' Nathan acknowledged. 'What else did he say?'

'Nothing much, except he likes your ideas about the specialized stuff. Italian songs. Jewish songs. Nostalgia must be pretty high right now with immigrant families, especially the older generation.' Dan smiled. 'But it might be a while before you clear fifty grand.'

Tim was confused. Before he went home he was sure of who he was and what he wanted. Now he was not sure of anything. Maybe his mother's death was partly an act of God, designed to make him stop and think before he made an irrevocable decision. He sat in the empty church and gazed at the ornate altar. He looked around at the twelve stations of the cross. Was he being tested? Jesus was tested. St Peter was tested. Why shouldn't *he* be tested?

He could get up now, walk away. He could walk up to Hannigan's where he knew he could find a temporary bed. But that was silly, he told himself. He was just being melodramatic. He knew he could always sleep on Dan's floor. Dan would feed and clothe him, take care of him as he always had. But he was on his own now. He must make up his own mind on this. It was his decision, his alone. He went outside in search of Father Pat but Father Pat was not there. The only sound was the muffled, sporadic conversation of the workmen on the roof.

Tim knocked lightly on Father Pat's door and looked in. Father Pat was sitting by the window, his Bible open in his hand. For a moment Tim thought he had intruded on his daily meditation, but Father Pat looked over the tiny spectacles that were secured on one side by a thin twist of wire and beckoned him in.

A coal fire glowed red in the polished blackleaded grate. There was a sofa, a deep armchair, a sideboard with a new-looking radio, and a small bookcase the parishioners had bought for him to mark his twenty-fifth year at the church. There was a row of books on theology and pastoral work and several of the slim white diocesan newsletters that arrived every month. On the bottom row there were several cowboy books by Zane Grey and others.

'Have you fed yourself today?' Father Pat asked.

'Yeah, yeah, thank you, Father,' Tim said. 'I've been with our Dan.'

'Good boy Dan,' the priest said for no particular reason. 'What does he have to say for himself?'

'Nothing much,' Tim said. 'I told him about O'Hara and the roof and he said you're right to take the money.'

Father Pat nodded.

'And I should lay off O'Hara.'

'And will you?'

Tim shrugged. 'Maybe.'

'You got other things to think about right now. That it? You're having doubts, so you are, and that's how it should be.' Father Pat put the bible down and looked at Tim searchingly. 'You're having doubts about the priesthood.'

Tim nodded. 'I don't know if I could ever be a good priest. I don't know if I've got what it takes.'

'Oh, you got what it takes. It's whether it's what you really want.'

'I don't know if I'm smart enough,' Tim said. 'I make mistakes.'

'Well now, that's a great start!' Father Pat smiled. 'If you actually *know* you make mistakes that's half the battle. Some people are never wrong. Some people think they're infallible. They think they're the Holy Father.'

Tim glanced at Father Pat quickly, looking for a hint of a

smile. He could never tell what Father Pat was really thinking. At times he didn't seem like a priest at all. 'Do you make mistakes?'

'Oh sure,' Father Pat told him. 'Sure I do. I made a pretty big mistake over Tony O'Reilly. But it's too late now.'

'What did you do?'

'I wrote that letter to the newspapers, didn't I? It was wrong. I shouldn't have done it.'

'It was good. Sure you should have done it. Let everyone know what it was like, how awful it was.'

'Let everyone know how awful it was? You mean, like Tony's ma and little Francis?'

Tim nodded, understanding.

'I may be a priest, Tim, but I'm a man, too. Just a man. I get things wrong. Being a priest doesn't change that.'

They were silent for a moment then Father Pat said, 'I don't know what happened when you went home. Something did for sure. But that's your business not mine. If you believe you're being tested then you probably are. We all get tested along the way. Some of us come through it, some of us don't. For some, what there is gets broken and can't be mended. For others, what there is gets broken but the break heals and what was broken is stronger than before.'

# TWENTY-FIVE

FRIDO'S WAS A small diner on the corner of Grove Street and Bedford. The correct pronunciation was *Freedo's* but the neighbourhood kids who terrorized the little Italian owner called it 'Friedeggs'. Jimmy Pickles would arrive there most mornings for what he liked to call his brunch because that was what the nobs on Park Avenue called it. It came after the breakfast rush but before the lunchtime crush so he often had the place to himself.

This morning he ordered his usual 'two fried sunny-up with a side of hash browns' but before he could sit down Frido himself came from the kitchen and handed him a piece of paper. 'Hey, Jimmy,' he said. 'Guy wants you to call this number.'

Jimmy Pickles knew the number well. He went into the booth and closed the door. 'Pickles,' he said.

A low gruff voice. 'Any of the boys with O'Hara?'

'Should be at this time. Two, I guess.'

'Tell 'em to get out of there fast. Then you go home and stay home. Now, OK? We'll be in touch. You got fifteen minutes.'

Pickles rushed from the booth. 'Sorry, kid,' he told the waitress who was about to deliver his order and he raced along Bedford Street to O'Hara's place. Few people were about mid-morning and the house, too, was quiet. He went in silently and down the passage to the back room where two of the boys were lounging, one asleep, the other with his head in the *Daily News*.

'Come on, fellas,' he said quietly. 'You got to get out – fast.'

The sleeper came awake as the other asked, 'What's going on?'

'If you want to live you got to leave now,' Pickles told him. 'Go on, beat it. I'll be in touch.'

The two looked at each other then took off – fast. Pickles was about to follow when the door to O'Hara's 'office' opened and O'Hara appeared.

'Hey, Jimmy!' he said. 'Come in here.'

He went back inside and Pickles followed dutifully as he always had.

O'Hara had an open suitcase on his desk, the door to the wall safe hung open and the safe looked empty. 'I want you to go home, pack a bag and bring the car round. Fast as you can. You and me, we're going to take a little vacation.'

Pickles nodded. He was anxious to leave. Time was running out. 'Sure, boss,' he said and he turned to go.

'And Jimmy.' It was not a hot day but there were beads of perspiration, Pickles noticed, on O'Hara's forehead and upper lip. O'Hara looked at his watch. 'Ten minutes, OK?'

Again Pickles nodded and he turned and ran. But he didn't go home and he didn't pack a bag or bring the car around. He ran across the road and into a dressmaker's shop where he stood by the window with a good view of the house.

'Can I help you, young man?' the elderly seamstress asked.

'It's OK, ma'am,' he said apologetically.

She knew who he was. Most people in the neighbourhood knew who he was. Nervously she went back to her sewing but, her hands trembling, she couldn't pick up where she left off.

The boys had got the message and they had left the house in a hurry. Now he, too, had run away. Rats leaving a sinking ship came to mind, but Jimmy Pickles had no qualms about that. He knew his boss had something going with the stock market and he knew the big boss was involved. But O'Hara had never cut him in. If things had gone wrong – and he had heard the rumours – then maybe it was just as well.

Across the street a black Buick drew up by O'Hara's house. Two men in trilby hats and overcoats got out, leaving the driver with the engine running. They might have looked like a couple of businessmen but without making any attempt to conceal it one was carrying a Thompson sub-machine-gun.

Resolutely they walked up the steps and the first man kicked open the front door. O'Hara was in the hallway. He knew at once who they were and why they had come.

'Hey, fellas,' he said desperately. He was holding a small case and he balanced this on one knee. 'Look,' he said, 'I know what this is all about but we can make a deal, can't we?' He opened the case slightly to show them it was packed with dollar bills then he closed the case up and held it out. 'You boys can keep the dough yourselves. You can say you just missed me. I already left.'

The first man took the case and stood aside as the man with the machine-gun stepped forward. O'Hara's fleshy mouth dropped open and he turned and ran. He ran for the stairs but calmly the machine-gun was levelled and he was less than halfway up the stairway when the bullets ripped across his broad back. He turned to look at the gunman but then he fell, his large bulk crashing to the bottom step.

The man holding the case walked forward, turned O'Hara's body over with his foot and, to make absolutely certain took a .38 Smith & Wesson automatic pistol from inside his overcoat, aimed at O'Hara's forehead and pulled the trigger. Then, as quietly and as swiftly as they came, the two men left.

Jimmy Pickles heard the muffled sounds of gunshot and dashed from the dressmaker's shop. His instructions were to go home and stay there and he ran there now. He had only been home a few minutes when the same two men walked into his apartment.

He was scared now, not sure what would happen. 'I got the message,' he said brightly. 'I'm just waiting for Bluey.'

'Bluey won't be coming,' one said. 'We sent him to Trenton.'

'And he won't be coming back,' the other told him quietly.

Jimmy was really scared now. Jimmy Pickles, whose true name was Pickering, had been recruited almost from school by O'Hara's predecessor, Patsy Doyle. It was Doyle who first called him Jimmy Pickles and the name had stuck. Then when the big boss was in hospital convalescing after someone took a shot at him, Doyle got a little too ambitious and made it plain he planned to take over. But the big boss recovered and Doyle was swiftly eliminated. Vin O'Hara took his place and he kept Pickles on. Pickles knew he had made many enemies during O'Hara's rein but O'Hara had been his insurance.

The first man was at the window. He was looking out across the dismal rooftops, but the second man had somehow got in behind Pickles where he deftly removed his Italian silk scarf, slipped it over Pickles' head and pulled it tight around his throat.

Pickles struggled madly for several seconds, his hands clawing at the scarf, but it was no good. The man's grip was too strong and the life slowly drained from Pickles' slight body. Calmly the strangler removed the scarf and put it back around his own neck. Then, as quietly as they came, the two killers left.

It was front page news. *GANGLAND KILLINGS! TOP GANG BOSS MOWN DOWN!* Cloth-capped newsboys waved special editions at passers-by. 'Extra! Extra! Read all about it!'

Mrs O'Reilly nodded. But it was not, she said, going to bring her Tony back. Frankie punched the air in delight. The man was dead and no one, not a soul in the Irish community mourned his death.

At the church Tim Dolan held up the evening newspaper. 'I hope you didn't have anything to do with this, Father,' he said with a grin.

'The power of prayer,' Father Pat said.

It had worked perfectly but it was on Dan's conscience. He had made a phone call he knew might result in another man's death. That the man was evil and deserved to die was irrelevant. He just wished it could have happened in some other way, a way in which he, Dan Dolan, was not involved. But when he mentioned this to his boss all Baker said was, 'World's a better place without O'Hara.'

'The world is full of O'Haras,' Dan said. 'Plenty more like him.'

'Oh, sure,' Baker agreed. 'But he was *our* O'Hara.'

It was a quiet afternoon and for once they were in the office together. On Joe Baker's instructions Dan had come back from the Exchange earlier than usual. Apparently Baker was setting up some deal and he wanted Dan present.

Dan had noticed a change in his boss. It was gradual at first, now it had become more obvious. Not for the first time, Baker had decided not to go down to Wall Street. That morning he had remained in the office with a mumbled excuse about calls he needed to make. He had told Dan to go without him and report back, Dan guessed he was simply dodging the brisk walk down the avenue he had made for years without getting out of breath. Some days he seemed to struggle now to breathe and sometimes, though he thought no one noticed, he would hold on to the back of a chair for support.

Sitting behind his wide desk he picked up the paper Dan had brought in. 'Gangland killing!' he read aloud and with an air of amusement. 'The most feared gang boss in NY City was rubbed out today.' Baker laughed. 'Most feared gang boss? Whoever wrote this stuff ain't met The Englishman.'

He looked at Dan over the top of the newspaper and Dan saw, in that instant, just how much he had aged these past two years.

'Yeah, well,' Dan said, 'I'm glad it's over.'

'It ain't over yet,' Baker said. 'I want you here at three.'

'Fine,' Dan said. 'Are we meeting someone?'

'Yeah,' was all he would say.

Dan looked in Paul Merrick's office although he could see there was no one in. The glassed-in cubicle seemed abandoned. The desk was clear and there was nothing on top of the two filing cabinets. Paul was not the tidiest of men and his office was usually chaotic with letters and files all over the place. Dan stood in the doorway, looking back at Harry. 'Where's Mr Merrick?'

Harry stood up and came forward with a frown. 'I don't know, Mr Dolan. He's gone. Packed up this morning and left.'

'Left? Did he leave a message, a phone number or anything?'

Harry shook his head. 'He didn't say much. I asked him if he was OK but he just said, "Goodbye, Harry. I'm through here".'

Dan went down to the café round the corner, just off Madison. He looked in the back room, asked the girl behind the counter but she said she had been on all morning and Paul had not been in. He can't just walk out like that, Dan thought, a bit hurt and surprised Merrick had left without leaving him a note or anything.

He ordered a sandwich and a coffee and he made the coffee last until it was time to go back to the office. He wanted to be a little early in order to ask Baker if it was true Paul had left and if so why didn't he know about it.

Baker was still behind his desk and it didn't look as though he had moved since before lunch.

Dan sat at his desk in the corner as Baker studied yesterday's prices in the *Journal*. He sensed that Baker didn't want to talk, but he couldn't resist saying, 'I see Paul Merrick has gone.'

'Yeah,' Baker said.

'He didn't say he was leaving, not to me anyway.'

'He only heard this morning.' It occurred to Dan that Baker might be about to wind up the company, get rid of everybody, retire 'for health reasons'. But Baker went on, 'His three years were up. I was supposed to keep him on three years and I did.'

'Did he have somewhere to go?'

'I didn't ask,' Baker said.

There was a brisk knock at the door and Barbara Baker put her head round. 'Dan, hi!' she said lightly, coming in.

Dan stood up instinctively.

'Si' down,' Joe Baker said. 'I want you to hear this.'

Dan sat down, curious now.

Barbara pulled up a chair. 'What's goin' on?' she asked, a little unsure of herself. O'Hara's death had unnerved her. She had been involved with O'Hara since she was just seventeen when he offered to push her career in show business. It had soon become obvious she had no talent as a dancer or as anything else on stage but she was decorative and, though she had never got along with Jimmy Pickles, O'Hara had brought her in as a member of his gang. Now, since Baker's health had begun to deteriorate, O'Hara had been urging her to get him to marry her. We would then inherit his considerable loot, O'Hara had said. And he was right, she told herself. Joe couldn't have long to go. Though he had refused to discuss his illness with her it was obviously something serious. Now, with O'Hara gone, getting that ring on her finger was even more important.

Baker opened a drawer, drew out a banker's draft and handed it to her across the desk.

Barbara's mouth dropped open. 'Fifty grand!'

'For you,' Baker said.

Her eyes lit up. 'Fifty grand? For me? What did I do to deserve this?' She made as if to go round the desk and embrace him but he waved her away, back to her seat.

'You didn't do anything to deserve it,' he said coldly. 'You *don't* deserve it. I'm giving it to you now you can get lost, get out of my life and don't come back.'

'What?' She looked back at Dan accusingly as if he had something to do with this. 'What are you talking about?'

Baker regarded her with loathing. 'You go home. You pack your bags and all that expensive junk you filled your wardrobes with, you get out of my house and you don't come back. I don't care where the hell you go but you stay away from me, my home, my office. I don't want to set eyes on you ever again. You got that?'

'But—'

'No buts. Just go. And you cash that within five days or it's dead. Understand? Now for the last time, get out!'

She stood tall, her face pale beneath her powder. She swung her silver fox fur around her neck and her lip curled. But before she could speak Baker thrust a business card at her across the desk, a card with the name and number of his lawyer.

'You know Jim Paley,' he said. 'If you have anything to say, say it to him. Now go, get out!'

Barbara turned on her heel and left, slamming the door.

Baker slumped forward in his chair as if relieved it was over, then he went into a bout of coughing.

'Well?' he said, looking quizzically at Dan as he brought the cough under control. 'Say something.'

Dan spread his hands. He wasn't sure what to say. 'Was that wise? Sending her back to your place? She might wreck the joint.'

Baker laughed and set off another bout of coughing. 'No chance,' he said at last. 'I asked Mrs Heine to be there, see she takes only what's hers and nothing else.'

Dan nodded. Mrs Heine, who took care of his apartment, was a large, formidable lady. She had no time for 'Mrs' Baker whom she believed was unworthy of her exalted position. Everything, it seemed, was under control.

'You have a hospital appointment tomorrow,' Dan said. 'I think I should come with you.'

'Hold my hand?' Baker said wryly, but he didn't dismiss the idea. 'Listen, son, I need to talk to you, put you straight on a few things.'

Dan moved up to the chair Barbara had vacated.

'I want you to understand,' Baker went on, 'that what we did with O'Hara was not our style. Helping to manipulate the market at the expense of the little guy is not what we do or what we've ever done – except on this one occasion.'

Dan was nodding in approval.

'Now there are some guys, members of the Exchange, who have no scruples. If they can build up a stock to a phoney level then make a killing, they will. They don't care what harm they do. Well, I reckon the market is overheating, too many little people investing all they have. They are led to believe they can't lose, this crazy boom will go on forever. Well, it can't. We've had good times now for ten years but it's running out of control. It can't go on. It ain't based on anything.

'What happened with Radio stock was down to these specu-lators. They gang up and form "pools". They buy together in a big way and everybody else piles in. Then they pull out. They all sell at the same time leaving those who are not in the know taking the loss. They make their killing and run. Well, they got away with it this time with Radio stock, but one day, and soon, the whole goddamn works is going to blow up in their faces.'

'So what do we do?' Dan asked.

'We sell up,' Baker said decisively. 'We cash in what we've got and put the proceeds into long-term bonds. I'll show you which. It's low returns, yeah, but safe. I reckon there's a stormy period ahead. So I say we get out now. Most of the companies who owe us are doing OK so we call in the debts and we don't lend any more dough for a while.'

'You want me to sell everything?'

'Yeah, starting tomorrow morning. Don't talk about what you're doing. They'll think you're crazy. Just do it.'

'And tomorrow afternoon I take you to the hospital.'

Baker nodded, 'Sure, if you want to. But there's not much those guys can do for me.'

# TWENTY-SIX

A COLD WIND was blowing up from the Hudson and Tim Dolan was back walking the streets of the parish. He felt at home here. People knew him now. He had just stopped to exchange a few words with Officer Healey the neighbourhood cop who knew everybody and was almost as well known as Father Pat. An old man searching the sidewalk for cigarette butts, looked up at him, grinned and said something he couldn't make out. He grinned back at the old man and went on walking.

This was far removed from Dan's world of high rollers and stock market wizards but it was his part of town now and he knew, sadly, he would soon have to make a move. Father Pat hadn't raised the subject but Tim knew he was waiting for the verdict. Had he come through his recent problems or was he going to quit his plans for the priesthood? Trouble was, he didn't know. He was still debating with himself. But soon, he knew, he would have to decide.

Frankie O'Reilly was having trouble raising the back wheels of his buggy out of the gutter and up on to the sidewalk. Tim stopped to help him and together they levelled the cart. Then Tim raised the cover and saw the buggy was piled high with cobs of coal.

He laughed. 'Better watch out. Officer Healey's about.'

'Was him told me there'd been a spill,' the boy said.

'So how are you, Frankie?' Tim asked as they walked along.

'I'm OK, I guess.'

'And ma? She OK?'

Frankie looked at him sideways. 'Well, y'know. She never will be.'

'I guess not,' Tim acknowledged. 'So it's up to you now. Stay out of trouble. Make her proud of you.'

'You sound like Father Pat.'

Tim smiled. The boy was growing up. He was more self-possessed, more confident. 'Has he been bending your ear?'

Frankie sat down out of the wind on the bottom step of the block where he lived, his coal buggy drawn up at his feet. 'More than that. He gave me a lecture about the two sides of the law and which side always wins. I said what about the guys who beat the rap? And you know what he's like. He says they don't win. They get theirs when they go upstairs.'

Tim laughed. 'He's got an answer for everything.'

'Yeah,' he said. 'And now he's got me doing extra school-work.'

Tim was impressed. 'I reckon that's no mean feat. Getting you to do extra schoolwork. Getting *any* kid to do extra school-work.'

'Yeah well, Father Pat and me, we've got plans. I'm going to be a lawyer, see. Like Dennis.'

'Dennis Casey?'

'Yeah. Dennis is a kid from round here like me. Father Pat took me to see him and now he's teaching me stuff about the law. That's what I'm going to do. I'm going to be a big-shot lawyer like Dennis.'

'Well, I think that's great, Frankie,' Tim told him. 'I really do and I wish you all the luck in the world.'

Later that day Tim called into Dennis Casey's office. He wanted to applaud what Casey was doing and thank him.

'Don't thank me, Tim,' Casey said. 'It's Father Pat's idea.'

'Well, it's good for Frankie. Especially after what's happened. I expect he's a long way to go but he's a bright kid. Let's hope he makes it. All the way.'

'He'll have every chance. He's getting extra tuition already. Father Pat has this guy comes in for a couple of hours two nights a week, help him with his schoolwork.'

'That's great,' Tim said. 'And it's good of the Church to help out.'

Casey shook his head. 'Nothing to do with the Church. Father Pat pays for it himself.'

'That so?' Tim was even more impressed. 'Now that's real good of him. You mean, he pays the man out of his own pocket?'

Casey nodded.

'Can he afford to do that?'

'He's done it before,' Casey said.

Tim laughed, shaking his head. This Father Pat never ceased to surprise him. 'He's done it before?'

'Several times. Sees a bright kid, boy or girl, and he does what he can to help them.' Casey paused for a moment then he said, 'It goes back years. At least twenty to my knowledge. My old man was no good. He'd come home now and then when he had nowhere else to go. And he didn't work, never had a real job, so there was never much money at our house.'

'You mean, he did it for you?'

'Sure. He saw me all the way through. I've tried to pay him back a number of times but he won't hear of it. He's in a league of his own our Father Pat.'

The consultant came out to where Dan was waiting to take Joe Baker home. He was a grey-haired man in his late fifties, cheerful and friendly and willing to talk whilst Joe was getting dressed.

Dan was hoping for a word, some indication of how Joe was progressing but he had to prompt him to get it. 'It's bad, Doc?'

The doctor nodded. 'I guess so,' he said. 'But, at least, he knows it. He's a tough old guy, been a fighter and a survivor all his life, I'd say. But this is the toughest battle he's ever had to fight, son, and the odds are stacked against him.'

'How long?' Dan asked.

The doctor was surprised at the directness of Dan's question. He hesitated, then he said, 'Who can say? Month, maybe two.'

'A year?' Dan asked hopefully.

'I can always tell when people are talking about me,' Baker said as he emerged fixing his tie. 'No need to look guilty, fellas. I know the score. From where I'm standing I can see the Old Reaper.'

'Don't say things like that,' Dan said, genuinely concerned.

'The queue's getting shorter,' Baker insisted.

'Getting shorter for all of us, Joe,' the doctor said with a smile.

They shook hands and Baker grinned at Dan. 'He tries to pick my brains, you know. He's always asking me what stocks he should buy.'

The doctor looked at Dan and shook his head in denial.

'I tell him to get out,' Baker went on, 'Sell everything. Cash in while he still can. The market's overheating.'

'Is he right?' the doctor asked Dan.

'He always has been,' Dan said.

The doctor patted Baker on the back. 'See you in a couple of weeks, you old rogue,' he said. But he didn't. This was Monday and Joe Baker died during the night the following Friday.

Dan was with him when he died. He was at home in his smart apartment and his breathing was so bad Dan refused to leave. At times he seemed to be in pain but the nurse on watch gave him enough of what Dan guessed was morphine to help him sleep. Before she left she said she would be back early the next morning. Joe was sleeping peacefully, but the nurse warned Dan that he might not wake up. Around midnight, sitting at the bedside, Dan fell asleep.

It was just after two o'clock when he suddenly came awake and realized where he was. Joe was still asleep. The heating had gone off and it was cold. Dan touched Baker's hand but it felt warm enough. Then, still half asleep, he drew an armchair nearer to the bed, found his overcoat, drew it over himself and fell asleep again.

The second time he awoke it was just after six. He sat up straight. The room was still and so was Joe. Dan had the strange feeling it was the silence, the absolute stillness that woke him. And he knew at once that Joe was dead.

He called the nurse who said she would come right over. She would 'take care of things', she said. Dan was thankful for that because he had no idea what he should do. Would he stay there? was all she asked. A doctor would be called, she told him, to certify that Mr Baker had passed away.

Dan stood at the bedside, looking down. He felt that he knew Joe well and that he didn't know him at all. He had come into Dan's life some five years ago and in many ways he had become like a father to him. Few people seemed to get along with Joe Baker but Dan liked him from the start. There was something tough, unpretentious and – what was the word? –*indomitable* about him. But even after seeing him and working with him nearly every day since he joined the company Dan felt he still knew very little about him.

He wandered down the wide hallway to the room Baker used as an office. Big desk. A bookcase. A dark-green filing cabinet. On one wall a print of a small town with minarets, a tall spire and a line of cyrillic letters across the bottom like a travel poster. But there were no other pictures. Dan sat at the desk and picked up a slim white envelope. It was addressed in Baker's scrawling handwriting to Dan Dolan with the instruction: Not to be opened by anyone else.

Dan picked up the shiny gold-plated NYSE letter opener and sliced open the envelope.

*Dear Dan*
*When you read this I'll be on my way up into the wide blue yonder or maybe they'll send me the other way, who knows? I guess I never told you much about myself yet I made you tell me everything I could possibly need to know about you. Well, maybe when you read the attached you might get an idea why I was such a tight-fisted bastard, why I never met a girl and married her, why I got no family of my own. I envied you, I really did. You had a couple of brothers. Something I never had and I wished I had. Even if one was a crooner and the other was a crazy Bible puncher.*

*What I really wanted was a son or a daughter. And it was my own fault I never got one. Not until I got you, that is. I wish we'd met earlier when you were just a kid. Maybe I could have adopted you. But we did meet up – about the only thing I have to thank that Barbara for – and I soon saw in you the son I never had. I watched you when you first came to us and I saw that you were a good man, the sort of man maybe I would have liked to have been myself.*

*Anyway, what I want for you now is that you find the right girl, marry her and have kids. Life is not worth living without a family. So don't leave it too late. OK? See you in Heaven – maybe.*

*Pops*

Dan smiled. That was Pops. Still giving instructions. He looked at the single sheet attached. It was a brief account of Baker's life from Ellis Island to Park Avenue. His name was Josef Bakke. He had come to America with his mother and his little sister from the Ukraine. There was an address in Shevchenko Street in Kiev. On Ellis Island he had sailed through all the health and other checks but his sister had a problem. She had developed an eye infection and on the voyage over it had worsened. Baker wrote:

*I understand the officials suspected it was trachoma and they wouldn't let her in. I was already through. I was waiting for them at the place they call the Kissing Steps. My mother was calling me back but I wouldn't go. I was in America. I had my immigration card with the address of some second cousin of my mother and I absolutely refused to return to the Ukraine. It must have been tough for my mother, torn between me and my sister. So I thought I would make it easier for her. I was fifteen years of age and I believed I could take care of myself so I just ran off. But, of course, she had no choice anyway. She had to go back. I wrote to her often, hoping my sister would be cured and they could try again. But they never did and one day I heard my mother had died and my sister was in a blind institution. There was nothing I could do about that. I was broke. Didn't have a dime. So I spent all my time, every minute of every day learning how to get rich. Then, when I could afford to bring her over and prove to the authorities she would not be a burden on the state, I found she had died, too.*

The note went on to say he had worked at a variety of jobs and he eventually realized he was a good salesman. His best move was when he joined the NY Curb Exchange. This was a job selling stock on the sidewalk in Broad Street. He never stopped working and saving and when he had enough hard cash he bought his seat on the much more prestigious NY Stock Exchange.

The funeral was a strange affair. Baker had left instructions with his lawyer that he didn't want anyone from the Exchange or from his trade association. He just wanted Dan Dolan, Harry and Lois from the office, his housekeeper Mrs Heine, the lawyer Jim Paley and Mrs Paley and that was all. For a man so widely known in business circles it seemed to Dan a very odd send-off, but his last letter to Paley was adamant – just his closest friends and associates.

Joe had specified he wanted a non-religious ceremony yet he had joked in his last letter about meeting up in Heaven. Dan thought about the first day he walked into the office on Madison, his cloth cap, collarless shirt, worn jacket, work pants, heavy boots. He was scared of Joe Baker then but he needed a job and he was willing to do anything, anything legal anyway. The way things turned out could not have been better.

'What I want is a Mark Antony not a Brutus,' Joe had told him. Dan had read the play, seen it in an off Broadway production and he wondered now why an uneducated kid from the Ukraine would be familiar with *Julius Caesar*. Well today, he thought as the plain wooden box passed by, 'I come to bury Caesar *and* to praise him'.

Dan had power of attorney over Baker's affairs and the first thing he did was close the office as a mark of respect and give Harry and Lois a week's paid leave. Dan and Jim Paley paid their tributes and that was it. Brief and without fuss as Joe had wanted. Then, as they came away, Paley drew Dan aside and told him they must meet as soon as possible. He had some very important news for him. Dan agreed to call at his office the following day.

# TWENTY-SEVEN

BEING A PARISH priest was tough, Tim acknowledged, at least in a parish like this. And you had to admire Father Pat. His church had a brand new roof, the workmen had gone and so had Vincent O'Hara.

Tim was a lot clearer now on what he wanted. Maybe going home and discovering what had happened to Kathleen had been good for him. According to Father Pat some things are sent to test us. If that's so, Tim had said, it was a bit tough on Kathleen. But as always, Father Pat was ready with his answer. That young lady will walk straight into the house of the Lord. Why, she'll be as welcome as the flowers in May. Tim could only shake his head in wonder. Father Pat was no different to the nuns in primary school who told the wide-eyed infants in their charge not to be sad when a three-day-old baby died. That baby was very lucky, they said. His little soul would be as pure and as white as snow. He would walk straight into the Kingdom of Heaven, so he would.

A load of rubbish, Tim thought. Or maybe not. But whatever it was he wanted to be part of this world of service and dedication to the community Father Pat operated in. He had seen the frenzy of the stock market, the obsession with making money. It was not his world and, as he walked up the gradually darkening path to the church in the early evening, he paused briefly to listen to the choir practice. This was where he belonged. This was where he wanted to be. He was sure of that now.

'What I want to know,' he told Father Pat later that night, 'is where you get the money to help kids like Frankie O'Reilly.

Do you have a private income or something? Or do you creep out at night and gamble on stocks and shares when no one's watching?'

Father Pat laughed and sat back in his armchair. The chair was so big and deep it made him look like a gnome, but it was the most comfortable chair in his sitting room. 'Why do you ask?'

'Because I might want to be able to do the same one day.'

'Well, there are several ways,' Father Pat said. 'Sometimes I bribe the politicians into helping out, especially if they're from round here. I promise them my parishioners will vote for them *en masse* the next time they come up for election.'

'You can't do that.'

'I know, but they don't know I can't.'

Tim shook his head.

'And there's always the fellas who have pulled themselves up out of the gutter. If they're from round here and they're doing all right professionally I can usually count on them for a little contribution.'

'People you've helped in the past?' Tim asked.

He nodded. 'Sometimes.'

'Well, what about Dennis Casey? He said you wouldn't let him help, you would never accept money from him.'

'Dennis is different. He's always stayed close to his roots. He set up his office here and he often does work for free. I'd never put the squeeze on Dennis.'

Tim looked at the priest thoughtfully and for a long moment. It was as though he wanted to say something but he didn't know how or where to begin.

Father Pat held his gaze then asked quietly, 'Does this mean you're coming through your troubles, you're ready to go ahead?'

Tim nodded. 'I think maybe I am, yes.'

'You know you have to be absolutely sure it's what you want.'

'I *am* sure, Father. It *is* what I want and it always will be now.'

Father Pat hesitated, then he said, 'Well, that's good. Because there's a place for you at the seminary. I got a call this morning.'

'When?' Tim asked eagerly. 'When do I go?'

'September. If all goes well.'

Nathan's music company had got off to a good start, due mainly to the success of one record. The vaudeville entertainer, Sophie Tucker came from a Russian Jewish family and she'd had a huge hit with her recording of *My Yiddishe Momme*. It had proved surprisingly popular right across the various communities. Jewish, Italian, Irish, everyone was aware of it. Nathan had been quick to seize his opportunity. He had recruited a young Jewish singer with a fine voice to record the song in English on one side and Yiddish on the other. His sales across the Lower East Side and beyond had soared and the record had gradually become a big success with Jewish families nationwide.

He had called his record label Olde Favourites and the brand name was quickly established. Older people with fond memories of the parents and grandparents they had left behind enjoyed the nostalgia the music evoked. Nathan had high hopes now for his next project, an Irish tenor singing *The Mountains of Mourne* on one side and *The Rose of Tralee* on the other.

Anxious now to know what would happen to Joe Baker's stake in his company he called Dan to express his condolences and to ask tentatively how things were. Dan was unsure of himself as yet and he didn't want to make any decisions until he was ready and he knew what he was doing. 'You want to know what happens now,' he said. It was a statement not a question. 'Well, I'll tell you. Nothing happens now. Things go on as before. Keep finding hits like *Momma*, we might want to invest even more.' He had no grounds for saying this but he wanted everyone connected with the business to stay calm, give him time, because right now he was a little apprehensive, not knowing what might happen next. Perhaps after his meeting with Paley he would have a clearer view.

Paley's office was just a couple of blocks away on the fourth floor of a tall narrow building. Dan strolled there in the bright sunlight of that September afternoon. Not knowing what to expect, he had toyed with the idea of putting Paley off, telling him it was not convenient just then and making a date of his own choice. This Paley had given him no clue as to what he wanted and he objected to being summoned to his office as if he had been granted an audience with the Pope. But he knew it wasn't really like that. What concerned him were the many letters and documents he had signed and counter-signed at Pops' request and he was wondering what, if anything, he had let himself in for. For all he knew Pops might have run up huge debts that would wipe out the business and him with it, leaving him bankrupt for years to come.

Jim Paley was a tall slim Bostonian, his silver grey hair brushed back, his pencil moustache giving him an air of distinction. He showed Dan to a seat before his imposing desk and offered him coffee which Dan declined a little ungraciously. But as they talked Paley began to seem more like an amiable uncle than some hard-nosed businessman and Dan decided his earlier assessment had been wrong. Pops, he knew, had held Paley in high regard.

Paley opened a bulky file on his desk. 'You know, he was very fond of you. He told me so.'

'I was fond of him, sir. He gave me a job when I first arrived here and he treated me far better than I could have hoped for.'

'Well, I have to tell you,' Paley said with a smile, 'Joe Baker has treated you better than you could possibly imagine.'

Dan raised his eyebrows.

Paley picked up a sheet of vellum from the file. 'This is the Last Will and Testament of Mr Josef Bakke.' He looked up at Dan. 'It's very simple and straightforward. *I leave all my worldly goods and possessions to my good friend Daniel Dolan, signed Josef Baakke, September 1, 1929.*'

Dan looked worried, confused. 'Mr Paley?'

'Shall I read it again?'

'No, no,' Dan said. 'I just can't take it in.'

'You were not expecting this?'

Dan spread his hands helplessly. 'It never occurred to me for a moment. I mean, why? Why would he do this?'

Paley laughed. 'Well, he couldn't take it with him, he had no family and you were obviously his closest friend.'

Dan was still stunned by the news.

'I understand this may well be a considerable surprise, even a shock for you. But you are a very wealthy young man. Joe Baker has left you several million dollars.'

'Is there no one else?'

'Absolutely no one. I dealt with Barbara what-was-her-name? She came to see me but she has no claim on Joe. He treated her very generously – which, as I told her, he had no need to do. But no, there are no beneficiaries other than yourself.' He laughed again and opened a side drawer. 'You look as though you need a drink, son.'

On the Monday morning when the office reopened Dan called Harry and Lois together. He was not sure where things would go from here, he told them honestly, but the business would carry on. If they wanted to leave and find something that might seem more secure he would understand. But he hoped they would stay.

'Will you take Mr Baker's seat on the Exchange?' Harry asked.

'I hope so,' Dan said. 'I have to go before the committee later this month.' He smiled. 'So they can decide if I'm a gentleman, an honest upright citizen, or not. It's important to us. If they turn me down it would damage our investment business, but we would still have the commercial side. Lots of people out there looking for the capital to expand right now.'

'Well, I wish you all the luck in the world, Mr Dolan,' Harry told him, 'and I'd like to stay.'

'Me too,' Lois said.

So that was settled. Dan planned to be down in Wall Street by ten o'clock, but first he asked Harry if he had any idea where Paul Merrick was living. Harry said Mr Merrick had phoned in with an address in the Village in case there was any post for him.

Dan moved round the floor of the Exchange seeing and being seen. Michael Meehan and several other members offered friendly words of encouragement and he spent much of the morning smiling and shaking hands. Then, just before noon when things went a little quiet, he made his first move. He sold his company's entire holding in US Steel. It seemed an odd thing to do, even to him, US Steel had risen steadily all year and now in late September it was at an all time high. But this was Pops' instruction. Sell everything and do it quietly and discreetly.

'US Steel got a long way to go yet, son,' a tall, thin man who was watching nearby told him. 'Time's not right for selling.'

Dan smiled politely and moved away. He didn't want to get into a discussion just then and certainly not with this fellow about whom Pops had once warned him. In Pops' estimation the man was 'not entirely trustworthy'.

'Listen, maybe we can help.' The man had followed him. 'Maybe you should join up with me and my partners. We'll put you right.'

Dan smiled again. 'Thank you,' he said. 'I'll bear that in mind.'

In the course of an hour he sold US Steel, General Motors and Westinghouse, all good solid investments, and just when people were beginning to notice he left.

That afternoon he went to the address in the village Harry had given him. But he was too late. Paul Merrick had moved on. Did he leave a forwarding address? he asked the tough-looking lady who ruled the rooming-house. Oh sure, she said and she squinted at a little red notebook in which she recorded her weekly rents. 'Here it is,' she announced. 'Place over in Brooklyn.'

Dan made a note of the address. 'Why did he leave?' he asked. 'Has he got a job over there? Or maybe it's cheaper than here.'

The landlady made a derisory noise in her throat. 'If it's cheaper than here it must be quite a dump.'

It turned out to be a woodframe house in a long street of drab, nondescript houses. A wooden sign with the word

ROOMS in faded white paint slanted sideways on a small patch of worn grass. Another landlady, tired-looking and bored. 'Yeah, he's here,' she said, 'for now. But he won't be next week if he don't pay up.'

She let Dan into a dim and narrow hallway and called up the stairs. 'Hey, Merrick. You up there? You got a visitor.'

Paul Merrick appeared at the top of the stairs. He looked down at Dan, surprised to see him and embarrassed at his straitened circumstances. But then he called down, 'Dan! Please come up.'

Dan looked to the landlady for permission but she shrugged and went off down the hallway. Merrick's room was small with a single bed against one wall, a battered desk, a dining chair and not much else. A grimy window looked out on to a few yards of unmade road, a row of neglected houses across the way and that was it.

Merrick offered Dan the only chair and sat down on the edge of the bed.

'You OK?' Dan asked.

Merrick shrugged.

'Are you working?'

'I am between jobs. I am like an actor. I'm resting,' he said grandly. Then, more seriously, he said, 'I've tried a few things. But it's no good. I can't stay here. I have to move on.'

'You through with the investment business?'

'The investment business is through with me, Dan,' he said. 'But I don't want that kind of work anyway. I never did. I've told you. I want to work in the movies. Talking pictures. I have enough for a train ticket West.' He looked at Dan frankly. 'And I have to go. Begin at the beginning.'

'Doing what?'

'I dunno. Scene-shifting. Anything.'

'What about your friends?'

'Well, the last I heard they were doing fine. They don't need me. Unless I can find the money, of course.'

Dan stood up and went to the window. 'You hear about Pops?'

'What did he do? Buy General Motors?'

'He died,' Dan said. He turned to look at Merrick and saw that his reaction was genuine.

'I'm sorry to hear that. Really,' he said. 'I mean it. He was … well, he was a good man. A better man than me. What I did was wrong.' Then he asked, 'Are you running the office?'

'I guess so,' Dan said, a little sheepishly.

'Well, you can do it, Dan. I'm sure of that. Just watch out for the people at the Exchange. Joe always said they were crooks – all of them.' He laughed. 'But not him, of course.'

'Listen,' Dan said. 'I'd like to stay, go for a drink or something. But I have to get back. I need to see Harry before he goes home.'

Merrick stood up. 'It's good to see you, Dan, and it was good of you to come and find me, I appreciate it. But if you've come to offer me my job back, it must be thank you but no thanks.'

'Actually,' Dan said, 'I came to give you this.' He handed over a cheque for a thousand dollars.

'What's this?'

'It's to help you find a place out West and to make an honest man of you. Before you go you can pay your landlady what you owe her.' He handed Merrick a second cheque now, this one for *fifty* thousand.

Merrick held the cheque gingerly, his hand beginning to shake. He looked at Dan in amazement.

'It's what you should have had in the first place.'

'I can't take this,' Merrick said.

'We're in the investment business,' Dan told him. 'See it as an investment and don't forget to send me tickets when your first talkie hits New York.'

Merrick was sitting down on the edge of the bed again, his hand shading his eyes.

# TWENTY-EIGHT

THE NEXT MORNING it was hot and humid. To Dan, the people at the Exchange seemed restless and there was a tension in the air as if the heat was building up to an unsustainable level and was about to burst with a shattering thunderclap.

He carried on where he left things the day before, clearing out the company's holdings and cashing in relentlessly. It was noticeable now but nobody interfered. He was a young guy who didn't know what the hell he was doing and the older, more experienced simply shook their heads and carried on trading. Michael Meehan might have had something to say had he noticed what was happening to his old friend Joe Baker's portfolio, but he was too absorbed in the steady revival of his Radio stock and most of the day Post 12 was surrounded by eager speculators.

Everything was still on the up and even later that month when there was what most investors saw as a temporary hitch and prices fell slightly and looked unsteady the general air of optimism was not shaken. Stocks had dropped before but always they had recovered. Falls had been followed by a sharp rise and prices had climbed even higher. 'Smart' operators saw such minor setbacks as opportunities to snap up bargains.

Dan Dolan was seen now by most of the Exchange's members as a young man who had struck lucky, taken over Joe Baker's business and was intent on stripping the assets, cashing in and getting out. At the office even Harry questioned the logic of what he was doing. 'Prices are still going strong,' he said. 'Are we right to be pulling out just now?'

'It was Mr Baker's advice,' Dan told him.

Then Harry asked the question that was really troubling him, 'You're not planning to wind up the business?'

Dan assured him he was not. He was simply following the instructions of the man who always knew what to do.

At the Exchange just one man, a Mr Weber, approached him with approval and encouragement. He was a quiet man who didn't seem to have many friends or associates and he was seen by most of his fellow members of the Exchange as a boring pessimist, an unwelcome prophet of doom.

'You are doing the right thing, son,' he said. 'I've been telling them for months now. Things have gone too far. Everything is overvalued and it can't last. I tell them but they don't listen. No one *wants* to listen. They are all mad with greed.' He lowered his voice. 'And we will all have to pay one day.'

But prices regained their balance and started to soar again and Weber's gloomy predictions didn't come true until several weeks later. Then, on Thursday, October 24, the unthinkable happened. The world of high finance woke up to heart-stopping news. Dan heard the first rumble on the radio as he shaved at 7.30.

In the last hour before the closing gong the previous day there had been a frenzy of selling and some stocks dropped as much as fifteen dollars as no one stepped in to buy. A radio announcer, intent on sniffing out a big story, exaggerated what had happened citing an alleged report of a man jumping from a skyscraper and traders being rushed to hospital with suspected heart attacks. None of this was true but it was obvious that something momentous was happening on Wall Street and this time it was not good news.

As Dan went down to the Exchange the streets seemed strangely quiet. It was as if a bomb had dropped in another part of town and people were waiting for news of survivors. A crowd had gathered by the spot where the country's first president, George Washington, had been sworn in. On Wall Street, at the entrance to Broad Street and in front of the imposing façade of the J.P. Morgan building the crowd was swelling to record proportions. Dan had literally never seen anything like it. Yet the crowd was strangely quiet. Men and women stood around with anxious eyes as if waiting for a lead, an announcement to say it was all a ghastly mistake or a signal to start a race to offload their holdings and grab what crumbs they could.

Dan had to ease his way gently through the throng to reach the main entrance on Broad Street where the sergeant on duty opened the door only slightly, noted his card and let him in, hurriedly closing the door behind him.

Police officers were prominent on every street corner as the crowds were contained by officers on horseback and movietone news cameras were set up at various vantage points. But this was no festive occasion. It was more like a wake and there was a general feeling of foreboding that things were bad and were about to get much worse.

Inside the Exchange prices were falling dramatically and the trading floor was filled with frantic traders crowding round the posts and waving pieces of paper, anxious to sell at whatever price they could and at least salvage something from their shattered dreams. A short fat man whose normally red face was now almost puce glared at Dan with a pained expression as if to imply Dan had known something and had failed to pass this information on to his fellow members.

At Post 12 Michael Meehan, inundated with people wanting to sell, was unable to trade. There were no buyers. It was the same at Post 2 where sellers were frantically trying to offload US Steel and it was the same with General Motors at Post 4. The anxiously watched ticker-tape machines simply could not keep up and by noon the prices were hopelessly behind. Anyone checking with the telephone quotation service to find if things were really this bad found they were infinitely worse.

Dan was beginning to wonder why he was there. He had sold all the company's major shareholdings at a handsome profit. The stocks the company still held were minor investments and, though they had suffered with the majority during the day, they did not add up to any great loss. He decided to get out, away from all the anxiety on the floor of the Exchange. But then word went round that something was happening. Thomas W. Lamont, senior partner at J.P. Morgan and a highly regarded financial adviser had called a meeting of the city's leading bankers.

The meeting lasted less than an hour and a decision was reached that the banks represented would inject up to $100 million into leading stocks in an effort to halt the slide. Immediately, with the bankers' backing, the Exchange's most senior officer on duty that day, Richard Whitney, went straight to Post 2 and ostentatiously placed an order for 25,000 shares in US Steel at $205 a share. The crowd around Post 2 cheered loudly. Whitney then went from Post to Post placing orders for millions of dollars and the whole mood inside the Exchange changed. Leading shares began to bounce back and investor confidence was gradually restored. People were buying again and things were looking up. But by seven o'clock that evening when the ticker tapes at last caught up it was clear that the losses incurred were calamitous. Prices had fallen by almost $3 billion.

Dan didn't go back to the office until the next morning where Harry met him with a grin. 'You had a visitor yesterday. Lovely lady.'

'Oh, yeah?'

'She waited for a while but I told her things were happening on Wall Street and I didn't know if you would be back. She said her name was Sue and she wrote you a note.'

He handed Dan a small envelope. Dan went into his office and sat at Pops' desk. '*Dan*,' he read. '*I'm leaving tomorrow with the rest of the girls. We're doing a tour of the Mid-West then I'm going out to LA and I won't be coming back. It was great fun, as they say, but maybe that's all that it was. Yours always, Sue. ps: We leave Penn Station at eleven.*'

Harry hadn't met Sue before but Lois had. The one other time Sue called Lois was there on her own and they had got along fine. Lois knocked lightly at the door now and breezed in. 'There you are,' she said brightly. 'I saw your girlfriend yesterday.'

'She's not my girlfriend,' Dan said.

Lois looked at him knowingly.

'She's not,' he protested. 'She says it was fun but that's all that it was.' He held up the note for her to read.

Lois peered at the note, reading it carefully. 'She doesn't mean that,' she told him. 'She wants you to get over to Penn Station and beg her to stay.'

'I don't think so,' he said with a laugh.

'Sure she does,' she insisted. 'Why do you think she's telling you what time the train leaves?' She looked up at the clock on the wall. It was only nine o'clock. 'You got plenty of time.'

Dan smiled and shook his head. 'I have things to do.'

In the last couple of years Joe Baker had begun to buy land and property. Dan and Harry spent some time now going through and listing these acquisitions to get a clear picture. Then at 10.15 Lois brought coffee in. She looked at Dan plaintively as if willing him not to throw away his opportunity. 'There's still time.'

Dan nodded, knowing what she meant. But he didn't go to Penn Station. He went down to the Exchange to see what the new day had brought.

Business leaders were playing down the disturbing drop in prices and reassuring themselves that the worst was over. Stocks would recover as they always had, they declared, and a move to close the Exchange for a period of quiet readjustment was defeated. Most members felt that such a move might create more panic.

In Washington the President, Herbert Hoover, was being urged to comment on the state of the markets, to say something positive. Hoover himself was not convinced that the worst was over, yet he was anxious not to say anything that might make matters worse. Mr Hoover did not trust the many speculators whose only motive was a quick profit. The President believed that cynical manipulation of the markets had raised the novice investor's expectations to unrealistic heights and he was seriously concerned for the millions of little people who had been spurred into risking their life savings by exaggerated reports of people like themselves who had 'gotten rich overnight'. But in many cases it was not only their savings they were risking. Many were gambling with borrowed money, money they could not afford to lose.

In the boom years more and more people, most of them new to the market, borrowed money to buy stock. Everyone was in debt, or so it seemed, but as long as prices continued to climb the debt diminished. Brokers borrowed more and more from the banks to lend to customers and even when the rates of interest went up the borrowers were not deterred.

The nation's bank, the Federal Reserve, wanted to keep this mass speculation at acceptable levels but some city bankers refused to listen and increased their levels of lending to the brokers. The mad climb continued and was fuelled still further when some of the large corporations, eyeing the high level of interest rates, decided lending to the market might prove more profitable than the business they were actually in. Soon they, too, were lending large sums to brokers. But as the demand for stock spiralled out of control no one seemed to notice that fewer houses were being built, the sale of automobiles had tailed off and steel production had slowed to a walking pace.

Compared to the previous day that Friday was quiet on Wall Street. It was, as one optimistic commentator reported, as if the City had picked itself up and dusted itself off. Yet for the thousands of investors new to the market it came as a shock, a salutary warning. Stocks could go down, just as dramatically down, as well as up. Inevitably, as margins diminished, there were many calls for cash and brokers were forced to sell the holdings of people who were unable to cover their debts.

Few investors were immune and there were many high profile losers. The cosmetics maker Helena Rubinstein lost well over a million dollars in just two hours. Comedian and singer Eddie Cantor lost his entire savings and allegedly was left with only sixty dollars in his pocket. He fuelled the myth about suicides jumping from skyscrapers by joking on stage that as he booked a room in a New York hotel the desk clerk asked, 'Sleeping or jumping?' Another star comedian, Groucho Marx, also lost his life savings. Groucho went deep into debt trying to meet his broker's calls for cash. But, unlike Cantor, he could see no funny side to the situation and he fell into a severe depression that lasted for months and prevented him from working. Yet there were even bigger showbiz losers. Songwriter Irving Berlin lost an estimated $5 million.

Throughout the next day, the last Saturday in October, the enforced selling of the holdings of people who could no longer cover their losses went on. More and more small investors lost everything. The many hopefuls who had rushed out to reap the benefits of the boom years were learning a bitter lesson. A few of the more cautious players, a very small minority, had seen this coming but many big investors had not, or perhaps had not wanted to, and some had suffered multi-million dollar losses that left a question mark over the future of several of Wall Street's best known institutions.

Members of staff at the brokers' offices in and around the Financial District worked through the night now to unravel the tangle of falling prices and to attempt to decipher the hundreds of hurriedly scrawled entries they had made in their books. Many were literally exhausted and had to be sent home. Now, as the true picture emerged, it became clear that the chaos of these last few days had left many casualties.

# TWENTY-NINE

ONE DAY LAST week Dan had spent an interesting after-noon with Jim Paley, Pops' lawyer friend. As well as lawyer, he found, Paley had acted over the years as a kind of sounding board, a second opinion in money matters. He was conservative, wise and prudent at all times. The kind of man who, though he would never make a big killing, would never make a huge loss.

The estate was more or less settled, he told Dan, taxes covered, the will proved and Dan found he really was a *bona fide* dollar millionaire. Paley counselled caution. 'A lot of people are going to be short of cash right now and some of them might come knocking on your door. They may claim to be old friends of Joe. They might even say he owed them money. Don't listen,' he told Dan, 'and don't let them in. In fact, anybody gives you money trouble refer them to me, OK?

'It might be a good idea,' he went on, 'to keep all this to your-self for now. If you haven't already, don't tell anyone apart from your closest family.'

It was good advice. He hadn't mentioned his good fortune to anyone, not even Tim. He wanted time to think about it. For one thing, it didn't seem as if it was his money anyway. He thought of it as still belonging to Pops, as if he was just a guardian and it was his job to see that it was not lost or wasted. At least he could take care of Harry and Lois as Pops wanted.

He was pondering these matters when he arrived at the office that Monday morning to be met by Lois who was still treating him coolly. The incurable romantic, she was convinced he had been a fool to let Sue go and she was certain he would be sorry.

'Mr Shaw's been on this morning,' she told him. 'Y'know, your friend Nathan.'

'What does he want?' Dan asked, more interested just then in what was going on at the Exchange than anything else.

'He says you're to call him the minute you get in. It's *very* urgent.'

Dan raised his eyebrows. Most things were urgent where Nathan was concerned. But *very* urgent? 'Better get him for me Lois.'

Seconds later she handed him the phone. 'Nathan,' he said.

'Dan! Where the hell have you been?'

'Does it matter?'

'No,' Nathan said. 'Listen, you got to come over here, right away.'

'Where are you?'

'In my office. Please. Come over. Now. Call a cab.'

'Are you going to tell me what this is all about? I mean, whatever it is, can't we do it over the phone?'

'No,' he said decisively. 'You have to come here. It's important.'

Nathan was renting an office on the top floor of a six-storey, cold water block just beyond Tenth Avenue, not the most salubrious of neighbourhoods, he admitted. But, as he said, it was the best his company could afford for now. Dan climbed the twelve flights of stone steps, two to each floor. Out of breath when he reached the sixth, he realized he might be out of condition, too.

'You better get out of here while you can still walk.'

'Nah,' Nathan said. 'I do those stairs twice a day and that's all the exercise I need. Keeps me fit. Come on in. Welcome to this hive of industry.'

Nathan was very much a one-man band. He couldn't afford a secretary, he said, or any kind of help. Not yet. But he was doing all right and he had bought himself a second-hand Model-T so he could call on the agents and buyers and distributors and anyone else who might help him build his business.

His office was poorly furnished, but at least he had a desk large enough to accommodate a heavy-looking phonograph and still leave desk room. 'I couldn't lug this monster over to your place, could I?'

'You got me here to listen to your phonograph?'

'Yeah, I did,' Nathan admitted. 'Now sit down and tell me what you think of this.'

'Nathan,' Dan protested, 'I'm no judge.'

'Shut up and listen,' he said, as he wound up the machine. 'I did well with the Jewish track and the Irish track is just taking off. So now I need an Italian job and that means I need an Italian singer. Some guy who can sing the old Neapolitan love songs real good with a bit of Italian thrown in. You know what I mean? Maybe the chorus in English and a couple of verses in Italian.'

Dan listened patiently but he failed to see how any of this could possibly concern him. 'What...?' he began.

'Wait, wait, wait,' Nathan said. 'Let me finish. So I need an Italian guy, OK? So I let the agents know what I'm looking for and I get this demo track in the post. It's from some agent in Los Angeles. Sends me this Italian guy who, he says, is going great out West. Guy called Johnny Roselli. I never heard of him but he sure can sing.' Nathan placed the record on the turntable, cranked the phonograph up a bit more, looked at Dan intently and said, 'Listen.'

Dan was quietly amused. Nathan was gradually becoming a sharp-nosed showbiz entrepreneur with a hard-edged accent to match.

The record crackled into life then evened out with the sound of violins followed by a voice and *O Sol Mio*. Nathan's eyes never left Dan's but he waited until the music slowed to its melancholy end and only the quiet whirr of the record remained.

'So who is it?' he demanded.

Dan shrugged. 'Some Italian guy.'

Nathan was rewinding furiously. 'God Almighty,' he muttered. 'Listen, man.' And he set the record in motion again.

Dan sat forward on the one spare chair and this time he did listen.

Nathan was smiling. 'It is, isn't it?'

'You think it's Michael.'

'Don't you?'

'I don't know,' Dan said. 'It could be, I suppose.'

Nathan was winding furiously again. 'Sure it is. It's obvious. I wish Tim was here. He'd know right away.'

'What about the name?'

'Everybody changes their name over here. You said so yourself.'

They listened again and this time Dan nodded. 'Could be. Yes.'

Nathan picked up the telephone. 'Long distance,' he said, a note with the number he wanted in his hand. There was a short wait then, 'Yeah, that is this number. Yeah, yeah. Thank you for nothing.' He put the phone down. 'My credit's not too good just now with the telephone company. We need a pay phone.'

They went down the stairs and across the street to the drug-store but it was approaching lunchtime and the place was crowded. Both phone booths were occupied. Nathan's Model-T took them uptown to Dan's office. Long distance took seven or eight minutes person to person but Nathan couldn't wait. He paced up and down until Dan said, 'Sit down, for God's sake. It probably isn't him anyway.'

Nathan grabbed the phone. 'Yeah, this is he. Thank you. Hi, this Mr Johnny Roselli? This is Nathan Shaw from li'l ol' New York. Nathan O'Shaughnessy to you.'

He laughed and listened for a moment. Then he said, 'Well, hold on. There's a guy here like to speak to you.'

And he handed the phone to Dan.


That morning as soon as the gong opened the day's trading the stock market took a massive dive. Now it was not just the lesser known shares. Blue chip stocks were equally in trouble. General Electric, Telephone & Telegraph, US Steel all dropped points and the big drops seemed to be getting bigger. The banks were watching closely but there was no sign they were prepared to get involved, no sign they were prepared to step in and help out and the gong at 3 p.m. closed trading on the market's worst day ever. An estimated $10 billion of investors' money had simply drained away. *The New York Times'* headline next morning read: STOCK PRICES SLUMP $14,000,000,000 IN NATION-WIDE STAMPEDE TO UNLOAD with the hopeful corollary *Bankers to Support Market Today.*

The severity of the fall came as a shock and a surprise. Whilst many in government believed stocks had been valued too high there was concern now that the fall in values was far too steep. Prominent businessmen and leading bankers tried to reassure the public business was strong and banks *were* willing and able to step in. They urged newspapers to sound an optimistic note yet at the same time some of them were actually fuelling the panic by selling their own stocks short in the hope of buying them back cheaply.

But most bankers did their best to raise expectations. Things will be better tomorrow, they said. There will be many bargains to be had and there will be many buyers. The market will surely recover. But on Tuesday morning, the day that came to be known as Black Tuesday, a great flood of orders to sell poured in and threatened to sink the Exchange. In the first minutes after the gong opened trading, thousands of shares were sold or offered for sale. Radio, US Steel, General Electric, all fell dramatically. Arguments and even fist fights broke out on the Exchange floor as clerks pushed and jostled each other in their frantic attempts to find buyers. Hysteria gripped many as less than an hour after the opening gong stock values had fallen by more than $2 million.

Large crowds were again gathering outside, anxious to sell to meet their margins. Savings banks were overrun by people wanting to make withdrawals. Insurance companies were inundated with policy holders wanting to cash in their policies. Pawnbrokers were swamped with requests to pledge valuables.

Once again the tapes could not keep up with the volume of trade and out in the brokerage houses, though they were stunned already by the falls, investors found there were even bigger shocks to come. The collapse came like an earthquake and the tremors were felt across the world. It was the biggest financial catastrophe of all time.

Near to the closing gong there was a slight rally reviving hopes that the worst had passed. Already the chaos and the devastation seemed somehow unreal for those able to survive such severe losses. But the reality was all too clear for ordinary men and women forced now to mortgage their homes, to accept the fact that this ill wind had blown away their life's savings in the mounds of paper that littered the floor of the Exchange and that, for many, the 'safe' investments prudently made to provide for a modest retirement had gone and they would have to start looking for work in a world where thousands, perhaps millions, of jobs would soon be lost.

Dan Dolan left the Exchange that Tuesday afternoon saddened by the sight of so much anguish. A detached observer, he had noted how swiftly the flimsy cloak of civilization could fall away. True, he was insulated from the turmoil, thanks to Pops, but the consternation and the hint of madness in so many eyes had disturbed him deeply.

The party was clearly over. The good times were gone, the joyful sound of jazz music was fading fast and only a slow dirge would bring this crazy decade to a close. From now on things would be very different.

There were two letters on the doormat, one from Tim who was settling in to seminary life and wanted to know what problems, if any, the Wall Street troubles had given his high flying brother. The other came in an embossed envelope with the name of a prominent New York judge on the back and an address out on Long Island. Dan ran over in his mind what misdemeanours he could possibly have committed recently but remained nonplussed. The letter, equally embossed, contained an invitation to a 'social evening' at the judge's home. Dan consulted the only other legal man he knew well enough to ask.

'Ah,' Jim Paley said with a laugh. 'A bit premature perhaps

but that's Andy. Judge Peterson is an old friend of mine. Your name came up at one of our meetings and he'd like to meet you.'

'One of your meetings?'

'Judge Peterson is chairman of your local Democrats.'

'I'm not being indicted then?'

Paley laughed again. 'No. Come over at lunchtime for a bite to eat if you can and I'll tell you what's on his mind.'

Judge Peterson was in his seventies. He was a distinguished judge and a leading player for the Democrats around New York. He had been a longstanding friend of Joe Baker. Andriy Petrenko had known Joe Baker when he was Josef Bakke more than fifty years ago and they had remained firm friends. 'But he was never able to draw Joe into politics,' Paley said. 'Joe was always too busy. But that was understandable. He came to this country with nothing and he had to keep making money to reassure himself he wasn't poor. He'd been poor and he knew what it was like.'

'I came to this country with nothing, Mr Paley,' Dan said, 'and I've been incredibly lucky. I want to preserve that good fortune in Pops' memory. I intend to take good care of the business.'

'Sure you do,' Paley said. 'But this country is going to need the Democrats and the Democrats are going to need bright young men. Things are in a mess right now. It's young men like you, Dan, who can help put things right. If this country has given you something good, maybe you should give something back.'

Dinner at Judge Peterson's house at Great Neck turned out to be a much more lavish affair than Dan expected. There were several young people present, men and women of his own age. The young men, he guessed, were Democratic Party hopefuls, mainly interested in political advancement. The young women, as far as he could tell, were mainly interested in the young men.

It was a black tie affair, the uniform that hides one's roots. All the men were dressed the same, Dan noted, and no one could tell how or why they came to be there. Judge Peterson spoke to Dan briefly and told him he had heard 'good things' about him.

He hoped he would enjoy the party and maybe *join* the party. Jim Paley and Mrs Paley were with a group of older people and as the judge moved on, Dan was left alone, drink in hand, his starched collar stiff against his neck as he surveyed the scene.

What would it cost, he wondered, to bring the regulars over from the Drummers and get them to gatecrash the party? The thought made him smile and his involuntary expression caught the eye of a girl nearby. 'Hi,' she said. 'You're new.'

'To this place,' Dan said. 'Yes.'

She laughed. 'Pamela Peterson,' she said, holding out a slim, bejewelled hand. 'The judge is my gran'pa.'

'Dan Dolan,' Dan said. 'Pleased to meet you, Miss Peterson.'

'You can call me Pam,' she said. 'Everyone else does.' She took his arm. 'This is a cattle market,' she told him. 'This is where up and coming young Democrats – the rich ones anyway – are invited to flaunt their egos and meet suitable young ladies. In other words, this is where they let the bulls loose on the cows.'

Dan glanced at her and caught the impish glint in her eyes.

'Well, that's what it's all about,' she said, unrepentant. 'See that big hunk of beef over there?' She pointed out a large, red-faced young man who appeared to be swapping stories with five equally libidinous-looking others. 'I'm marrying that in a month's time.'

'Good luck,' he said with a wry smile.

Pamela laughed at the implied hint that she was going to need it and she led him away to introduce him to some of her friends. He was here to socialize, he gathered, to meet people, and he began to realize that Jim Paley and the judge had plans for him.

The parties and social gatherings continued month after month and showed no sign of abating as the hard times came in though much of the talk was about the fallout and the consequences of what happened on Wall Street. The crash itself was not the main cause of the mess we're in, was the general consensus. There had been a serious downturn in business long before last October. But what happened then had undoubtedly accelerated the massive recession the country was now facing.

As Dan drove out to one or another of those white mansions along the Sound in his almost new roadster, bought half price in what had become known as a 'Crash' sale, he saw many hostile and defeated eyes turn to note his passing. He knew what poverty cloaked in resignation looked like. He had seen it sitting on front doorsteps at home in Ireland and it was sitting there now on the porches of the rundown houses dotted along the highway. To Dan these people suddenly looked older and thinner, though in reality they had not changed much. What had changed was that along the hedgerows there was now a proliferation of signs. *NO WORK. NO JOBS. NO HANDS NEEDED.* It was as if the new spring trees had sprouted dead brown leaves.

Yet, as he turned in at a long, well-kept lane that ran alongside a wide green lawn and came to a spacious parking place where an attendant in a dove-grey uniform guided him to an available slot, the stylish tinkling of a piano and the sound of laughter danced on the evening air. It seemed there were two worlds living side by side, the one getting by in a sullen silence, the other gracing these exclusive enclaves where there was still laughter and even some of the old gaiety, though the laughter was, perhaps, a little more muted and in quiet corners there were sometimes hushed whispers of suicides and ruined millionaires.

The truth was, as the lawyer Jim Paley insisted, there had been no more suicides in 1929 than in any other year. It was simply not true that people were throwing themselves from skyscrapers. But, as always, people chose to believe what they wanted to believe. True, there was great hardship nationwide, but most of the people who had always been rich were still rich and able, as before, to host their parties in their white mansions and make their periodic trips to Europe. As the song said, *The rich get richer and the poor get poorer....*

# THIRTY

FINGERS WERE POINTING now at yesterday's heroes. Men who had presided over the dizzy climb in stock market prices were today's villains, in some cases their activities revealed as fraudulent. In 1930 an investigation into the workings of the Stock Exchange by a Senate committee began with a series of hearings that would go on for the next two years. The Banking and Currency committee, as the committee was called, soon unearthed evidence of greed, abuse of power and insider trading. The pools formed to boost prices to unjustifiably high levels, the bribes paid to financial journalists, the favourable stock deals given to men of influence – all were exposed.

The Senate prosecutor, Ferdinand Percora, said the committee's investigation had resulted in 'a shocking disclosure of low standards in high places'. The chairman of National City Bank, the nation's largest bank, Charles E. Mitchell was questioned relentlessly about the selling of overpriced securities. The chairman of Chase National Bank, Albert Wiggin, was questioned about the way he promoted the bank's prospects and at the same time was secretly selling short his own holdings in Chase National.

Mitchell had authorized many dubious deals and, inevitably, as these disclosures were made public he resigned. He was arrested later on a charge of illegally evading taxes. After a long trial he was found innocent, but the impression remained that he was a man who had profiteered at the expense of his bank's many small investors.

When Albert Wiggin retired in 1932 he took with him a

pension of $100,000 a year. This was at a time when retirement pensions were relatively rare and the number of jobless was growing daily. When the news of his enormous pay off leaked out there was a general outcry and he quietly agreed to relinquish his right to the pension.

After the Senate hearings new standards were drawn up for all who dealt in the stock market. A private syndicate, insider dealing or any kind of market manipulation was strictly forbidden. Michael Meehan who had promoted Radio stock with great success in the Twenties was now accused by the recently formed Securities and Exchange Commission of violating the new code of conduct. The SEC, as the new commission was known, was created to monitor trading practice and the information issued about the various stocks and bonds. Meehan was accused by the SEC of attempting to boost the price of a small aircraft company. Most traders thought he had done nothing wrong but the commission took this as an opportunity to expel him from trading on any American Stock Exchange. It was seen as his comeuppance for some preconceived notion of earlier misdemeanours but many believed his expulsion was unjustified.

Vice President of the New York Stock Exchange during his boss's long absence, Richard Whitney fared worst of all. Whitney was a poor investor. He had lost $2 million, money borrowed from his brother. To hide his losses he began to steal from his customers and in desperation he even stole money from a Stock Exchange fund. Exposed as a common criminal he was sentenced to three years in Sing Sing.

Years later when he visited the Stock Exchange, Groucho Marx stood on a chair in the public gallery and at the top of is voice started to sing *When Irish Eyes Are Smiling*. Traders on the floor stopped work to look up at the clown in the gallery. When told the police would be called if he didn't behave, Groucho shouted down, 'Listen, you crooks, you cleaned me out of two-fifty grand in '29. For that kind of dough I'm entitled to sing.'

*

The awful reality of the financial disaster fully came home to
Dan Dolan in the spring of 1931 as he walked in the early
morning sun to his office on Madison Avenue. Groups of discon-
solate, defeated men of all ages, moving around the city in a
fruitless search for work had become a common sight in recent
months. But now there was something else. A new, even more
disturbing sight: bread lines. Grown men standing in line for a
bowl of soup and a slice of bread.

Columbus Circle had the longest line, winding away block
after block, an open truck with people on board ladling out hot
soup from big cauldrons, others handing out chunks of bread.
The Hearst Corporation provided that one and there were
others where men waited patiently as the morning ticked by.
And they were not all blue-collar workers, Dan noted. There
were office managers, clerks, salesmen.

He felt like an intruder and an impostor. It was as though his
smart jacket, his shiny shoes, the money in his pockets were an
insult to the less fortunate. He stood still for a moment when he
caught sight of himself in the dark window of a department
store. He thought he knew what poverty was. He had been poor,
very poor, but it had never been quite so bad as this. He had
never had to stand in line for a slice of bread.

He moved on and as he turned off Fifth Avenue to cut
through to Madison a young workman was standing on the
sidewalk. Their eyes met briefly and for an instant Dan felt that
this young fellow was about to approach him. But he didn't
pause. He walked on. Then he saw this young fellow again, this
time in his mind's eye. Flat cap, collarless shirt, work pants tied
with string, a labourer's boots. It was himself he saw now. He
had attempted to approach a well-dressed young gent once,
simply to ask directions, but the man had looked straight
through him and walked on. And that was exactly what he
himself had done just now.

Dan came to a halt, turned and walked back. He wanted to
give this young fellow a helping hand, a twenty-dollar bill
maybe. He had looked as if he might be 'just off the boat' with
his honest, hopeful eyes bright with the promise of a fresh start

and all that was new. But the young fellow was nowhere to be seen.

It was almost eight years since he and his brothers arrived, since they were just like that young fellow. But that was in the Twenties. Things were different now and it was not a good time to be coming off the boat. Yet the drunks and the dreamers at home would still be singing *Give my regards to Broadway* and *Tell them I'll be there*, filling impressionable young heads with the residue of their own broken dreams.

He would get Tim to write to Father Delaney, ask him to tell them not to come. There were no jobs and the bread lines were getting longer. But he knew they wouldn't listen. Back home this was America and America was still the promised land.

Lois was waiting for him as he ran up the stairs to the office. 'You're going to a wedding,' she told him.

'Lois,' Harry said reprovingly.

'You getting married, Lois?' Dan asked.

'Fine chance,' she said. 'I'll get Mr Shaw, your friend Nathan. He knows what it's all about.'

Dan went into his office as Lois put the call through.

'So you're getting married?' he said with a laugh. 'Congratulations, and about time, too.'

'It's not me, you dope,' Nathan said. 'It's Michael. He's been trying to contact you.'

According to Nathan, Michael and Annie were planning to come up from Los Angeles in two weeks' time and whilst they were there they hoped to stay for a while and get married. They had not been able to come sooner because Michael had contracts to honour. He was doing OK as Johnny Roselli, making a name for himself in a small way out there on the coast, but he had big plans.

Nathan had not used him on the Italian record. He had found a genuine Italian. But he had an idea he might try a new departure with Michael. It would be a chance for the company to branch out. It would be his first shot at a fully commercial record, aimed at the market as a whole, Michael singing one of the great new ballads that had just come out or one that was just about to come out, the ballad on one side and Michael with a really swinging big band on the other.

He also wanted to put the record out under the name of Michael Dolan, stage a comeback for the singer many on the East Coast would still remember as 'Everybody's Favourite Singer'. But he didn't know how Michael would feel about that.

First, though, there was the wedding. Annie wanted to be married in church and the suggestion was that Father Pat might be persuaded to perform the ceremony. Tim was still away and not yet qualified to solemnize marriages. In Tim's absence, Nathan said, Michael wanted Dan to make the necessary arrangements.

'I'll call him,' Dan said. It was noon in New York, nine o'clock in the morning in Los Angeles. He spoke to Michael and later that day he went to see Father Pat. A long line of men, women and children were waiting patiently outside the church hall. Yet another bread line. Dan left the roadster two blocks away and walked back.

In the hall Father Pat and two elderly nuns were ladling hot soup and handing out bread. 'I need to talk to you, Father,' Dan said.

'And these little villains need their soup,' Father Pat said.

Two small boys aged about seven were looking up at him, their eyes wide, their mouths open, like little birds waiting to be fed.

One of the parishioners took over his ladle and Father Pat walked Dan back to the church where they sat on the bench outside.

'So what can I do for you, Daniel?'

'It's my brother, Father. Not Tim. My other brother. Michael.'

'The crooner?'

Dan laughed. 'Yeah. He wants to get married and we'd like you to do it, if you don't mind.'

'Mind? Why should I mind? Good time to get married. Things can only get better.'

'You think so, Father?'

'Sure, now they're locking up all the crooks. So who does he want to marry? A nice Catholic girl, I hope.'

'Er ... yeah,' Dan said, though he was not sure if Annie was a Catholic girl or not. 'She's Italian. I suppose if they waited long enough Tim could do it. But they don't want to wait.'

Father Pat glanced at him. 'Shotgun?'

'No, no,' Dan said with a laugh, although he was not even sure about that. 'There is one thing, Father, I think I should tell you.'

'There often is, son,' Father Pat said. 'So what's the problem?'

'Well, Annie, that's Michael's girlfriend, she wants to get married in white and I'm to ask you if that would be all right.'

'And why wouldn't it be?'

'Well, they've been sort of living together for a year or two now, ever since O'Hara ran them out of town, in fact. She thinks it may not be acceptable.'

Father Pat shook his head. 'Sure and the Lord is not interested in fashion, Daniel. He'll look at what's in the girl's heart and soul, not at what she's wearing.'

'So it's OK?'

'They must come to Confession, ask for forgiveness, both of them. And you can tell that Michael he's supposed to wait until he gets a licence.'

President Hoover was campaigning for a second term but the Democrats seemed unstoppable. Franklin D. Roosevelt was the man of the moment and the nation wanted a change. The crash could not have come at a worse time for Mr Hoover and, though he was not to blame for what happened, people were ready to blame anyone and everyone. The gloom of the Depression was deepening and getting deeper every day and, despite efforts in some Republican quarters to suppress it, the song most often played at that time, the song that spilled out of windows and doorways, the song that mirrored the general malaise was Yip Harburg's *Brother, can you spare a dime?*

The nation was gripped by an all pervasive gloom. Then in December, 1933, the Volstead Act was revoked, Prohibition was gone and for a little while the rush to drink and get drunk took over. But only until reality returned. There was really no money for booze and not much money for anything else.

The whole of New York City, it seemed, was Democrat now as Dan Dolan involuntarily put himself forward for one of the seats on the Manhattan Council. Asked at one of the Long Island parties for his views he surprised himself and the people he was with as, only slightly inebriated, he launched into a tirade at the way things were. 'Empty pockets, empty plates, empty faces on our streets – we cannot allow this to go on. The nation must get back to work.'

He couldn't remember exactly what he said but whatever it was it met with nods of approval and even some mild applause. He was then backed into a corner by a distinguished-looking elderly man who urged him to run for office on the Upper West Side. He had everything going for him, Jim Paley told him later. He even had an office on Madison Avenue and a couple of willing helpers in Harry and Lois.

'And a business to run,' Dan reminded him.

His main concern just then was Michael and Annie's wedding. It was all planned. The banns were read in the parish in Santa Monica the prospective bride and groom gave as their home base. Michael and Annie said they would arrive at Penn Station and Dan booked for them a suite at the Waldorf Astoria. It was his treat, he said when they protested at the expense. A wedding gift. But Annie said they would have their bridesmaid with them. Dan simply booked another room.

'Is it Sue?' he asked Annie on the telephone, not knowing if Annie was aware he had once had something going with Sue.

'No,' Annie said. 'Sue's gone to Europe with the troupe.'

Dan was not sure if he was relieved or disappointed. At least, it was one possible complication out of the way. But nothing was ever straightforward with Michael. When Dan and Nathan arrived to greet the happy couple at Penn Station they were taken aback to see a baby boy standing between them, holding their hands and obviously theirs.

'We wanted it to be a surprise,' Annie said with a laugh.

Dan laughed. 'It's that all right,' he said and he lifted the little boy high in the air as Michael introduced them.

'Danny,' Michael said expansively, 'this is your Uncle Dan. And this other wise guy is your Uncle Nathan.'

'He sure looks like a Dolan,' Nathan said.

Annie laughed. 'We'll take that as a compliment.'

They would be staying in New York for a while, Michael said, maybe take an apartment. There was no urgency about a honeymoon, he added with a smile. It was not as if they were just getting to know each other. Anyway, he said, Tim was back to assist Father Pat. Everything was set including the reception.

Dan had planned to book a banquet room at the Waldorf but Tim wanted them to have the reception in the church hall and Michael and Annie had already said yes.

The church was full, standing room only, as if most of the parish had been invited. Father Pat and Tim were robed and ready at the altar, the organist playing softly in anticipation of the big moment when the bride appeared.

The previous night Michael had stayed at Dan's apartment. Now, when they arrived in Dan's roadster, they were met by Nathan who was intent on marshalling ushers. He had been discreetly drumming up advance publicity for the return of Michael Dolan and fans who remembered Michael from his previous incarnation had turned up to watch his arrival.

Nathan was looking at Dan curiously.

Dan raised his eyebrows.

'Just be prepared,' Nathan said.

Prepared for what? he wanted to ask but Michael needed help. He was surrounded by well-wishers and he was having trouble extricating himself. Nathan urged Dan to get him into church.

Michael and Dan, bridegroom and best man, were standing at the altar when the organist hit the chords to announce the arrival of the bride. Dan glanced over his shoulder. Dressed in the white she wanted, Annie was on her father's arm. A single bridesmaid, tall, slim with a tumble of black curls was close behind her.

It was only when the vows were made and Michael and Annie moved to the vestry that Dan came face to face with the one bridesmaid and her thick black hair and her dark laughing eyes. At first glance he had guessed she was Italian, like Annie, but now he was sure she was Irish.

'Hello, Dan,' she said.

He looked at her for a long moment. It was yet another big surprise, for Dan the biggest surprise of all. He couldn't take his eyes off her. 'Caitlin?'

She laughed, took his arm, steered him towards the vestry. 'Aren't we supposed to sign something?'

'You look lovely,' he said. 'Beautiful.' Then: 'Why didn't you tell me you were coming?'

'It was Tim and Michael. They wanted to surprise you.'

He couldn't speak. She was that lost little girl on the dock in Liverpool. And now she was this young woman. This lovely young woman. Tim was watching, smiling.

'I'll deal with you later,' Dan told him, and he turned back to Caitlin. 'It's not the fourth of July.'

'You remembered,' she said.

'I remember everything,' he told her.

They were outside now. A photographer, his head bobbing out from under a black cloth and back again, was marshalling people into groups, waving others aside.

'How long are you here?' Dan asked as they stood hand in hand and other guests milled around them.

'Depends,' Caitlin said. 'My folks go home early tomorrow.'

'Well, you can't,' he said decisively. 'We have to have afternoon tea at the Plaza.'

She laughed. 'Then we have to cross the road, see if we can spot the diamonds in the fountain.'

'So we do,' he said.